I'd like to give thanks to my friends and family that have supported my obsession over the past few years.

A very special **Thank You** to my sister-in-law Nicole Hornbaker-Langston and my Dad for their wonderful feedback and critique!

Ed, thank you for helping me wake up my creative brain cells on numerous occasions with your hypnosis videos! (www.Eddini.com)

And of course, my husband, Nathan, who has always been encouraging me and indulging my inner science-nerd for years.

Beyond Bermuda: Prelude

Hal's feet sank into the marshland with every exhausting step. The land surrounding him was barren and dead as the leafless trees hung low, their branches dipping into the soil, and a cold, murky fog lingered just above the ground. There was no wind and the only sound came from the mud as his feet penetrated its surface.

The thick fog clung to his skin as he passed through, paddling his arms as if it would help push it out of the way. The dense moisture settled on his skin, leaving an unusual residue that trailed down his arms and bare chest with gray streaks. It was calm now as he cautiously peered through the haze, but he knew that could change at any moment.

He glanced down at his watch and smeared away the film that covered the glass. The arms stood still, as did the compass, which he'd grown accustomed to after so many days, yet he still held out hope that some sort of normalcy or measurement would start ticking again.

The sky was dim and gray, giving an omnipresent gloom over the land that never seemed to change. There were no significant landmarks or objects that stood out among the rest, just a never ending marshland in an ever present time. There were no day or night cycles either, and without a functional clock, he could only guess how long he'd been lost.

"Forward, just move forward," he told himself.

He felt the jolt as time began to shift. It was an odd sensation, one that he would describe much like a punch to the head. There was the twist, almost painful, as the feeling slammed into your body. Then there was the slow motion as you absorbed the shock, temporarily forgetting the unusual sensation. Lastly, the recoil as your mind snaps back, the pain of the impact and the struggle to find your center of gravity again.

Hal felt as the shift began and crouched down, gripping his knees as he waited for *the push*. Time slowed and he breathed in, closing his eyes as the bright flare of light sparked. It was an unexplainable phenomenon that had been happening every couple of hours. He wasn't even sure if the event was real or psychological, but for several days they'd been occurring consistently. After a dozen times, he'd learned to recognize the signs and brace himself for the shift.

All movement seemed to pause and the first spark of green light appeared, flickering ever so briefly. He frantically looked to his side, trying to catch a glimpse of it, but it vanished too soon. The chaos was about to begin.

The second phase slowly faded in as a low horn began to resonate over the land, echoing off the trees from every direction. The peaceful land that stood still below him was now awakening as the roots began to stir and writhe through the soil.

He steadied his footing and squinted, trying to see through the green haze. The horn itself was a mystery. It came from no particular direction, but he'd witnessed it too many times to ignore it. The needles of his watch began to spin frantically on its axis as the horn steadied its loud, steady pitch. It was a wake up call. The earth had found its prey and was calling out to the demons that resided. It was an alarm for transition.

Panic rose in his chest and his feet instinctively sprinted forward. A second burst of light sparked to his left and he flinched. His vision faded with the flicker and he slowed to orient himself. Vines wriggled through the soil and the branches that sulked and penetrated it were now heaving out of place.

Like a bright camera flash, Hal squinted his eyes and waited for the blinding glow to fade. He slowed his pace but didn't dare stop as he cautiously stepped forward.

A lashing pain struck his side and he stumbled. He gripped his bicep, feeling the warm trail of blood as it traveled down his arm to his fingertips. The panic paused and his feet halted as he watched the droplet fall, flowing through the air before colliding with the ground, instantly shattering the moment into chaos.

The mother beast wailed and the ground trembled with her shriek. The shock wave startled the surroundings as the branches heaved and retreated. The vines below fell stiff under his feet. She was alerted.

"Run." Hal whispered to himself, dodging forward without a second thought.

The marsh came alive more than ever now, whipping its branches as they searched for prey. The soil gave with every step, stirring below as the roots gripped his bare feet, pulling him farther.

A blinding flash sparked before him, dulling his senses. His pulse was deafening in his ears and he swung his arms for balance before falling. He slid on his back as the cold soil slithered over his skin, covering his arms and chest.

With his limbs slowly growing immobile, he steadied his breath as his vision faded back. The fog settled, no longer rushing behind in his wake. His warm body quickly grew cold, covered in the mud. He lay still, listening as the footsteps came closer.

A disfigured foot slowly appeared through the fog and then paused. Although he'd heard the shrieks before, he'd never seen her this close. He held his breath and remained still as he gazed forward.

The beast took another step, piercing through the green haze and becoming fully visible. Her structure was almost human-like, but horridly mutated. She balanced on two main legs that extended forward. The feet were more like claws, sinking into the soil as they pierced through. A third leg protruded out the back with an inverted knee. Its foot was flat, used to steady the mass directly above. She walked more like a crab as her spinal cord bent forward at the pelvis, extending upward to a sunken stomach cavity. Large bones stretched the milky white skin of her enlarged chest and what looked like breasts drooped to the sides. Bulging collarbones lead to the massive shoulders and her long arms fell downward, touching the ground. Her hands were claws, with two long fingers and a thumb, curled into fists that pummeled the ground as she ran.

She took another step forward, sniffing the air and Hal's eyes migrated upwards. Black veins could be seen through her white, thin skin, rising up her chest to the neck. Bulbs grew on the surface, throbbing with her pulse.

She balanced awkwardly on her limbs, shifting back and forth as she tried to pinpoint her prey. Her nose had decayed, leaving two small holes where the nasal cavity would have been. A protruding brow overshadowed the sunken holes of her eyes below, but Hal could see the large, black bulbs as they darted back and forth. The skin on her face was torn with open gashes that exposed a dark fluid underneath. Patches of bone stuck out from the jaw bone and chin, which had mutated into a large, calcified surface.

She paused only ten feet away and the fog fell still. She was nearly within arms reach, and yet didn't seem to be aware he was there. The soil beneath him, however, continued to move and its grip tightened.

The echo of the horn stopped, and there was a sudden jolt. It seemed as if time itself halted. He let out a huge exhale of relief when the transition occurred and the creature froze in place. Everything just stopped.

The beast now looked like a milky white body hovering in time, completely motionless and still. The sunken eyes had a hollow white glaze over the dark spheres but remained in place, no longer searching for a target.

The grip of the soil also froze and finally allowed him to break free. Pulling his arm from its grasp, he gazed at his watch, which had now stopped its frantic spinning. His body was torn and a deep cut above his left eye blurred his vision even more. Its warmth was almost comforting as a stream slid down his cheek. For the time being, it was a little reminder that he was still alive and able to move.

Pulling his other limbs from the veins of the soil, he sat up and tried to orient himself. His breathing was now calm, and he stared at the unbelievable creature as it remained paused in time. No one ever had this close of an encounter, but he'd heard the groans and wailing from an unseen distance. He'd never believed she existed, or at least not quite in this form.

Another blinding flash appeared again and he flinched, holding an arm up to cover his eyes. The light remained and was no longer merely a spark. He strained as his iris' accepted the whiteout. His hearing perked as he faintly heard a man's voice in the distance. The words were muffled but calm and Hal focused as he tried to make out his words.

"Hal Brent, can you hear me? Mr. Brent?" The echoes quieted as his vision came back. The brightness faded and Hal's hearing fell mute again. The flash came and went, and as before, it lingered. The voices also returned, quietly at first, and then coherently close.

"Hello?" Hal spoke, but unable to hear his own voice. "Can anyone hear me?"

"Get the oxygen, his lungs are strained," the man's voice came again. The feeling of chaos and movement brushed against his skin. He could feel hands touching his chest and the warmth that came from them. His sensations were fading in and out. One moment the man was close, even touching him, then another moment everything fell numb.

The light disappeared and his vision slowly focused on the surrounding trees and brush of the swampy land. He leaned forward, putting his hands on his knees for support as his head continued to spin. Was this a new transition? He breathed heavy, again trying to focus on that brief moment of contact, but it didn't come.

Several moments passed and the world around him became his reality more and more. Was it a hallucination? Was it something new in this bizarre, hellish nightmare he couldn't wake him from?

He swallowed in protest as he accepted the reality of the cold mud engulfing his feet. His body was completely covered in the muck and the fog still lingered towards him. The surroundings of the marshland hadn't changed, and he'd been running for so long in so many directions, there was no way to tell which way he was facing. This was unknown territory, and the fog was different, somehow. It was a pale green and drawn to his body, creating a thicker cloud in a small radius. Maybe it was causing these hallucinations.

"Hello!" He screamed, desperately hoping for a return as his voice echoed off the trees.

These new flashes came and went, and the further he went into the fog, the longer they lasted.

He wasn't sure if it was his imagination. The man had known his name. Here he was, alone, in the marshland, miles away from anyone, yet the voice seemed so close.

The flash came again. Unlike before, the light remained and Hal's focus was instantly lost.

"Forty five years of age, former Air Force pilot. He's unconscious at the moment." The voice was so close now. He felt as if he were asleep and he could hear the man next to him, but his mind refused to wake.

This was real. Hal could feel the warm blood from the cuts on his arms and chest, and the bruises on his bare feet. His arms were outstretched, desperately searching for any nearby surroundings, but with each swing he found himself spinning out of balance. There was nothing to catch himself, nothing to hold onto. His breath slowed and the blinding light slowly began fading to black.

"Hold him! Hold! Mr. Brent you need to calm down… We're losing him!" The voice faded out and his vision went from blinding white to silent black. There was a deep calm and release as the pain of his wounds disappeared and the pulsing in his ears quieted.

Chapter 1: The Waking

"I told you, I cannot induce him to wake up. His body is under immense stress right now. If I do," he paused, "You won't get any answers." The hesitation was self-explanatory.

There was a sigh of frustration on some sort of speaker phone, followed by muffled conversation. Everything felt numb and a light directly above him blurred any attempt to focus. The voices in the room, the lights, his aching limbs and throbbing in his skull, it was all present, but yet numb.

He laid still, unable to move his arms, but also lacking the strength to do so. He listened more intently, focusing on the man's voice. He was in the room, maybe twenty or thirty feet away. There were other voices, two men and a woman. He heard the tones, but not the words as they increased in volume, engaged in an argument.

Hal groaned and tried reaching for his face. Everything still felt intact as his palms patted his skin. His eyes ached as his fingertips touched an adhesive cloth covering them. He gently pulled, wincing and letting out a sign of pain.

"Claire... I think our patient just woke up." The man's voice was only a few feet away now. Hal immediately stopped and turned defensively. Even with his eyes covered, he could sense the man approaching.

"Mr. Hal Brent? Can you hear me?" His tone was gentle. "Here, let me help you with that."

A warm hand touched his face and Hal jolted back, swatting away the doctor's hand.

"Stay back!" He was not going to volunteer any information. "Why am I blindfolded?"

"Mr. Brent, I'm Robert Prossman. I'm the station's doctor here." He sounded confused but didn't make any second attempts to touch his face again. "You're on a research base here on Soldier Key. We found ..."

"Soldier Key? In the Atlantic?" He interrupted him. Had he landed somewhere in the Florida Keys?

"Mr. Brent, please, let me help you with those so you can see." He reached again for Hal's face, and with a slight flinch, Prossman pulled a slim piece of webbed tape from his eyelids. "I'm sorry about that. You had a seizure when you first arrived, and your pupils were dilated. The webbed tape was to keep the light out."

It was overwhelming. He hadn't seen florescent lights or sunlight for quite some time and it took him a few moments before he attempted to open his eyes.

"Robert?" A woman's voice came through some sort of intercom system.

"Yes, Claire?" The doctor replied, turning towards the intercom. "He's awake. I don't think this is a good time to tell Troy, though. He's very disoriented. Let me finish treating him before Troy hears about this."

"I can't stall him for very long. If it's OK, I'd like to see him," she paused. "I'll be there in a minute."

His vision was blurry, but he could see the doctor walking around what looked like a sterile sick-bay. The room was well-lit. A little too well-lit. On the second level he could see a faint glow of electronic equipment. A single workstation stood out from the rest, littered with snack bags and pop cans, but the rest of the room was sterile enough for surgery.

The doctor had a crooked step, but busily walked towards his littered work bench. He pulled something that looked like a clipboard from the pile and began touching the illuminated surface. That was new. Hal had seen tablets before, but these were different. The entire surface was transparent and lit up the doctor's wrinkly face.

"You said I'm on Soldier Key. Has my crew been found?" Hal began to sit upright, gripping the padded bed for balance.

"Excuse me?" The doctor turned and looked at him with a puzzled face. He was a frail looking, older man and with the exception of a dozen white hairs, he was completely bald. Gravity had had some effects over the years, shown in his slight hunch, and he definitely wasn't a physical threat.

Hal was beginning to focus more clearly on his surroundings. "How long has this place been on the island? This is a large complex for Soldier Key."

The doctor laughed. "I wish I could take credit for building it, but I'm not as sturdy as I once was." The man proudly held the clipboard to his chest and puffed up, as if showing his strength and

10

stability. "My building skills are with smaller things... genetics." He smiled, but he didn't seem to understand the question. "No, no, there was a large construction team some years back. Most of the complex is actually underwater." He lifted his eyebrows with interest.

"What?" Hal frequently flew over the Keys and surely would have noticed a complex this large before.

"Ah, I bet you have some catching up to do." The doctor looked down at his clip board and touched-in a few things before laying it back down on the pile of desk junk. "You see, you're at a research base on Soldier Key. This is A&H headquarters. We dabble in a little bit of everything now, but a few years back there was this indestructible glass, Sealo-Pax." He began to fidget. "I know it's a stupid name, but the makers wanted their names to be known for the breakthrough. But anyway, the construction industry, oh! It's revolutionized how we build!"

Hal closed his eyes tightly and put his hands over his eyes. "Wait, when did this happen? Why am I on a research station that makes glass?"

"Oh, we found you." His voice was chipper, like he was some sort of prize. "You were floating on a piece of wreckage in the middle of the Atlantic."

Hal's hands dropped and his eyes were wide open.

"We had a search team out towards Bermuda looking for two of our freighters. They were heading towards St. George to another small facility, but mid-way, they lost power and just disappeared off our radar." He looked down at his hands as he began to fidget his fingers. "I'm not really at liberty to talk about it, but during our search we found you gripping onto some floating wreckage. Although, we're still not entirely sure it was part of our ship." His eyes wandered downward in disappointment as he recalled the lost ships.

The doctor still hadn't explained much, and what he had said didn't make a whole lot of sense to Hal. Why a glass company? A genetic research doctor? Was he heavily medicated or having some sort of hallucination?

A knock at the door interrupted his thoughts.

"Is this an OK time?"

Hal could tell by the voice that she was the same woman from the intercom.

"Yes, come on in Claire. Our patient has come to life." The doctor lifted his arms with enthusiasm as if some miracle had just happened and he was now presenting Hal to the new audience.

The woman smiled politely at Hal as she took a seat in the doctor's chair, holding a clipboard against her chest. She had dark red hair that was loosely held by a clip. She wore business pants and a white collar shirt under a lab jacket. "Mr. Brent, I'm Claire Kass. I'm one of the employees here. You're on a science research station called A&H."

"Your doctor here filled me in, but I still don't understand. Why am I here?" He looked down at his arms where there were new bruises and scratch marks.

She clasped her hands together. "This is going to sound a bit confusing." She paused, fussing a little with her pen, then making eye contact. "I don't know how to say this, Mr. Brent, but you died on August 21, 2013."

Hal froze. He looked forward, not sure if he'd heard correctly. There was a long silence and all his thoughts paused, realizing she was completely serious.

"You look really good for a dead guy." The doctor remarked. "You should be seventy-one years old by now." Claire quickly spun around and he immediately realized it wasn't funny. "Well, I mean... never mind."

"Mr. Brent, you were lost at sea and presumed to be dead." Claire rephrased her comment. She paused, considering the news must have been devastating, but it was only a small piece of the puzzle. "That was over twenty-six years ago."

Hal tried to grasp what was just said. The words were echoing and he still wasn't sure he'd heard them correctly. With blank thoughts, he looked at her, and then to the doctor. Her expression seemed concerned and anticipating. Doctor Prossman shuffled behind Claire anxiously. He looked at Hal with fascination, trying to hold back his eager questions. He held off for a few seconds, biting his lip. He was fixated on Hal.

"It's like a time warp." He stared for a moment.

Claire dropped her head at the remark. Prossman was a curious man and although his humor wasn't always sympathetic, she couldn't help but smile at his ridiculous idea. The shocked stranger didn't show any reaction. "There are going to be a few gentlemen coming in soon to ask some questions. I know you have a lot of your own, but if you can help us, we may be able to find some of those answers."

Hal continued to look forward, just staring in a general direction without movement.

There wasn't much she could say. There was a dead man sitting on their lab table, and aside from the ancient facts on paper, there was no explanation for his arrival.

"My passengers?" His voice was monotone. "I had passengers on my plane."

His report was fairly short, giving a brief history of his military career, and an even shorter blurb about the flight school he taught at just outside of Miami.

She sat back down on the bench across from him. Hal was still in a daze, but he seemed to be listening. "Your plane disappeared from radar about a mile off the coast, near Bimini. The waters are fairly shallow in those areas, but no one ever found wreckage or... your passengers." She avoided using the word bodies. He had enough for his mind to digest. "I'll leave you alone for a while. Doctor Prossman will stay here in case you need anything." She wasn't always the most comforting person, but she leaned forward and tried to assure him things would be OK. "You're safe here. We'll do what we can to figure this out."

Honestly, she was only trying to be optimistic.

Chapter 2: Findings

Not much was known about Hal Brent, except for what was on paper from twenty-six years ago, but it was hard not to feel sympathy for him. The report summarized how his plane, which carried himself and four student pilots, had disappeared just off the coast of Bimini. The water surrounding the area was very clear and shallow, but there were no remains or wreckage found, leading officials to believe he'd lost direction and crash-landed further from shore. The search had lasted a good two weeks, which was longer than most in such shallow waters, but they were left with absolutely no evidence or clues about the plane's last location. It wasn't that uncommon for pilots to get lost at sea, especially at high altitudes, because all the scenery looks the same. The waters between Bimini and Florida, however, are very shallow and in most cases you can see the ocean floor.

Hal was an experienced pilot, having flown in the Air Force throughout his 20's and 30's. He retired early at thirty-nine and worked as a pilot instructor in Miami for six years when he just vanished off the radar. It was the only blemish on his entire flying record. That wasn't the biggest mystery, though. He'd been missing for over twenty six-years, and it didn't look as if he'd aged a day.

Prossman was fascinated. He believed time warps and distortions of space were possible, and here he had a dead man in his lab. Hal's arrival was unusual for a number of reasons, and not many on base had known about it, but for good reason.

A&H was recently under pressure to find two cargo freighters that had disappeared while in transit to Bermuda and despite a week long search party, there had only been small fragments of wreckage found in the water. There was no evidence supporting that Hal had anything to do with the disappearance of the ships, but the timing and location made him a very suspicious guest.

The freighters were carrying research material from their base on Soldier Key to a smaller and more remote location just off the coast of Bermuda. Only a handful of people were even aware the transport was being made, and of that handful, only four people knew what it was carrying. Somehow Hal landed smack dab in the middle of it.

He was a mystery. They knew absolutely nothing about him up until two days ago and what little they did know didn't make sense. Dr. Prossman did have a point, he looked good for a dead guy. Even if he had survived his plane crash somehow, he certainly didn't look seventy-one years old.

The A&H building was a large complex and at 2:00 AM the place was completely vacant with the lights dimmed. Claire was heading back to Troy's office to get an update on his new conspiracy theory about the situation and any association between the freighters disappearing and Hal.

Robert Troy was the new CEO of A&H, and although he didn't own the company, he was the only recognizable face associated with it. He was the name that brought media attention to their research. He'd been a spokesman for the company since the beginning, but had gone unnoticed until an unfortunate accident eight years earlier where his spinal cord had been severely damaged during an interview. He was promoting the use of Sealo-Pax glass as a shielding device on modern military craft and vehicles. As he arrived at the demonstration area, a bomb was detonated and blew shrapnel right through the walls of the vehicle. Unfortunately, the transport car wasn't meant for the demonstration and Troy was left with severe spinal damage, paralyzing him from the neck down. It did however serve as a demonstration, as the neighboring vehicles that were Sealo-Pax protected received absolutely no damage.

Regardless of Troy's circumstance, the event brought worldwide attention to the company. It almost seemed staged. A&H went straight to the top, skyrocketing passed their competitors and became more than just a construction company. As it grew, so did the research. From civil engineering and construction, to military protection and bio-chemical warfare, the face of A&H had changed in less than a decade.

Claire was brought in eleven years ago and had seen most of the growing pains the company had endured. She was an integral part in the physics department and the recent turmoil of the missing freighters had left her at center with its stress. She'd spent the past three years working with a small team on a project called ARCA. The device was still in its experimental stage, but was intended to be used for radioactive waste removal. Bermuda had been devastated by a nuclear attack in 2022, leaving it uninhabitable indefinitely. It was the perfect test zone for the ARCA, but the transport freighters simply disappeared just miles off the coast. Up until now, A&H had every available resource searching for the wreckage or survivors. And then they found Hal.

Claire felt conflicted and exhausted as she walked down the long hallway towards the atrium. She didn't know what to think. They'd known for several months that information on the ARCA was being leaked to various news sources, which she partly believed may have been Troy's intentions, encouraging investors to dive in, but there was something else going on that made her feel uneasy. She just couldn't place her finger on it.

Groups that opposed A&H and their research weren't unheard of, and just eight years earlier an anti-technology cult had planned the Sealo-Pax bombing. It was unsettling to think that her research had caused so much stress and concern in the world, and the media spin, along with the protest groups, only worsened their image.

She shook off the unsettling feelings as she entered the large atrium, lit by the moonlight above that shined through the massive ceiling dome.

Things just didn't add up. Hal was a weird, unexplainable phenomenon at the moment, but there was absolutely no evidence to suggest he'd had anything to do with their current crisis.

Claire found herself standing on the top level of the atrium, pausing with dread as she looked at the only remaining light still on. Troy's office. He and his servant-man were still here.

There was no point in stalling. He'd been watching the live camera feeds like a hawk for the past week and surely he was aware that she hadn't left. He'd expect a debriefing.

"Claire Kass, report to room A1," Troy's voice echoed through the empty halls. The intercom system wasn't necessary. She was already on her way, and he knew it.

Crossing the last entrance way, she turned towards his office and knocked. Troy was a private man and preferred everyone to knock for permission, even if he was expecting you. His servant, Harley Brack, appeared at the glass door and nodded before opening it.

"You called?"

16

"Status? Is he up?" Troy didn't look in her direction as he gazed at his computer screen.

"Yes, he woke up about ten minutes ago and the doctor is still trying to help him get oriented."

He began to cut her off before she finished. "So what's he said? Why was he on my property?" Troy usually never let anyone finish a sentence, but lately he hadn't even tried listening.

"What? He isn't even aware of anything."

"You mean he hasn't told you about the hijacking." He wasn't asking like it was a question.

"A hijacking? No, Troy, he doesn't even know what year it is." She knew he'd been working up a conspiracy theory over the last few days, and this was it.

"He's lying. He wouldn't actually tell you the truth." He began to back up his electric wheelchair and come around his desk. Brack, his second in command, followed closely behind. "We'll speak to him. Kass, I need you to come with us. If he's traumatized, we need your face to give the environment some familiarity. You did speak to him, correct?"

Troy never complimented anyone outright, and most of the time his remarks were disguised as an insult. He didn't particularly like Claire either, only referring to her by her last name even though they'd worked together for more than a decade. They'd bumped heads on a number of issues, and ever since she was moved to the physics department, her team's research was failing his expectations.

Following closely behind Troy and Brack, Claire could hear the two quietly droning back and forth as if she wasn't even there. She was just as alone now, in their company, as she had been five minutes ago when it was quieter. The hum of the electric wheelchair, accompanied by mumbles of both men and the sounds of computers in the far hallway were all white noise.

Wait, there was something else. She stopped and listened intently as a slight tapping noise echoed off the walls. The two men continued their stroll down the hallway, completely oblivious to the fact they'd lost a party member, and even less aware of a foreign noise.

"Stop." She spoke aloud, but neither heard her.

Brack glanced behind briefly to see her looking up towards the glass overhanging window in the atrium. He heard it too now and stopped.

The tapping continued, but it was now accompanied by a smoother, more fluent sound, like footsteps. Claire and Brack were both stalled in place.

"Troy, we need to get you back to A1." Brack was the only person Troy ever seemed to listen to, and he was the only one whose opinion mattered when it came to personal issues.

Troy didn't speak. He turned his chair and saw both Claire and Brack staring at the ceiling dome. The lights were dim in the atrium and hallways, and anyone looking in would have had a difficult time seeing inward. They all gazed at the dome now, only seeing a clear black sky, dotted with a few specks of light. The noise now shifted its direction from the west and was directly overhead.

A quick flash of light could be seen through the dome and Brack immediately reacted. His job was to keep Troy secure and protected. He grabbed the back handles of his chair and deactivated self-control.

"Claire, get to the firing deck and release the tranquilizer guns from the test range. We want these son's-a-bitches alive." Brack was only seen as Troy's henchmen, but when it came to quick judgment and orders, you knew he was the real man in charge.

Troy had been concocting another theory before Hal's arrival that a band of terrorists had hijacked the freighters, and although the prototype of the ARCA was on board, much of the research was held at their on-shore base. Whoever had made the move to steal it would surely be coming back for the rest. His paranoia was warranted.

With Troy in his care, Brack swiftly ran back towards the only room with its lights on.

Claire sprinted towards the stairs. The shooting range was a flight down and functioned as a place to test shielding equipment, new types of weaponry and ammunition, along with personal practice for handling a weapon. The whole complex was built to serve as a multipurpose facility.

Her feet flew down the stairs. The bottom level was dark, and she lost her balance as she twisted around the turn of the railing. Her sneakers slid out from underneath her on the tile floor and made a quick squeal as she fell to the ground. It took a moment to adjust to the lack of light and she stopped to catch her breath.

Kneeling, she could hear footsteps, now two stories above, and there were shadows crossing over the dome window. A red light flickered steadily, and listening carefully, it was accompanied by an in-sync beep. Someone had the intention of blowing a hole through the window.

Most of the windows and rooms throughout the complex were reinforced with Sealo-Pax glass, which was for looks more than functionality. The glass was nearly indestructible from bullets, fire or most explosions. There was a weakness, however, and only a handful of people had known about it, until the recent leaks. The glass functioned as a conductor, which is where its strength came from, similar to metals, but it was also had one weak spot. If an electrical burst made contact at the right frequency, the material would vibrate and cause the glass to shatter. It was one piece of information that had mysteriously been leaked to an outside contact, and the list of suspects was very short.

Looking up at the blinking red beacon, she could see it was counting down in quicker intervals. Information of A&H research was being leaked from the company, and whoever was staging this attack may very well be the receivers. Crouched in the shadow, she watched as the blink quickened. Three, two, one. The noise of the explosion wasn't loud, but the vibration of the glass resonated a high pitch before shattering into a rainstorm of shards. Directly below, she fell to her side and slid across the floor under the cover of a nearby desk. She wrapped her arms tightly around her knees and ducked her head as the shower of glass ricocheted from all directions.

The storm stopped after a few seconds and she pulled out from the table's protection. The window of opportunity was closing, and she needed to get to the firing deck.

Darting down the hallway, a warm flow of blood trailed down her left shoulder blade. Her senses were numb. She'd caught some of the bouncing glass, but was unsure how bad the damage was.

The first level of the complex was built mostly underground, and extended almost a quarter mile before merging with another section. The entrance to the firing deck was the last door down the hallway.

Claire came to a skidding stop. There was a quick flash of light and the familiar high pitch of the resonating glass in the corridor directly ahead.

A light pointed in her direction, blinding her as a man shouted. Raising a hand to block the beam from her eyes, she could make out two figures. She dodged backwards and grabbed for the nearest doorway. Every room in the complex would be locked at this hour and require a palm scan to enter.

Placing her hand on the digital reader, it blinked red – negative. The blood from her shoulder had trailed down her arm and now covered her hand. She slid her palm across the lab jacket, leaving a long smear as she desperately tried to clear it. The light blinked green and the door flung open with her force. She gripped the handle from the inside to keep her balance as she spun into the room. The door slammed just in time as a man's face appeared in the small glass window of the door frame.

He was an Asian man with a cloth draped over the lower portion of his face. He winked, in an odd gesture, before darting towards the center building with his partner.

With her bloody hand pressed against the doorway, she looked down and caught her breath. Although Troy was paranoid, no one could have guessed some sort of invasion was about to take place. And for what reason?

Chapter 3: Failing Answers

"Bob, you need to lock down now!" Claire's voice came through the video-com into the doctor's office. "There's been a break in. They took off for the atrium and might be heading toward the west wing."

The doctor had been trying to catch Hal up on some recent history. He didn't know much about his personal situation, but he was talkative about his own. Claire's voice had startled him and he spun towards her call.

"Claire, you're bleeding," He made a short observation. "Have you been shot?"

"Lock down NOW!"

The doctor clumsily hurried towards his desk, swept the snacks onto the floor and pulled a retractable glass plate from the underside. The glass illuminated, displaying a series of buttons and text.

"Initiate shut down in Wing 4. Authorization Prossman." With a final touch on the screen the lights shut off. Emergency red lights flickered on and illuminated the room. The sounds of rolling beams hummed around the room and the hiss of air came from the hydraulic door lock. Prossman circled as he observed the lock down go into effect. He gazed at Hal, who also watched the transition from an uncomfortable florescent office to a red, air tight prison.

"I think someone else is aware of your arrival." There was an unsettling fear in Prossman's voice. He shuffled, looking back at his surveillance screens. One screen now displayed Claire, who appeared to be looking right through to the doctor.

"They breached the glass, Doc." Her voice wasn't fear so much as surprised.

Prossman just looked at his console. "That's not possible."

She sighed and shrugged, "Yes it is." There was a long pause. This was news to the doctor, who was staring intently. "A few weeks ago during one of our trials, Marcus was testing different frequencies on the ARCA. We found a weakness."

"The accident? That wasn't construction failure?" He was puzzled, raising his hands behind his head.

"No, different vibrations, frequencies from the ARCA can break the glass." She sighed again, looking down and then back at Prossman. "Only eight people know."

"I guess not." Prossman almost found it humorous as he glanced around the room he'd felt so protected in before.

She only gave him a look of disappointment. Hal and the doctor were watching her shuffle on their screen. "If they know about the glass, they might be able to get through our security. Locking down might only slow them. We need to move Hal now. This isn't about the ARCA. They wouldn't attack us here if it was for the research. They're here for him."

"Why would they want Hal?" The doctor was completely out of the loop with Troy's conspiracy theories.

"Doc, just do it!" Claire shouted back. She didn't believe the conspiracy, but if there was a chance that Hal was involved, they couldn't risk him being captured.

Hal hadn't had much time to get a grasp on reality yet, and here he was in the middle of a lock-down in some crazy science lab, which had just been invaded by kidnappers who were here for him. And now, there was an escape plan being formed.

Claire glared through the screen at Hal. "Do you think you can run?"

Hal looked shocked. "What?"

"If Prossman can open to ventilation hatch, do you think you're able to crawl through to the next room and make a run for-"

"He hasn't even stood up yet Claire!" Promssman abruptly interrupted. "What if they have weapons?" He obviously didn't like where she was going. "Where is he going? Troy? You think that cripple is going to fight off..."

"Brack's office. It's like a bunker, Doc. If there's any place that can't be breached, it's Brack's. Whoever is staging this... we can't let them find Hal." She was insistent, and unfortunately correct. "I was within shooting range and they didn't fire. I don't believe they're armed."

"So why are you bleeding?" Prossman huffed.

"I was in the atrium when the ceiling came down. I'm fine, don't worry, but we need to move Hal now." She wasn't concerned about herself.

"The ceiling is down? God almighty! And you don't think they're armed?" He didn't expect an answer but was astonished that such a strong window could have merely been taken down.

He didn't like taking orders, especially from friends, but he hurried over to a closed office doorway and disappeared into the room, making noise as he did.

"Hal, do you think you can run?" She was still looking directly at him through the screen.

Hal had been sitting upright, but hadn't tested his balance since he'd woken up. As he shifted to the edge and began to stand, the ache of his old wounds were making themselves known. He was on two feet though.

"If it's any encouragement, the last thing I remember doing was running for my life." He smiled, although somewhat distracted by his pain.

Claire let out a sigh, relieved that he was somewhat willing and a hint of humor still existed. "That's good to know, Hal."

"That will be funny later, right?" He smiled out of the corner of his mouth. Given the situation, he was at least comforted that she was more concerned about his safety than accusing him of being part of the chaos.

Before she could answer, Dr. Prossman marched out with some clothing and equipment in his arms.

"Here, these will at least keep you somewhat covered." He handed the clothing to him before pulling out a small round device. "This will go into your ear. It's a com system. You'll be able to hear Claire and me, and we will be able to hear you. We'll direct you to Brack's office."

Hal quickly put on the clothes. They looked like someone's gym suit, but they were dark and would give him an advantage with the lights out.

"I'm sorry, I don't have shoes." The doctor had a regretful face, as if he'd just given someone a gift they greatly disliked.

"It's OK. How do I use the ear piece?"

"Oh, yes." The doctor had already partly forgotten. "Let me see your ear." Hal leaned in and turned his head as the doctor inserted a small blue ball and tangled the rubber piece around his ear, stringing the rest of the wire down the side of his neck and attaching the sticky-

23

microphone to his neck. He waddled back to his desk and spoke in the general direction of his screen.

"Can you hear me, Hal?"

"I think so." He reached to adjust the ear piece a little.

"Can you hear Claire?" The doctor asked. "Claire? Claire, can you hear me?" He looked at his screen, but she was no longer on it. "Claire?"

"Yes, I'm here. I need to call Brack. He's barricaded himself in by now and needs to know the plan. Hal, exit through the ventilation shaft in the doctor's storage closet. That will take you to the opening of the food court. The hallway going east will bring you to the atrium. On the third rise, there are four offices. You'll need to get to the last one. There won't be any lights on, but if you can get to the last door, Brack will be waiting for you. Be careful, both of you."

Hal was now dressed, but barefoot, and looked intently at the doctor. Prossman didn't know how to apologize for the shock Hal had woken up to. "Wait, before you go, you may need something."

Prossman scurried back into his closet and Hal followed. The doctor opened some shelves, which were now lit by the red caution lights. He pulled what looked like a mechanical needle for injections and six vials of a yellow liquid before loading them into some sort of side cartridge.

"Here, these are for some of the aquatic life we've sometimes had to neutralize during expeditions." He handed the mechanical device to Hal, which felt like a very lightweight hand gun. "I suppose with your background you know how to use something like this. The darts are mainly used underwater and haven't been tested on humans, but I suspect the outcome is the same. If you encounter anyone, these injections should paralyze them within 3-4 seconds. It's sort of like a cross bow, but the mechanics are much smaller. The drug works almost instantly and targets the nervous system, rather than the blood stream, so the delay is much shorter."

Hal felt a sense of comfort holding a weapon again. Albeit, it was a tranquilizer gun, it was a sense of security he hadn't felt in a long time.

"Come, in here." The doctor grabbed a screw driver gun and began to dismantle the cover to the ventilation shaft. "This goes to the food court. The doors should be unlocked, even during an emergency.

Take a left at the entrance and you'll be headed in the right direction. If you get lost, talk very quietly. The ear mic is sensitive and I'll be able to hear everything around you." He stood up, gesturing towards the opening and gave Hal a look of 'good luck' as he moved aside.

Hal smiled and gave a quick look of thanks to the doctor and then got on his hands and knees to fit into the shaft.

Chapter 4: New Encounter

The shaft was tight, closing in on his shoulders as he wiggled forward. He'd been through some rough training before, which luckily helped him overcome any previous claustrophobia. The tunnels were dark, and the only light he could see came from the red reflections ahead and behind him. His hair was much longer than he'd remembered it ever being. Rather than his short military cut, he now found himself brushing strands behind his ears simply to keep it out of his face. It was an adjustment he wasn't used to making and was now hindering his sight.

He had crawled twenty feet or so before there was a bend in the vent, which led to an even tighter tunnel. As he began to make the turn, he was relieved to see the ending vent cover. He quietly approached, unsure whether or not someone would be waiting on the other side. Pushing his hair aside, he peered through the tiny horizontal vents of the wall cover. A shadow moved passed, about thirty feet ahead.

"American Cuisine," a man mumbled with a heavy accent as he stood in front of one of the vending machines.

Hal waited, watching the man's intentions and his gestures as he shifted. He had a mask over his mouth and jaw, and a red sash over his shoulder. His attire was unique, draped over his torso, making it difficult to see whether or not he might have a weapon concealed underneath. Several seconds passed and the man started to pace, shifting his hands to his waistline, and the glimmer of light reflected from his belt. He was indeed carrying something, although still holstered. They may not have had the intention of shooting Claire, but they were armed and the only way Hal was going to be able to make it out of the room was to sedate him.

There was no graceful or easy way to do this, as the ventilation cover was screwed in from the other side. Hal reached for the tranquilizer gun that Prossman had given him. The vent holes were large enough to push the launching needle through. Very carefully, Hal wedged the device in one of the cracks and gazed through the open slat above. There was no sight on the weapon, but the aim and feel of a gun was something he would never forget. He pulled the trigger, which was soft compared to the weapons he was used to firing, but it hit its mark.

The man spun around, alarmed by the sudden pinch at his shoulder. He reached for his weapon, clumsily grabbing it with one hand. "What the fuuuu..." His body quickly grew weak as he slumped to the ground, still conscious enough to brace his fall before blacking out completely.

Hal sighed with relief. He'd been thrown into this confrontation so quickly without any choice or time to think. He'd never tested the weapon before and was afraid the doctor's estimations would have been exaggerated. It did the trick, though, and much quieter than he'd anticipated. He waited, still, to see if the man would awake or anyone would come to his aid. After a long minute, the coast remained clear.

With a swift hit, the ventilation door bowed, followed by three more hits before the pressure finally took its toll on the upper screws. Bending it to the floor, Hal could finally get a clear view.

The room was a majestic red hue and appeared to be empty. The knocking of the vent door hadn't alerted anyone, or at least not yet, and he scurried behind one piece of furniture to the next, anticipating anything or anyone.

There was no movement within the room and the shadows remained still as he worked his way to the paralyzed man on the floor. His gun was still in his hand, but it was unlike any model he'd ever seen in his time. The barrel was long, but had no silencer. It didn't appear to have any insert or clip either.

Hal held the weapon out and a flicker of the yellow caught his eye. Looking more closely at the side, he hit a release button, which opened a small cartridge that slid out of the bottom to reveal vials similar to his own pistol. Whoever these people were, they didn't come with the intention of killing.

Closing the cartridge, he pocketed the gun into the loosely fit pants. At the very least, he would have additional ammo.

The double doors to the food court were closed, but he could see through the small glass windows. The hallway looked empty, dimly lit with the red glow of the emergency lights. He opened the door cautiously, peering down the long hallway to the open atrium that glistened from the shards scattered along the floor. Tiptoeing outward, he slid his back along the wall, hiding in the shadows. Two voices could be heard to his right further down the hallway, but the whispers were foreign. He couldn't tell how many for sure, but there were at least two of them.

Hal paused and leaned into the the nearest doorway frame. The door was locked as he pressed against the handle. A small window in its frame glowed from nearby computer equipment and more emergency lights. He ducked to avoid creating a shadow.

The voices had stopped and he knelt down, concealed by his dark clothing as the footsteps approached, pausing at each door. They were inspecting the rooms.

Hal peered around the corner and could see a pair of men. Both were similarly dressed as the man in the food court and each held a weapon weapons. If he made a run for it now, they'd spot him.

He propped his elbow onto his knee and steadied his aim. The first shot was silent, and the man grabbed his neck before falling to the ground. The second man, now alarmed, ran towards his partner uttering something quietly as he placed his hand on his chest. Hal recognized his language as Japanese, but wasn't fluent enough to make any sense of what he said. He shifted his aim and fired a quick, silent shot. The man was clumsy as he spun around, returning fire with a shaky hand and striking the wall about three feet from Hal's position.

The second man resisted for a few seconds before collapsing to his knees and sliding to the floor.

It wouldn't take long before someone started to realize these men weren't responding. He sprang to his feet and started towards the open atrium.

A million shards of glass lying on the floor sparkled from the moon light above and the offices surrounding them were all dark. The last door on the left was Brack's office, and it was the furthest from him.

"Claire, does anyone know I'm coming?" He waited, pressing the earpiece further in hope of an answer. It was silent."Doctor?"

"Yes, Hal?" he answered.

"I'm two hundred feet from the doorway. It looks unoccupied." He didn't want to make a run for it only to find himself locked out in the middle of a very large, well lit room.

"Claire, can you hear Hal?" The doctor was now asking the same question. "Claire?"

"I don't want to be a sitting duck, do I go or not?" Hal anxiously looked back and forth through the open atrium.

"I... Claire? Can you hear me?" The doctor paused, now frustrated. "I don't think she can hear me."

Hal crouched. What was he supposed to do, just sit and wait? Maybe Claire had cut the radio contact. He was watching Brack's office window and door. There was absolutely no movement. If there was anyone in that office, they were either dead or incapacitated.

Movement down the hallway caught his attention. There was a shadow moving quickly from an adjacent hall. Hal backed against a wall. With his naked feet and dark clothing, he was silent and well hidden. The shadow became elongated as the person approached the atrium and Hal held his breath.

"Mitsuya?... Mitsuya?" A man in similar dress appeared in the light. He frantically glanced in every direction, when his focus stopped on his fallen comrades. His hand went to his weapon, although he didn't draw it.

Hal drew in a silent breath in, and sliding along the wall he ducked into the indent of the doorway.

The man looked straight at him as he passed, peering through the darkness but unable to see him. He slowed, and then stopped. The throbbing of Hal's heartbeat should have alerted him by now.

There was a gasp from the man as he grabbed for his own shoulder. He glanced away, looking into the atrium before collapsing. Through unconscious reflex Hal threw out his arms to catch him and gently slid him to the floor.

"Hal?" It was Claire. He could hear her voice in the room and through the earpiece as she ran towards him and ducked into the same doorway.

She looked at him as best she could in the darkness. "I know this isn't what you expected waking up, but we can explain it later. We need to get to Brack's office."

He looked at her confused. Not expected? That was a loose way of putting it. He looked down at his tranquilizer gun. She had one as well, which was covered in blood from her shoulder wound.

"The door is just down this hallway. I've counted six men so far and..." She glanced down the hallway to see the other two men laying on the floor, "two more."

"Three. There was a man in the food court."

Claire peered her head around the corner and gazed up towards the shattered ceiling dome as new movement could be seen on the roof.

"I think we're going to have to make a run for it." There was no telling how many men were there, which wasn't the only entry point.

The third level of the atrium was covered in a thin layer of glass. It was well lit from the moon above, and the shimmering glass on the floor was not going to make this a covert escape.

"On the count of three?" Hal almost sounded as if he were joking.

Claire just looked at him as if she were reconsidering.

He took that as a yes, because either way, they couldn't stay in the hallway with three unconscious men suspiciously laying on the ground near them. "1, 2, 3."

Hal grabbed her wrist, partly to help keep balance, but also making sure she didn't get left behind. He knew her hesitation was out of fear, regardless of how tough she might have looked carrying a weapon.

The dash was painful. Her sneakers crunched the glass below, but his bare feet did not.

They reached the office door, and no one had seemed alarmed. She scanned her hand on the door entry pad and it blinked red – rejection. She frantically pressed again. Red again.

Hal grabbed her wrist and pulled her hand towards him. She didn't resist. The panic and fear in her eyes was showing. He took the cloth of his shirt and wiped her hand and wrist. Placing her hand on the scanner, it blinked red again.

Hal swung his gaze around the room. They were in bright moonlight and could have easily been seen. A voice from above was returned by a yell from below. Shit.

He turned his face to Claire again. She was paralyzed with fear. Her eyes were glued to the shadows above, and a stream of tears could be seen on her cheeks.

Hal pulled her hand back towards him. He spit onto his shirt and roughly wiped her hand the pushed her to the side slightly and wiped the scanner, which was also bloody now. One last shot at this before a whole team of men converged on them.

He pulled her hand onto the scanner. Red.

The door swung open and a large arm reached outward and grabbed Claire by the shoulder. She was still gazing upwards as she was pulled into the room sideways.

Hal grabbed the inside ledge of the door frame and spun to the other side. His feet were wet, and he slid, clinging to the wall. The door hissed with a slam as they disappeared into the dark.

Hal was pulled backwards, his mouth covered by a large hand.

"It's him!" Claire gasped. "It's Hal."

The hand released and the grip loosened. The room was completely dark, and he turned to face the people behind him, but couldn't see their faces.

The main windows were covered with blinds and only a small stream of light filtered through the tiny window in the doorway. With an arm still around Hal's chest, he was pulled backwards into the dark.

"Come, sit." It wasn't exactly a welcoming invitation, but he wasn't going to argue.

Hal backed up and was released. He knelt down, sliding even further until his back hit a wall. Shallow breaths came from another occupant just beside him.

Chapter 5: The Welcome Party

Aside from the sounds of breathing, he could hear Claire sniffle and shuffle as she wiped her face. Brack must have been the man with the firm grip next to him. His breathing was steady and unchanged. He didn't even sound the least bit agitated. There was a glimmer of yellow as Hal recognized the loaded tranquilizer in his hand.

"Are you hurt?" Brack asked.

"I'll recover." It was a quick remark. Claire on the other hand was bleeding badly. "I think she caught some falling glass."

Still covered in darkness, it was hard to see movement right next to him. Brack shuffled towards her and a glimmer of green goggles now gave more light to his position. He could see Claire faintly in the glow and the horror on her face wasn't hidden by the smear of tears and blood.

"Let me see your back." The man's tone was more gentle towards her. With a firm grip, he tore the back of her clothing off. Even with the lights off, the green glow reflected several small fragments of glass wedged into her skin all the way from her shoulder to mid back.

"I'm sorry, Claire." He paused before pressing his gun to the base of her neck and she instantly slumped forward.

Hal wasn't entirely sure what was happening at that moment, but his fear was suddenly paralyzing. Having been in the darkness for about a minute now, his eyes were beginning to adjust and able to make out his surroundings.

Brack stood and reached for the nearby desk. His hands slid along the underside and retracted a glass panel that was now illuminating the dark room. With a series of hand gestures, a hydraulic hiss sounded from behind.

From the outside, the sudden gleam of light must have attracted attention as shadows quickly fluttered passed the small window. A man's face suddenly appeared, spotting the targets.

The hiss of the door stopped as it opened, letting more light out of the glass elevator chamber.

"Get in." Brack wasn't asking. The other occupant, who he could now see was in a wheelchair began to roll backwards into the

32

cage. Hal was still crouched down and quickly followed. Brack pushed the glass slate back under the desk and picked up Claire before stepping into the chamber.

The hydraulic hiss sounded again and a pane of glass slid down in front of them. The face in the doorway was infuriated and made the gesture of 'I see you' before the cage descended out of view.

The glass cage was cramped and Claire lay limp in Brack's arms. Fluorescent lights hung on the dirt walls descending downward. By his guess, they must have gone down at least ten stories.

"Do you have a history with them?" Brack didn't even glance in his direction as he asked.

"Who?" Hal was still crouched down, holding his tranquilizer gun with a firm grip. "These men?"

Brack now glared at him with a blank face. It was hard to see any expression with his goggles on. "Yes, these men. The Yotogi."

"Who the hell are the Yotogi?" His expression was self-explanatory.

"Good." Brack was satisfied with his answer.

There was a long silence in the elevator as it continued its descent. Hal stood, now realizing they were out of reach from those above. His feet were bleeding from running on the glass, but his callused bottoms had held up surprising well.

The elevator came to a soft halt and the glass door opened before Brack took a few steps out. "Lights on." The room suddenly flickered to a brightly lit office, surrounded by steel walls and two metal tables.

"Clear a desk." Brack nodded towards one of the nearby tables as he carried Claire towards it.

Hal sprinted ahead of him, sweeping the clutter onto the floor in one large push.

"Help me roll her on her side." His night vision goggles still covered his eyes and he struggled to see as he tried to gently place Claire on her side.

Hal grabbed her ankles and helped position her. Her back was exposed and flickers of red light reflected from the shards of glass extruding from her skin. He glanced back at the other man who was in the elevator with them. His wheelchair slowly approached as he observed the woman, but his face showed no emotion.

Brack swung his head back, which caused his goggles to raise to his forehead. He reached into his pocket and pulled out a retractable small knife. At the same time, he reached inside the desk below and grabbed a small box. "Fill this with the water at the workstation there." He nodded towards the far wall that had a small counter top and sink.

As he lifted the lid of the box, he saw what looked like a blue mesh pile of medical gauze. As the water made contact, they quickly expanded to the top of the box.

The 'tink' of the glass hitting the metal table was the only sound in the room. Without conversation, Brack quickly removed the larger shards from Claire's back and laid the blue mesh material on her skin. Once the material made contact, there was an instant gel that began filling in the gaps.

"She's lost a bit of blood." Brack's voice was almost mechanical, but he knew what he was doing. "There are some IV needles and tubing in the drawer below the sink." He glanced back at Hal, with his goggles still on his forehead. "Please retrieve them."

As instructed, Hal sprinted toward the sink again and grabbed an armful of supplies. He was no medical doctor and wasn't sure what packages to be looking for, so he grabbed anything that looked useful.

He handed them to Brack, who ripped a package open with his teeth and attached a small needle to the end of a clear hollow tube before placing it into her skin on the side of her neck. Blood slowly began to rise in the tube, and Brack attached the other end of tubing to a needle and punctured a small bag of orange fluid that dripped down into her body. He held the needle in its position and placed the IV bag on a hook that clamped to a pole.

"Please pull a chair over for me." It was the first expression of courtesy Brack had shown.

The room was quiet as he sat, staring at his watch. He occasionally reached to feel the pulse in Claire's wrist and glanced back at the other occupant still staring from his wheelchair, unmoved.

"She'll survive." There was no reaction or concern on the man's face.

For someone that was quick to give orders, there was a side to Brack now being shown that was much more concerned. He reached down for a gauze and placed it over her neck before withdrawing the needle.

Hal felt suddenly uncomfortable as both men shifted their gaze to him.

"It's about time you woke up. We have a few questions." Brack removed the goggles from his forehead, revealing a red imprint where they had been.

Hal took a seat against the adjacent desk and took a deep breath. So far the only questions he'd been asked were from Claire and the Doctor. None of which made sense.

"These men, we believe they were after the cargo on board cargo freighters 48 and 49. We had equipment related to a project ARCA we were conducting here." For a company so concerned with secrecy, Brack was giving quite a few details, but there was no emotion or look or recognition on Hal's face.

"Do not give him information!" The other man in the chair finally spoke up.

Brack abruptly turned towards him. "This is Robert Troy, head representative of A&H here." He made a gesture towards him. "The information is not secret anymore. The project has been compromised for some time now, and you know that. This veil of secrecy and your orders have failed." Brack stared in Hal's direction, but spoke to the man behind.

The man in the chair retracted and backed away. Brack rolled his eyes in frustration before bringing the focus back to Hal.

"I do not believe that you are a member of the Yotogi, nor do you have an agenda to destroy our research, but they have a definite interest in you, and I want to know what that is." He shifted in his chair and crossed his arms, expecting an answer.

Hal took a moment and rested his head in his hands. "The last thing I remember was running through a wooded area in dense fog." He lifted his bare feet to show callused bottoms, hardly marked by the same shards of glass that had left Claire badly injured. "I can't explain it to you because I don't know." He paused, desperately trying to remember anything in between. "Before that, I was flying a standard route from Miami to Bimini with four student pilots before we were engulfed in a storm cloud of some sort. Our instruments were disabled and we were unable to make contact with anyone at either base." He lowered his head again and sighed. "I ordered everyone to bail out with an inflatable boat before blacking out. Those are the last events that I can remember."

"I believe you." Brack's answer was surprising. Perhaps Hal had been in the military too long, but questioning a subject, especially one who may have committed sabotage, would have never been taken for his word. Troy was most certainly upset with his reaction, but for some reason Brack was satisfied by the lack of answers.

"How can we believe him? He was on the wreckage!" Troy had a limited tone capacity with his paralysis, but his wrath wasn't at all restrained.

Brack was not one to be questioned and his response was equally defensive. "No, you were not on the search team, and the wreckage was not determined to be from our ships. Our ships are designed to sink when tampered with." He pointed directly at Hal while speaking to Troy. "And had he been on it, we'd have a body on the ocean floor." He lowered his hand and now gazed at Hal. "If the Yotogi had left a man behind, and I don't believe they would have, he would not be alive."

The note struck home with Troy and he remained silent, although not composed.

"I don't understand. You believe these Yotogi sunk your ship?" Hal was now the one asking the question.

"Yes. It's no secret that they have started protesting our research, but this was a violent move for them. They've never before taken physical actions towards us, at least not that we can prove. Even with the power behind their movement, we lack any evidence against them." Brack had become more relaxed, and he was no longer looking at Hal as an outsider. "They wanted you alive. I want to know why they'd make such an attempt."

There was a long pause before anyone spoke again. Both men were staring at him expecting some sort of a response, but he had nothing. In a way, it was the best answer he could give, as Brack looked for any signs of defense or self-preservation, but there was none. He put his head in his hands and closed his eyes. Why him? What did they expect from someone like him? "Could it have been someone on the plane I was with? Would they have had something on

36

board that could have triggered our crash back then? I've never heard of any groups called the Yotogi before."

"Not likely. Your passengers were never found in the area you were flying over." Brack was mild-toned now. He knew the circumstances of his disappearance, but not much more than that.

Hal had a sinking feeling and turned away. He didn't know whether or not they'd even made it to shore after they bailed the plane with the parachutes and boat. "So they were lost at sea?"

"That's what's in the report. But I think it's highly unlikely the Yotogi had even formed a small congregation then or knew of your crash."

Hal was beginning to feel a slight bit of anger. His head pounded with frustration and disbelief, feeling the panic rise up as the non-reality started to become real. What the hell was happening? Here he was on a research base that was under attack in 2039! He'd lost four students on a plane and these men were now asking him questions about a terrorist organization? What about him! What about those kids?

"I understand your frustration." He could see Hal's anger growing, and in a way, he understood that the circumstances he was now finding himself in were, to say the least, confusing.

"You don't understand! What about those men? Those kids! They were just kids! Have they just been missing for twenty-six years? Why am I even here?" Hal sat down on the edge of the adjacent desk again and began to rock back and forth. "Am I in the middle of a nightmare? This can't be real."

He paused and put his face in his palms. There were no memories. He thought back, reliving the event in his head, second by second. "The radio is static. We were at a thousand feet. I could see the water right below us." He took a long breath in. "The radio just started screeching for no reason. There was no communication before it started malfunctioning. Everyone took off their headsets and I continued to listen but it was just noise. Our instruments went off the boards. They said we were declining in altitude hundreds of feet, but the plane wasn't moving. We were holding steady, visually. The students realized something was wrong and began trying for the radio, but there was no response."

Brack seemed interested, but Troy just stared angrily.

"Movement was fine. The steering and handling was fine! I would have felt the vertigo, but there was none. Our instruments were telling us something was terribly wrong." He looked at Brack expecting him to have a theory or an answer, but he remained silent. "There was a sudden flash of light and it was if we'd all blacked out simultaneously, but I didn't sense any change in altitude. When our vision came back, we were heading into what looked like a storm cloud." His tone had changed, having recalled this much.

"Were there any changes in the weather before you took off?"

"No. None. It was the perfect day for flying. You can see for miles in the air, and fly by sight if you're only a few hundred feet above the ground." Hal knew where he was going with this, believing he may have misjudged the weather. "I would have seen a storm miles away. I'm certain it was not there. Even if it had been, I've handled circumstances much more hazardous."

"I've read your record. I believe you." Brack was suddenly retracting his accusation. Hal had nearly a perfect record and could fly an eight ton cargo plane with one failed engine. His record was never in question, but given the circumstances, it had to be asked. "Please continue."

Hal could sense Brack's interest as genuine, and if he were in his position, he would have asked as well.

"We couldn't see the ground after we entered the cloud. I tried to turn back but our instruments were jammed. It was as if everything had completely stalled. Nothing responded." He shook his head. None of it made any sense. "The plane just went out of control. We had nothing on the stick, our gauges were going in circles. We had no way of telling how high we were anymore. Everything just failed all at once. Even my watch, which had a compass and altitude gauge. It's as if we had flown right into an electrical storm."

Brack and Troy perked at the words electrical storm. Their interest had finally changed from simply listening to something that they now recognized. "Were there any charges going off? Sparks of electricity?"

Hal raised his eyebrows. "Yeah, there was. I'd never seen anything like it before." Something about Brack's inquiry had suddenly helped him remember. "We were seeing flashes of blue and green on the windshield when they made contact with the plane."

Brack now looked at Troy who nodded. "We've seen similar results during certain tests in our lab, here." He made a gesture towards the metal gray metal door.

Hal stood and approached the door, noticing a faint glimmer from scratch marks. "These marks." Hal tapped the metal material, a strong steel. "Are they from an explosion?"

"Yes." Brack's answer was quickly followed by Troy's discontent for saying it, which was ignored. "We had an incident about five weeks back. Some of our instruments malfunctioned and one of our containment chambers simply burst. We've been investigating the accident, but so far we haven't been able to pin point the cause." Brack's voice had changed now to a somber tone. "One of our surviving lab technicians reported the glass began sparking just before it exploded."

"Surviving techs?" Hal could sense the gap in his story, which must have been a sore spot.

Brack choked, and cleared his throat. "Yes, there were four casualties in the accident. Kyra was the only one within the lab that made it into this room before the initial blast and flooding." There was another pause before he glanced at Claire, still laying motionless on the table. "She's Claire's lab partner."

He shuffled and stood. "Those marks are from the initial explosion and where many of the electrical sparks landed. Thankfully the door held." He was still holding something back.

"And what of the other technicians?" He was beginning to wonder whether or not there had been any evidence on the bodies of the other people inside.

Troy was approaching in his chair before. "We're not discussing the condition of our faculty here. I want to know what you were doing at the last known location of our ships, and why the Yotogi have such an extreme interest in you."

"You're asking me? With all your science equipment, you can't find two boats and you're side-stepping my questions. What happened to my crew, my plane!" Even though Troy's figure in the wheelchair was no doubt devastating, he was not the victim here.

"We have not found our employees." Brack stepped in, trying to shift the discussion. He knew Hal wanted answers just as much as he did, especially regarding his fellow colleagues. "The flooding came to eight feet and all of our technicians have been trained for deep sea diving. There were no exits, aside from the room we're currently standing in, and we do not have their bodies. I can't explain the disappearances, just as I can't explain yours, but I assure you my desire for answers is just as valid." He was now standing between Hal and Troy. "So please, if you recall anything else..."

Hal took a moment to breathe in Brack's plea for answers. "There's nothing more. I told the crew to pack up and jump with a life raft. I assumed that they'd at least have a shot paddling to the shore. The rest is blank. I simply can't remember if I passed out or if there was an explosion, or a crash." Hal sat on the desk, placing some distance between him and Troy. "I just don't know."

They had more in common than he'd considered, and it wasn't so much a question of who to blame as much as it was a need for closure.

The timing couldn't have been better when the hydraulic gate lifted from the elevator shaft. Both Hal and Brack spun to face its direction, holding their tranquilizer pistols. Through the glass, he could see Doctor Prossman, shaken at the sight of having weapons pointed at him. He immediately and sloppily held both hands in the air. Hal lowered his gun but Brack did not.

The door lifted and still, Brack held his aim. "Are you alone?"

"Why yes! Stop it! I wouldn't bring anyone else down here. What kind of guest do you think I am?" Prossman was a comical relief, and Brack let his guard fall.

"How did you get into my office?" There was only one elevator leading down to this room, and the other entrance was from the room behind them.

"You left your door open." He twitched and smiled from one corner of his mouth. "I don't believe I have a key to your office."

"No, you don't." Brack was now off guard. "The door was locked."

Prossman glanced backward and almost spun off balance. "Are you sure?" His mannerisms were like a child asking an adult whether they'd left their keys in a locked car.

"Were you followed?" Brack was now walking passed him and glanced up at the ceiling of the glass elevator.

"Well, no, I don't think so. I couldn't get communication through our com system so I waited until the boat left the pier." He pointed at a screen before approaching it and turning on a camera feed showing the ocean outside.

"A boat?" Apparently this was news to both Brack and Troy, as they came closer.

"Yes, they've been there for about a day. I figured it was one of ours, until the lights started going out." He was waving his hand around, as if he'd been the only one smart enough to have noticed something as obvious as a foreign boat at the front door. "Once they left, I walked right out and saw your door was open."

Brack was wide-eyed at the statement. Here they had been under scrupulous watch for anything unusual, and there had been someone's watch dog just outside the front gate.

"Oh, and we have a new guest!" The doctor was peppy with an announcement. "I found a gentleman in the food court and with some extra zip ties, I chained him to one of our dinner tables. Mind you, I thought it'd be rude to leave him without something to eat."

Everyone looked at the doctor now with a sense of relief and astonishment, of which he proudly put his hands behind his back and nodded.

There was a long pause before Hal shrugged and laughed. Brack followed with a chuckle of relief and the doctor contently turned to notice Claire on the table.

"Oh my gosh! Is she...?"

"She's sedated. She's lost some blood and will need some stitches. Do you think you can manage this while we entertain our new guest?" Brack glanced at the security feed one more time before pulling away and walking towards Claire. "I'll take her to the medical bay, and Hal, meet us back there when you're ready."

Troy was now glaring at Brack with what looked like jealousy. There was a sense of understanding between Brack and Hal, and he had no similar part. He did a full turn in his wheelchair and faced away from the two before quickly zipping into the elevator shaft. Brack very carefully picked Claire off the table and walked into the glass box before the hiss of the hydraulic door shut and proceeded upwards.

"Are you OK Mr. Brent?" The doctor who had been abnormally peppy turned towards him with a look of concern. His gaze shifted to his feet, which were dark with dry blood. "I'm sorry I didn't have anything for your feet."

"I'll be fine." He smiled and put a hand on the doctor's frail shoulder. "Thank you for the clothing."

His wrinkled cheeks lifted and he shrugged. "I like to prepare for anything, but I don't exercise much, so the clothes are always there. Come. We'll get you something a little more formal upstairs."

Hal gazed around at the room as the doctor walked towards the elevator. He hadn't paid much attention at the time, but this must be part of the underwater complex.

Looking around, he could see water damage in the ceiling corners. The steel walls were matte, with the exception of those spots. The lights flickered every now and then, but didn't go out. Overall, it was a sterile, empty, metal box. The two desks and metal cabinets were the only pieces of furniture that occupied the large room. The hiss of the hydraulic door interrupted his interest and he followed Prossman into the glass box.

Chapter 6: Recovery

Hal sat in the same place he first found himself. He was perched on the soft exam table in the doctor's office and Claire lay on the neighboring bed next to him, still unconscious and breathing heavily. The doctor had removed the rest of the glass shards and stitched what needed to be. She had a large blue bandage covering her neck and most of her back now. The damage had only been skin deep, but according to the doctor would leave a nice battle scar.

He wasn't sure how to occupy himself. He kept playing the events of his plane crash, or blackout, but they were sporadic images that lead to no answers. Nothing more could be remembered beyond what he had already told. He just kept thinking about his passengers. Not one of them could have been more than thirty years old, and they had just vanished.

It was now almost eight in the morning. He wasn't sure where to go or what to do. There was a new *guest* in the food court where Hal had left him sedated, which the doctor had so proudly contained with zip ties.

The Yotogi were still unknown to Hal. He had never heard about them before, or at least they weren't an establishment that he could remember. Brack and Troy had left out many details and the doctor seemed relatively clueless. He merely described them as anti-technology wackos and left it at that. The question still burned Hal, though. Why were they interested in him? He had nothing of value here. He didn't even have a valid passport anymore, much less any piece of valuable technology. They came in with tranquilizers, not weapons, which he was pretty sure still existed in 2039.

After the initial shock had worn off, he found himself bored.

The door quietly opened and Brack strutted in, followed closely by his controller, Troy, who had remained silent since their last exchange of words. Now, having a closer look in better light, he could see what a sad figure he really was, and perhaps his sense of giving orders was the only grip of control he had over people. Troy was an older man, somewhere in his early sixties, Hal guessed. His posture was poor, indicating some sort of neurological injury at a high level. He maneuvered his power chair with the use of several fingers, but it was still very weak control at that. His neck and right cheek had some slight scarring, possibly from burns.

"Our guest still remains unconscious, so maybe it's time we fill in some of the blanks." Brack was referring to him now, and his tone had been much more mild than before. Formality had been moved aside, and with his recent interest in his own missing colleagues, perhaps he was seeing some mutual benefit if he played nice.

Hal adjusted himself, crossing his arms over his chest and leaned back against the exam table's backrest. "I can't remember anymore about the crash. I've rolled it around in my head a thousand times, and I just... it feels like my memory has been wiped blank."

Troy looked upwards at Brack, as if that were somehow the answer he'd been hoping for. "We believe that may have been their intention."

Hal simply looked at Troy, not entirely sure where he'd be going with this.

Brack came closer and sat on the edge of the neighboring exam table where Claire lay, still unconscious.

"We believe that someone may have been holding you as some sort of hostage. It would explain the memory loss, had they intended to keep something a secret, such as your location or what you may have witnessed." Brack was sympathetic, but his skepticism in Troy's theory was also showing.

"I'm sorry, what? You believe I was held captive somewhere as a prisoner? What would anyone want from a retired pilot?"

Troy began to speak, but paused before being able to catch his breath. His paralysis had affected his breathing and speech. "The Yotogi may have used you to make a point." He adjusted himself in his chair as much as possible. "They are believers in paranormal activities, and poor magicians at that." He paused to breath in. "If they can make others believe in these activities with someone who has come back and forth, they will become a stronger opposition force for us here."

Troy's beliefs always focused around the 'good of his company' and never stopped to consider outside motives. Hal had never met the Yotogi formally, or even observed them on TV, and the idea that he was abducted was ridiculous right off the bat.

He gave Troy a doubtful look as he squinted. "For twenty-six years? How can you explain such a time gap?"

Brack had obviously already asked this question as he quickly responded. "We're not entirely sure. It is possible to suspend life in various forms. We do it here, sometimes, testing on various types of sea life."

"But I thought you said the Yotogi have only been some sort of establishment for a number of years. Is it possible they could have somehow, I don't know, abducted my crew and I that long ago?" Hal was considering the possibility, but only because it was the only explanation to go on so far.

Troy again was anxious to speak. "It is possible, yes. They may have been a small group long before anyone realized. There are several leaders that have opposed various types of advancing technology for decades."

"You mention going back and forth. Back and forth to where?"

"The Bermuda Triangle." Troy was serious as he spoke, and Brack simply put his head down. Hal looked between the two, both of which just stared with silence.

Hal found himself torn between laughter and anger. Was this some sort of joke or was he serious?

"I'm sorry. The Bermuda Triangle?" His eyes were wide from the ridiculous answer.

"Why yes! That could be!" Now the doctor's interest had also been perked, completely oblivious to Hal's sarcastic response.

"No, I did not say it *was* the Bermuda Triangle. I said that the Yotogi would like to make people think it is." Troy was as loud as his paralysis would allow, but the point was made. "They're trying to frame you for being some sort of anomaly, which is why they want you in their custody – to publicize this false event."

"But if I was in their custody, why would they have simply let me be taken in by you?"

"They may not have let you. Your last memory was some sort of chase. You were running through a green fog in the woods. It sounds very much like the environmental conditions currently on Bermuda." This was Hal's first history lesson in 2039, where the island of Bermuda had apparently seen some catastrophic nuclear activity.

Hal shifted uncomfortably. He wasn't sure if it was a cruel joke, but his memory had somehow been erased and he couldn't explain it. This may be the reason why the Yotogi had intended to capture him alive rather than in a body bag.

"So, what do I do now?" All immediate thoughts of his current life were erased. He had no family, no friends, and on the record, he was a dead man.

"We don't do what they expect us to. We keep it quiet." Troy was referring to him as *us*, now considering he might be somewhat valuable.

"You're their token for publicity, and as much as I hate to play their game and keep you as a hostage, I think it's for your own safety." Brack was genuinely concerned for a number of reasons, whereas Troy was merely focused on his own company's interests.

"So is this some sort of witness protection?" He looked around at the men who, despite giving the invitation to stay, were inconvenienced by his presence.

"We'll provide you with quarters down below. Most of our staff lives in a complex nearby and all the provisions will be available to you here." Brack reached into his slacks for something hidden in a back holster. "This should be a familiar tool for you." He handed Hal a hand pistol similar to the tranquilizer gun he'd had earlier. "We're not taking chances with them again, and you will have access to many other tools we have here to keep you safe, but the resources you're being exposed to are to remain confidential"

Hal gripped the weapon with one hand, surprised at how much heavier it was than the one the doctor originally provided. Adjusting his grip, the familiarity of a hand weapon was still instinctual to him. A laser sight was fitted on the top, along with a silenced barrel that added about five inches to its frame.

"It's quiet and holds a sedative round capable of tranquilizing an elephant for twenty four hours. It should neutralize any threat immediately." Reaching into another holster, he pulled out something he still recognized – a tracking device and wire. "For your safety, I would like you to wear this on your person at all times." He handed the devices to Hal, which were smaller than the technologies he remembered, but were similar enough.

Hal took them and looked around on his body for a means to attach them, but on his current doctor-provided exercise pants, there were none.

"Clothing has also been provided." Brack went to the back of Troy's chair which held a small leather pack, no doubt filled with stylish goodies and trinkets. "You'll also find some various equipment you may find useful, along with a security key pass for the mess hall, your quarters and the firing range, in case you'd like to tone your skills. You have all the freedoms of our entry level technicians here, along with a transponder which will give you communication with Claire, the doctor and myself," he said as he handed the bag to Hal. "It's a large complex. You will be monitored where ever you go, for your own safety, of course. More importantly, you will have the resources to protect yourself if needed. We will try to give you as much freedom as we can in these circumstances."

Hal was grateful that he would at least be allowed to wander outside the medical bay, and was comforted by the fact he would be holding a weapon again, although he wasn't entirely happy they'd be monitoring his every move and activity, it was a sign of mutual trust.

"In the meantime, I'd like you to stay here until Claire has come out of it and when our other guest has awoken, I would like you to be present during the questioning. If they know you're cooperating with us, he may be more forthcoming." Brack shrugged and began to stand. "I am more interested in his reaction than his answers though. The Yotogi are notorious for being cryptic, and I'm fairly certain he won't outright admit you were their prisoner, but nonetheless your presence may send a message."

There was a moment of pause before they both nodded in agreement. Brack turned to Troy, inquiring his next order to take.

"We'll go back to the holding area and alert you once he is awake." Troy had begun to make a move for the door before finishing his sentence. Even now, he was annoyed at Hal's presence, but he would have to make due until he was no longer needed.

"This may be our only chance to find one of their leaders and finally see what their intentions were." Brack quickly turned to Troy and followed towards the door.

Chapter 7: An Answer

In the pack, Hal found a pouch filled with green vials, which were similarly shaped to his previous ammo cartridges, but with a slight color difference. He'd expected the clothing to be more formal than what was provided, which contained an undershirt and short sleeve cotton t-shirt. A black over-jacket was a material he'd never felt before, much like denim, but much more flexible and puncture-proof. The pants were standard blue jeans, one size too big but a belt made them fit reasonably well. They apparently still had comfort and practicality in the future.

Once dressed, Hal continued to rummage through the bag, finding more trinkets than he knew how to use. The doctor intently watched as Hal explored these new devices, quickly offering his insight on their function. There was a sleek arm attachment that could be seated on his forearm and indicated direction, altitude, body temperature, heart monitor and injury status, heaven forbid he ever needed a device to alert him. It fit like a fingerless latex glove that extended up the forearm and responded to the touch of his fingers. The surface was illuminated by the wiring and display, which showed its readings on various meters. It amazed Hal how technology had evolved to the point where it could simply be worn like a glove, and did not hinder movement in the least. The sheer material stretched with his movement and only responded to his 'bio-signature' as the doctor quoted it.

The other device Hal found was the transponder, which fit onto the shoulder of his left arm, wrapping around his chest. The material was the same, and had a small buckle that sat comfortably on his chest, just below the neck. An accompanying ear piece was optional, and fastened to the device when not in use. All in all, Hal felt as if he'd suddenly been upgraded and dressed in the most up-to-date gear this day and age had to offer. For the first time since he'd woken up, he felt a sense of control and security for his own being. His grip on this new reality was still difficult to grasp. The disbelief of it all still wouldn't let him so easily accept it, but at the moment, he was at least physically prepared for whatever might be thrown at him.

Claire mumbled and began to stir. The doctor turned his focus from his computer screen, which was now showing security feed that everyone had been examining for the past four hours.

"I think she's regaining consciousness." It was an obvious observation, but at least there would be something different to focus on.

The doctor grabbed her by the shoulder to help wake her, and also help steady her on the table. She slowly opened her eyes and sighed at the ache of her neck and back.

"Good morning Claire." The doctor smiled as she slowly responded to his touch.

She lifted herself into a somewhat sitting position and looked around groggily.

"You're in sick bay. How do you feel?" He already knew, judging by the dark circles under her eyes and pale skin, but his inquiry was out of innocent concern.

"I feel pretty shitty right about now." Her response made him giggle lightly. Hal too. She sat up completely now and lifted the garments over her shoulder for cover. "Are we still under lock down?"

The doctor just shook his head and patted her hand.

She was facing the doctor and looked over her shoulder at Hal, who sat staring at her exposed backside covered in blue mushy gauze. "I'm sure it's not as bad as it looks. The enzymes will help tissue rebuild in a day or so."

She stood from the table and stretched. "Anything from the cameras? Do we know why they are here on base?"

The doctor looked at Hal, "I think they were here for him. Hopefully we can ask them soon, though."

"Really?" She was pulling at her hospital gown now, which covered her front side, but not the back.

"Yes! They left one man behind, and I managed to capture him before they realized it, I bet." The man had already been heavily sedated by the time he found him, but he failed to mention that.

Hal remained silent on the table as he watched the doctor comically tell the story. The sunlight was coming through one of the windows, and he'd forgotten the feel of daylight on his skin. He also found his gaze directed at Claire. Her dark red hair was no longer pinned back and fell past her shoulders. Her back was exposed and left a small window to her lower half. She was a pretty girl in her mid thirties and in the sunlight her tanned skin was drastically different from his own. A quick glare from the doctor caught his attention and he realized how inappropriate it was to be staring.

"Troy and Brack have already been in to see Hal. They were kind enough to give him some new equipment too. Although, I don't think it was Troy's idea." The doctor obviously wasn't very fond of Troy, but he seemed to have a neutral opinion of Brack. Then again, he hadn't met anyone fond of Troy, yet. "They gave him quarters down below and expect you to give him the tour, I believe."

Claire smiled at the doctor and looked down at her garments, realizing she was somewhat exposed. She reached for the back of her draped-on medical gown and walked into the doctor's closet.

The doctor smiled and winked at Hal as she left, completely aware that he'd caught a glimpse of her more inappropriate side, but he remained quiet.

When she came back out, she was wearing a loosely fit exercise shirt, covered by a short sleeve white lab jacket. Standard black working slacks and sneakers weren't exactly how he'd pictured futuristic woman's clothing, but practical. Her hair was again pinned in its normal style, tied back in a loose bun. She made a hand gesture to come along and follow.

Hal got off the bench, again taking notice at how nice the flexible shoulder and arm equipment felt. He followed her out of the doctor's office, casting a glance of thank you towards him before heading out the door and continuing down the hallway towards the atrium. The building was much brighter during the daylight hours, and the lack of red caution lights made him feel a little less on edge.

"So, did Brack and Troy ever give you a theory on your..." She paused, "I'm sorry, I'm not sure what to call it."

"My appearance here?" He looked downward, also unsure what to call it.

"Yeah, your arrival." She looked at him with interested, but tired eyes.

"They think I may have been an experimental subject for the Yotogi, or something along those lines." His response was new to her and held a look of surprise. "I'm not sure what to make of it. I don't remember being in any sort of captivity, and until yesterday, I'd never even heard of the Yotogi. Brack's theory just seems... it just feels so far-fetched. "

She perched her lips and thought about the idea for a moment. "You want to know what I think?"

"Yes, I would." He was partly joking in her playful response, but he was also genuinely curious for a sane person's opinion.

"I think it's as plausible as anyone's theory so far. It's just all so... I don't even know how to put it. When you first arrived, our main concern was your survival. We had no idea who you were at the time, let alone how long ago your last flight was. This past week has been such a whirlwind, I haven't had time to stop and think about just how confusing and unrealistic it all is. The mere fact that you're here... There has to be foul play somewhere. " She shrugged, partly knowing it was some sort of wacko idea Troy came up with. "The Yotogi are extreme believers in various types of world anomalies. Everything from the Bermuda Triangle to the ring of fire. They believe it's mother nature's way of protesting our growth." She paused, thinking about what other information Brack and Troy may have given him.

"They believe that the recent turmoil with Russia and the disaster on Bermuda was a result of conflicts with the Earth. Messengers of mother Earth, rebelling with violent actions to protest any sort of progression and regularity," she sarcastically added. "I'm not saying I believe it, but with fanatics, you can't really find legitimate reason either. Their support has been growing. I don't know why. They never even make public announcements or statements, and yet they keep recruiting more and more. Could they have had something to do with your disappearance, then held you in some sort of stasis? Then how does that get connected with our freighters and research disappearing?" She shrugged, trying hard to sort through the possibilities.

They reached the atrium and paused, looking down as three men cleaned the remaining glass shards from the lower levels. She leaned onto the guardrail causally and watched, partly recalling the night's events.

"We've spent the last decade trying to clean up the world's disasters. We're trying to reverse the damage mankind has done to our planet and to help protect the general public. Sealo-Pax is used to reconstruct old concrete buildings, subway tunnels, even underwater passageways. We're in the business of protection, and with that, our military as well." She looked up at him, not sure how much he'd be able to absorb. "I know Troy and Brack have mentioned our recent project - the one everyone is so paranoid about. I'm not sure how much they've told you, but by now you've at least heard of it. The ARCA was going to be used to remove chemical waste. The details of it are complicated, but Bermuda was going to be our first testing ground. We've had some instability problems with it, but its potential is... it's so much more than they know. The Yotogi, these protesting groups, if they only knew what they were preventing..."

Hal leaned on the guardrail casually and closed his eyes as the sun came in through the open ceiling. It'd been so long since he felt the rays of the sun on his skin and he was relaxed as he listened to her describe some of the world's recent history.

"We found a way to displace matter, to move it out of our living frequency and in essence, remove it from our world." She was proud of her work as she described it.

"Are you sure you should be exposing so much of your research to a stranger?" He nodded his head at the mention of the ARCA. It was something he'd heard of, but Troy had almost immediately interrupted Brack from explaining further.

"It's no secret anymore." She pointed to the new hole in the ceiling. "One of the hazards we accidentally found with the ARCA is that its frequency disrupts the Sealo-Pax." Her tone shifted to a much more somber one. "A few weeks ago there was a test that had some very negative results. We believe one of the frequencies may have continued to resonate within glass containment chambers down below and..." She trailed off.

"There was an explosion." He had heard the story from Brack a few hours earlier while they were in lock down.

She was surprised Troy allowed him that much. "Yes. We lost a few of my close colleagues. I guess that's no longer a secret either." She stood up straight again. It was obviously a sore subject for her, but she was comforted that someone wasn't calling her life's work a failure for once. "That's when we had decided to take the ARCA to a new testing ground on Bermuda – a place that wouldn't have potential casualties. But the equipment just – it vanished." She looked over at Hal. "I suppose that's why you're such a suspicious guest here. If the Yotogi had somehow known about us relocating our work, and *somehow* they were using you as a test subject..." she shrugged as she paused. "I don't see a connection., but I have to admit, the timing was pretty shitty."

They both giggled and took a few more seconds to dwell in the sun before she made a motion to continue. They walked around the top atrium level towards the front, which overlooked the wide blue ocean. A&H had quite a nice piece of real estate, which was no doubt chosen for its isolation than view. The entire front-side of the entryway was a pane of glass with a beautiful view. A large concrete walkway stretched from each side and continued around most of the complex. Below Hal could see a dock expanding to the south where several boats were anchored. Some were obviously company vehicles with the A&H logo boldly displayed, but most looked like casual riding cruisers. Hal supposed a speedboat was considered normal when you worked on a secluded island.

They continued on the top level of the walkway that circled the atrium below. Several doors lined the top floor, which were most likely the administrative offices.

They reached the end of the hallway, which lead to two large doors, and Claire tapped her hand on the control panel next to them. After several seconds, the smooth glass cage rose to their level. The doors slid on a circular guard lining the cylindrical elevator and they stepped in. She tapped the letter 'B' and the doors swiveled shut before gently descending.

Hal watched with fascination as the surroundings changed. The cement walls of the shaft were disorienting. There were no distinguishing markers or indicators about their depth, only lights that passed every twenty or thirty feet.

The door again opened to a long concrete chamber. It was sterile and cold as the fluorescent lights hummed above.

They continued silently down the long hallway towards the door at the end, which lead to another gray room, surrounded by concrete walls. At the center of the room was a pool with a large, egg-like glass capsule.

Claire stepped out onto a small docking area that faced the capsule and motioned towards the object.

"What is it?"

She knelt forward and laughed, forgetting that the ways of today's transportation didn't quite exist in his time. "It's a submarine. There are four underwater complexes here and these are the trolly vehicles we take back and forth. "

Hal looked at her cautiously. He hadn't realized that they were now actually under the ocean and that this transparent capsule was the future's submarine. He approached it, stepping onto the platform where he assumed one would board, but he wasn't even sure where the door was. She smiled and walked towards the glass egg and placed her hand on the small box-like decal. The device immediately became active, opening the door and turning on a string of lights lining the bottom. Hal could now see the interior, which had three rows of seats, allowing up to twelve passengers at a time. He stepped in, carefully positioning his feet as he felt the vehicle shift slightly.

Hal suddenly found himself rather anxious as to where they were going, and this was surely a new method of transport for him. He moved along to one of the front seats and looked downwards where part of the vehicle was already submerged.

"Hold on." Claire was watching with amusement.

The capsule softly jolted as it began to descend into the water. It took Hal by surprise and he found himself lifting his feet, anticipating the subconscious feeling that water would rush in.

Completely submerged, the capsule stopped on a metal rail and a doorway in the front of the circular pool opened, revealing the dark expanse of the ocean. There was a string of lights that faded out of view along the rails that the submarine traveled on and it marked the path forward.

As they slowly progressed, Hal stared in fascination. The ocean was a dark void, but the string of lights faded in as they gained momentum. He hadn't imagined they'd gone this far down and there was little to be seen. The silhouette of a fish occasionally flickered passed, which was hard to see until it was almost touching the window. He gazed around the vehicle at the darkness, completely amazed to think they were so far beneath the surface.

Claire smiled. She knew this was a new experience for him and she wasn't going to waste words while he was in awe. Patiently watching, she took note of his features. His picture in his military profile showed a very clean cut style and uniform. Now, his once dark hair was equally spotted with gray, long and unkempt. It was tucked behind his ears to keep out of his face, and he had about four days worth of stubble on his chin and cheeks. She guessed he was of a Hispanic descent with his dark brow and eyes, but his lighter skin might have suggested differently. He hadn't lost his military figure, albeit a little on the thinner side, he still had an athletic build.

In the distance, Hal could see a larger light approaching. They had only been in the submarine for two or three minutes before the next complex came into view. It was massive and he would have never guessed such an impressive building could have been constructed under the ocean.

"We're almost there." Claire had gotten out of her seat and was moving toward him now. "This is our seclusion center. It's very difficult to pick up radio transmissions or communications under the water, which is why we keep most of our research here."

"And guests?"

"Yeah, guests who we don't want making outside communication." She nodded.

They approached the outside doorway, which slowly opened and the capsule moved inward. As the cabin was lifted out of the water, Hal's ears popped and he squinted to adjust to the brighter lighting.

Brack and Troy waited just outside the doorway. "He's asked for you by name. So far, he won't talk to either of us."

Hal was a bit taken back. So far these men were strangers and now one of them had specifically asked for him by name? There was definitely some legitimacy behind Troy's theory now, and the expression on his face was clearly satisfied.

Chapter 8: The Questioning

Hal followed behind Brack and Troy as they continued down a long cement hallway. The walls vibrated with a low hum, and without windows to the outside world, it was a reminder that they were now several stories underwater. Air was ventilated through the hallway, giving an ever present breeze flowing passed them. Claire walked alongside, looking downwards with her arms crossed. There was anticipation, but in Troy's presence no one felt at liberty to talk about it.

Up until now, he had been running for his life in a whirlwind and now, he was being led to a holding cell to question a prisoner. He hadn't even had time to think about what he was going to ask. Judging by his request to speak with him only, Hal felt like he was going to be the one questioned.

They passed a dozen doorways before reaching the end of the hallway. Troy stopped abruptly in front of two large steel doors, allowing Brack only enough room to side-step close enough to reach the handle and quickly push it from his grasp as the wheelchair moved inward.

The room inside was dimly lit in comparison to the fluorescent hallway. There was a long dark glass panel with lights on the other side. As they approached, they could see another man reclining in an office chair. He was staring at several screens, each showing different camera angles of their prisoner.

The man behind the glass nodded at Brack as he looked down. Leaning over to push a button with a standard prison-gate buzzing sound that released the lock, allowing Brack to hold it open for Troy. Claire caught the door as he released it and walked inward.

Holding the door for Hal, Claire gave an empathetic look, not knowing what kind of circus they were about to walk into.

They stood in the observation room and Brack made a motion for Hal to enter the next door.

"What am I supposed to ask him?"

"Try to keep him on the subject of their invasion. What is it they were after and how they got the information regarding the Sealo-Pax." He crossed his arms and glared through the glass at the prisoner.

"And Hal, the Yotogi have always been somewhat... cryptic. Don't take it personal."

Hal wasn't exactly afraid of his feelings being hurt, but Brack had obviously meant something by it.

He turned towards the door and with a familiar buzz, the door latch clicked and he entered.

The man behind the table simply looked downward at his hands resting on the table. He was cuffed to two small eye-bolts coming up from the bottom. His hood hung low and covered his brow, but the majority of his lower face was exposed.

Hal glanced back at the one-way window. He knew he wouldn't see the others looking on, but somehow expected some sort of coaching.

"You are looking for the wrong answers, Mr. Brent." The calm voice had a slight accent.

"How do you know my name?"

"I knew all of your names. Cyrus, Kleo, Harnagose..."

"Stop." Hal interrupted him. He was giving the names of his crew from the plane crash.

The man tilted his head to the side, then leaned back. His eyes were now staring directly into Hal. "You, Mr. Brent, are asking the wrong questions. So much time has gone by, but it was not lost. You have made it back."

Hal felt a deep sense of guilt as the man spoke. He knew about his crew, and how he had failed them as a pilot. And now, he was here amongst the living while they were not.

The man's words had struck a nerve and he bit down hard, lowering his head and clasped his hands together. The man across the table was observing this, but he didn't show any satisfaction the way a terrorist would. Turning his gaze upwards, the man actually had an expression of compassion. Although quirky, his eyes and stance hid no malicious intentions.

A noise in Hal's ear abruptly interrupted his thoughts. He'd all but forgotten the com-system in his ear, and he could hear Brack's voice.

"Stay on the subject of their invasion."

The man behind the table shifted again. "They will watch you." He nodded towards the glass, completely aware that someone was behind it. "Let them."

He again assumed his original posture, looking down at his folded hands, hiding his brow. "The answers I offer are not to them, but to you, Mr. Brent. Heed my warning that a war will rise amongst the smallest of armies. You are the beginning of what must end."

He lifted his eyes to meet Hal's again. With a slight movement of his jaw, he appeared to bite something in his mouth. His eyes slowly began to change to a solid black and as if some switch had been flipped, tears began to stream down his face. The man slowly began to slouch and the clear tears were now sliding down in black streaks.

Hal jumped, his eyes fixated on the man. The door buzzed and lurched open as Brack burst in.

The man maintained his gaze at Hal and gave a terrifying smile. The tears gleamed down his face and quickly dripped onto the table surface. "We've been waiting for you." He leaned backwards as his hood slid back off his head, exposing his whole face.

Hal stood in a trance, staring at the man cuffed to the table. The noise and movement around him became a blur. Claire ran around the table to the opposite side of Brack, as he felt the man's neck for a pulse. Everything seemed to happen in slow motion as he watched. Claire was yelling for the guard with a set of keys. Fumbling, she managed to un-cuff both hands.

Brack pushed her aside as she finished, picking the man up and laying him on the table's surface. Leaning in, he pressed his ear to the man's mouth before beginning CPR.

Claire stood in shock with her hands over her mouth. There were tears forming in her eyes as she watched a perfectly healthy man slip away right in front of their eyes.

Brack repeated his motions as he tried to revive him. He grew more and more frustrated with every failed attempt, pumping harder and harder on his chest. After several minutes, the effort was exhausted and he placed his hands over the man's eyes.

That was it. The shock was fading and noise began to come back as Hal helplessly watched from the corner of the room. What the hell did they just witness? The man now lay lifeless on the table before them. Claire stood in shock with both hands over her mouth to contain her horror.

"You didn't ask a single question and now he is dead!" Troy's brash ignorance broke the silence.

Hal simply looked down at Troy. He was a pathetic man on the inside.

"You couldn't ask a single, useful question!"

Hal felt his nerves come to an abrupt crack as he pulled the com system from his left ear, slammed it onto the table. He gave a look of empathy towards the prisoner. Whoever he was, he'd known more about his disappearance than anyone had lead on. His heart sank, feeling as if part of his memory had just disappeared further into oblivion.

Hal lowered his head before taking a step backwards, nudging the chair behind him as it crashed to the ground. He couldn't breath as he felt pressure build in his chest and he bolted for the door.

He didn't know where he was going to go. He felt a sense of panic take over as he drudged forward into the hallway. His head was dizzy as he stumbled a few feet, reaching random door handles as he passed, but unable to open them. He was under the ocean with no windows, no light and no exits. He felt more claustrophobic than ever and the room spun. The air was thick, his feet ached and his head throbbed. The light flickered to a bright white and he moved his hands to protect his eyes, but it remained. His knees caught the ground with a heavy thud, standing on the cold tile below as he slumped forward. He heaved heavily as the light intensified and then dimmed, fading in and out. The throb in his head was nauseating as the world spun around him. He was unable to focus. Footsteps thumped behind him, as if shaking the floor below. He began to wheeze and could only hear his pulse as it echoed through his skull. The burden grew heavy in his chest as he slid onto the cold floor surface, feeling a calm pass over before he blacked out.

Chapter 9: The Recurring Dream

Hal lay on his back and let his tired eyes slowly open. His vision was blurred and he raised his hand above his face as it faded in and out of view through the thick fog. He flinched as movement from underneath snapped him out of a daze. The soil slithered against his skin as he sprang upright, trying to balance and get his bearings.

The haze was thick and heavy, only rising about two feet above the soil where his feet disappeared beneath. He peered through the marshland, squinting in every direction for anything he recognized. Several barren trees dotted the landscape as far as he could see in the marshland.

Checking his body, he brushed away the mud that clung to his bare arms and chest. His feet were also bare and cold, and what remained of his pants were badly torn.

An oscillating noise occupied his head, vibrating in circles as if he were spinning.

Muffled and slow, he yelled, "Can anyone hear me? HELP!"

His actions felt as if they were playing in slow motion with his voice low and distorted. Slowly, other sounds began to stir. The wind rustled past his ears, whispering and whirling in a high pitch. The forest around him seemed to breath, crunching sticks and the quiet tap of footsteps on the rocks came closer. He turned, slow and cautious towards the disturbance. Something felt wrong. He waited, listening intently for a response, but as the noise drew nearer, he felt anything but relief.

The fog that engulfed his feet had begun to swirl passed. The roots from the soil were crawling outward away from its movement, churning beneath him as he stepped back and held his breath.

A loud shriek startled him and he fell backwards to the ground, knocking the wind from his lungs. A dark mass flashed above him as a creature leaped over and quickly vanished again in the dense fog.

The shriek came again from his side but darted swiftly out of view, only leaving a wake in the fog to be seen. The creature was fast, but it wasn't simply hunting. It was stalking.

A rip at his side tore into his skin and he twisted forward as the warm trail of blood began to flow. He rolled to his side, cradling the new pain. His pulse became heavy and he pressed his hand over the wound.

A low groan came closer to his front, and he grimaced as he shifted his focus away from the pain. The fog was thick and distorted his view, but the beast could be heard, slowly closing in as it tiptoed through the mud.

Hal looked for anything to defend himself with. The branches and roots beneath him had a life of their own, slithering through the muck. He grabbed one as it writhed in his hand, and with a hard tug, it broke loose and fell stiff again. He tightened his grip on the root, now holding it like a bat as he waited silently, shifting in anticipation.

The beast lunged forward with a snarl and Hal's instincts kicked in, swinging the branch-like a club and making contact with a loud thud. The creature's momentum continued forward, plowing into his chest as its mass sent them crashing to the ground again.

He pressed upwards, lifting the creature's limp body and gasped for breath. He heaved and forced the mass down, slumping it onto the ground beside him as he jerked away. He reached down to his side and picked up the root, holding it firmly as he cautiously crouched down to get a closer look at the body. It was unlike anything he'd seen before. Two front legs were small and attached to a rugged torso that looked somewhat like a wolf. The fur was thin and patchy around the shoulders and welts covered most of its flaky dark gray skin. Its hind legs were bulged and at least a foot longer than the front limbs. The hunch of its back revealed extruding spinal disks, leading down to a boney tail with some sort of wire or sharp twine wrung around it.

Hal cautiously stepped around to get a look at its head, which twisted at the neck, now broken from the impact of his swing. The face was similar to a dog, but extremely distorted. One brow was swollen and bone was exposed. The under-jaw extruded, revealing three fang-like teeth. Blood from its mouth was a dark red, which gave a deep contrast from the skin and mud that covered its face. Black metallic whiskers were spread thinly on the majority of its surface.

A loud horn echoed in the distance, and he covered his ears, failing to mute the sound. He slowly stood upright and gazed around. Nothing stirred, not even the soil beneath him. A flash of light suddenly blinded him as he moved his arms to block his eyes, but it did no good. As the deafening echo pulsated, the disturbing sensation hit him. He remembered this. The feeling of deja-vu had never been stronger.

He was temporarily blinded and his heart began to race. He couldn't place his finger on it exactly, but he'd witnessed this event before, somehow, and he covered his eyes instinctively.

He spun with his arms outstretched for balance, tumbling in no particular direction as he reached out for anything solid. The world around him vanished with his sight. His hands swung, searching for something, anything, but with every attempt, his grip flew through the empty space.

Then, like a switch, the white light disappeared and his hearing faded back in. The world was dim and he struggled to focus again. The echo of the horn continued through the fog as an ever present hum and got louder with every second. Again, he couldn't ignore the feeling that this was all so familiar somehow. He fell to his knees and placed his hands over his ears and closed his eyes. He knew the flashes would return.

He tried to slow his breathing in anticipation. Sure enough, it flashed. There was no sound now. Even his breathing had become mute. Although he was afraid, the silence was peaceful.

Chapter 10: A New Day

A blurry light began to flicker in, and with a gasp, his eyes shot open. The light was dim, but his eyes were unfocused and teared. He sat up and gazed around in a panic as he began to make out the familiar surroundings of the doctor's office. The nearby computer screen illuminated and Hal could see himself from another angle as a camera gazed down from the corner in the room.

He swung his legs to the side and halted as his stomach ached with pain. He instinctively reached for it and pressed hard, his eyes opening wide in shock as the warm stream of blood flowed over his hand.

"Doctor?" His voice was weak as he attempted to yell. The room was vacant, but he helplessly hoped someone might be lingering in a nearby room or over the com system.

He wearily placed his feet on the cold floor and stumbled the short distance to the computer screen at the doctor's work station. "Can anyone hear me?"

With a flicker on the screen, a new window came up as Claire's tired face adjusted to the illumination. "You're awake?"

"I think I need to see your doctor." He choked the words out.

On the screen he could see Claire gaze around her room. "I'll page him and be there in a few minutes. Is everything all right?"

Hal stumbled backwards, his head dizzy and disoriented. For a second he'd lost his balance and backed into the neighboring medical bed.

"Hal?" Claire gazed into the screen, focusing more intensely as she realized the emergency.

"Prossman, to the medical bay immediately." Her voice was nervous as the echo resonated throughout the speaker system in the building.

Hal's senses faded in and out, unable to focus on the screen any longer. He continued to lean against the desk and attempted to sit in the chair beside him, but the wound to his side screamed in rebellion as his muscles rejected movement. He gripped the side cushions for balance, but the harder he tried to remain upright, the lighter his head became. Blood was now running down his pant leg and onto the floor. The contrast in temperature was dramatic as he felt the warm liquid slide over his foot, briefly warming the skin as it grew numb. Unaware of his balance, he shifted and tipped, reaching for the bed, but his slippery, numb hands were weak. The shock of the fall was almost mute compared to the pounding pulse echoing through his skull. With every beat, he could feel the warmth of his blood begin to cover his skin. The brief feeling of nausea lingered, and he knew it wouldn't be long before he couldn't fight for consciousness.

Minutes went by and he blinked slowly, quietly listening to the sound of his heartbeat slow. His breath had become shallow and the darkness was almost comforting.

The lights flickered on abruptly and his eyes flinched at the change. Claire appeared at the doorway and immediately noticed Hal laying on the floor. She rushed to his side, skidding on the slick tile that was covered in a thin layer of blood.

"Oh my gosh, Hal, what happened?" She pulled his hand away and lifted his shirt. "Hal?"

He squinted at her with blurry vision, but was unable to reply.

"Hal, I need you to lay down." She pressed her hand on his shoulder, slowly easing him onto his back. "Hold your side."

She reached up and grabbed the cloth sheet that was on the medical bed and pressed it to his side, drenching it almost immediately.

With Hal now laying on the floor, she got to her feet and ran to some nearby shelves for equipment.

The door swung open again and Doctor Prossman stumbled in. "What's going on? It's four in the morning," he spoke in a confused tone. His eyes darted around the room before landing on Hal. "Good Lord! What happened?"

Claire rushed back to his side and began unwrapping the packages she'd retrieved. Cutting the shirt from his belly to his chest, they could see a large gash tore into his flesh from the bottom of his side up to his ribs.

"These look like claw marks!" She looked up at the doctor who was standing over them in confusion.

The doctor stumbled over to the counter and grabbed a small monitoring device that looked like a sheet of glass. Claire grabbed it from his hands and held it over Hal's stomach. It was a small X-ray device and Hal could see his organs from the other side of its reflection.

There was a short pause as she moved the device above his wound. "There's no damage to his organs, but he's lost a lot of blood," Claire said and looked at the doctor. He nodded and stumbled towards his storage closet.

"We're going to use some general anesthesia to numb your side and stitch this." She was pressing on his side, and all Hal could focus on was the pulsing in his head from the lack of blood.

"Stay with us, Hal."

The doctor emerged with a bundle in his arms. Coming up beside Claire, he knelt down and began filling a syringe. There was a slight pinch as the cool fluid entered his skin and began to numb the wound.

"Do you know your blood type, Hal?" The doctor's voice was quiet now.

His hearing was starting to fade. "B Positive."

Prossman looked at Claire, who shook her head. The medical bay seldom functioned as a blood transfusion lab and didn't carry much in the way of a supply bank.

"I'm O," she said and began rolling up her sleeve.

Prossman looked at her with concern and knew her intentions. Like it or not, it was the only option they had at the moment.

"Put a tourniquet on and get started. I'll proceed with the wound." The doctor now sat on the ground next to Hal and Claire moved further to the side.

She grabbed Hals arm and stretched it outward. The pinch of a rubber tourniquet gripped tight and the cold needle slipped into his vein. She did the same to her own arm, and there was a rush of warmth as the tube between them quickly filled with blood. Her adrenaline and his lack of blood pressure was enough to siphon the flow.

The doctor was busy at work, but the numbness from the anesthetic made it painless. He was quick with his hands and within several minutes he'd tied up the last stitch and trimmed off the remaining thread. "That's finished."

Hal's senses were returning and he cast a glance down at the doctor who was now applying the blue mesh gauze. It bonded with his skin instantly and began to cool the surface.

"Hal?" Claire tried to relax as she positioned herself closer to his shoulder. "What happened here? Was someone here with you?"

Hal raised his other hand to cover his eyes. There was a long period of silence as the memory of his dreams scattered into confusing fragments. "I don't know. After the questioning... I just couldn't take it. I don't know what we witnessed, but something that man said to me, it was like he knew me. I just lost it." He trailed off, envisioning the man's suicide and immediate reactions. He shuttered at the thought and moved passed it. "I needed out. I needed air. I was in the hallway and all I remember were these sparks of light. They were overwhelming and the echo... I felt like I was fading out, somehow."

"You collapsed in the hallway, but you weren't having a seizure, or at least not that we could tell." The doctor paused, now looking at Claire again. "But that was twelve hours ago."

Claire sat adjacent from the doctor, still attached to the lifeline between her and Hal. Her mind was weak and cloudy as her blood count continued to dwindle, raising her free hand clumsily, she pointed towards the fresh wound in Hal's side. "These look like claw marks. Were you attacked? Was something here with you?"

Hal's memory finally hit a clear note. He closed his eyes and could remember the creature that lay on the ground. That was a dream, though. Wasn't it?

"Hal, what is it?" The doctor could see Hal's face flinch with recognition.

"It can't be reality. It's not," he trailed off, whispering to himself. "It was a dream."

Everyone now had the look of confusion on their face.

"Just before I woke, I remember being in the woods somewhere. There was this... this thing that was stalking me. It looked sort of like a canine on all fours, but it wasn't like any dog or wolf I've ever seen. I was dizzy and alone when I heard it approaching. It lunged and attacked me here." He placed a protective hand over his side. "It was so vivid, I felt it. But it was a dream. It had to be."

Both the Doctor and Claire fell silent. There was no explanation for what had transpired here or for the wound that left Hal bleeding to death on the floor, but the seriousness of his injury was no dream.

"You've been under surveillance this entire time. If anyone or anything happened to you while you were here, we should have footage of it." The doctor began gathering the materials and stray packages that lay on the ground around him as he stood up.

Claire was still at his side, and from the paleness of her skin, the lack of blood was starting to take its effect on her. She remained, though, and slumped back against the nearby medical table.

The doctor was now at his desk rewinding the last hour of surveillance footage.

"You should disconnect." Hal's voice interrupted Claire's thoughts and she looked down at her arm, which was growing pale.

"How are you feeling?" She asked, but made no movements to remove the needle.

"I'll live." He was now stable, although far from feeling well. She on the other hand was beginning to fade.

"Yes Claire, you should disconnect and lay down," the doctor echoed his voice without looking in their direction.

Her hands were slow as she pinched the tube before pulling the needle from her skin. She leaned forward and did the same with Hal's, then curled his elbow and rested his hand on his chest.

She shifted around, sliding on the floor as she stretched and fully reclined on the ground next to him. They were both dizzy from blood loss and tired.

"Thank you." His senses were returning and he began to think clearly about the mess that had just transpired.

Claire rolled her head to face him and smiled. It was obvious that the physical and mental stress had taken its toll on her, yet she tried her best to hide the discomfort. "You're welcome."

There was a long period of silence as the doctor glared at his screen with confusion. There were several huffs and sighs as he watched the recent footage, but nothing promising.

Hal and Claire both lay on the floor in an awkward silence. How weird this scenario must have been for everyone involved in it, and not only to himself. He had his own questions and issues, but up until two days ago, this place, this time line was normal. The people who had just saved his life were never attacked or bleeding to death until he arrived. Despite where he came from and the trouble that followed, Claire and the Doctor had put their lives on the line to save a stranger. He felt a great sense of guilt, but also gratitude. None of this had any explanation or justification, but here they were.

"Doc?" Claire was now looking in his direction.

"Yes?" He quietly responded, still staring at his screen.

"I think we need some cookies," she almost chuckled, realizing it was a little out of place to request cookies.

"Oh yes, that makes sense. You both should probably eat something." The doctor pulled away from his computer and waddled over to the two invalids on the floor. "I'll go to the mess hall and grab something." He searched his pockets, pulling out some sort of plastic card, presumably some form of payment to a vending machine. He made one last glance to them before turning towards the door.

"This wasn't exactly how I pictured the day starting." She was unexpectedly optimistic as she spoke. It surely wasn't how anyone had pictured starting their day. Or week.

Hal chuckled at her sarcastic tone. He was lying next to a woman he knew almost nothing about, yet found its awkwardness just a tad funny.

"No, I think it's safe to say no one did."

She was still pale, but her smile was warming.

"I'm sorry for this." He had been confused and distressed since he'd awoken, but was beginning to consider he wasn't the only one.

"It's OK. Believe it or not, this place is usually pretty boring." They both let out a restrained laugh as their exhausted bodies protested.

She began to shift her legs and turn towards him. "You know, you're the biggest lead we've had to the Yotogi. They've declined all offers to communicate directly and never openly faced the company. Even with the interview last night, that was the longest conversation we've ever had with one of their members."

Hal looked a bit puzzled. He'd had no relation to the Yotogi or their cause. A&H themselves were unknown, albeit not hostile, he'd never even heard of the company's existence until two days ago and now he was a temporary resident.

"I don't understand, though. Why me?"

"The Yotogi are, well, Troy will tell you that they're terrorists, but they've never been openly aggressive." She rolled her head on the hard floor as she spoke, dizzy and barely coherent. Her hair was a dark contrast from the white flooring, but her skin was just as pale. "They've been an establishment for years, protesting technological advancement that could *end the world*," she sarcastically emphasized. "They believe the research we're perusing here, among other places, will eventually tear some sort of rift in our existence. I don't know. They've never really been clear about their motives or explanations and I don't pretend to understand them. They normally protest our expos and public announcements when we're promoting a product, but never anything like this."

"So why now?" He was curious.

She shrugged. "I'm not sure. We produce equipment for construction, for protecting our military and waste clean up. I've never seen a connection for their cause. When our freighters disappeared near Bermuda, we naturally suspected they had somehow disabled our radio frequency. We lost connection and waited for hours, but it was never reestablished, so we sent out a search team about a day after the incident. We had sonar, satellites, manned and un-manned search teams scouring the ocean floor for days without a single thing... And then you showed up," she paused again. "I'm not sure why or how you fit into all this, but the Yotogi have never shown this kind of interest, even with our most promising projects. They protest peacefully, or at least they always had, but for some reason they played a different hand of cards in an attempt to contact you." She continued to look directly into him, curiously asking what the hell he meant to them.

Hal wasn't sure how to respond, but how could he be? He remained silent, trying to think of an explanation, but there was none.

She continued. "I'm sorry. I don't mean to scare you. I just don't know what to think. We're resourceful and yet we don't have any answers for you. But that man downstairs, that man acted like he *knew* why you were here. He knew something we don't. "

It was a lot to think about all at once, and Hal was again without words, but Claire had a point. They had a lead, or at least some sort of vague connection, however unfriendly.

The door buckled and the doctor waddled back in with a large tray of food in his arms.

"I wasn't sure what you liked, but some glucose will do you both some good." He approached them and placed the tray on the office chair near-by.

The thought of food was appetizing to Hal more than ever. He couldn't actually remember the last time he'd eaten, and although he'd been a guest here for the past two days, eating was one thought that hadn't yet crossed his mind.

The doctor carefully sat his fragile body on the ground next to them and began to open a large bag of chips. "There is some left over casserole that the chef made in the fridge and various snacks and juice."

Claire reached for a bottle of juice and cookies before handing the tray to Hal. His side wound was now just a throbbing ache. The anesthetics were in full force and did an excellent job masking the pain, but the dizziness from blood loss was still echoing in his head.

Without thought, he quickly began devouring everything on the tray, spooning in mouthful after mouthful of noodles and tearing into several packaged cookie bags. His hunger was without realization.

The silence wasn't long, as the food quickly disappeared. Fluids and blood count were on the rise. The party of three was weak and tired, but on the mend.

"At least we have cookies," Claire joked as she finished her last one. It was an awkward get-together, but she still found a humor in the ordeal.

"Ha, I suppose," the doctor chuckled in response as several small chunks of potato chips escaped his dentures. He had a habit of talking with his mouth full, but at the moment it was comic relief in the near death situation.

After several minutes of munching, Claire began to shift around in an attempt to stand up. Using the bed as support, she managed to steady herself and lay down onto the softer surface. It was almost 5 AM and the bright peaking sun was just starting to light up the ceiling windows. This would be his second full day here, and no doubt there would be more questions asked before the end of it. His body and mind were exhausted, and as Claire made herself more comfortable on the neighboring medical bed, Hal fumbled around on his weary limbs to do the same. The floor was cold and although the blood had dried, he was still damp.

"Do you have any other clothing I could wear?" Hal asked the doctor, who was still situated on the floor.

"I believe so. I'm not sure they'll fit, but we usually keep some spare clothing in the closet." The doctor was an older man, somewhere in his 70's and had a difficult time propping himself into a standing position before wandering off into his closet.

Hal figured now was as good a time as any to get off the cold floor and stumbled as he tried. His recent wound left him weaker than he thought, but with a dizzy head he managed to stand and lift himself onto the bed.

The doctor emerged several minutes later carrying an armful of clothing, including sweat pants, another t-shirt and two blankets. He handed the clothing to Hal and turned to place one of the blankets over Claire, who already lay motionless. Her eyes were closed and her breathing was heavy. Pure exhaustion left her no other choice.

"Rover will be here to clean this up in a minute." The doctor made a gesture to the blood on the floor. "I'll go wake him."

Hal was a bit confused at first, but as the doctor wandered off into the corner and turned on a robotic machine, he realized Rover must be the janitor of modern day.

Times had changed and a mop and broom had been replaced by a very complex, motorized scrubber. Everything from a standard computer to janitors had all evolved into much more advanced machinery.

He remained on the bed in a semi-upright position, carefully peeling off his old clothing and exchanging it for the new garments the doctor had provided. The surface was soft and warm as he reclined downward and let gravity pull him farther into the cushion.

He turned his head and watched in fascination for several minutes as the bot completely polished the floor and bed side where he'd fallen.

The doctor was lost at his computer screen, intensely staring at the surveillance footage, rewinding and playing the short segment of film.

"Is there anything there?" Hal asked.

"No, not that I can see. I mean, your movements indicate you're in REM sleep, no doubt, but I don't understand. You simply stand up and you're bleeding. It's as if whatever happened to you in your dream is actually affecting you in reality. I've read of similar stories where subjects can scratch or even attack themselves while sleeping, which leaves them pretty scratched up, but it's nothing like this." He was puzzled. There was nothing on the camera to indicate an attack, and the room was completely empty. "We also have the infrared feed. You were completely alone."

He exchanged glances with Hal, and his face was sad with disappointment. He wanted to offer at least a little comfort in finding an explanation, but there was none. Even so, Hal did find comfort in his presence, and Claire's too.

"You should try to sleep, Mr. Brent. It's early, and this place will be awake again in a few hours. Get what rest you can. And here, put this on." He approached Hal with the arm band he'd had on earlier in the day before. "This should monitor your heart rate and bodily behaviors. If at any time you go beyond normal levels, it'll alert the staff here in the medical bay and we'll wake you."

Hal began to place the band around the lower half of his arm. It fit like a perfect glove all the way to his elbow and was completely flexible. It was another piece of amazing technology that had surely only been a dream back in his time. Strobes of light were active on the circuitry, which displayed everything from heart rate, body temperature, sugar level, time zone and geographical position.

"Here, this should help." The doctor gently placed the remaining blanket over his body, pushing the edges snugly under his sides. "Good night for now." His wrinkly face smiled and his eyebrows lifted before he backed away, headed towards the door and turned off the lights.

Claire lay on the bed just adjacent of him, sound asleep already. He had no idea if he could sleep, especially after his latest incident. His dreams were haunting, and the glimmer of what he remembered seemed all too real. He recalled it like a memory, not a dream where segments start to immediately disappear once you awake. He could remember everything about it. The fog, the smell, the creature that lay on the ground. It was more like a memory he'd relived.

The questions were repeating themselves in his mind, and he slowly lost focus as his eyes began to close. He was exhausted, and without realizing, he slipped into sleep again.

Chapter 11: Starting Anew

The room was peaceful and quiet as Hal began to stir. Sunlight came in from the ceiling windows and he opened his eyes to see the surroundings of the doctor's office that were beginning to feel comfortable again. Beside him on the neighboring medical bed lay Claire, asleep and curled into the fetal position. Her dark red hair partly covered her face, and her normally tan skin was much more pale.

Hal simply lay still, afraid his movement would wake the other occupant. It was awkward, sleeping next to someone he'd only known for a day. They'd never had much of an introduction, and yet she'd already saved his life twice.

He glanced at his arm band and the digital watch read 12:06 PM. It was already past noon, and he'd had a good seven hours of sleep, but now he was restless.

Without much to focus on he stared across the gap between the two and began to wonder what role she played in all of this. By now he'd learned that A&H was much more than a construction company, although that's where their public market was, but that they had grown into a military contractor for protective equipment as well. She didn't quite fit the description of a mad scientist, dabbling in the unknown mechanics of physics, or at least not how would have pictured it.

She twitched as she slept, still reeling from the trauma. Her skin was a drastic contrast from the dark rings circling her eyes, and the sedatives Brack had given her still lingered. Physically, she was a mess.

Hal considered himself for a moment and wondered how mangled he must have looked as well. His skin was also pale and was completely absent of any tan. He lifted his hands and felt his hair, which was much longer than he would have ever preferred it. He was used to a crew-cut, military style, and now it fell past his ears and almost touched his shoulders. He'd developed a habit of tucking it behind his ears, and it naturally began curling that way. It was thick and tangled as he tried to brush his fingers through it.

He remained quiet as he restlessly pondered what the day would bring. He'd been through the events a hundred times now, and the only consistency was that nothing was certain. This was no dream world he was stuck in, and the unexplainable circumstances were now his reality. Last night was unusual, to state the obvious, but it had given him a new perspective. Ever since he'd awoken, his only focus had been on himself and the student pilots he'd lost. He'd been so distraught over his own confusion that he'd failed to consider the new strangers extending their hand to him. Even after all the inconvenience he'd caused, they hadn't given up on him. As he looked over at the woman on the adjacent table, it was the first time he realized and appreciated what that must have taken. This wasn't just about him anymore. A&H was a powerful, resourceful company, and whatever the link was between them and his crash, they needed each other.

His thoughts were interrupted as Claire began to stir next to him and let out a sigh. She reached to move the hair covering her face, and then to her shoulder, which was still no doubt a lingering pain. She looked at Hal as he gave a slight, humble smile. He'd wanted to thank her and the doctor, but at the moment he suddenly felt like a stranger again.

Propping up on her elbow, she gazed around the medical bay, which was quiet and calm, despite it being so late in the day.

"Morning." She was groggy and distraught.

"Morning," Hal replied, feeling more awkward than before.

"How long have we been here?" She asked as she looked around the room.

He glared at the new device on his wrist with fuzzy vision. "About seven hours."

"Remind me to never volunteer for testing those tranquilizing drugs again." She shrugged before shifting her weight and sitting upright. Her sneakers were still on her feet as she swung her legs over the edge and stretched.

No longer afraid to make noise, Hal perched himself to a sitting position on the bed, but his side wound begged him not to push any further.

"I'll bet you could go for some more anesthetic," she asked, noticing as he protectively wrapped one arm over his side.

"Yes, please." He tried to ignore the sudden rush of imbalance as he sat up quickly.

Claire slowly and sloppily stumbled over to a cabinet before rummaging through some of the doctor's poorly-organized materials. After a minute or two of searching, she came back to Hal's side with two bottles, some cloth material and a syringe.

"Let me see your side." She gently reached and lifted his shirt as he leaned to the side. The blue gauze material was now dried, but unlike a band-aid, it easily parted from the skin.

"This is going to sting a little." She applied alcohol to a piece of cloth and he flinched as it made contact with his skin.

"I'm sorry," she winced.

"It's necessary." He was grateful, although it was impossible to pretend it wasn't painful.

She backed away and put the bottle on the neighboring bed and picked up the needle. "Now this is going to sting again." They both smiled as he prepared for another painful jab.

He lifted his shirt higher and took a deep breath in. Normally he wouldn't have blinked at the sight of a needle, but with several places of injury, he was a little more intimidated. The pinch came quickly as the cold fluid entered his skin. It was a cool relief that spread within a matter of seconds and faded to a dull throb.

Now numb, Claire finished applying the blue bandage adhesives and pulled his shirt back over the wound.

She walked away with the materials before grabbing the doctor's chair and sliding back over to him. "Now let me see your feet."

Stiff and achy, he obeyed. A few hours earlier the doctor had applied the bandages to his feet bottoms, and although they still ached, the wounds had made remarkable progress.

He relaxed on the bed, leaning back against the wall as Claire removed the bandages and again doused his cuts with alcohol before wrapping them back up. The lack of pain was a complete change. Even his side was numb now, and his muscles were no longer protesting his movement.

"I'm going to check about getting you some sort of living space for now." She moved over to the doctor's main desk and brought up his workstation. "Paging doctor Prossman to the medical bay."

A few minutes of silence passed and Hal simply remained as calm as his body would allow. He was tense, although not entirely sure why. He was comfortable for the moment and no one was shouting orders or asking questions, but he had a feeling the traumatic experience wasn't over yet.

The door popped open and the feeble doctor appeared. He wore a long blue lab jacket and slippers.

"Good evening!" The doctor was chipper, as usual, but his enthusiasm wasn't returned. "I came in several times and you were both out, so I made myself useful downstairs. Hal, we've made you some accommodations down below. I'm sure you'll want some time alone to get oriented best you can, but there's some talk going on here among the staff. Needless to say, some are wondering about the, um, how do I put it? The reconstruction of our facility." He made a hand gesture towards the ceiling, recalling the atrium window.

The doctor continued to pace around the room, shifting his focus back and forth between the two.

"I've had some time to catch up with Troy and Brack, and they both believe it is best to come up with a cover story for your presence here so that the other employees won't continue to ask questions that we still don't have some answers for."

He glanced over at Claire, who nodded in agreement, although unsure of the plan.

"Brack proposed that you accompany Claire for the time being as security detail. If anyone asks, you were hired as an outside security measure to protect those closest to the ARCA project," the doctor said, clasping his hands together. "You won't be expected to know anything about the project, but many have now heard of it and will know it's off limits with their clearance. You're merely here to ensure the safety of the employees, and nothing more."

Project ARCA had been mentioned a few times and he probably already knew more about it than most of the staff. Nonetheless, it was supposed to be hush-hush, and those who were curious enough to ask about his background would, hopefully, discontinue.

"Sounds good enough for me," Claire chimed in. With her as company, it would be a lot easier to redirect suspicion as well.

"Now, I'm sure you're both anxious to get out of the medical bay and get a little more comfortable around the building. Troy has admitted you the same permissions Claire and I both have, but most importantly you need to keep this experience to yourselves. He's already under a lot of pressure from the staff for an explanation, and the best we can do is to keep the subject as quiet as possible. I'm sure you understand the importance of this." The doctor wasn't firm with his point, but Hal knew the pressure was coming from Troy, not him.

"With the formalities addressed, I brought some different attire for you that might help you fit in a little easier." He pointed to a nearby desk as he approached and picked up a uniform.

Nicely folded, it looked like a fairly standard security uniform, minus any bandages. Hal stood from the medical bed and carefully walked over on his new foot bandages to examine it. There was a standard black cotton t-shirt and slacks, along with a leather vest and gun holster. Inside was the same tranquilizer pistol Brack had given him the previous night and some other small details. An over-jacket covered them both and looked fairly casual.

Hal lifted the items from the table and began to size them up to his build. They were almost an exact fit, with the exception of the pants, which were a size too big around his narrow waist.

"We have a showering room here, Hal, if you'd like to make yourself decent." The doctor was again in his peppy mood, anxious to see what a nicely groomed man hid under the scraggly mess he'd become overnight. "I can even cut your hair!"

"No, Doc." Claire quickly entertained the idea. She glanced at Hal briefly. "You don't want him to cut your hair."

"I cut my own!" He said defensively, as he gestured towards his head, which was only occupied by a couple dozen strands.

"Precisely." She smiled at the doctor and began to stand. "You have such nice hair. You wouldn't want anyone with the same style."

"Well, I suppose." He was a little let down by her comment, then shifted his focus back to Hal. "Let me show you the showering area. Mind you, we normally use it for washing various types of aquatic life. It's not the largest, but the water is warm and it has a hose."

Right about now, Hal had considered wading in the ocean for a while, but a warm shower hose was a welcomed alternative. He followed the doctors into a small adjacent room, which looked more like a dog washing tub than a shower. With a pile of clothing in his arms, he shut the door behind him and began to undress the torn clothing that hung from his body. The soreness of his side was still subdued by the anesthetic, but his muscles still reminded him to be gentle. Sitting on the bench, he felt the cold water hit his body, which soon warmed. It was the best feeling he could remember, and for several minutes he simply sat and absorbed the comfort. The water fell over his chest and he relaxed his core. His long hair clung to his face and neck, which was unfamiliar. So much time had passed that he couldn't remember letting it grow long and it seemed foreign.

After several long minutes, Hal had completely wiped away a lifetime's worth or grime and dried blood. He stood in front of the small mirror and for the first time looked upon a man he hardly recognized. His hair had grown uncomfortably long, and was equally gray as it was dark. His eyes had sunken in, from what he remembered of his old self, and his cheeks were now gaunt. He was malnourished and had little padding over his bones. His muscles had grown, or at least it appeared that way in his new skin and he was a completely different man on the outside, now.

Looking around, he saw that the doctor had provided some other grooming utensils. A razor and buzz clipper lay on a steal table beside a tub sink and some hand soap. Hal pumped a handful and lathered his face. As he began to shave, he was able to see scars he didn't remember. There was a long scar on his left cheek, extending down to his jawline. It had completely healed, and had obviously been there for a while. Another scar appeared under his chin, following down his neck to his collarbone. He tried to remember where or when he'd incurred the injuries, but it was a void. There was no recollection except his plane crash and the recent dreams that followed.

He grabbed the buzzer and selected a longer than normal cut of about two inches. As the hair slowly fell from his head, he could again begin to see his old self in the reflection. He was never one for anything stylish, but the shadow of his former self felt awkwardly distant. This was his new life, or at least immediate new-life, and with it, a new hand of cards.

He finished dressing and stepped into the main office again, groomed and refreshed.

"By golly! Is that the same man?" Prossman asked as he set his eyes on the gentleman that walked out. "I'm not sure anyone is going to recognize you."

Claire had since left. It was now just the doctor and himself. The bandages from his wounds had been removed, and his bare feet were cold on the tile floor.

"Ah! I got those for you as well." Prossman motioned towards his feet. "I guessed you're a size twelve?"

The doctor wandered over to the table again where his clothes were laid out before and picked up some standard white socks and pilot boots.

"You'll need some new bandages until those heal. Come." He patted the bed for Hal to sit.

The doctor's hands were weak and gentle, but also a little clumsy. Unlike the gauze material from before, he used some sort of aerosol spray on the bottoms of his feet. It felt tacky at first but quickly formed a latex-like shell to keep the wounds closed and sealed. He applied the same spray to the side of his stomach wound, which allowed much more movement than the bandages had.

Hal was completely dressed and again familiarizing himself with the shoulder harness and arm band from before. He'd always been fascinated with computers in his time, but fast forward twenty six years later, he was now wearing the most powerful, flexible and advanced piece of technology on his skin. Back in his day a simple navigation tool belonged on a touch screen and attached itself to a dashboard. Everything from his heart rate to geographical location was now being displayed on a transparent glove that could flex circuitry. It was quite the upgrade.

The room grew quiet as Hal continued to sit idle in the doctor's office. Prossman was occupied with his daily activities, mostly staring at his computer screen.

He began to stir and lay down again on the medical table, which was now uncomfortable. He hadn't noticed before, but the bed was a cheap thin pad on a metal surface with little support. He'd slept off his exhaustion and was still full from his meal before. He was grateful for the peace, but at the same time uncomfortably bored. He'd already been betrayed by relaxation and he anxiously waited for another emergency to arise, as it already had a dozen times in the past twenty-four hours. What would come next?

The door opened, and he sprung into a sitting position, ready by reflex. It was Claire, dressed and stressed. She too was still strung out from the recent events, but recovering.

"Wow, the doctor did you up good." It took her a moment to adjust to the new stranger.

The doctor spun around. "Ah! Claire, good to see you doing well again. How's the shoulder?"

"Almost healed, but a little stiff. I'll be on desk duty for a week or so." She carried a transparent tablet under one arm and approached Hal. "Are you ready to become an official A&H employee?"

He stood and glanced to say goodbye.

"I'll see you in a few hours. I have some work to finish here, but I'll catch up with you before the night is over." Prossman was casual, and nodded back towards them both before turning to his potato chips.

Chapter 12: A New Mission

Hal followed Claire out of the office and glanced down both directions of the hallway. The complex was much noisier than the night before, and with the sunlight coming in from above it appeared much larger. Several bystanders in the hallway grew silent as the two passed, shifting their attention to the new member. It wasn't just the sudden silence that made him uncomfortable. They were all dressed in formal white lab jackets, including Claire, and his attire made him stand out like a sore thumb.

"Remember, you're new security personnel and are here to observe." She spoke quietly to him with her head lowered.

The uncomfortable silence remained, but he tried to play his role and held his shoulders straight as they continued down the hallway to the atrium.

"I'm meeting with one of our lab partners who is aware of your situation. She's been with me for nine years and was the surviving researcher during the ARCA accident, so she's aware of your arrival and position. I trust her, so if there's any details shared between you and me, she's of equal knowledge." As she spoke, she remained fairly quiet. The mention of Project ARCA was still somewhat hush-hush to many.

The atrium was quiet and occupied only by three other people at a front desk on the middle level. They hardly took noticed as they approached and walked to the front entrance on the bottom level.

Hal squinted into the sun as they exited onto a large cement patio looking over the ocean. It must have been mid-day by now and although the sun was still bright in the sky, a storm was brewing to the east.

They continued to circle around the west side of the building. Around the corner Hal slowed in amazement as he saw the monster complex expand a quarter mile in front of them. In the distance was another large building that looked like an apartment complex of some sort, accompanied by a recreational area with six tennis courts and two basketball courts. Several people occupied the area, which he assumed were permanent residents and employees at A&H, but no one took notice of them in the distance.

Claire called out to him. "Hal, you coming?" He had slowed a good fifty paces behind her while pausing in awe at the recent construction, but quickened his step to catch up.

"I had no idea such a large complex could be built on such a small island." He was still gazing at his surroundings.

"It's amazing, isn't it?" She too took a few seconds to admire its construction as well. "A&H started construction here in 2024 and has been expanding ever since. We also have two more bases in Maryland and a smaller testing facility on Bermuda. Most of the residents here live right off the base." She pointed towards the housing complex, which was a grouping of apartments surrounded by a few smaller house-like buildings. Judging by its size, he was guessing there were over two hundred occupants that either worked or lived on the base. There was a large dome greenhouse to the west. All-in-all it was a quaint self-sustaining island.

They followed the walkway to a small secluded picnic area with metal benches and tables, which was occupied by a dozen employees on their lunch breaks.

As they approached a table, the woman sitting on the opposite side stood to greet them. She walked around closer and opened her arms to hug Claire. This must have been Kyra.

"How are you feeling?" She had a heavy Russian accent as she spoke.

"Better. Still a little stiff, but I'm recovering." Claire's tone was more comfortable and soft as she spoke to the woman. "This is Hal Brent." She shifted and made a motion towards him.

As he extended his hand out to greet her, she approached and instead held her arms open and gave a gentle hug.

"Thank you for protecting my friend. It's a pleasure to meet you." Kyra was a pretty woman, somewhere in her mid to late thirties with blonde hair and a thin frame. She backed away from them both with a smile and gestured for them to have a seat.

Claire smiled and winked in Hal's direction. She knew it wasn't the type of introduction he was used to, especially considering his previous greetings with Troy and Brack. Kyra was friendly and had a compassionate face. He was instantly comforted in her presence, although he still felt a little awkward hugging a stranger.

"Claire has filled in some of the details about the Yotogi break-in and your arrival here, and there's been some talk among the people." She pulled a cigarette to her lips and lit it. "I've worked here for almost ten years and never have we had anything so..." She paused and shifted around, thinking of a word to describe the situation, "well, exciting. Many of the workers have been off-duty for two weeks now. After the freighter disappearance, we figured Troy was going under lock down until the mystery could be solved. It's our first day back and there's been a lot of talk about the reconstruction inside." She smiled and exhaled.

"Troy will be making an announcement to the workers in a few hours. He's going to leave out the details about the Yotogi and make the atrium window incident look like faulty construction in the surrounding frame work, but not the glass itself." Claire explained to Kyra. "He doesn't want any more information to get out about the recent weakness we've found in the glass."

"Understandably." She huffed in sarcasm. "Troy wouldn't want any of the contractors to pull the plug on his product." She glanced in his direction. "Always the lying businessman. So, Mr. Brent, tell me about yourself." She was more interested in his opinion on matters than those of her employer. "You probably know more about our company in the last two days than most of us here. What are your thoughts so far?"

"I think I may be stuck in a nightmare."

They both smiled and adjusted to his response. "I believe you. I can't imagine this being the kind of wake up party many would have hoped for." Kyra was compassionate and wasn't looking for answers so much as an opinion. "Nonetheless, I'm quite sure this is our reality. Perhaps you're just stuck with us for now, but it's not all bad. After all, you're on one of the most beautiful islands in the Atlantic."

It was beautiful here, and he remembered a time when he was a pilot he often visited the Florida Keys.

"I just wish it could be explained." He lowered his head, again being briefly reminded of his past before coming back to reality. "I don't have the answers that Troy is looking for. I knew nothing of the Yotogi, in my time, and I'm now his number one suspect. He believes I'm a spy or a victim to one of their experiments, but I honestly can't remember anything beyond my plane crash decades ago." He shifted and crossed his arms over his chest. "I know I am not a spy." If there was any one fact he was sure of, it was that alone.

"Good. Then you have nothing to fear from him. As paranoid and relentless as that man is, he's not stupid. He knows there is nothing to gain by pursuing you, which is why he's letting you have free range here, I'm assuming." She exhausted her cigarette and pressed it out in the nearby ashtray. "The Yotogi would not have let you escape if you were merely a test subject, and especially not a spy. He knows that. The Yotogi have an obvious interest in you, though, and I'm guessing that is also one of the reasons you are still here."

Claire pulled her tablet from under her arm and began to touch in some information. "That brings us to our next matter of business." She slid the tablet across the table for Hal to see. There was a man displayed in the image, dressed in the familiar Yotogi uniform he'd seen the previous night.

"We're trying to make communication with this man, Akira Eiji." As she spoke, Kyra gave a huff of sarcasm across the table. Claire simply continued. "We believe he was in charge of the attack. He's one of the leaders within the group and often organizes protest rallies when A&H comes out with a new product. One of our contacts in Miami has informed us that he's currently in the city, presumably overseeing the recent events we just had here."

Kyra interrupted, somehow angered by his mention. "And how exactly does Troy intend to make contact with Eiji?"

Claire looked at her before shifting focus back to Hal. "Well, that's what we're here to discuss." She put her hand on Hal's wrist in comfort. "Hal, no one is ordering you to do this for us, but this man," she pointed to the face on the tablet, "if he staged this attack to retrieve you, I believe there might be a connection between your disappearance. I don't know how, but these men knew about you when no one else did. Troy may have other motives right now regarding his freighters, but this could mean answers for both of us."

Kyra began to stir with frustration even more. "So Troy plans to use him as leverage? Bait?"

Claire was annoyed by Troy's decision as much as she was, but what other option did they have? Just wait it out and see what the Yotogi next move was?

"I'll do it." Hal also didn't see any other options. He didn't care for Troy or A&H's business deals, but if it meant he could have some closure about his plane crash, that was all that mattered. As it was, he didn't have any family ties to go home to; no long forgotten wife or children and no occupation to resume his new life. Like it or not, this was his new life, and the only friends he now had were those immediately surrounding him.

Claire looked a bit shocked and smiled at his willingness. Kyra on the other hand still didn't seem pleased. Her reaction was understandable. Troy was only interested in his company's image and everyone knew it.   What Hal wanted was to get information from this Eiji fellow, and if Troy or anyone else put him within arms reach, that was what mattered to him.

"Really? You're really just going to bait yourself out for these..." Kyra paused with an expression of annoyance. "These men are terrorists! They've done nothing but harm to the world and God only knows what else."

"I have nothing to lose. From what I've learned in the past two days these men, these terrorists, have been the only ones who know more about my own disappearance than I do and the students who were with me when my plane went down. Troy may only care about his company, but I don't. I want to know why I'm here and those boys are not." His rebuttal wasn't rude, but more like an explanation for his choice.

Kyra took the hint. She was so focused on her anger towards Troy, and probably her colleagues who had been lost during the ARCA accident, she hadn't considered his personal motives.

"I realize. But still, these men have never produced anything good in the world. I just don't see how that changes here. I mean, why the interest? What could they possibly gain from you when you yourself don't know anything?"

"I don't think they mean to harm Hal," Claire interjected. "When they trespassed two nights ago, they were armed with tranquilizers. They want him alive. "

Kyra tried to interrupt and dispute it but Claire continued. "In the interrogation room, the prisoner knew more about Hal than we did. He knew his age, knew of his death, his passengers... Maybe this isn't about A&H. Maybe the Yotogi know something about these disappearances that we don't. Troy may want our research back, but we have no proof it was the Yotogi who stole it. We only know that they knew something was wrong. They knew Hal was here, and for screwed up reasons, they know more about it than we do!"

Her point was made and Kyra backed down. She was right. This wasn't just about A&H. In the past few months two freighters had disappeared, an explosion took the lives of several people and a dead man showed up. Things were off and there was no explanation for it. But now there was a possibility for an answer, and even though they were about to befriend an enemy, it was a miserable action that couldn't be ignored.

Kyra sighed. She had seen one of the most bizarre occurrences with her own eyes. Her colleagues vanished from their stations with no explanation and she hardly escaped with her own life. Every cell in her body told her this was a bad move, but the Yotogi weren't the cause of these problems. She didn't know what was, but somehow they had some piece of information that they needed.

"So, how does Troy purpose we actually get this information?" She lit another cigarette.

Claire went back to her tablet and pulled up something he still recognized in today's world. Downtown Miami had changed quite a bit and a hotel was at the center of the photo. Although Hal couldn't recall the name from his time, it was now one of the largest buildings on the stretch.

"The Yotogi have recently been seen in the surrounding area of the Mirada Hotel. We believe Akira may be staying as a guest under the alias of Jose Palino for a little over three weeks. This places him there before and after the recent events and our contact says he's been seen numerous times in the area." She pointed again to a new picture on the screen showing a man who looked more like a thug than a professional contact.

"This is Howard Westford. He'll be working with us to get you inside the hotel, among other things." Her inquiry was left open, suspiciously. "Times have changed since you've last been in the city. With the Yotogi presence, local law enforcement has been minimal. The Yotogi don't exactly blend in and we suspect they're well armed – not like they were two days ago here, but with something more. Their robes cover much of it, but they're definitely concealing something larger than a pistol. The police are scared and won't touch them. Marshal law doesn't want a violent mess downtown and although the Yotogi won't shoot first, they won't just turn a blind eye and run if they're shot at." She looked up at Hal, knowing that he'd be going into a hostile city he no longer recognized. "That's where Howard comes in. Tomorrow night he'll be at a cafe just near the Mia Marina docks. A&H can't supply you with much because of possible repercussions, but Howard can."

"Do you think the Yotogi intend on shooting to kill now?" He agreed to this initially, not realizing the new circumstances.

"No. I still don't. The Yotogi don't want a public mess on their hands any more than law enforcement does, but we can't deny that their presence here seems to be more hostile, perhaps defensive. Still, if they'd wanted you dead they would have had you by now." She continued to scroll through some photographs on the tablet before turning it back to him.

"You will be going in alone, and whatever words are exchanged are off the record. I'll be the only one in your ear, but I have no doubt Troy will be listening. There's going to be some communication problems." She glanced back at Kyra who nodded with understanding. "Troy won't be able to contact you, so this will be your choice. I understand your need for answers, but you don't have to find ours if you choose not to. I won't ask you to do that. After all, you owe us nothing." Her tone was somber. It almost sounded as if she didn't want any answers on behalf of the freighter disappearance.

Hal was comforted that this was at least his choice. He didn't quite know how he'd be getting into the hotel unnoticed, but once there, he wouldn't be pressured from a third party. Perhaps the Yotogi would be more forthcoming with this in mind.

"So, is this normal for A&H to conduct business meetings with an enemy? Or is it just Troy's desperate attempt save some money by retrieving stolen research?" He asked sarcastically, trying to shake the cold feet suddenly creeping up on him.

"Neither," Kyra abruptly implied. "The prototype of the ARCA is still in our possession. It's only a matter of producing more of them. Troy wants the Yotogi to be disassembled. He thinks that Akira is the man in charge of the organization and wants him taken out of the picture."

Claire didn't object.

"It's key that we keep communication open between the Yotogi. Troy is stupid to believe Akira is the only one with power in the group, and although it would cause instability within, the outrage would be much worse than he realizes." Claire shifted her gaze towards Kyra. "This may be the closest we've come to a peaceful connection."

Hal took some time to consider his position. These men were roaming free in an unguarded city with possible assault rifles, and this was what they considered peaceful. Still, given the recent fiasco he'd been running through, perhaps the open city might be more welcoming and at least he'd be somewhat familiar with the surroundings.

"So, where do we start tomorrow?" He wanted to get as many details to plan for as he could.

"We're going to drop you off on the dock near the Miami strip. From there, Howard will meet you in the cafe and get you whatever materials you feel are necessary. We can't arm you with much more than a tranquilizer gun but if you feel the need for something more, it will be available through Howard. Unfortunately, there isn't much more planning than that. We've only had a day, but Howard has been in the city for months watching the Yotogi activity. We know they've occupied two floors in the Mirada and some of the surrounding clubs and restaurants. They've been relatively peaceful within the city until two days ago. It can't be a coincidence. They were planning this attack all along, and now that it has failed, they can't outright leave the city without obtaining what they came for. They've been discovered, though, and have heightened security. The timing of it all makes perfect sense. We know they're linked, somehow." She looked at Hal, still allowing him a chance to retreat if he wished.

"How will I know it's Howard and not someone else?" Hal didn't want to back down.

Claire tried to hide her smile at his enthusiasm and continued. "He'll find you, and as I said, the Yotogi have occupied floors 18 and 19. Howard will have a key card that allows you access to his, um..." She paused. Everyone knew she was going to say it, but legally she was prohibited.

"Tools?" Kyra sarcastically implied.

"Yes. Anything you might need will be provided. We don't know exactly how many Yotogi have occupied the city, so once you're in and get a glimpse at the surroundings, you can better gauge what you think is necessary." Claire looked back at Kyra, who smiled at the thought of bypassing A&H regulations. "We'll be meeting with an additional security team tomorrow and get updates on anything new."

Kyra nodded and exhausted her cigarette before giving Claire a friendly hug and continued on her way back to the complex.

"You can still decline." Claire looked at Hal wearily, half expecting him to. The details they'd acquired within the last two days were sketchy. Howard was an outsider, and from the sounds of it, A&H didn't approve of his involvement. However, being on a secluded island made it difficult to monitor any sort of outside activity, and their options were limited.

"I'm in," he nodded, almost excited. There was reason to hesitate, but Hal hadn't seen much action since his days in the Air Force. Even after he retired from the service and became a pilot instructor, he'd always longed to be with his team again in the field. Granted, this was more like walking into a civil war zone, but he began to look forward to the nostalgic challenge of it.

Claire nodded back, feeling relieved that the lack of details hadn't scared him off, and his willingness was an added assurance.

The meeting was agreed upon and Claire indicated for him to follow, as he was instructed for the remainder of the day. His job wasn't complicated yet and he followed through her daily work paces.

Chapter 13: A New Home

Claire's research team was stationed in one of the smaller underwater complexes and as they traveled down the elevator shaft to the mini submarine, he again felt amazed that such a large piece of architecture could be built out of sight from the rest of the world. It was much different from the night before, when they traveled alone to an almost vacant building. Now he sat alongside three other occupants in the submarine car. None paid any attention to him as he watched out the window in fascination. The dark sea was illuminated by a string of lights that attached to the travel rail below. Claire, like the other occupants, stared down at her tablet screen. All of this new-world transportation wasn't so new to them, but Hal couldn't shift his focus as he watched the lights from the neighboring complex come into view.

It was much larger than he remembered the night before, split in two levels that stacked onto each other. Small windows lined the building side, showing the inside hallway and several people passing through.

Once again pulling into the docking bay, they exited the submarine into another large hallway. There was an ever-present breeze due to the added ventilation being pumped throughout the bottom levels.

Following Claire into the laboratory, he found himself immediately uncomfortable as he found himself the center of attention. Five people now looked at the new member in concern. This was a private lab, and with Hal's security uniform, he didn't exactly fit in with the rest of the lab nerds.

"This is Hal Brent. He's been assigned as security detail for our protection, given the recent incident with our freighters. Troy has assured us that our work is to remain classified and that new security measures are being taken seriously with that consideration. Please resume work as normal." Claire stood next to Hal at the top of the stair case that overlooked the main work area below. Her announcement was comforting to the workers, and Hal as well. Everyone immediately shrugged off whatever suspicion they had and continued to occupy themselves.

Kyra approached from the right and again smiled to greet the two. "Welcome to the project. Come. I've set up a station where you can pass the time. We're not exactly the most exciting bunch down here, but there's probably a great deal of history you'd like to catch up on."

Hal nodded in acceptance. He hadn't spent much time thinking about the past twenty-six years worth of world events, but the mention of it did spark his interest.

He made himself comfortable at the small workstation, which was more like a transparent cubical than a comfortable office. Three five-foot high walls formed a cube formation around him. Along the lining of the glass were LED lights, which gave off an ever-present and ultra-bright work light. The underwater laboratories were nothing like he'd seen up top. They were cold, sterile and always well lit. It felt more like a square tanning booth than a workstation, which was probably by design to make sure no one fell asleep.

The average day of an A&H employee meant spending eight to ten hours in an underwater lab, quietly piddling away at a tablet computer or running calculations on a virtual simulator. He shifted his focus back to the resources in front of him and tried to ignore the background noise of complicated physics equations going on between the technicians.

The internet had only grown since his day and age, and with it, mass media had pretty much published any possible topic someone could hope for. It was oddly one piece of technology that hadn't changed much; the ability to do research via the web.

History was never one of Hal's main interests, and as he sifted through articles, he was surprised at how little had changed from his time period. There hadn't been any major wars, which was rather surprising to him, but several nations had separated from the UN. Russia was a looming threat to Japan, and Hal wondered if that might have been when the rise of the Yotogi had formed. Although the US seemed to still have one of the largest military forces in the world, other nations had also been rising, which was worrisome. Politics hadn't changed much since he last remembered either.

His attention dwindled quickly with the overflow of history articles displayed before him.

The laboratory was artificially lit and a few small windows lined the room, looking out into the dark ocean. It was difficult to gauge time here with a lack of sunlight and after several painfully boring hours of reading up on recent events, Hal glanced at his watch and was relieved to see it was nearly eight o'clock.

"We're closing down for the night," one of the techs announced. Nobody immediately moved, but it perked Hal's attention. He was dying to stretch his legs and move around.

Kyra walked around behind him as she approached the door. "We shall see you tomorrow."

Claire swiveled around in the office chair where she'd remained for the last two hours. The technicians all eagerly gathered their things and headed out, leaving them alone in the empty laboratory. The computer systems hummed quietly and the lights were now dim.

"I promise things will be more eventful tomorrow," she smiled.

They both laughed and Hal stood and stretched. His feet had grown uncomfortable, as had his side, from the new injuries.

Claire noticed as he restrained his motion. "Why don't we go up top to the food court and get some fuel. There's still a few things I'd like to go over with you before we finish planning tomorrow night and we can get a new dressing on those wounds."

The hallway was brightly lit as they made their way to the elevator. All the workers had since left the underwater labs and it was quiet. A little too quiet. Having been down this same hallway two nights ago, he was leery. He half expected the place to go pitch black at any moment and they'd be running for their lives again.

The main atrium was engulfed in a red sun-set tone. It was September and the sun was just settling at 8:30 PM now.

Several occupants were still on the main level. Most were in the adjacent rooms just down the west hallway, but no one took notice as they approached the food court. As they entered, several people at the tables glanced over in their direction. Ironically, Hal had been prepared for a swarm of curious questions, and yet no one seemed fazed. Troy was paranoid that the workers would be suspicious of a new face, especially one dressed in a security uniform, but not a single person had even approached him.

The menu was bland with a mix of cheesy noodles and bacon bits, a salad bar and fried chicken. Hal chose it all. Somewhere buried in the back of his mind his body ached for food, reminding him that it shouldn't be taken for granted. He couldn't remember why he felt so desperately eager to eat. He wasn't even that hungry, but it was more of an instinctual reaction that he couldn't help but feel. Judging by his weight loss, there was probably a good reason for it.

Claire was modest with her dinner. She chose a small plate of noodles with a salad. They sat across from one another at the same table and she was more amused by him than her own meal as he shoveled mouthful after mouthful without much pause in between. He was thin, but not emaciated. The last photo from his old life showed him with about 40 lbs more than his current weight. At 6'3" he was a tall man, and he probably weighed about 190 lbs now. A few hundred extra calories in every meal would do him some good.

The room emptied after about ten minutes and there were now only three other people present. A man dressed in a black suit stood out from the other workers. He was completely absorbed by whatever was on his tablet screen and took no notice of them.

The chef was cleaning up what was left and another younger man approached their table. He was dressed like most of the other workers and wore thick black-rim glasses that partially held up the mop of hair curling around his face.

"Hi Claire. Can I join you?" The man didn't even take notice of Hal as he asked.

"Sure Bean, have a seat." She patted the bench next to her and he was a little too eager to accept. The expression on her face was friendly, although you could see in her eyes that she wasn't in the mood for his company.

"Hal, this is Forest Bean. He's one of our security techs that maintains the video and alarm systems here." She motioned towards him and Hal held out his hand to shake.

"Hi, Hal. I'm Bean! So, what's with the remodeling in the atrium?"

94

Claire looked over, somewhat annoyed that she had to lie about it. "The support beams up top collapsed and there was a shift in its weight. It just gave out."

"Oh. Geeze, I figured we built things tougher than that." He looked over at Hal. "Are you part of the reconstruction team?"

"No, he's not." Claire spoke for him, trying to take the focus off their new guest. "He's here as security. With the windows open, A&H hired a few private security contractors as an added measure. It's nothing serious, just a precaution."

"Well, I feel safer. I've been watching the security feeds over the last few days, and there's something abnormal going on." He looked at her, waiting to fill in the blanks.

"Oh?" She fell silent. Troy had erased the recent footage of the Yotogi invading, but from the sounds of it, Bean had seen something he shouldn't have.

"Yeah, I was wondering if you knew about it. There's been a whole bunch of men in black suits wandering around freely." He nodded towards one of the men who'd been sitting in the corner. "They're all over the place." He now looked at Hal. "So, are you guys all here to guard the open window?"

Bean had completely misunderstood. He must have gotten the impression he was just a window watcher, which was fine, really. He didn't care what the man thought, but it did make him suspicious of the other guy. Claire picked up on it too.

"Actually, Bean, I'm not sure who that man is."

Troy hadn't mentioned anything to anyone about added security, other than Hal, and she was being left out of the loop. Something else was going on.

"Hmm, it's not like Troy to add so many personnel in one day. I mean, we had a few days of leave, but these guys are, like, super armed and stuff." For a man who watched monitor screens all day, it was probably the most excitement he had in years.

Claire looked at Bean with one eye brow up. "Oh?"

"Yeah, they've been in the firing range for the entire day! It's like an army down there."

Troy must have been taking these recent precautions a little more serious than he led on. All three now had their eyes fixed on the man. It caught his attention as he nervously packed his tablet under his arm and headed for the door.

Claire tilted her head and stood. "Maybe we should go ask them?"

Bean remained in his seat. "But, wait. I don't want to instigate anything."

"You're not."

Hal also stood. He actually liked the idea of going to the firing range. He hadn't fired a real weapon in years and the mere mention of it was intriguing. Although he was confident in his aiming capabilities, he had hoped for some target practice before tomorrow evening. Bean on the other hand seemed to shy away from the whole idea of being in a room full of loaded firearms.

Claire led the way down the hall and Hal closely followed. This was the most excitement he'd felt since arriving, at least in a good way. Something about holding a weapon had become instinctual in his previous career. He wasn't sure what type of weaponry the future had for them, but judging by the types of research A&H frequently dabbled in, it would be a welcomed education.

Bean squandered off into a nearby office without a word. Surely he'd watch the episode from his camera lens somewhere in a dark room, accompanied by his cheese noodles.

The hallways were dark and empty now. Muffled gun fire could be heard as they approached the neighboring section.

It was the only occupied room throughout the level and a stream of light came through the small glass window in the door frame. Claire scanned her hand and a green light flashed before the buzz. The noise instantly hit them as the sounds of several assault rifles echoed in the small space.

A dozen faces turned to greet them as they entered and the gunfire stopped. They all looked the same, aside from their facial shape and color. Bald, blank and dangerous.

Claire didn't seem to mind. She walked over to a nearby closet, all eyes watching her, and pulled out a large drawer with various types of hand pistols. A glass cabinet lined the back wall with assault rifles and long range firearms. Knowing the new guests were watching her, she pulled out what looked like an M4. It wasn't quite the M4 Hal remembered, but it was the closest he could compare it to.

"Take your pick." She winked at Hal to choose his destruction.

The room was still silent and she approached one of the nearby doorway openings. Hitting a tab on the floor with her foot opened a gate in the distance and the paper lining of a human figure moved forward to about seventy feet. It was the farthest target on the range and with a few pops she hit several marks, while missing a dozen others. Her aim wasn't bad, but not great either.

Hal gazed at the firearms with excitement and chose a .45 hand pistol. Although the variety was large, he chose something a little more modest. It wasn't any type of weapon he'd recognized, but the caliber was the same and much lighter than he guessed. Claire watched as he stepped up, hit the floor pad and moved the target to seventy feet. With a squeeze, a single round jolted his grip. It had more bite than he was used to, but his aim was square. A single shot hit dead center in the chest. As Hal turned, the men in their suits shrugged and cornered a smile of approval, including Claire. He hadn't lost his touch, although he'd have to get used to the kick.

The surrounding audience quickly resumed, now accompanied by two other gun-wielding comrades of mutual interest. A silent competition started among four others who quickly reassessed their firearms to match Claire's assault rifle. It was a mad house of gun fire and Hal quickly exhausted his rounds into the skeletal drawing from afar. Claire continued to miss hers. Her work was generally more desk-heavy and shooting wasn't a mandatory requirement, but she was still well versed in their handling.

She emptied another thirty shots into the target, which had moved closer now, and she lowered her aim to reload. One of the guards approached her and inquired about something of interest while glancing at Hal. She nodded. The conversation was muted by the surrounding chaos, but she smiled with good intentions before gesturing for Hal to accompany her out the doorway. He had fired a good twenty rounds or so and had had his fill of excitement. It was a huge release and felt good to re-familiarize his instincts with a weapon.

He followed behind as the two exited the room into the hallway. The door clicked behind them and his ears adjusted to the sudden lack of volume.

The man extended his hand for Hal to shake. "I'm Simon Ortiz. I'm the leader of a private military contractor, hired by Harley Brack. My men and I were briefed this morning about the added security detail after your recent attack. I've been told to follow any orders you or Mr. Brent here have for us. Although I report to Brack, we're here as an extra measure and are at your disposal. Some of my men will be on the ground with you tomorrow Mr. Brent, and our main objective is to make sure you're in safe hands. You won't see us outside of this complex, but I assure you we're there."

Hal shook the man's hand firmly. He was in command of a small, well trained private military and he wasn't even aware of it. "Thank you. It's appreciated."

Hal wasn't sure if they knew his circumstances, but having seen their skill, he felt both secured and a bit frightened. This man was shaking his hand and addressing him as his superior. Either he'd missed a memo or wasn't yet filled in, but with more than a dozen military units on his side, he was either being watched or heavily guarded. He wasn't entirely comforted by the feeling.

"Please excuse us for not being informed. I haven't spoken to Brack in several hours and haven't heard any updates." Claire was trying to gauge how much of the situation he knew.

"Surely. Please, follow me where we can discuss matters." He put his hands behind his back and with a strict walking stance, he placed his palm on a nearby doorway scanner and opened it.

The lights immediately illuminated the interior of a conference room. With a hiss and click of the doorway behind them, he paced over to a nearby terminal and unplugged the security camera.

His stance became casual. "Please, sit. Brack has contracted this work outside of Mr. Troy's knowledge, which is why you haven't been briefed. He's currently tied up in other business and hasn't had the chance to inform everyone of the additional security. We've been hired to ensure your safety, Mr. Brent, as well as the scientists here on the base. This is being made to look like a private interaction within the company, but several agents will be on the ground tomorrow night and at your disposal. Mr. Brent will be meeting with Akira Eiji in the Mirada Hotel and we're here to ensure he gets to his target and out safely. We also have a mole within the Yotogi that has verified this information, along with several undercover agents to help with the extraction if needed."

Claire looked concerned suddenly. "Are you really expecting so much resistance?"

"No. Our insider has indicated that the Yotogi have tightened security, but they're still recoiling from their recent failures to obtain Mr. Brent. They've regrouped in the hotel, but don't seem to know of these future plans. They have about two dozen members within the city and are easy to spot, but Brack is concerned with how many have gathered. We're here as an added measure in case they become..." He paused, choosing his words, "agitated."

"You mean hostile?" Hal already had one encounter with the Yotogi and they seemed more than a bit agitated.

"The Yotogi are known for non-violent protesting. It's their image. They have no intentions to harm you, but with your lack of history, you're already a dead man. There are no suspects if a dead man disappears, which is why we're taking these precautions. We're also here to provide whatever back up is needed that the local law enforcement won't uphold. I'm comforted that we have one of our own in this operation. You know how to handle a weapon and this isn't merely a duck and cover run."

Hal was flattered. Ortiz knew of his military record and was addressing him as a superior.

"How much do you know about my arrival here?" Hal was curious.

"Professionally, I've been told of your death in 2013 and that you may have been held in some sort of suspended animation until now, presumably by the Yotogi." Something in his tone was hiding something.

"Professionally?" Claire sensed it too.

He looked back at Hal. "Yes. Personally, however, you were a friend of my father, serving in Iraq before your retirement. I met you when I was a boy in Puerto Rico. I must say your disappearance was a loss to our family and it's an honor to have you back."

Hal was taken back a bit. He remembered his father Carlton Ortiz and could see the resemblance now. This was personal to him, and although their attachment was distant, he was touched.

"My late father would have wanted this, as would I, if the Yotogi did hold you in some sort of captivity. I'm not so quick to believe they did, but they have an interest in you, and for whatever reason, they've set aside their public facade to obtain you, which makes them my enemy. You're a free man, Mr. Brent and I intend to ensure that."

Simon was just as patriotic as his father, and although times and politics had changed, he looked up to him as a father figure still. It was a compliment and a curse. Hal hadn't been around when his fellow soldiers had passed away, and now here he was being protected by their offspring. It was a bizarre feeling of gratitude and sadness, but his presence among this new generation was welcomed.

There was a minute of silence before anyone spoke. Claire felt out of place as two strangers reunited.

"Is Brack aware of your history?" She placed her hands on her lap and reclined.

"No, and he doesn't have to be. Our job is the same either way, but I wanted to address you both beforehand. We'll meet again at 9:00 AM for a briefing." He held out his hand again to shake Hal's. "It's good to see you again, friend."

Chapter 14: The Calm Before the Storm

Before ending the night, Claire applied new bandages to Hal's side and feet, then escorted him down to his temporary living quarters below. It was risky having him stay in the above quarters, given the previous few nights. The underwater complex was much less accessible to anyone outside the company.

The new living quarters were much more comfortable than the doctor's office. He had about nine hundred square feet of living space with a full bathroom and cooking area. The room was vacant and completely lacking much decor, which was how he preferred it. He wasn't sure how long he'd be welcomed here at A&H and didn't want to feel too comfortable. He had nothing in common with the other residents and was about twenty-five years behind any technological research they were conducting. He tried to avoid the thoughts about Troy and how long he'd be useful to him. For all he knew, they'd just dump him on an island somewhere when they were done with him. It was a scary thought. He trusted Claire, for the most part, but how far would that go in the long term? His future lingered and now alone with his thoughts in this empty, office-like living space, he had no choice but to consider it. Even if things worked out, he was still a lost, outdated and worn out military man. There was little attachment to this world. Not that his previous world had many attachments, but who would want him when this was all over? Would it ever be over? Even this mysterious group called the Yotogi would find his *knowledge* useless when they realized he had no part in their cause.

He told himself he should be grateful to simply be alive, but he still found the situation depressing. In a lot of ways, he was already dead. The only real connection he had was with Ortiz, who was only a shadow of a memory now. The last time he'd seen him he was just a child, but still, he was hopeful. Ortiz wasn't the type of man to abandon his fellow soldier, and he was the best thing Hal could hope for at the moment.

The day was exhausting, even though he'd accomplished nothing. His body ached and his blood count was still low. Although he'd well exceeded his daily calorie count, he was starved. A few meals occupied the mini fridge and within the hour he'd completely devoured every single one of them. Food. It was something so simple that he'd been missing and every cell in his body felt the need to hoard it. There was something psychological in his brain telling him to consume as much as he could, for fear that the next day might not provide it. He couldn't explain it. He'd never felt such a need to gorge until now.

His energy didn't return, which was comforting. Modern conveniences had been a missed luxury, but again, he couldn't explain his new found appreciation for them. Hot water, hot food, the soft carpet and sofa-bed were all like new to him. Even in this empty, dismal-gray storage space, the weight of his body felt light as he lay on the futon. The blankets were rough and the pillow was a little less than soft, but it was his space for now.

His mind wandered but slowly ran out of fuel as the food and comfort began to settle. His future was uncertain, but tonight he was warm, fed, bathed and in capable hands. More importantly, he felt a sense of being needed, or at least for the next forty eight hours. The thought ended as he slipped into a deep sleep.

Chapter 15: A New Purpose

The lights were low as something stirred in the room. He struggled to open his groggy eyes and squinted at the dim lights in the kitchen area. The stir came again to his side and he quickly shifted to face its direction. The floor was cold on his feet and his balance was off as he fought for stability. The movement in the room had stopped and he held out his arms in defense as his eyes continued to adjust. His nerves were on high alert, and all the comfort he'd just experienced quickly vanished.

"Who's there?" He blinked and focused on the figure that slowly crept towards him out of the darkness. The silhouette of the creature moved into a hunched position, but it wasn't quite a human shape. It slowly began slithering forward like a shadow, voiding out the light. He blinked and in that instance it was gone.

"Who's there!"

A gust of air moved past and he spun to face it. Still off balance, he fell to his knees and he grasped the futon. The figure was now slithering over the surface of the couch towards him. There was no form to it, just darkness that consumed the light around. With his fists clenching the mattress, he watched in disbelief as it crept up his knuckles and wrists. He lurched back, trying to free himself from its grip as it solidified and rose up his forearms like vines, twisting over his skin.

This wasn't right. He looked down at his arms calmly, realizing this wasn't his reality. This is a dream, he told himself. I'm not awake. "Wake up Hal!" He yelled, his eyes still glued shut. "Wake up, now!"

A screeching sound resonated in his ears as the light in the room suddenly vanished. He sprung to a sitting position, clasping his hands over his ears as the ringing continued to fade. His hair was wet and his heart was beating ferociously in his chest. He swung his arms from side to side, now able to move again. The only light in the room came from the wrist band on his arm, which was now bright with an alarming message. He focused on its readings, which gave a pulse rate of 185. He was gasping for air and he checked his limbs for any abnormal injuries. The blankets and sheets were damp with sweat, but nothing was damaged.

He exhaled with relief as the nightmare faded. Sleep was an abnormal thing, now. He was being haunted by something, but unlike the last time, he was at least aware of it and the noise from the wrist band was irritating enough to snap him out of it. As his heart rate settled, the noise ceased.

His eyes had now adjusted to the lack of light around him. The small bathroom door was open and the light from within gave a dim illumination to his surroundings. The place felt more foreign than ever. He was alone, and for the first time he felt scared to be so. The last nightmare had left him bleeding out from an unexplainable wound to his side, and sleep was no longer to be trusted.

He glanced again at his wrist band for the time, which read 6:43 AM. He'd been out for about eight hours, but still felt exhausted.

A light flickered on a small work station desk and an image of Doctor Prossman came up on the screen. "Mr. Brent, are you awake? Can you hear me?"

It took Hal a second to orient where the noise was coming from.

"I don't think this thing is working here." He could see the doctor shuffle around on the screen. His face was now zoomed in close to the camera. "Mr. Brent?"

Hal stood and walked towards the console. "Yes, can you hear me?" He had no idea how to activate the microphone and he spoke aloud hoping the message would get through. "Doctor?"

He could see the man shuffle around, still unsure of whether or not he was being heard. "Ah, yes. There you are."

Hal could now see himself on what looked like an infrared image, activated by his movements.

"Your heart rate is rather high, are you OK down there?" Prossman was still zoomed in on the camera lens, unaware of its depth perception. He didn't know how to use the camera or microphone either. "Did I wake you?"

"No, no, doctor. You're fine. I just..." He rubbed his eyes and walked closer to the console. "I just had a nightmare."

"Like before?"

"I don't know. I feel like something is haunting me. I can't seem to sleep without something attacking my memory." He relaxed, realizing that he was at least in the real world now and alone again. "I don't know how to explain it."

"What was the dream?" The doctor relaxed and backed away from his camera lens.

Hal glanced around at his surroundings half expecting to find the looming shadow figure behind him. "I was here. I was awoken by this dark figure on the couch and it was... I don't know. It was trying to consume me."

"Huh." He had an expression of concern and curiosity.

"It grabbed my arms and began to crawl into my skin." He brushed his clammy arms, feeling the area that had been consumed.

"Interesting. Is the arm band still in place? It should sound some sort of alarm when you're under immense stress." He motioned where the band should have been.

"Yes, it did." He sighed. "I'm fine now. I just need to get my bearings."

"Alright. I was to be alerted if anything unusual happened." The doctor was relieved. "I was afraid something similar to the previous night might occur."

Hal was touched. The man had saved his life at least once already and even though he wasn't in his medical bay now, he was still concerned for him.

"I'll be fine. I'm not sure I can sleep, though."

"I understand. If there's anything you need, there should be a communication option on your arm thing." He smiled. He wasn't well versed with the equipment Hal was wearing, and in a way, it was amusing that he wasn't the only one. "Get what rest you can. Mr. Brack will be assembling a meeting this morning at 9 AM. I'll come down for you before then." He nodded before Prossman's screen turned black.

He looked around the room and saw a small camera in the corner, which matched the direction his recording was coming from. The idea of surveillance was a bit uncomfortable to Hal. He felt more like a lab rat than a guest here, but the precaution was also to ensure his well being, and given previous circumstances, safety didn't allow for privacy.

It was quiet again.

"Lights on?" The room illuminated and he winced. He wasn't sure if the voice command would work, but he'd heard Brack give the same command a few nights prior, which did the same.

Sleep didn't come again. Hal found himself dabbling at the computer console, which was much different than he remembered in his time. Everything was voice or touch based. By simply saying the word "Help" a prompt came up and inquired his interest. He thought this would be a good time to catch up on some of the modern events taking place, and do a little research on this group the Yotogi.

They were only publicly established since 2024, fourteen years earlier, but there was suspicion that they'd been a small congregation since 2018, protesting military advancement and technological research. Various articles had been written about their supposed agenda, but what interested Hal the most was their origin. Their leader, Akira Eiji was Japanese and as Hal last recalled Japan was one of the World's leaders in technological advancement. It was ironic that one of their own would turn against a leading asset.

The group was accused of various attacks, including the promotional display A&H had for their shielding material that skyrocketed their popularity. The turmoil had only grown since then and along with A&H's success in the technology market, the followers for the Yotogi had also grown. They now had tens of thousands of followers, although many simply sided with their cause but hadn't shown any aggression.

Most of the articles and news bits were the same. They were from anonymous sources outside of the group, and none of the official members ever gave formal statements. It was amazing to consider how such a large group had become a world-wide organization without any of the members themselves promoting their causes to the public. And yet, they not only had thousands of members in Japan, but in the US as well.

Before long a quick beep of his new wrist watch reminded him that it was nearly 9AM. The doctor was expected to escort him back up top to the meeting, as he didn't quite know his way around the complex yet. It wasn't a long wait before a tap on the door came and he went to greet his escort.

Out of his pajamas, the doctor was dressed in his normal white, bland jacket and black pants, but he still had his slippers on.

"Ah, good morning sir! Did you get anymore sleep?" He was as chipper as they came.

"No, not really. Rest, but not sleep." He explained as he put his boots on carefully over his wounded feet. They were still sore from the glass cuts, but the spray-on fix-it had worked like a miracle considering how deep they were.

"Well then, lets go on up. They're running a little behind schedule with their meeting, but maybe we can get something to eat on the way," he said as he patted his belly.

The walk was shorter than he remembered down the hallway to the elevator tube. It felt like a tube, too, because the actual shaft could be seen through the glass walls.

The atrium was bright and clean again and there was a construction crew noisily buzzing away as the new ceiling dome was being installed. At the top balcony he could see both Brack and Troy overlooking the operation. Neither of them noticed their arrival from a hundred feet away, and doctor Prossman glanced at them suspiciously as they made their way toward the west hallway food court.

The food court was much busier and louder than the previous night, this time occupied by some familiar faces, but most were still strangers. He grabbed a tray and eagerly waited his turn in the line. Even though he'd stuffed himself last night, he was unusually hungry again. The variety was much better than the previous night as well. Pancakes, eggs, fried ham, sausage and bacon all struck his interest. Before he realized, his tray was overwhelmed. The doctor's was too. They grabbed a nearby table with two other occupants who he didn't recognize, and without conversation he piled in the protein as fast as his mouth could chew it. Prossman was also quietly occupied with his meal and didn't show much interest in conversation.

Hal had almost completed what was on his plate before a buzzing noise interrupted him. He glanced side to side, realizing the noise was coming from his body somewhere.

The doctor pointed at his wrist with his fork. "You're being paged. They must be getting started."

He pulled up his sleeve and saw something new. A screen came up asking to accept or deny a communication.

The image became larger and was expanded to a video monitor. It was Brack, grim as usual. "We're starting in ten minutes. Tell the doctor to bring you to conference room 8."

"OK, we'll be there in a minute." Hal hadn't yet adjusted to Brack's direct orders. Something about the man was very cold. He always seemed to be very direct and forward, but it wasn't that. His tone just sounded dead.

"Brack has requested that we go to conference room 8." He glanced around at the food court, which was now only half occupied.

"Right. Well, lets get going. When Brack says ten minutes he usually means now." The doctor picked up his tray and neatly piled his utensils to the side before bringing it to the trash can.

One of the new security members stood motionless outside the conference room. His arms were crossed and he merely nodded his head as they approached the entrance.

"This will be it Hal, good luck." The doctor made a motion for the door, indicating he wouldn't be following.

He entered and saw some familiar faces. Claire sat at the far end of the table and made a motion for him to come and sit. Ortiz stood across at the other end of the table in front of what looked like a translucent screen. Among the crowd Hal recognized Brack, Troy and two other security men he'd seen at the firing range the night before. Two other men walked in and sat around the table on the other side.

"Now that everyone is here, we'll get started." Ortiz motioned for the last man that entered to lower the lights, and the screen before him illuminated.

"The man we're trying to contact is Akira Eiji, who we believe is leader of the Yotogi. A source within the group has consistently reported his involvement in numerous protests, and with his recent presence so close in Miami, we have reason to believe he was staging the attack here at A&H." The screen changed to a close up photo of their suspect as Ortiz continued. "Eiji has been seen at some of the local establishments by various contacts within the city, and members of the group have been lingering as well. Within the last week, however, their numbers have grown. We estimate anywhere between sixty to seventy members are located in the immediate downtown area on the strip."

He glanced at Hal, now focusing his attention directly to him. "Until now, they've shown little aggression towards the public or law enforcement. However, within the past forty-eight hours their security and presence has become a little more worrisome."

He flipped to another photograph showing two men dressed in the same black cloaks they'd seen the other night. It was difficult to see what kind of transaction was taking place, but there was definitely some sort of new equipment concealed under their attire. "We believe these men are now carrying weapons of some sort. They're not large, but that's why we're here. In the event that they become aggressive, or their stance has changed from their previously peaceful protesting, we're here to ensure your safety. It's still unclear what interest the Yotogi have in you, but they are now making more serious approaches to make contact. The recent events here have proven this, but I assure you my men will not allow them to take measures further than mere communication."

Brack began to approach the spotlight where Ortiz stood. "Our actions through A&H are limited. Our intentions are to make contact with Akira Eiji and, hopefully, establish a baseline of communication. So far they've refused to make any sort of public announcement or direct communication with us, and what we heard and witnessed the night of the attack, it seems that they've chosen you to be our medium." His tone remained cold, as usual, as he spoke in Hal's general direction. "We believe they were involved in the recent sabotage of the shipment freighters heading towards Bermuda. Over the past several years we've been making an effort to help improve the environmental conditions on the islands, and they've organized protests at every attempt. They may not protest the actions of A&H directly, or publicly claim to, but this has been an ongoing effort for several years involving various corporations working towards technological advancement that would allow us to continue our work. What we are asking, Mr. Brent, is that if you can establish any sort of contact with Eiji, or any of the leading members for that matter, to try and get information to prove this. Our research that we were conducting on Bermuda involved certain equipment that had not been fully tested. Project ARCA has been compromised, but it is more important that we can reclaim the equipment that was lost. If it were to become public or fall into the wrong hands, it could be used for something much more devastating than what it was designed for."

Everyone shifted in their seats at the mention of Project ARCA. It was a key word that seemed to make everyone uncomfortable, including Troy who was anxiously tapping his finger. The word was out. Project ARCA was out of the box, although Hal barely understood what it even was. He suspected as much among most of those also in the room. So far, it had only been a lingering secret with a code name, and now that it was being brought to the public, everyone shuttered at the mention, yet no one was still really sure what the hell it was.

"We will be dropping you off on the Mia Marina docks, just north east of the Miami strip. The docks are vacant during the late hours, aside from those who live on their yachts or fishing boats, and we'll blend in. My men are already scattered around the city and will know your exact location at all times. A&H is taking precautions and will only be arming you with a stun pistol, prod and carrying knife, but I assure you my men will be able to *deal with* anyone who has an intention to harm you." Ortiz was obligated to hide the fact they'd probably be carrying machine guns, but for the purpose of public image on A&H's behalf, he couldn't come right out and admit it.

There was a brief moment of silence as everyone slowly shifted their gaze towards Hal. That was it? Just a drop off? Hal was confused and suddenly under some pressure to speak now.

"So, if he's staying at the Mirada Hotel, what exactly am I supposed to say when I get there? I mean, is there a plan to actually find him or his room suite? Do I just ask at the front desk?"

Brack hadn't really planned that far ahead and nervously shifted on his feet. He had figured Hal to be a resourceful man, and he was, but still, it had been twenty-six years since Hal had even set foot in the city of Miami.

Claire could sense the strain on Brack and his lack of answers. "Eiji is staying in a suite under the alias of Jose Palino. There are five main entrances into the hotel, two in the front and one on each side. There's also a back entrance, which doesn't have a security camera and from our surveillance we haven't seen any frequent guard members patrolling. It might be the best way in, and an outside contact in the city can probably get you a security pass." The mention of this *outside contact* made both Troy and Brack annoyed. This was supposed to be a closed operation, but it was no secret that Claire had some of her own *friends* outside of A&H, and with the lack of planning on their behalf, they couldn't really object.

"The Yotogi seem to be occupying both the 18th and 19th floors. Each floor has sixteen rooms, and among them, Palino's signature for room service has been shown for 18C, 18D and 19H, so we can only assume he's located in one of those three."

"It's likely that the Yotogi will recognize you on sight," Ortiz chimed in. "In which case they may actually seek you out, rather than you finding them. This wouldn't necessarily be a bad thing. We know that whatever their intentions are, they don't show any desire to harm you permanently. They want you alive."

The room stood silent. There were no more details, and everyone felt a little nervous at the lack of information Brack and Troy had been cooking up. They'd been dealing with the group for years, and on numerous occasions, yet over the last three days they'd been planning some sort of interception, and this ten minute debriefing was all they'd conjured up.

When the meeting ended Claire escorted Hal to the firing range to get some more *exercise*, as she called it. There was no mention of weapons and what he would be carrying into the hotel, but he was under the impression that other means of defense would be provided once he was in the city.

The exercise was welcomed. He had more confidence after several rounds, and although he'd never forgotten the feel and weight of a weapon, these new types of ammunition were different compared to his time. They had less kick and more accuracy, and several hand held pistols had multiple functions that he wasn't used to. Some carried different shells for different ranges. Others were designed for non-lethal neutralization.

One weapon in particular took to Hal's liking. It was an eight inch barrel pistol, similar to the one he'd carried during the initial attack, and it carried twenty two dart-like cartridges with tranquilizers. There was little to no kick once fired, and the dart could travel up to a hundred and fifty feet without sagging. Once the target was hit, there would be a one-to-two second lag before the opponent was completely paralyzed. This effect lasted for several hours and was the most accurate and quiet in the bunch. Hal hadn't yet formed much of an opinion towards the Yotogi, but he figured they'd be more useful alive than dead. Not to mention that they'd go down without a sound and any sort of life supporting monitor wouldn't be triggered. Best yet, it was the only weapon within A&H that they could hand him directly. More would be provided by this *outside contact* but weren't immediately available.

The day went by surprisingly quick, which was welcomed. After being cooped up for several days, anxiously waiting for the next crisis to surprise them, he felt as if he would soon be able to take the aggressive stance and get some answers without someone else waiting for clearance.

He joined Claire, Kyra and the doctor one last time in the medical bay where a small, private dinner had been planned. The little details were being filled in by the only people who seemed to be on top of things, and Hal felt a genuine sense of care among them. Tension within the company was apparent before Hal's arrival, but here among the others, he felt as if his objectives were their primary ones as well. He was somewhat of a stranger to them still, but regardless of what A&H gained, they were motivated to find Hal his own place among them.

Chapter 16: A Visit to the Past

The lights of Miami could normally be seen for miles over the ocean, but the weather was dismal and a lingering fog made even short distances difficult to navigate. The rain was light, for now, but the winds were picking up from the storm just south east of them.

Hal was equipped with some new gear, and thankfully it was weather proof. He wore a long jacket that was almost a foot longer than his waist. Not quite a trench coat, but its length covered the items on his belt, along with the vest that carried the tranquilizer pistol, several clips of ammunition, a carrying knife, and a billy club specially modified with a stun prod at the end for any close encounters. The vest he wore underneath was also an added feature for the mission. Interwoven with a slim, flexible version of the Sealo-Pax material, it would stop any small caliber bullets, as well as some with a larger caliber. It was puncture proof and had metallic wiring throughout that bridged to a small dis-charger in the back. In the case of electric shock, stabbing or tranquilizing, his chest and arms were immune.

The small yacht they were on carried Claire, Kyra, Ortiz and two of his men. Claire and Kyra both sat at the front near the controls and computer systems. They had a microphone and headset piece that snaked around their ears to the small insert that allowed them to hear everyone on the system. Hal had one as well, but it was smaller and couldn't be seen easily.

As they approached the dock, Claire's voice came over the mic. "Mic check, can you read me?"

Several people gave the affirmative.

"We're at fifty feet, closing in," Ortiz read back, although the dock wasn't in sight due to the fog.

There was a splash, and before Hal could realize, Ortiz was in the water.

It was amazing how thick the fog was over the ocean. As the boat closed in, he jumped the four foot gap to the dock and landed sloppily on his feet

"We're going to move south and dock at the neighboring pier. Back up is already on the ground, but they're scattered. If you need any assistance, call it in over the mic. They'll have your position at all times, and we'll extract you if things get rough." Claire's voice was nervous.

Hal was almost excited. His adrenaline was high and for once he felt like he was the one in control. He was well armed, and even with the brewing storm pushing from the east, the protective gear made him feel immune from its force.

He casually made his way down the long dock, which hadn't changed much, although the real estate and boats that were now lining them were much more sophisticated than he would have thought. The boats anchored to the docks were like small houses, and no doubt some of the occupants lived here most of the time.

The place was vacant and dark with only a few lamp posts that lined the pathway. Many of the lights had gone dark due to neglect and bad wiring. It was a perfect place for the drop off. The fog and turbulent winds made it easy to remain unseen in the constant movement surrounding him.

The fog lightened as he approached the city, but the rain had begun to pick up. The streets were nearly empty with less than a dozen people in sight. They quickly ran from one roof covering to the next, which was a pointless effort as the wind threw the rain sideways.

Directly in front of him was the cafe that Claire had mentioned. Its bright neon lights shone through the fog and the cloth overhang above the doorway whipped violently in the wind. He could see six people inside, one waitress and as far as he could tell there were no Yotogi members, or at least not in their usual attire.

Without trying to look suspicious, Hal lowered his head and approached the front entrance. He gazed from side to side, cautiously inspecting his surroundings as he walked. Two men stood in the distance near the walkway overlooking the ocean and beach, dressed in black long coats. He could only assume they were members of the Yotogi based on their location and dress, not to mention that they were the only two people just tolerating the weather outside. They didn't seem to notice him from three hundred feet as he approached the cafe.

"Psst. Hey you, man."

Hal was about thirty feet from the door when he saw a man sitting on the sidewalk, his knees curled to his chest and he sat under the cover of the eaves trough.

Hal paused and glanced around before looking back at the man.

"Yeah, you man." He waved his arm to call him closer. His hands were covered with fingerless gloves and he wore a dirty beanie hat over the mess of hair that came out from the sides. "I got something to tell you."

"Is this part of the operation?" Hal whispered into the mic.

"No, he's not one of ours." He heard Ortiz whisper back.

"Negative, not one of our contacts either," Claire confirmed.

It would look suspicious if he didn't approach the man now, so Hal quietly and discretely strolled over to him.

"Hey man, I know something is going on here." The man with the beanie hat extended his hand to meet Hal's, which he accepted and helped him to his feet. "I could help you out."

Hal looked behind him at the two men who were still standing at the overlook.

"Those men over there. I know they have something that you might be interested in. Whaddya say?" He'd apparently been watching the same men.

"Can you be more specific?" If the guy wasn't a member of Ortiz's team, and he wasn't part of A&H, then he was either looking for a hand out or he was bait.

The man was also looking around with suspicion. "I've been following 'em, man. I know where they meet down in the alley. They've been fighting over something. They're angry dudes, if you know what I'm saying." He nodded and his eyebrows raised with a look of crazy. "They've been gearing up for something. I see them everyday watching this shipment box on the north side. I figure they be watching something valuable in there."

"And how can that help me?" Hal was interested, but he wasn't sure what the man was offering.

"Hey look, man. I don't have anything. I just wanted something to eat and a place out of the rain, but they pushed me out. That's mean, man."

Hal could see he wasn't an undercover agent of any sort. He was just a man, down on his luck and looking for a dry place to stay. Hal didn't know much about the Yotogi mannerisms, and apparently they weren't sympathetic to those less fortunate.

His earpiece was quiet. He didn't know what to do, and neither did anyone else. The man sat back down on the ground and covered his head with his hands. Hal felt obligated to help him, although he'd never been very charitable before. He felt as if he was looking at a lost soul, similar to himself, but no one was there to rescue him. He couldn't explain why he felt obligated to give this man something, but it was a new emotion of sympathy he hadn't really experienced before.

Hal knelt down beside the man. "I'm sorry, I don't have much now to give, but maybe you can help me."

"Yeah, man, anything. I just need something to eat. I know they have something valuable in there." He shivered as he spoke. He wanted to get into their shipping container and steal something worth selling.

"I went there a while ago and the guy was pushing me around. He dropped this." He patted his shirt and pulled out what looked like a credit card. "I think it's a key or something, but I aint going back there to try it."

He handed it to Hal. The tag on it had some hand writing in Japanese, which he couldn't read but he flipped it over and saw a small emblem he did recognize. It was the print logo for the Mirada.

"Actually, this is helpful," Hal gently spoke. "What do you want for it?"

"Hey, really? I just want something to eat man, and maybe some coffee. I haven't had coffee in, like, forever man."

Hal handed the card back. "I'll be back with something, but you hold onto this. Don't give it away now."

"Thanks dude, I'll be right here."

Hal stood and walked back towards the entrance of the cafe. He whispered, knowing those on the com system would hear. "I think I may have just found a way into the Mirada."

Claire immediately responded. "I heard. Listen, Hal, this man isn't with us. Talk to Howard before you consider using the card. We don't know if he's some sort of mole for the Yotogi. It doesn't sound like it, but just in case... be careful."

Hal glanced back at the man sitting on the corner who gave him a thumbs up and smiled. All but one tooth remained in his mouth.

116

"I doubt he's with the Yotogi." It was an observation you'd have to see to make the judgment, but if the Yotogi were hiring bums with no teeth and forcing them to shiver on the street corner, then they were desperate.

The cafe was quiet and the few occupants that were at the counter didn't take notice to his arrival. Hal scanned the place for a face that would stand out among the rest. If someone was anticipating his arrival, they didn't show it. The waitress was distracted by a nearby TV screen.

Without anyone jumping to their feet for an introduction, Hal quietly strolled over to a nearby booth and took a seat. He glanced over towards the TV screen that had everyone's attention. It was the weather forecast broadcasting the dismal rain they were beginning to experience. A large scale radar map came up and Hal got a glimpse at what everyone was so focused on. It was hurricane season, and just off the shore of the Florida Keys was what looked to be a category two swirl of clouds. No wonder the city streets were so empty.

His focus was on the television and he didn't see as a woman approached him. "Mr. Brent, I presume?" Her accent was foreign, but he couldn't place it.

He was startled and confused. This definitely wasn't Howard.

Without waiting for an answer she sat down across from him and lit a cigarette. Hal simply waited for her inquiry. She wasn't what he expected, and he wasn't going to volunteer his name to someone he didn't know.

Over the intercom he could hear Claire mutter something in the background. "Uh, Hal, this must be Ruby. She's Howard's main man... I mean woman. I wasn't notified of a switch, but if she has business for Howard, this is OK."

"Hello Claire, good to hear from you." She spoke to Hal, very well knowing who was on the other end of the one-way conversation.

Claire chuckled in his ear. "Tell her hello. It's OK Hal, Ruby is a good friend."

"She says hello." Hal responded for her.

Ruby relaxed in the seat and gazed at the TV screen as she took a long drag from her cigarette. The smoking ban in public places had apparently been lifted over the last several decades.

She was a pretty girl underneath it all. It was hard to tell with the dark makeup that circled her eyes. Her dark hair was a short bob-cut with streaks of bright red in the front. Long bangs covered her left eye and the side of her face. She was dressed in a tight corset-like ruby-red shirt and a skirt with a long slit barely covering her legs that were wrapped with long black lace that went from her stiletto boots to just above the knees. It was an outrageous look, but Hal assumed this was the natural progression of fashion.

She frowned at the corner of her mouth. "Ugh, the city is due for another shit storm soon." She shifted her gaze back to him. "You are well, yes?"

Hal wasn't sure if she was still talking to Claire or to him now, but with no reply in his ear, he answered. "I've never liked hurricanes, but yes, I suppose."

"Well, then, welcome back to the city. It's a shame you couldn't have seen it on a better occasion, but nonetheless, welcome."

"Thanks, I guess. I was supposed to be meeting someone else here and I don't think you look like him." He tried to play coy, just a bit, but he was mostly just confused.

"Right. Howard is currently tied up with a little business. He sent me in his place. Tell me, Mr. Brent, what have you been told about your *mission* here in Miami?" She used the term *mission* suspiciously.

"I'm not exactly sure what I'm supposed to mention." Everything was supposed to be hush-hush about his *mission* and he wasn't comfortable relaying information. As far as he knew, he was supposed to be the one taking orders, not sharing them.

"Good. I see they have you on their leash, then." It wasn't an insult, but rather an observation.

He didn't know how to respond, but he nodded with a smile. I guess that's what you could call it – a leash.

"Well then, let me tell you what I know. You are here for Akira Eiji, notorious leader of the Yotogi." She was sarcastic as she described him. "And what for? To find A&H's missing boats?" She huffed, finding something about the situation funny.

"Partly, yes. I have my own objectives with Eiji, though."

"Of course, but consider this. A&H is one of the most powerful engineering companies in the world. And yet they send you, a dead man, into a hostile city to question a man about two lost ships." She sighed. "A&H couldn't find their own boats in the water if they were sitting on them. Do you really think that is why they sent you here? No?" She tilted her head in objection.

Hal hadn't considered what this must have looked like to an outsider, but he also hadn't figured an outsider would have this much information on a supposedly secret operation.

"You seem to have your own theory?" he asked curiously.

She nodded and took a long drag from her cigarette while staring at him. "You are bait."

At that moment he could hear Troy come over the intercom and with the sudden volume in his ear, Hal quickly jerked receiver out. She was right about him being A&H's dog, and everything that Troy had planned since his initial arrival had either been accusing or put him directly in the line of fire. His input right now was not appreciated.

She chuckled. "Good 'ol Boy Troy must have sat this one out."

"Continue, please." Hal was encouraged to have someone else on his side.

"What motives do you think A&H really has for you? Do you think Akira would give you any information, if they even have it, that would *help* A&H?" She asked the question, although she already knew the answer, and so did he. "No. A&H wants Akira so that they can take the Yotogi out of the global picture. This," she motioned her hand all around, indicating the Yotogi overtaking of the city. "This is their reaction to being held back. Whatever they want from you, it is from you alone. A&H is using you as bait to lure him out of hiding. They want them to take a stand, preferably a violent one, to discredit their cause. With their interest in you, they just might."

"And what are your motives?" Hal had questioned A&H's motives from the start. They didn't have a solid case against the Yotogi, or at least not as far as Hal was concerned, but it also begged to question hers as well.

She anticipated this as well. "Claire is a dear friend of mine, and whatever her interest is in you is mine as well. I do not know your history here, Mr. Brent, but I assure you my loyalty to her is much greater than that of A&H. Whatever the outcome here, she wants you to leave alive."

119

There was a long moment of silence between the two as Ruby stared into him. She wasn't judging him, though. It was more like she was challenging him. She obviously didn't like A&H, and she was asking the same questions he'd asked himself a million times already.

"Regardless, you better get moving." She slid a small envelope across the table. "This isn't what you came here for, Mr. Brent. The Yotogi are merely protecting themselves, and whatever you've been told, it is only one sided. Be careful who you trust."

She stood and turned to face him. "I hope we can do business in the future. Take care of yourself." Walking towards the exit, she grabbed a long black leather jacket from the rack and left.

Ruby wasn't a fan of the Yotogi, and she wasn't under any orders from A&H, but her perspective was a wake up call. Again, Hal found himself doubting whatever the hell he was supposed to be accomplishing. But what else was he supposed to do? He hadn't made up his mind what to ask the Yotogi leader if he found him. He'd only been told that this would be a violent, military-like stand off between the two factions and somehow he was the key between the two. It didn't make sense. He was left with this unsettling feeling that he'd purposely been left out of the loop and information was being withheld so that he would take the bait.

He shook his shoulders. This was all the recycled garbage he'd already considered, and with the same results – nothing. He had nothing. He had no one. He had no money and no means to start a new life here and now. It was the lacking of anything that had made the decision for him. Logically, finding Akira Eiji seemed like the only step that might bring him closure regarding the student pilots he lost twenty-six years ago. Even with such a loose connection between the two, it was evident that the Yotogi had more information than anyone else.

He opened the envelope and pulled out two small plastic cards. One was semi-transparent and the print read "Storage bay 28C." He recognized the address listed at the bottom. It was an old storage center for many of the fishers and businessmen in the area just a block north, near the docks. A long time ago Hal had rented a small place there to keep his belongings between his flights back and forth to Bimini. This must be the location Claire had mentioned; the one

Howard was supposed to link him to for his *other* equipment that he might need.

The second card in the envelope was a credit card. Written on the back were the words "*Compliments from a future business partner.*" Odd. Claire wasn't kidding about the hand outs he'd have access to from her *outside contacts.*

Things were falling into place, or at least as well as they could. He had an entrance ticket into the hotel, and now he had a means to prepare himself for the welcoming party. He'd come this far, and it made no sense to turn back. He shook off the thought that A&H was setting some sort of trap. They wanted him alive, for now at least, and so did the Yotogi.

He placed the com system back into his ear and heard nothing. Whatever rant Troy had taken off on was over. That or he temporarily ran out of breath.

There was one thing left he had to do before leaving. He signaled to the woman at the counter and ordered some not-so-futuristic food – a greasy-looking burger and fry basket with the largest coffee on the menu; to go of course, and handed her the new credit card.

Less than five minutes later the woman dropped the to-go basket on his table and stomped off.

He grabbed his goods and headed towards the door without notice.

Still outside was the man on the corner. He saw him approach and smiled at the sight of his basket. Hal sat down on the sidewalk next to him and gleefully handed it over.

Hal gave him a few moments to satisfy his hunger and examined his surroundings. The weather was getting more and more miserable by the minute and the winds were picking up.

The two men at the overlook had moved on. Not even the Yotogi were out in this mess.

"Hey man, that's the nicest thing anyone's ever done for me." The bum smiled and again showed his lack of teeth.

"Listen, I need that card you had earlier. It's for the Mirada Hotel just down the street. If I can get in with that key, I can possibly get you a place to stay for a while." Hal felt bad making it a promise.

He didn't actually know if the credit card had a limit or was just for supplies.

"Oh, right, yeah. Here ya go, man." He reached into his jacket and handed the card over. "Can I come with you?"

Hal gazed around. There was no one in sight and he couldn't just leave him here as the weather degraded.

"Sure, but you have to promise me something." The man was listening intensely as he talked. "I'm here doing some dangerous business. If something happens, I need you to run back to this spot. OK? And don't talk to anyone. I have to go to the north storage area first, but it'll be quick."

"Sure, dude. I got it." He followed as Hal stood and cautiously started north.

The city had deteriorated since he was last here. The street shops had all been closed and boarded up, possibly for the storm headed their way, but it looked more like a line of wrecked shacks you'd see in a slum area.

The storage center was vacant and the hum of the fluorescent lights buzzed on every building corner. He counted the numbers of each row as they passed. On the far side he approached row 28 to block C, which was one of the smaller rooms in the group.

"Wait here for a minute." He motioned for the man to stay under the roof near the building.

Hal slid the card through and the light turned green. He was at least in the right spot. The door buzzed as it opened and the interior lights flickered on.

There were only two medium-sized crates in the corner. One box was like a chest freezer and opened from the top. The lid lifted and an interior light displayed more than his expectations. There was a row of hand held grenades marked EMP, Sleep and Fire. That was pretty self-explanatory. He pocketed four EMP grenades and two Sleep. He hadn't had any training or explanations about how these differed from his time, so he grabbed what he thought would be most efficient for a quiet approach. Hopefully he wouldn't need it.

With his pockets full, he looked at the variety of equipment in the box. There were various different hand held weapons, but most were too large to discretely carry. Howard or Ruby must have planned for an event much larger than what was actually unfolding. Better to be overly cautious, though.

He felt guilty as he considered heavy fire arms. He didn't know these men, and there was some serious weaponry in front of him. What the heck were they thinking? He could take out everyone in the city with what lay in front of him.

Still, he wanted something more than a tranquilizing agent or pocket knife and wrapped his palm around something familiar. It was a long barrel .357 revolver. He'd owned and fired one hundreds of times and he was immediately drawn to it. It was reasonably sized and snapped into the holster on his lower back. It would be his just-in-case choice.

The other box was a little less violent-themed. There was a small bag and several document-like folders that he quickly glanced through. They contained pictures and short descriptions of the men seen around the hotel and downtown areas.

Hal's eyes opened wide as he unzipped the bag.

"Uh, Claire, did Ruby specify what was intended for me here?"

"Everything you might need. Why?" She was still listening intently behind the boat monitor.

"I can't really explain it." He gazed down into the bag at the stacks of hundred dollar bills that filled it to the top.

"Is everything OK?"

"Yeah, fine. It's just... " He paused for several seconds. How was he going to explain thousands, possibly hundreds of thousands of dollars in the bag. Was he even supposed to mention it?

"Hal?"

He whispered back. "There's thousands of dollars here."

She took a moment to silently contemplate. "I was told that everything is at your disposal. Ruby owes me. If you need it, take it." She was firm in her statement.

He was still in awe at the offering. Surely inflation had gone up, but still, this was enough to buy a yacht. He wasn't sure how much he'd need, if any. It looked like someone's ransom was being carried. Maybe it was.

To be safe, he emptied half of the bag's belongings into the smaller box and securely zipped the remaining. That should cover, well, pretty much anything he might run into.

Hal exited with the door squeaking behind him. His companion hadn't moved. He stood under the neighboring roof in the shadow, his hands clasping the coffee cup for warmth.

"Are we good to go man? My feet are getting cold." He shifted, trying to generate some body heat.

"Yeah, we're good." Hal stepped to the end of the row and carefully peeked his head around the corner to look for anyone patrolling the area. He was actually surprised when he saw someone, dressed in a black gown. His face was covered and his hands were holstered firmly on his belt line. He was unmistakably a member of the Yotogi.

Suddenly Hal felt a wave of anxiety and adrenaline. Shit. He'd been preparing for this over the past two days, and now that he was only fifty feet away from one of them, he felt extremely nervous. He hadn't anticipated this. He ducked back behind for cover and made a gesture towards the bum to stay quiet. "Shh."

He nodded.

Hal clenched the tranquilizer pistol and took a long breath. He calmed. He'd done this before and he remembered the feel of the weapon. "Stay focused," he told himself.

He pulled the weapon out and swiftly shifted around the corner. His arms extended and with a jolt, he felt the dart exit. With the man's back turned, the dart hit his right shoulder, and he flinched, reaching behind, but the drugs were already rushing too quickly through his nervous system. He turned and fell to his knees, his arms outstretched to brace for the impact and he slumped over.

That was easy. Hal waited for a reaction, but there was none. No calls for help, no screams, and no noise. That was it.

After a minute he stepped out into the open, glancing in every direction. The fog was thick and the light was dim. It was the perfect position. The approaching storm was inconvenient, but it was a constant distraction and it was easy to blend into the chaos.

He approached the next aisle and took a quick look around the corner. Empty.

They made their way to the end of the row and approached the nearby intersection. Hal waited for several minutes to observe any potential patrol routes or if any new activity would transpire.

He lowered his head and pulled the collar of his jacket up his neck before making a run across to the other side.

They were about two hundred paces from the Mirada Hotel and he could see the front entrance. Two men dressed in the familiar black robes stood suspiciously with their hands on their hips, occasionally raising an arm to block the gusts of wind and rain. The bellhop for the hotel sat nervously on the nearby bench, uncomfortable with their presence.

Hal peered upwards counting the floors to levels 18 and 19, spotting two men on the balcony overlooking the streets.

There was a side entrance to the building, but if it were anything like the outlook in the front, it would be guarded as well. The only possible entrance would be from the back.

Hal turned to his new companion, who just stared at him idly, completely unfazed.

"You see that building over there?" He pointed to the Mirada.

"Oh hey, man, those are the same guys that were pushing me around. I don't like them." He knew what Hal was about to ask.

"No, no. They won't do anything to you over there. Just tell them you're getting a room to meet someone."

"Are you sure? They'll let me right in?" He looked at Hal with one brow suspiciously raised.

"Yes. Go into the lobby and make yourself some more coffee. I'll be there in a few minutes." Hal reached into the zipped bag and pulled out two hundred dollar bills. "If anyone asks, tell them your friend was delayed by the weather, but will be there shortly. This should get you some refreshments and just sit comfortable for a while."

He didn't ask any more questions as he happily accepted the money.

Hal watched as the man quickly trotted down the street. The Yotogi immediately took notice as he approached and, frightened, the man's pace slowed. The bellhop, on the other hand, was glad to see another face, particularly one that wasn't a Yotogi member, and he greeted him cheerfully. It gave the man confidence, and knowing that the Yotogi had no control over his entrance, he gleefully strolled passed them into the lobby.

"Good boy," Hal whispered to himself. He didn't know why he was leading the man into the building, except that he hoped it would be a temporary diversion, but at least he would also be out of the rain until the storm passed.

He went to the back of the building that led down a long alley. It was quiet as he cautiously walked past several back entrances. A door opened and Hal ducked behind a dumpster nearby as a young man in a cooking apron stepped out and leaned against the wall. He flicked a lighter several times before lighting a joint.

Hal stepped out from behind the dumpster, reaching into his jacket pocket for the tranquilizer gun just in case and approached him.

"How bout this weather?" He asked, shielding his face from the rain with one hand.

"It's something else." Hal relaxed. The kid was just trying to make idle conversation to a passerby.

"It's only going to get worse. I heard it's a category two now, but I think it's going to be a three by the time it hits." He took another drag from his joint.

Hal took a step under the small overhang that the kid was standing under. "Hey, can I ask you a question?"

"Sure, what's up?" He casually backed away from the wall.

"What's with all these men here? The ones in the cloaks?" He already knew who they were, but he wanted a stranger's opinion.

"Those dudes are just friggen weirdos. I've seen them on the news a couple times. They're all over the place for some reason. I don't know. Miami isn't exactly a vacation spot during hurricane season. You think they would've chosen someplace with nicer weather." He didn't sound too interested in them, which was probably a good thing.

"How long have you seen them around here? A friend of mine was being harassed by them a day ago." He was referring to the man he'd just met, kind of considering him to be a friend.

"That doesn't surprise me. They're assholes. They're terrible customers and they don't tip for shit." He rolled his head back in sarcasm. "They always want a private table when they come into the restaurant here and then they order shit no one has on the menu. The other day my manager sent me down to the market to pick up tofu. I mean, who the hell orders tofu at a steakhouse?" He took another drag. "I think they've been here for about a week. Maybe two. I don't know. I don't deal with customers much. They were all over the place a few nights ago. Something about them just gives me the creeps. You have an interest in them?"

"Not really. I just haven't been in Miami for a long time and didn't realize there was some sort of Japanese army taking over the city."

"I hear ya. Shit, I'm afraid of the gangs and such, but I'd hate to piss off these assholes." He made a gesture towards the hotel. He must have been paying enough attention to them to know where they were congregating.

"Are they armed?" Hal had been told that they might be, but still hadn't seen any weapons yet.

"I thought about that, but I've never seen it. But dude, they're wearing fucking robes. Who knows what type of foreign shit they're carrying under there. I think that's why no one's ever turned down their service. Everyone's scared stiff with them strolling around in an oversized, black bathrobe." He flicked what remained of his joint into the alley.

He reached out his hand to shake Hal's. "I'm Trent, by the way. If you're ever looking for a mean steak, we have the best ones in town."

Hal accepted his hand shake. "I'm just in town for a while, but if I stop this way in the future I'll give it a try."

"You here on business or something?"

"You could say that. I'm trying to learn something about these men. Find out why they're stationed here." Hal wasn't trying to be honest.

"Like a reporter or something?" He asked.

"Not really. Just doing some research. I've been a little out of the loop for a while and visiting friends. They've been concerned about them."

"Well, I don't know much about them, but I think your friends are concerned for a good reason. They're not friendly, and they've even scared the cops out of the city. We've had less than half of our normal customer base since they arrived. Their presence alone has everyone scared." He squinted his eyes and looked in the general direction of the hotel. "I just hope they finish up whatever they came for and leave. They're some sort of religious cult, I think."

"They're a global cult trying to push their opinions of anti-technology on everyone. So I heard." Hal was trying to push the subject into something more factual.

"Yeah, they call themselves the Yotogi. I remember seeing them on TV since I was kid. Always protesting research or some shit. I don't know. I don't follow the news much." He looked at his watch. "Well, I have to get back to work. It's been slow lately, but I still have to look like I'm doing something."

Hal again extended his hand and shook Trent's. "Thanks for the info. If it makes you feel any better, I don't think they'll be staying much longer."

The kid laughed. "Good to hear, I hope you're right."

Trent walked into the back entrance a little calmer than he left it, probably due to the joint more than any kind of reassurance.

It was good to at least hear another opinion of the Yotogi. They weren't very kind to anyone outside of their little club, and if the police were intimidated by them there was probably a reason for it. Claire had mentioned that the local law enforcement were somewhat scattered on the issue of their presence. They didn't technically break any laws, and they didn't appear to have any weapons out in the open, but their robes left everyone worried.

Moving further down the alley, he now had a good view of the Mirada. It was a thirty story building that hovered over the rest and almost every light was on. The occupants were probably trying to wait out the storm, but Hal was particularly looking out for the 18th and 19th floors. All the lights were on, which was a bad sign. They occupied the entire two levels, and from the looks of it they were all full.

There were several men standing on the balconies and they stood out like a sore thumb watching the streets below. Even if he made a dash for the back door, they would see anyone on the streets. He couldn't just blend in either, given that virtually no one was on the ground.

He made his way to the side and glanced around the corner. One Yotogi member stood near the side entrance door, but it was too close to the front. If he tried to take him out, there was the possibility that the affect of the tranquilizer wouldn't work immediately and he could run out to his buddies.

There didn't seem to be any way to sneak in from the ground level. He looked up and then down. No openings. He stood for a few moments and watched for any movement. They didn't leave their posts or cycle through any sort of patrol route.

The neighboring alley ways lead to another street and an open area, both of which he'd be spotted in.

"Claire, there are guards everywhere. They're on the roof, the street and directly in the entrance way. Are there any other ways into the building?"

"There's a sewer grate a little north of you. I hate to say it because, well, it's not the cleanest option, obviously. But if you enter the shaft, it has another opening that's about ten feet from the back doorway. Is that enough clearance?"

He gazed around and saw both opening hatches. The one farthest from him was right next to the eaves trough and there was a good amount of cover. The rain and fog created movement everywhere, and with the drain right above, there was a good chance it would go unnoticed. Like it or not, it way the best way.

He walked over to the grate and strained to lift it onto the concrete. He made a bit of noise as he did and he cautiously watched all his sides as he slid it far enough to slip in.

The sewer wasn't as bad as he thought, but with the lack of light he took a minute for his eyes to adjust. It was a tight corridor with a walkway on both sides. The rain water that came rushing in rose up to his ankles as he tip-toed through. As he made his way towards the other opening hole, he could see the faint glow coming in through its small openings and the light above streamed in.

Sliding the cover to the side, he opened the gap large enough to peak his head through. He couldn't see if anyone was above him on the ground, and he held his tranquilizer pistol in one hand.

Peeking his head out, he could now see the alley he was in. It was still empty, and the back entrance was unguarded. To his other side he could see the nearby corner of the Mirada. Its other side entrance was closer to the back, and as he slipped his torso out of the hole, he could see it was guarded by one man. He steadied his feet on the sewer ladder and slowly rose the pistol to his sight. A quick click and the dart hit the man's leg.

He clumsily turned and Hal fired another round, this time hitting his right shoulder. He fell to his knees, his arms now reaching for the ground before catching himself and slumping over.

Hal waited and held his breath, his pistol still at bay. He wasn't going to take any chances and fired one more round, hitting the man's side, but he didn't so much as flinch.

He shifted his focus to all of his sides. He couldn't see the balconies or the roof top above him, which meant they couldn't see him either.

He took a deep breathe of relief as he pushed his soaked hair out of his face. The rain was getting increasingly more violent by the hour and he was completely drenched. The winds rushed through the alleyway and water rushed in sideways.

The back entrance was well lit, but it was underneath a small overhang that hid its position from anyone above. Looking in through the colored glass window of the door, he could see a short empty hallway that bridged to another split hallway.

There was a key card locking mechanism and he swiped the card that the bum had given him. The LED indicator flickered red with rejection.

"Oh come on," he whispered frustratingly and wiped the card on his inner shirt, hoping it would dry before swiping it again. To his surprise, it flickered green and he turned the metal door handle and spun around to the other side, silently pressing it shut behind him.

The hallway glowed in the dim, beige lighting that most hotels had. Quiet waiting-room music hummed throughout as he carefully stepped through its entrance.

He had studied the building schematics the night before and proceeded to the laundry room to his right. It was a fairly large room, but unoccupied. There was a staircase at its adjacent side, and Hal peeked his head around the corner before entering.

There was chatter coming from above him within the stairwell and he listened carefully. He recognized it as Japanese, although he wasn't fluent enough to understand the words. The elevator would be a terrible entrance as well, and even if he were alone, anyone could pop in without notice.

He listened closer to their conversation, gauging their level without directly crossing their line of sight. They were at least five, maybe even six, levels above him. He quietly tiptoed up four flights with his tranquilizer in one hand as he moved through the shadows. If he went much further he'd be spotted, so he took the entrance to the level five hallway. It was empty, except for a cart that stood idly outside of one of the first rooms. He cautiously approached it and looked in the open doorway. The maid was in one of the rooms cleaning.

He stepped in, hoping he could sneak past or at least pause to get his bearings.

"Oh excuse me! I was just refilling your towels." The girl smiled at him, completely unaware that he wasn't supposed to be there. "Can I get you anything?"

"Uh, no, thank you. I just left something." He smiled back, trying to act inconspicuous.

"I was just finishing up. Here." She handed him some mints. "For your pillows."

Hal accepted, trying to act casual about the situation. "Thank you. Oh, and here." He reached into his zipped bag and pulled out several bills. "Good work."

She gazed down at his *tip*. "Oh, wow, thank you! Have a good night, sir!"

Hal wasn't sure what the common tip was nowadays, nor was he sure what the value of a dollar would be in this time, but she accepted it with great surprise. He figured that was either really good or sarcastically bad, but either way, she'd left in a hurry and he was alone again.

The door clicked and Hal found himself standing awkwardly in someone's space. It was warm and cozy, but he didn't dare stay.

He walked over to the balcony and slid the door to the side. The outdoors wasn't welcoming as a gust of wet wind slammed into him.

He stood at the edge and looked up. He couldn't see with the rain in his eyes, but he was still several stories below where he wanted to be. The balconies were in an offset pattern, and standing on the 5th floor, the 6th floor balconies were at each side, and the 7th story was directly above him. The scattered pattern made his line of sight that much better, and in between was the fire escape ladder. Hal grabbed for the cold, wet metal, which was difficult as the wind whipped past. His gear was soaking wet and exhaustively heavy.

He made it to the 16th story and sloppily jumped to the nearest balcony, landing with a heavy thud as his lungs begged for more oxygen.

He was exhausted and sat for several minutes to catch his breath. The noise around him was chaotic with the winds whipping and the rain pounding every surface it could touch. He focused on any other sound, any sort of conversation or movement. If there had been, it was completely drowned out by the rest.

From what he could tell, he was just outside room 16C, two stories below where he would look first. Some of the rooms were shared with an adjoining doorway. 16C was linked to 16B, and so were the floors above him. Looking in the glass doorway, he could see the room was vacant. The lights were on, but the bed was made and there were no belongings of anyone staying there.

He pressed the earpiece and quietly whispered, not that anyone would have heard him in the storm, but he couldn't help but feel extra cautious. "I'm at 16 C right now, just two stories down. I need to know if I can enter one of the rooms or if it's occupied."

There was a long silence and he pushed the earpiece further. "Claire, can anyone hear me?"

"Yes Hal, give me a moment. I'm going to see if I can set a reservation for that room. If it's vacant, you can use it as a staging area." It was Kyra who answered.

Waiting, he took note of his surroundings. He knew there were men on the balcony two stories above but he couldn't see. They all seemed to be centered around 18C, which made him believe that he was close to the target.

Looking over the edge, he could see a shadow being cast down over its ledge. If he could create some sort of diversion, redirect their attention, he might be able to climb to 17D's balcony unnoticed.

"What kind of range does an EMP have?" he whispered to himself, knowing someone else on the other end of the com system would hear.

Ortiz answered. "An EMP generally has a small radius, but in the right location, such as a fuze box, you could efficiently disable all power on several levels at once."

"16C is yours Hal. It's adjoined to rooms 16B and D. You have the full suite." Kyra came through on her promise. "I'm unlocking the doors remotely. Should only take a few seconds."

Hal watched the locking pad on the opposite side of the window. There was a flicker of green and he turned the handle.

He laid his bag onto the bed and flipped the light switch, now leaving him alone in the dimly lit comfort of a hotel suite. He pressed his ear to the neighboring room suites and heard nothing. Both rooms to his left and right were unoccupied, as they should have been, but he checked anyway for paranoia's sake.

He hadn't put much thought into exactly how he'd get onto the 18th and 19th floor, just the routes that were possible. There were several large air ducts that he could squeeze into and bridge the connecting rooms, but it wasn't exactly incognito sliding into one. The Yotogi occupied the entire two floors and anyone outside their organization would probably be forced to leave.

Hal strolled into suite 16B, which was the closest to the stair case. He'd spent most of the previous night studying the blueprints for the hotel and there was a fuze box every four floors. With the power out, he'd have a much better chance at slipping through any of the neighboring rooms without notice.

The hallway was quiet as he pressed his ear to the door. He could hear muffled chatter from some of the other rooms near-by and a couple was arguing, but those interactions were normal. What he was listening for was something abnormal.

He clicked the door open and cautiously peaked through. A maintenance cart stood still in the hallway outside the open room, but no people.

With his bag clutched to his chest he pulled his collar high and made his way to the locked closet just outside of the staircase. The door was marked for "Employees Only", and he shook the handle. Locked. The bottom was slightly lifted and gave a 2-inch gap between the floor. It was just tall enough to slip the cylindrical EMP under. Its shape was also convenient because it would continue to roll towards the back wall.

He knelt down as if attempting to tie his shoe and pulled out one EMP canister. It was a nifty little device. There were two main components; the device itself and the transmitter which allowed you to precisely control its detonation remotely.

The device rolled easily on the tile floor and he heard the quiet tap as it hit the wall at the far side of the other room.

No one had entered the hallway yet, but he continued to play coy as he glanced back and forth and continued to the elevator.

He entered and immediately hit the stop button once the doors closed. The ceiling had a service panel and he placed both feet on the railing, straddling the corner and lifting himself to reach for it. With his pocket knife he removed the screws holding the panel in place and threw his bag up. He swung off the railings, now hanging onto the edge and he gently tapped the number 17 with his toe before pulling himself upwards onto its roof. The elevator jolted and continued to floor 17, but from his position, he was now at eye-level with floor 18.

He pulled the transmitter from his pocket and closed his eyes as he pulled back the protective cover and pressed the button.

There was no real shock with an EMP. It was an instant, muffled burst, which was different than any type of explosion. He heard a quick snap, much like when you plug something into an electrical socket and there's an initial spark. It was slightly louder, but nothing to cause alarm. The reaction, however, did. There was no fluctuation, no flickering. It was just instantly dark, which was exactly what he wanted.

He could hear doors opening and people were walking around. Hal backed away from the vent as several people approached the elevator and tried the button.

A voice stood out among the crowd that had gathered in the hallway. The Yotogi had the entire floor and there were no normal guests within these two levels.

"The storm is approaching. Stay in your rooms. Power should be restored shortly." The voice came from a very low toned, calm man with a foreign accent.

Hal strained to get a better view, but his vantage point was terrible. He heard nothing in the hallway now. No footsteps or conversation, but he could see a long shadow streaming across the red carpet. Someone was just outside of room 18C.

There was a small opening for maintenance personnel along the wall of 18A. It was about four feet tall and Hal ducked as he entered. The shaft led to a small storage closet with cleaning equipment and tools. He pushed the buckets that lined the walls to the side and found a small vent shaft that led to the AC ducts. It was tight, about two feet in width, but it led to every room on that story.

Hal cringed as he knelt down on all fours and attempted to squeeze in. His shoulders cleared, but the equipment on his back made it impossible.

Struggling to be quiet, he backed out and removed his jacket and bag. He'd have to come back for them, but he still had his shoulder harness and most of his important gear still on his body.

His second attempt was easier and on his elbows he scooted forward to the bending in the shaft and made the turn. The long corridor extended about a hundred and fifty feet, but he couldn't tell as the light dimmed over the distance.

Without power, some of the residents had resorted to candles, which let in a trail of flickering light through the air vents.

There was quiet conversation in rooms 18A and 18B as he passed. It was all foreign and he knew he was in the right spot.

18C was unusually quiet. Light filtered in through the slim air vents and Hal could see several candles on the table, but no occupants stirred. He knew two men were on the balcony, or at least they had been before when he was in the alley. There were no shadows or movement now.

He had a terrible angle in the vent and was only able to see a small portion of the room in front of him. Although Eiji had signed for several room service deliveries from 18C, there was no guarantee he was still there. 18D was another possibility, which was adjoined to the same suite, but as he remained still for several minutes. Maybe they'd just gone to sleep for the night.

On that thought Hal grew impatient. They were well aware of his arrival in this reality, and whether they knew his exact location now, he was in the mood for confrontation.

Just as he built up the courage to move forward, he stopped. Footsteps. Someone quietly stepped along the soft carpet near the wall. They were outside of his viewing angle and they were also alarmed.

Hal drew in a silent breath and waited.

"Leave me," a man's voice quietly spoke in English.

His adrenaline spiked and he felt a burning sensation of nervousness take over.

The door latched shut and Hal calmed himself, knowing only one man remained.

He was now looking in through the small vent openings of 18D. A man with bare feet stood at the end of the bed, about fifteen feet away. The curved lines of the vent openings made it difficult to look up and see the man's face, but the attire and robes were all too familiar.

The man walked casually towards the balcony and Hal could hear the wind rush in as the doorway slid open. He could see the man's elongated shadow along the carpet as he walked out onto the balcony and closed the door behind him, muting the outside world again.

Hal took his screw driver from his vest and pried the door open. The screws were from the outside of the room, but the metal was flimsy and quickly gave way.

Bending it to the floor, Hal peered his head out and breathed a sigh of relief as he found the room was indeed empty.

The balcony doors let in a stream of light as lightning flashed. A silhouette of a man remained in place, soaking up the weather as it poured down on him. His back was still turned and Hal cautiously crouched in the corner of the room, hiding in the shadows, keeping his focus on the man and reaching into his shoulder harness for his tranquilizer.

The man on the balcony leaned forward over the edge and looked in all directions below and above him. He stood in that spot for a good two minutes, ears and eyes darting from side to side. It was as if he were gauging the fluctuations of energy around him. The Yotogi knew something or someone was out of place.

The man turned and slipped the balcony door open again. He squinted while cautiously inspecting the room before stepping inside.

This was Hal's opportunity he'd been working towards. The questions he'd rehearsed raced through his head, but he hesitated to speak.

Hal stood slowly, his arms raised and tranquilizer pistol at bay. "What do you want from me?"

The man shifted his head, but his body remained in place. Hal now had a good look at his face, which was uncovered.

The man smiled, but neither in a sarcastic or malicious way. "You are much more resourceful than I would have thought."

He held out his hands, showing that he was unarmed and turned to face Hal. This was Akira Eiji, there was no question.

"I did not think you would come to me. Please, do not judge so quickly. Our attempt to contain you was merely a precaution. We have no ill intentions towards you, Mr. Brent." He moved his right hand over his heart. The other was still outstretched to his side.

"You didn't answer my question."

"Your questions are complicated. There is not a simple answer." He tilted his head inquisitively.

Hal began to hear Troy's voice over the com system in his ear and he quickly reached to yank it out. It was his turn to do the questioning.

"Your friends are resourceful at A&H, but you're beginning to question their motives." He let his hands casually fall to his sides as he walked to the kitchen counter and poured a cup of tea.

Hal's vision didn't leave the scope of his pistol, which was aimed directly at Akira's back. Akira didn't seem fazed by it. In fact, he walked away, oddly tranquil.

Akira clasped his cup loosely and took a seat at the nearby table. He made a gesture for him to sit across from him, but Hal made no movement to accept.

Akira sighed and took a short sip before continuing. "You are a complicated subject, Mr. Brent. We are fascinated by complicated subjects, but I assure you we are not enemies. You have been told many things, most of which have led you to ask more questions. You're beginning to learn that A&H does not *like* to be asked questions."

"A&H rescued me from a shipwreck. You assume too much. Consider my position and what it looks like when your men stage a violent attempt to *kidnap* someone. Consider my reaction when one of your men gives me a cryptic warning and then commits suicide right in front of me." All the anger that had built up inside was now coming out in an accusing tone.

"I have." Akira still sat relaxed in his chair. "You awoke a dead man in someone's laboratory. Twenty-six years of your life have been lost, but that's not the reason you're here."

Hal immediately felt his heart sink. Akira knew it, too.

"You made it back, my friend." His tone was genuinely sympathetic. "And they did not."

Hal lowered his pistol. He let his guard down at the mention of his fellow pilots. Akira wasn't skirting the issue, but he wasn't demanding answers from Hal either. This whole time he'd been told that the Yotogi were a self-righteous clan of protesters working to sabotage technology growth, but so far they hadn't demonstrated any of that, or at least not towards him.

"So why did your men come for me? Why would they risk their lives to capture me?" He changed his tone.

"I cannot tell you here." He motioned towards Hal's ear piece that was linked to the com system for everyone to hear. "Let me tell you, though, that you are an extraordinary piece to a large puzzle. It's difficult to understand, at first. You are an anomaly that has never happened before. In the care of A&H, I fear your potential could be squandered."

There was a knock at the door, and they both flinched in reaction.

"Remain!" Akira yelled in the direction of the door, which immediately quieted.

"You best put that back in." He gestured towards his ear.

Hal was immediately made aware of the situation as he heard Brack's voice, "Go, go, go! Everyone in your place!"

Hal gazed at Akira, who already knew what was beginning to unfold. A&H was pulling the plug on the operation and ordering the PMC force into the building.

Akira extended his hand to Hal, and for some reason he accepted it unguarded.

"Until next time." Akira let go of his hand and walked towards his closet, grabbing a back pack and securing the buckles to his chest. He stepped onto the balcony and left the door open.

There was chaos all around them as men ran up the stairway and through the halls. Doors crashed open and he could hear the clutter of furniture being knocked around.

"Freeze!" Ortiz yelled with a loaded assault rifle pointed at Akira, who was now standing on the balcony railing.

"Do not forget the real reasons you are here, Mr. Brent." Akira was focused only on Hal and paid no attention to the men threatening his life. He closed his eyes, spread his arms and leaned backwards, kicking off the balcony rail and plummeting downwards.

"No!" It was a hopeless effort as Hal lurched forward, grabbing for something far out of reach. He ran to the edge, Ortiz right behind him, and looked down as a parachute opened and lowered him to the ground. It was a short jump from eighteen stories up and he saw Akira hit the ground with a thud. He was alive, but badly injured. All of Ortiz's men were on the top levels now, and down below he could see four Yotogi members rush to Akira's aid and carry him off down the alley.

Soldiers filled the room, which was now lit by the rays of their flashlight mounted guns. There was a noise, a puff.

"The room is rigged!"

The smoke that filled the rooms swirled in their flashlight beams.

Several men began coughing and falling to their knees. Others quickly grabbed a gas mask and promptly placed them on their faces. Ortiz reached over and grabbed Hal's arm. Pulling him to the ground, he took a breather-mask and placed it over his mouth and nose. Hal accepted it and Ortiz grabbed another from his pack for himself.

There were screams coming from all around. He could even hear the residents in the neighboring rooms coughing and gagging. Windows broke from the balconies as many rushed to the fresh air. It was chaos.

Hal stood. The soldiers here could handle themselves, but there was someone in particular that couldn't. With blurry vision, he made his way through the room and into the hallway. He held the mask tightly to his face and breathed deep. With a swift kick to the

139

maintenance door, the latches snapped off and swung open with force. He grabbed his belongings that he had left behind and dodged towards the stairwell.

As he arrived at level fifteen the smoke had dissipated and he removed his mask. He recognized the familiar smell of sleeping gas, which was non-lethal and those who were caught in its path would be unconscious for several hours, but there would be no fatalities. Still, it was the bold, violent move that A&H had hoped for.

He raced down the stairs and exhaustively reached the main level. There were a dozen or so occupants all standing in the lobby area, confused and coughing.

The bum was right where he told him to be, sitting casually on the lobby couch watching the hysterical crowd.

"Hey man! Over here!" He saw Hal and waved his arms in the air.

"I did just what you said," he chuckled. "It was funny. Those men couldn't stop me."

"That's great," Hal responded. "We need to get out of here. Something's wrong."

"Yeah, OK man." He acknowledged and followed Hal like a devoted buddy as they made a run for the front entrance.

In the streets he could see several black cars speed away and numerous Yotogi members run towards the docks to their getaways. Hal grabbed the bum's hand and ran south, away from the crowd. His instincts screamed that something was still horribly wrong. He couldn't place it, but they just needed to run.

They ran about eighty feet before a large boom shook them from behind. The shock blew them to the ground and Hal rolled over to look at the Mirada, which was now bursting with smoke. Shattered glass was falling from the top stories as floors 29 and 30 disappeared in flames.

Bystanders on the street were now standing in shock and some of them had their hand held recording devices pointed directly at the building.

"Whoa," the bum exclaimed.

"We need to keep going." Hal got to his feet and helped the man up.

Hal struggled to push onward. His bruised knees ached in pain as they limped to the end of the street.

Rain continued to beat down on them as they came to the corner and glanced around, spotting another hotel on the opposite side of the street. It was a smaller, less formal place than the Mirada, but it was somewhere safe to take cover.

Hal took the man's hand and tugged his tired body into the lobby. He stopped fifty feet from the entrance and took a long breath before walking into the building as casually as he could.

"Here. This is for your help." He handed the bag to the bum, which contained more money than he could have possibly imagined. "Get yourself a room and stay until this is over. A hurricane is coming, and Miami will be under marshal law for a few weeks." He caught his breath and shook the man's hand.

The man was left speechless. With dazed eyes he took the bag from Hal and his limp hand was shaken.

Hal dodged towards the door, leaving the poor man standing shell-shocked in the hotel lobby.

Sirens rang past him as emergency vehicles raced by. Hal pulled his collar up his neck and tried to casually limp back towards the docks. His earpiece was dead. His heart rate was no longer racing through his temples and he listened for any type of communication over the air waves. Nothing.

"Claire, Kyra? Can anyone hear me?"

It worried Hal. Maybe they'd cut communication to him. Maybe there was a malfunction. What if they'd been compromised and their location was exposed. He began to run, making his way towards the docks. The crowd was gathering now, shielding their eyes from the relentless rain that was falling.

Claire said they'd regroup at a new point on the southern pier, which was branched to the main line. He turned the corner and sighed with relief as he saw her in the distance standing on the dock. Her attention was on the hotel and her hands covered her mouth in shock. Kyra stood beside her, also bewildered.

He slowed as he approached, but his movement caught their peripheral vision and Claire sprinted towards him. Without thinking he held out his arms to grab her and she wrapped her arms around to embrace him. It was an unconscious reaction, and although they'd only met three days ago they had been through so much together.

"What have we done?" Claire again looked at the Mirada hotel, which was now billowing smoke from the roof tops. She was in shock, and a sense of guilt swept over.

Hal didn't know how to respond. He touched her shoulder and they all just stared in the general direction of the hotel.

"The com system is down. I can't make any contact to A&H or with Ortiz." Kyra approached, but fell mute in the chaos.

It took several minutes for Claire to get her bearings again. "We have to get back to the base. We'll regroup there. Ortiz can take care of himself and his men."

She turned back to the boat, her eyes still glazed in shock. It was the only logical thing they could do.

Chapter 17: Regrouped

As they approached A&H there were several new boats anchored to the dock and several people were stumbling towards the complex. Hal recognized some of the men, dressed in their uniforms. Many were coughing heavily and several of the A&H staff members were helping to carry them in. Doctor Prossman was among them, taking vitals and giving them oxygen.

Hal stepped off the boat as they docked. His knees were sore from the fall and his body was still in shock from the explosion, but his lungs were clear now. Things couldn't have gone worse. Not only was he the trigger that caused this mess, he came back with no information that could be helpful for these men. He'd completely disregarded Troy's objectives, but his meeting was so brief, what else could he have done? He felt both anger and guilt.

His guilt came from the feeling of failure, but he was also defensive. Yes, he had put his own interests first, but if it weren't for Brack's assault, all of this could have been avoided. He was already feeling unwelcome here, now, as the soldiers looked past him, coughing and wheezing.

Approaching the main entrance, he could see the shadow of Troy and Brack in the second story window. Their gaze burned into him as he entered.

The atrium was filled with about twelve or more people stumbling and coughing as they found comfortable places to get their bearings. Troy was yelling best he could at some of the men and Brack stood silent behind him, his head lowered in anger as he cast a glance to Hal.

"Follow me, don't look at him." Claire distracted Hal's attention from Brack, who was no doubt on the verge of charging at him.

The west wing was quiet and the echo of the atrium was now white noise in the distance.

Kyra shoved the door to the doctor's office. It sprang back with a loud clash. "What the hell was he thinking?"

She paced around the room, her arms crossed over her chest. Her temper was more intimidating than Brack's and the rage in her scared everyone into silence. Hal hadn't considered her as a key role in all of this until now. She'd put her life on the line just as much as anyone else, and she wanted answers for colleagues she'd lost. This was all just as devastating to her as anyone else, maybe even more so.

"The com system didn't go down! It was disabled! Our controls were terminated the second Ortiz's team took action." Kyra held her head, trying to contain herself. She stopped in place and took several deep breaths. She gazed at Hal and her expression turned from anger to concern. "I'm sorry, that was uncalled for. It's just... We *had* this. It was under control!"

She dropped down into the doctor's chair and rested her elbows on her knees.

Hal was beginning to feel calm again when it was rudely disrupted. The door flung open behind them and Brack stormed in, his face glowing red with anger.

"Don't you dare!" Kyra stood up and passed them. "You bastard!" She was on the verge of slapping him, but somehow managed to hold it back.

Brack stood in the entrance and opened his mouth to speak back.

"No! Don't you even start. Do you know just how many people will suffer from your judgments? You forget your place. You sit on the side lines behind the safety of your surveillance screen while your men are out in the field. You're so blinded by your hatred towards the Yotogi that you forget about the safety of your men. And for what?" She was trembling with anger. "We had them. He had them!" She pointed at Hal. "And you lost it!"

She glided past him quickly and exited before anyone could object.

Brack stood defeated and darted his eyes from Claire to Hal. There was nothing to be said as he quickly and shamefully left.

Hal still didn't have his grip on the situation. Now, standing silently in shock, they both just looked at one another, reverberating from it all. What happened? His head was so clear a few hours ago. He was in control. Everything fell into place. It was what Brack and Troy had been planning for, so why pull the plug so quickly?

Claire turned to the doctor's main computer screen and typed in some commands before a live broadcast appeared on the screen. A news anchor was discussing the situation, which was still *unknown* to the public, and without blatantly saying it, she was accusing the Yotogi.

"We did this," Claire said without emotion. "They wanted this."

"You think Brack planned this?" Hal thought the same.

She nodded. "They've never been violent. Just... just verbal. They wouldn't provoke this."

Throughout this entire mission Hal felt something was out of place. It made sense and Ruby had hinted at it as well.

He placed his hand on Claire's shoulder. "We were following orders. You didn't do this."

She placed her head in her hands. She knew this, but she couldn't help but feel some guilt in her role. She'd been misled and lied to, but still, her denial that A&H would plan something so malicious encouraged her to go through with it. They'd crossed a line, and now lives were lost. The death toll hadn't been announced, but a war was starting and they were now at the center of it.

Chapter 18: The Wake of the Storm

Hal didn't feel right. A sense of non-reality washed over him again. It was the terrible nightmare that wouldn't end, and his thoughts were a blur. There was no comfort here.

Claire sat beside him silently. The trust in A&H had gone. She'd been here and devoted her life to the *good* that was being done, but the tables had turned now and she questioned her place. In a sense, she was now in the same boat as Hal.

"So what next?" Hal couldn't stand the silence any longer. His body ached and he was exhausted.

She snapped back to some coherence and sighed. "We wait."

It wasn't what he wanted to hear. He wanted reassurance. Then again, so did she, but it wouldn't come tonight.

"Stay with me tonight. I just don't want to be alone when this breaks in the morning." She didn't mean anything sexual by it, but right now she wanted the company of someone who didn't have any motives or connections.

Hal nodded. He didn't feel alone with her and he couldn't sleep in his quarters here, locked in a dungeon below the ocean.

She stood with her arms crossed and made her way to the door.

The west wing was noisy compared to the doctor's office. Echoes of the chaos rolled through the hallway as they traveled to the back door.

The wind nearly sucked the air from the exit as the door opened. The rain had died down only to be replaced by gusts of sweeping wind. The apartment complex was well lit in the distance.

Hal felt like he was entering a frat house as they walked in. There was a small recreational room in front and a dozen people sat in silence as they watched the news on the main TV stand. Several other people had their hand held tablets and were watching or reading as the events unfolded.

Claire wrapped her hands around her chest and held her head down as eyes followed them.

They took the stairs up four flights before exiting into a brightly lit, sterile hallway. Dark tiles led down the path and the white walls made the entire place feel like a hospital, but at least it was quiet.

They entered the first doorway on the left and dim light comfortably illuminated the room. Her place was much more home-like than the rest of their surroundings. The lighting was soft, and her dark red furniture felt warm. It was a large apartment, probably about a thousand square feet of open area. It was one main room with the exception of the bathroom, which took up almost a quarter of the entire area. Her bed overlooked a large window facing east and it hid behind a shoji-style changing divider. A large glass TV panel hung on the wall across from the bed and red, fluffy couches with scattered pillows circled the main living area.

It was suddenly awkward now that they were alone in her private space.

"I'm going to shower and change. There's some food in the fridge if you'd like." She avoided eye contact with him unconsciously as she stepped into the other room.

Hal wasn't hungry and looked around for someplace comfortable. Her couches made an L-shape and had about ten pillows scattered on top. He plopped down onto them and sank in, which was like falling into cotton candy as its plush surface embraced him. His eyes were heavy and he let the room fall dark. It seemed like only a few seconds before he stirred again.

Claire's feet thumped across the carpet as she waddled senselessly out of the bathroom.

"There's a spare toothbrush and towels if you'd like to use the restroom." She sank onto one side of the bed facing the window and looked out into the nightmarish storm that slammed into the building.

It took great effort to pull himself from the couch and he took off his boots as he entered the bathroom to clean up.

The hot water felt good over his cold skin. Florida was normally hot this time of year, but the rain had chilled him to the bone and the air conditioning in the apartment was now uncomfortable.

He brushed and groomed, and now alone to process his thoughts, the events of the day were replaying in his mind. He felt used. This was what Brack had planned all along. He wanted Hal to make it into the hotel and staged the whole thing like it was a mission to extract information. He knew the Yotogi wouldn't resist, but with their lingering presence in Miami, the explosion would look like it was their doing and make them a public enemy. He succeeded.

He exited the bathroom and saw Claire laying on the bed watching the rain careen into the glass.

Claire turned and stared at him. He liked being alone with her. She'd been the only real attachment he felt to anyone here, now, and he didn't feel like he'd failed anyone in her presence. Even Ortiz was a distant connection, but it was merely a formal acquaintance. Ortiz still felt like a child to him. Although he'd grown into a respectable man, he still didn't have a connection like a comrade. Claire was different. She didn't pity him, and she was more intrigued by his circumstances than motivated by personal or company gain.

"Stay with me." She was quiet and moved the covers aside. It wasn't a sexual invitation, but she'd felt betrayed by everyone around her. People that she'd known for decades had put her in harms way and hurt many innocents in the process. She was a tool, a piece of the puzzle that was morphed and squished to fit into place.

Hal stood and crawled onto the bed with her. She simply didn't want to be alone and he wrapped one arm around her waist to pull closer.

Her small frame was comfortable, but she was stronger than she looked under a lab coat. Hal had spent his younger years married to his career and when he decided to retire from the military, he chose his love for flying over everything else. He filled the void of having a woman in his life with his plane and his students, who were much like himself and just wanted to feel the freedom of being in the air with the ocean beneath them.

Her back expanded as she breathed. It was a comfortable rhythm that Hal had never appreciated with a woman. At forty-five years old, he had little experience with any long term relationships. He'd had a year long fling with a woman in Bimini that he saw regularly on his flights back and forth, but nothing ever lasted. He had his plane and was always on the move. He never saw himself settling down, but then again he never considered his mortality until recently either. His attachment to this new world started with Claire, and although they hadn't known each other long, laying here now, he didn't want to let go or think of the future outside of A&H. At least not yet.

The rain was peaceful hitting the window, and even though the storm was approaching, there was a sense of calm.

Claire stirred, backing into him further. She was already asleep as Hal brushed her hair to the side. He wondered what a girl like her was doing inside A&H. She was a petite and pretty woman, and yet she spent her days in a basement laboratory under the ocean working on an experimental physics project for a world-class company. She had a small frame, about 5'5", 130 lbs, and although she was thin she definitely wasn't frail. Her back and shoulder muscles could be seen through her tank top and she had a lean waistline that Hal wrapped his arm around. She wasn't the stereotypical physics nerd you'd find in a basement. Not that it mattered, but it made him wonder how a woman like her ended up in a place like this.

His thoughts wandered. He was exhausted, but his mind was anything but. Part of him was afraid to fall asleep out of fear that another nightmare would take over. The wrist band was still around his arm, which was supposed to have an alarm system and wake him in case of a sudden increase of blood pressure or pulse rate, but it had little effect last time.

Thunder rumbled in the distance, and with it, the added sense of comfort. Having spent many years in Florida and the Keys, he'd grown fond of the rolling thunderstorms they often had. The rain was peaceful, and he focused on it, trying to change the subject in his mind. It was the last thing he remembered hearing before finally dozing off.

Chapter 19: A New Day

Light streamed in from the window and Hal shifted.

Claire was shuffling around in the kitchen area quietly, unaware that he'd woken. He glanced at his arm band, which read 7:48 AM. It was the first night he'd slept without a nightmare occurring.

"Good morning," Claire spoke on the opposite side of the counter. It wasn't a chipper greeting, but given the circumstances, everyone was still a little on edge.

"Morning."

He crawled out of the comfortable bed and looked out the window bays. It was a dismal sight. The sky was gray, which could barely be seen through the fog and heavy rain. The gusting wind whipped against the building and you could almost feel it shift.

Claire sat at the bar table and quietly drank her coffee.

"Anything new from Troy or Brack?" He was curious about what she was thinking.

She simply shook her head.

Hal stood and tried to stretch as his back and knees protested. He'd taken a bad fall running from the Mirada and the bruises were setting in.

"The Yotogi are scattered. They're probably trying to flee the city by now." She held her head down in shame.

"They don't blame you." He tried to be comforting, although he knew it probably wouldn't ease any guilt.

"It's not that. I know they don't, but this is going to change everything." Her head suddenly picked up as a new thought crossed her mind and she stumbled over to the console on her desk. "Call Westford."

A blank screen popped up in the center of the display.

"We still have a mole inside the Yotogi. If he made it out, he would report to Howard for cover." She glanced back at the screen and tapped the desk impatiently.

After a minute or so a man appeared on the screen. This must have been Howard. His hair was pulled back into a pony tail and his masculine profile was what Hal imagined he'd look like.

"Claire, my dear. Sounds like you guys stirred up some trouble in the city." He was already well aware of the situation.

She put her head down in shame as he reminded her. "Howard, is Michio with you?"

"Actually, yes." He looked away from the prompt and yelled something in Japanese.

Howard stood and walked away as another man's face appeared on the camera.

"Oh thank God, Michio." Claire was happy to see him unharmed.

"A&H is going to kill me now." He wasn't asking it as a question. "If the Yotogi don't find me first."

"The Yotogi still don't know, Michio."

He looked surprised hearing this. He was under the impression that this whole ordeal might have actually been because of him.

"So, what happened then? Why is there no communication coming in from them? We should have regrouped by now." He was still lost in the chaos of it all.

"Listen, I need you to stay with Howard for now. Even if you get a call from the Yotogi, you need to stay. This is A&H's doing, and they'll be going after them. They can *not* find you." She knew what A&H's next move would be. "You're the only link between the company and the Yotogi. I think Brack has a personal vendetta with Akira, and he's lost it. What happened at the Mirada was staged... by us."

"So now what? Do I just stay here with these... these thugs?" He whispered and glared behind him where Howard must have been standing.

"Hey! We heard that." Howard laughed in the background.

"You make me uncomfortable." Michio humored back.

He glanced back at her through the camera. "I don't like it here."

She smiled. Michio was used to a much more peaceful crowd. "Hang in there. At least until we know it's safe."

"Wait. Why would A&H have a stand off in the Mirada?" He didn't question whether or not Claire was part of the ordeal, and he trusted her, but this was a surprise to him that the company would be so aggressive.

151

"Brack lead us to believe we were trying to bridge some sort of communication between them. He's out of his mind. I don't know for sure, but I think this was what he wanted. He wants there to be a public outcry again the Yotogi all together." She was holding something back, knowing this wasn't a secure line.

"There's been no word through our normal channels. We're scattered now and have no way to regroup." He was shaken and nervous as the crowd behind him laughed. "If I get any word, I'll have Howard contact you."

She nodded, although not happy by the news. "Take care, Michio. I'm glad you're all right."

He smirked. He was safe, but not *all right.*

The screen went blank and she turned to Hal. "I need to find out what A&H is planning. If they find out there's still someone connected to the company and this disaster..." She paused, shaking her head. Hal knew what she was implying and how Michio would be at risk from both sides.

She took off towards her closet and quickly undressed before grabbing her typical lab coat and putting her formal outfit on. Hal did the same. His clothing was still damp from the rain last night, but it wasn't like he had a spare set to change into. Come to think of it, these were really the only clothes he currently had.

The outside weather was frightful. Wind pushed them from side to side as he tried to hold his jacket close to his chest.

They entered through the side door of the west wing and shook off the rain in the empty, dark hallway. Work as usual had been called off due to the storm, but a few occupants were still in the building and food court. They passed the doctor's lab and looked in. It was vacant, and they continued to the atrium. Hal looked up at the new ceiling dome that had already been completed. They were definitely a company with resources and fast labor.

Room A1 was Brack's office, and to their surprise it was also vacant.

"Locate Brack." She spoke in Hal's direction, and he felt confused. "Your arm band," she pointed.

"Oh." He lifted his jacket sleeve and a small display was shown with a topographical map of the building.

"He's in the conference room." She passed him and headed towards the north hallway.

She approached the door and scanned her palm before it chimed and the green light flickered. The door swung open and they found themselves suddenly being stared at by twelve unsuspecting faces.

"What's going on?"

"Welcome Claire, have a seat." Brack glanced at Hal, but there was no similar invitation.

She didn't obey and remained in her place with her hand on the open door handle.

Hal felt enraged suddenly. He knew this was coming. There was no place for him anymore, and although he was surely part of the discussion, Brack did not want him to be included until they'd decided where to place him.

Ortiz stood from across the room and angrily began to pace towards the door. Two other men followed behind him.

Whatever the hell was going on here, these men were *not* happy, and with the dismissal of Hal from the group, it must have been the last straw. Ortiz had a personal connection to Hal, and despite it being a distant one, his loyalty was not to his paycheck.

"Stop." Brack put his hands to his head for a moment before looking back at the group. "Sit. All of you."

No one moved as they glanced back in his direction.

"We fucked up." It was the first admittance that they had done something they couldn't control.

"No, you fucked up." Ortiz spoke back, just as brash.

"Yes, I fucked up. I made a call that was premature. I lost sight of our objectives and Eiji was..."

Hal cut him off. "He was giving me answers that you couldn't provide."

"No, he was brain washing you to think this was done on purpose. He was trying to convert you." He stood his ground, trying to hold onto whatever creditably he had left.

"How? I was in there for less than five minutes. All you were after was information regarding your freighters. Was it so much for me to ask about my own circumstances? Twenty-six years ago I lost the lives of four student pilots. Can you blame me? We had good communication with their leader. I would have gotten to your damned boats!" Hal angrily spat back.

Brack took a moment to compose himself. He was furiously brewing inside but no one moved to support his argument. "It's more complicated than that." His tone had changed. "We have another situation at hand. Please, sit."

Like it or not, the meeting was going to include Hal, and everyone slowly took their seats.

The turmoil quieted and Brack calmed himself. "This is classified information. No one beyond this room must speak about it." He glanced around the room as several of the people nodded their heads. "Project ARCA has been located. It has a built-in homing device that's been activated, but not by us."

Everyone glanced around the room, suddenly nervous. He continued. "The ARCA was designed to activate a security protocol when it's been tampered with outside of our facilities. It's no secret that the mechanism is unstable, and we added this design to ensure the device would be deactivated entirely if it defected."

"So it's disabled?" Claire asked suspiciously, knowing something was being left out.

"That was the intention, yes. But someone with the ability to reactivate it can bypass it. Kyra Boshcov has gone missing."

There was a silence among everyone as he spoke.

"We have known for some time that there has been a mole within the company. Information about the project has been leaked to various news sources, and we naturally suspected the Yotogi were the recipients. We still suspect this, but Kyra's actions have led us to believe she has been the main cause."

"She wouldn't..." Claire muttered under her breath, but the expression on her face portrayed doubt.

"Kyra has always had sympathy for the Yotogi. At this time, all communication with her is terminated. She is not wearing her location device, and given her involvement with the project, if you or anyone is to have physical contact with her you are ordered to incapacitate her by any means necessary." The anger that everyone felt towards Brack had already been forgotten.

"So where is the homing signal coming from?" Hal was surprised to be the only one asking the question.

"It's in the Atlantic heading towards Puerto Rico. The US territory is close, and we're assuming that she's intending to make a transaction there. It's our last prototype of the ARCA." Brack was somber. This was an embarrassment to him and the company.

"Wait, this wasn't the research on our freighters?" Claire asked.

"No, she stole our last prototype from the base here last night." Troy strolled forward to include himself.

There was a long silence for several seconds before Claire spoke. "So we go after it." Her tone was angry now. She'd been betrayed enough times already, and now she'd just found out that her best friend and partner was the real perpetrator.

"We're planning that now. Ortiz and his team will be on a stealth ship under the water. Hal, the reason we didn't want to include you in this meeting was not out of spite. What you did for us last night... You've paid us your dues. You are under no obligation to us here, and I couldn't risk this information getting to the media more than it already has." Brack had changed his tone from defensive to apologetic.

Here he was again, put into a situation that he could just walk away from and he had no further obligations to his rescuers. He looked at Claire who was quietly brewing with anger. She'd worked with Kyra for nine years side by side and all this time she'd been part of the opposition, stealing the company's research.

"I'd like to help." Hal wasn't motivated by Brack or A&H's objective. He still hadn't found his place in the world, and he had nothing to go home to. He had Claire and Ortiz here.

"Good. We dispatch in two hours. You can join Ortiz and his team on the ship headed towards Puerto Rico."

There was no arguing or oaths to the company. He'd proven his usefulness and his training gave him a unique set of skills A&H couldn't deny when they were made available.

Brack looked at Claire who was still contemplating her role. "Claire, you'll stay on base and monitor the situation with us."

"No. I'm going with them." She was defiant. "You said the ARCA is active, despite the homing device being set off. I'm the only one who can disarm it from the ground."

Brack wasn't comfortable with her response and he began to object.

"The ARCA can't be shut down remotely. It has to have a registered DNA signature to switch controls. If we can find it, I can shut it down indefinitely."

Troy strolled forward. "This is our last prototype. If it goes down, we won't be able to repair it."

"Then we'll rebuild another one!" She was outraged. Troy wasn't even considering the havoc the device could have if it fell into the wrong hands. All he wanted was the device to come back, in one piece, unharmed. To hell with anyone who was injured in the process.

"It's something to consider, Troy," Brack objected. "This will put you directly in harms way, Claire. Who knows how the Yotogi will react to us now."

She stood angrily, but it wasn't directed at him. "We don't really have a choice." She looked at Troy. "And sitting here on my ass while you discuss the implementations of the ARCA and what it could do in the wrong hands... You're wasting time we don't have. We'll deactivate the device and bring it back. We'll rebuild it from scratch if we have to."

She shifted her focus back to Brack. "I have training. Give me something we can use to disarm it and I'll go in with Ortiz and his team." She looked over at Hal, happy to see at least one loyal face among them.

"Done. Meet with Ortiz in the firing range and take whatever you think is necessary." He grabbed her arm as she turned to leave. "*Whatever* is necessary."

Chapter 20: Go time

Launch time was scheduled for 1 PM and Hal stood on the pier next to Ortiz and ten of his men. They were heavily armed with assault rifles, pistols and grenades. Hal still wore most of the gear he had acquired last night, which was much less intimidating than those around him. He had several sleep and EMP grenades, his tranquilizer pistol and the .357 revolver, which was the only deadly firearm on him. He still felt secure in his ability, but as he glanced around at the other men, he felt somewhat inadequate.

Claire and Brack were walking down the pier to meet them and get their last orders. She was dressed in what looked like a black diving suit. The outside lining shimmered as a thin layer of Sealo-Pax laced the exterior for protection and a dark long jacket covered the rest. A shoulder harness wrapped around her chest and held onto a long range sniper rifle. As her jacket lifted from the violent winds, Hal could see her carrying two hand pistols, several clips of ammunition, a stun prod and twelve inch combat knife. If he were the bad guy in all of this, he'd fear her the most. Ortiz's men had the same reaction as they approached.

She joined their ranks and stood next to Ortiz. She was a good five inches shorter than anyone, and yet carried the biggest rifle. It would have been humorous if it weren't for the situation they were in.

"We aren't sure what ship Kyra is on, but it's not fast. At her current speed you should be able to reach her in twenty minutes or less." Brack pointed at the ship they were about to board.

"The Shadow is a stealth ship and can travel underwater undetected. It's electrical signals should go dark two miles out. You'll be flying blind once you're in that radius. We'll be on channel 1400 using the com system, which is out of reach for standard radios. Kyra is no doubt aware that we'll be attempting to repossess the device, and the Yotogi will be hostile." He turned to leave in dismissal before adding one last thing. "Destroy the ARCA if you have to."

Everyone nodded in agreement before stepping onto the ship.

It was tight as twelve occupants crammed into the small quarters and submerged. Hal felt like he was with his old group during his military days. The red hue of the lights illuminated their faces, most of which were covered in camouflaged paint. They were excited, and this was more like a game to them than a mission. It was the secure sense that he'd only felt while on a mission with his men, and it was where he belonged at the moment.

Claire was quiet, her head resting in her hands and she perched her elbows on her knees. She didn't need to be comforted, though. She was raging on the inside and completely in control.

"Four minutes until contact. We go dark in two," Ortiz announced.

The room was quiet and several members checked their ammunition supply and primed their chambers.

"Two minutes," he announced again. The room fell dark as the red lights went out. The only light came from some of the headsets Ortiz's crew was wearing and LED bulbs attached to their firearms.

The Shadow surfaced and Ortiz opened hatch as a gust of air rushed in, spraying the fearless passengers with ocean water. They were now in the midst of the hurricane's wrath, swaying back and forth as the wind rocked the waves all around them. Any small boat in this weather would easily be overturned.

Ortiz moved up the ladder and out the hatch to get a better visual.

"Up top, men," he yelled.

Single file, they piled to the top of the ship, lights off and quiet. They were a mile from range and Hal could see bright lights of what looked like a cargo freighter through the fog. The ocean was in turmoil and the small ship bounced with the waves. Hal followed behind the last man and fell to his knees, grabbing hold of a metal beam lining the exterior. Claire was the last to exit as she squeezed out of the small hatch and also braced herself against the winds.

She paused in shock as she looked at the *boat* they were approaching. "That's our freighter!" She pressed the ear piece and spoke into the com system. "Brack, she's on our freighter!"

There was silence over the com system. They had been expecting to board a small vessel, manned by only a dozen or so men, but as they got closer Hal could read the A&H logo on the side. It hadn't gone missing after all.

"That bitch!" Claire swore.

"We'll get her," Ortiz yelled back, his voice echoing through the ear piece of every team member.

The Shadow approached the docking area of the large freighter and Ortiz shot a grapple hook towards the hull. With a clank, the hook penetrated and the Shadow tugged forward as they reeled in closer to the ship's emergency ladder. One by one they climbed to the main level of the freighter.

Ortiz went first and jumped the railing, quietly crouching as the rest of the team followed.

Hal held out his hand to help Claire get her grip. The ladder was about thirty feet long and wind slammed from side to side, trying to tear them from the surface.

Hal was the last man to spring over the railing and he looked around to see the others scatter. Dressed in black, they all hid in the shadows.

Scoping the surrounding areas, he could see several men on the balcony of the higher two levels of the ship towards the front. Hal counted four total, and lights could be seen from the inside windows. Even though the ship was large, it still rocked on the violent waves and most of the occupants on the boat were weathering the storm from somewhere inside.

Hal grabbed his tranquilizer pistol with his other hand and held it in front of him, focusing through the attached scope to get a closer look.

Claire crawled on the ground, her sniper rifle perched on the surface and she peered through the scope to do the same.

"Four on the balcony, two at the side entrance. There's an opening just inside the main door. The windows are fogged. I can't see how many are inside." Everyone could hear her through the com system. On the bright side, with this being A&H's cargo freighter, she knew her way around. "The ARCA is being held on the third level from the bottom. We can enter the hatch from the surface here, or take the side entrance and work our way down the staircase."

"Are there any open areas from the top hatch?" Ortiz asked.

"Yes. We're five levels up and just below us is a large storage area. If the ARCA has been moved, it's most likely on level two or three. They're large, open bays, and when the ship was sent out it was carrying very little. You should have good range of sight." She looked over to Hal who was crouched down about two feet behind her. She tossed a pair of night vision goggles in his direction.

It took him a moment to orient himself through the lenses as they automatically zoomed in to focus on the various targets.

He paused. Something was wrong here.

"These aren't the Yotogi."

Claire looked back at him in surprise before looking back through her own scope. She lifted her sight from the lens and then back at Hal. "No, they're not."

Hal focused in on some of the men standing on the balcony. They most definitely were not Yotogi. They wore a white uniform and were carrying assault rifles. Several of them had goggles on as well. He focused on one man in particular and suddenly felt a rush of fear sweep over him.

There was a yell from the balcony in a foreign language and several other men rushed to his position. Shit.

"We've been spotted. Move!"

Claire lunged to her feet and swung the rifle to her back before grabbing Hal's shoulder and running towards Ortiz's men. Shots were fired as they approached.

They swung around a large beam that supported a life boat above them. The ting of the gunshots ricocheted from the other side and Ortiz's men returned fire.

Claire spun across the beam and laid on the ground, her rifle perched as she steadied her sight on the balcony. She was covered in the shadow from above and a loud shot released from her weapon. Hal could see through his goggles in the distance as a man flew backward. Another shot fired and another man fell.

Hal glanced to his left where three of Ortiz's men were also positioned with their rifles. They followed Claire's lead and continued firing until all six men on the balcony were down.

Shadows streamed through the windows in the distance as the chaos unfolded. They were taking positions.

"We have to move." She glanced at the hatch that was forty feet away. She swung her rifle strap over her shoulder and made a run towards the hatch.

The hatch cover was heavy and Hal grabbed one side to help lift. The pressure release hissed as it opened and toppled to the side.

She swung her legs into the hatch and slid down the ladder, gripping the side shafts with her feet and hands. Hal followed behind and ducked inward just as a bullet struck the deck inches away.

His feet landed on the metal floor below. He tilted his head back, lifting the goggles to his forehead and they ducked behind a cargo container.

"There's a stairwell to our left, about a hundred and fifty feet. We need to go down a level." She pressed the ear piece in. "Ortiz, where are your men?"

"We have three up top, two on level four, two are heading towards the control room and I'm with Smithers and Logan heading towards level three." He was interrupted by the sound of gun fire. "We need backup."

Ortiz was on the same level as they were, heading towards the stairwell. Hal could hear the gun fire over the com system, which was delayed a fraction of a second from the sounds in the room.

Claire crouched down and began to sprint towards the stairs. She grabbed her back pocket and pulled out a small grenade, pulled the pin and flung it towards the front of the ship.

There was a spark of green and blue that arched over the containers before the emergency lights turned off. Static filled their ears for a few seconds as the discharge of the EMP traveled throughout.

They made it to the door and flung it open as the muzzle flash from Ortiz's men illuminated the downward spiraling staircase.

"Smithers is hit!" His voice echoed off the walls.

Hal glanced over the railing downward. There were several men on the bottom level firing upwards at Ortiz.

"Hold your breath!" Hal yelled as he threw one of the sleep grenades Ruby had provided him. Ortiz looked up and saw it fall down the shaft as they took a breath in and retreated upwards to their position.

Five seconds later there was a puff of sound, almost mute in the chaos, and coughing pursued. Hal looked at his wrist band and counted. It took nearly twenty seconds for the gas to take effect and the ringing in their ears was suddenly comforted by silence as the gunfire stopped.

Smithers had his arm around Ortiz's neck for support with his left knee curling. A bullet had ricocheted and grazed his leg. Nothing fatal, but paralyzing, all the same.

"The shadow is still tethered to the freighter. We have to bring him back up top. We weren't prepared for this much resistance!" Ortiz looked over at Logan who nodded.

"There's a life boat at the back of the ship. If you get your men back to the Shadow, they'll think we're retreating. I'll stay and make sure the ARCA is disabled," Claire said as she reloaded her pistol.

"I'm staying." Hal felt like a member of Ortiz's team, but he couldn't leave her here. "I have nothing to go back to."

"See you on the flip side." Ortiz patted Hal on the shoulder before pulling Smither's weight onto his back and retreated up the stairwell. Logan took the lead and made sure the path was clear.

Claire had time to pause and the reality of what they were doing was beginning to sink in. She'd handled a weapon before in training, but the expression was clear. She had killed someone for the first time tonight.

"We're almost done. Remember what we're here for." Hal patted her shoulder the way a comrade would, and she snapped out of it, nodding her head. She could dwell on this later.

"This is the second level. One more down." He looked at her, blanking out any emotion.

"Got it."

The stairwell was silent and they crouched down in the darkness near the entrance of level three. They waited, listening to the chaos unfold up top. These men on the ship would have their focus on Ortiz and his team trying to retreat.

Claire was still numb. She'd turned her reality off and was still with intense focus.

A new voice came over the com system and jolted them out of suspense. "We have to leave now!" There was argument in the background. "Ortiz and Smithers are down. We're not going to make it back."

Shit! Hal's heart sank.

They waited and the ship fell quiet. There was no more radio contact, and hopefully the remaining group had successfully made it in the water to their escape. It was only them now.

An alarm went off and the red emergency lights went out. Hal jerked his head forward, bringing down the night vision goggles that were perched on his forehead. He could see Claire in the dark struggle to put hers on.

A loud speaker echoed through the hallways in a foreign language.

"Russian?" he asked, and Claire held up her hand to listen.

The message was brief, and Hal recognized some sort of countdown as the man spoke.

"They're verifying it's clear on levels one, two and five." She was fluent in the language. "That still leaves three and the main dock open for patrol."

The door swung open, revealing their hiding spot. Claire swung her leg out, sweeping underneath the man and bringing him to the ground. She rushed to his side and held her hand firmly over his nose and mouth.

"Clear." She whispered to him, repeating it in Russian for him to understand. Her grip was firm over his airways and he began to struggle. She repeated the order to him and grabbed his communication device from his neck, forbidding him to use it until he obeyed.

He held up his arm in surrender and she released. He gasped for air and she held a pistol to his chest before repeating the order again.

He murmured it back to her and nodded before pressing his communication device back to his throat. She didn't give him a second chance to reconsider his words as she fired a single shot to his chest.

Hal grabbed the man's feet and pulled him out of the open doorway as it shut behind, leaving the three of them alone in the dark stairwell. The dart from her tranquilizer was still stuck in his chest and Hal continued to drag his limp, unconscious body out of sight from anyone passing by.

He searched the man's chest for ammunition and other weapons. He was only armed with a semi-automatic pistol, but one thing was clear. These men had the intent to kill.

The com-speaker echoed again, repeating that all levels were cleared and they breathed a sigh of relief.

"There are heat sensor cameras at the front and back of this level. We're going to need to avoid the one in the front, but the back swivels on a thirty degree axis. If we can get to it, we can lock it in position staring at the wall." She reloaded the one cartridge she expelled into the guard. "The ARCA is towards the back, but it's heavy. I'll need about three, maybe four minutes to deactivate it. The front camera will be on me the entire time. If you can reach it, take it out with an EMP. It'll take them several minutes to send in reinforcements and we'll have to make a run for the stairwell up to level five, then out the stairwell."

She leaned into the doorway and opened it a few inches to scout out the third level. It was quiet, but the fluorescent lights strung along the ceiling didn't offer many places to hide. She lifted her goggles and made a motion to come closer. "On three. One. Two. Three."

They bolted towards a nearby storage container and Hal checked one corner as Claire checked the other.

She reached into her jacket for a makeup compact and shone the mirror above their heads over the top of the container. "There's the camera."

He watched as it panned around in their direction and then back. "Stay here."

He grabbed the ledge and pulled his weight over it and watched. It took about eight seconds to rotate from one position to another. He counted down and on the eighth second he swung around to the other side of the container, ran in a crouching position and ducked under a workstation, still counting.

Again he made a dash for the next hiding spot behind another workstation. Something immediately caught his attention to his right and he swung his tranquilizer pistol, firing a shot before his brain could catch up to his reflexes. A man dressed in a white uniform grabbed his throat as the shot struck. It took three seconds for the drug to paralyze and he fell to the ground. Patrols were still walking the paces and making sure the place was clear. Thankfully he'd fallen just outside the doorway and out of the camera's line of sight.

Hal watched around the corner and again began his counting as it reached its far angle. He made a run for it and lunged over a table, jumping a four foot gap and grabbing the ledge of the closest storage container directly under the camera and out of its vision angle.

Claire's mirror watched from a distance. "When the camera is at angle zero, facing the wall, give it a quick jerk clockwise." Her voice was quiet in his ear piece.

The cycle seemed slow now and Hal impatiently waited for the eight seconds to pass. He gripped, trying not to shake it too soon, and then jerked. It stuck.

"Good. Now the second camera." Hal had already begun his descent off the container as she gave the next order.

"The second camera doesn't move. If we set a small EMP discharge near it, it'll go blank and they'll come running. Be ready." She nodded at him and then in the direction of the camera. "Wait." She reached behind under her jacket and handed him a grenade, which stuck to his arm band as he touched it. The outside jacket of the grenade was a foamy glue that instantly clung to whatever surface it touched.

He swooped the corner and shifted the grenade in his palm, trying to keep it from making permanent contact.

There were no hiding spots from this direction, but with a good swing, the grenade would land within an effective radius. He closed one eye and narrowed his vision, pulled back his right arm, aimed and swung.   It hit the wall with a satisfying thwack two feet from the mark and a blinking LED light could be seen as the five second countdown began.

Hal ducked back behind the corner. He'd set an EMP off before at the Mirada, but he hadn't actually witnessed its discharge. He had no idea whether it would be blinding or loud out in the open.

The burst was quick and sounded more like a storm of static zaps. The lights above flickered, and those within the immediate radius were completely dark.

Claire bolted towards the large display in the open floor and ripped off a black tarp, revealing what looked like a large assault rifle inside a thick glass tube. This was the ARCA. It looked like a large gun with a harness that the operator wore to support the two foot long, six inch wide barrel. The top had three canisters mounted to it, illuminated by the power cores that spun slowly inside. All this time he'd heard about the ARCA, he hadn't quite envisioned it looking so much like a weapon.

Claire typed in some commands in front of the console attached to the chamber and there was a hiss as the glass shield slid down.

She climbed up onto the control pad and crouched over the device to hit in some commands on the top console, which was mounted to gun device itself.

"Shit! It's been reprogrammed!" She shouted in Hal's direction. He stood on guard, not sure how to respond.

"Can we destroy it?" He knew it wasn't the desired action, but if it couldn't be disabled they'd either have to carry it out or kill it.

"Yes, but we need to get it out of here. If they can reprogram it, they can rebuild it."

Kyra knew almost as much about the device as she did, and even if they could disable its function, they would be able to reverse engineer the pieces.

Hal shuffled over to the front entrance and slid a heavy desk in front of the doors. It opened inward and would at least slow anyone's intrusion.

"Help me carry this down," she ordered and he rushed over to help dismount it.

To his surprise it wasn't that heavy, but for Claire and her small frame, it was more than she could casually lift.

The clamps released and four mechanical arms opened and separated, letting go. They wobbled it off the stand and she pulled the harness over her shoulders.

"Get the door." She pointed towards the side entrance stairwell they entered through.

A clash of noise came from the front entrance to their left. The door shoved into the desk, screeching along the floor as the men behind desperately tried to break through.

Hal ran into the exiting door, swinging it inward with his force. Claire was struggling to run with the heavy load, but she wasn't far behind.

"There's a life raft up top on the back of the ship. Go! Unlatch the reels holding it in place. I'll be right behind you," she shouted.

He hesitated. Splitting up wasn't a good idea, but the guards were heading towards level three and would still have ground to cover. The raft would need to be lowered, and they'd be wasting time if it wasn't ready to release once their objective arrived.

He nodded and sprinted up the stairs, gripping the railing to pull himself up faster.

He slid against the door and pressed his ear to the surface. No commotion came from the outside and he peered out the small, open crack.

He dodged towards the pulley that lowered the boat. It came down to deck level and he dragged the chain with him before stepping aboard.

The boat swung in the air from the turbulent winds and he looked down at the ocean, which was about three stories below him.

He heard the door clash open as Claire burst out, almost stumbling to the ground. His vision shifted towards the movement behind her as four men with guns raised were running in her direction.

She darted towards Hal, clumsy and exhausted as she fell to her knees. Her eyes widened with shock as she was struck. Fighting the paralysis, she extended her arms out to catch herself.

"No!" he screamed.

The men advanced. Hal fought with the chain and yanked to hold the boat in position, but it was too far to make a jump as it swung backward with the wind.

The men lowered their weapons as they reached Claire, who was still protesting the tranquilizer. One man leaned over and unwrapped the harness from Claire's chest before lifting her up into his arms.

Kyra burst through the staircase exit and frantically gazed around before her eyes stopped on the ARCA, then on Hal, who was helplessly out of reach. She smiled at their failure. There was a hint at something more, though. They not only had the ARCA in their possession, but they also had the one person who could finish it – Claire.

Kyra approached the pulley arm for the life raft and gripped the wheel. "I'm sorry you fell into this, Hal, but you don't belong here."

With a swift pull on the chain it released and Hal's end went limp, sending the boat downward with a sudden jolt. Hal fell to his knees and gripped its hull as the boat collided with the ocean's surface. He bounced off the floor and water rushed in from all sides, but it remained afloat. The waves were tall and lifted the boat carelessly into the air and back down again. He got his grip and crawled to the side, looking up at the rear of the large freighter that was quickly accelerating away from him.

He flipped over onto his back and gripped the suspending wires, holding onto dear life as he thrashed back and forth, up and down with the angry waves.

"Brack, this is Hal. Can anyone read me?" He listened, praying to God someone would hear him. "I repeat, this is Hal Brent! I'm on a life raft. Can anyone hear me?"

"This is Logan with the Shadow. We hear you Brent and we're heading towards your position." He recognized the man's voice from Ortiz's team. "Intercepting in three minutes."

Hal felt anger growing in his chest. Not over the ARCA, but Claire. They had no idea what they were walking into, and damn it, he shouldn't have gone ahead without her. Ortiz and Smithers were lost too, but unlike her, they were probably dead. Claire was different. Although not an ally, she was useful. The ARCA was unfinished, or at least unstable, and she was the only one fluent enough in its mechanics to repair it.

A light lifted from the water forty feet away and Hal struggled to get his balance.

"This is Logan, we have eyes on you and we're approaching." The voice was barely audible with the surrounding noise.

The Shadow was nearly ten feet within range when the hatch opened.

Hal sloppily stood on the fluctuating floor and dove into the water. The waves threw him from side to side and he struggled to swim the short distance. A dip in the waves sucked him down below the surface and he frantically pushed forward with his arms, reaching for anything to grab hold of. His hands slid across the surface of the hull as he was thrown back upward with a returning wave.

A hand grabbed his jacket and yanked upward. It was Logan.

"I got you!" He heaved to pull him onto the surface. "Where's Claire?"

"She's gone." He muttered. "She's gone! They got her," he painfully yelled out.

There wasn't time for Logan to react as he quickly pulled Hal towards the hatch and inward.

There were now eight men waiting in anticipation as he fumbled down the ladder. He looked back at every one of them in disappointment. There wasn't a need for explanation as they quickly realized they'd all failed. Ortiz, Smithers and Claire were lost to them and they'd failed their mission.

Chapter 21: The Masked Enemy

No one came out to greet them at the dock as they reached A&H headquarters. News had already spread and there was no need for the welcome party, because let's face it, there was little to welcome.

Hal stood at the entrance as the rest of Ortiz's crew walked in with their heads down. The hurricane was in its most violent stroke and the wind pushed him in the doorway.

"They're not in the conference room," Logan said, meaning Brack and Troy. "Alright men. This has been an exhausting day. Sleep it off. We'll regroup in the morning at 8AM and get ready to head out unless A&H has another objective for us. If not, we'll head back to base in the afternoon. I'll deliver their belongings to the families."

Hal was left alone in the atrium as the men somberly picked up their remaining equipment and headed towards the lower levels. He didn't belong here, and as far as A&H was concerned, he was useless.

With nowhere to go, he walked towards the doctor's office in the west wing knowing it would be the only door open at this hour. To his surprise, the lights were on and streaming through the small window in the door frame. Someone was still awake.

The room was dimly lit. Brack and the doctor sat with their backs turned to him as he entered.

"Come in and sit, please," Brack asked somberly.

On the table was a bottle of whiskey and they both cradled a glass in their hands as he joined them. Brack poured Hal a tall glass and slid it across the table.

"This was supposed to be a celebration when the ARCA project would be made public but," he held his head down, looking into his glass. "I'm sorry you had to be a part of this, Mr. Brent."

Brack was sincere for once. Maybe it was the drink that knocked his ego down a bit, or maybe it was the humility in his failure. He had no reputation or facade to protect any longer. He didn't care about the loss of the project anymore, or at least not in comparison to the loss of his colleagues.

Hal sat quietly in shock as he looked back and forth at the two, never once making eye contact. There was a long silence and he took a large sip of the whiskey, dulling the feeling of guilt.

The doctor raised his glass. "To Claire."

Brack reciprocated the gesture. "To Claire."

Hal quietly did the same and they clanked glasses before shooting a mouthful down.

The three men sat quietly, nursing their whiskey and mourning their losses. It was out of their hands now, and they all felt helpless and betrayed.

Hal's mind wandered. The silence was deafening, and the whiskey helped mask Brack's feelings, but not his.

"Is there any way to track the freighter? To track Claire?" Hal spoke up.

Brack looked up and tears bordered his eyes. "No, the signal went dark, as well as Claire's tracking device. There's something masking it. Something we don't have access to."

"They took her alive. I don't know about Ortiz and Smithers, but Claire was incapacitated. She had the ARCA in her possession before..." Hal trailed off.

This was news to Brack, surprisingly, and he perked his head up. This whole time he'd been under the impression they'd been killed. There was no briefing afterward, when they arrived at the dock, and he was still in the dark about the details.

"What?" He asked.

Hal looked back and forth between them. "Claire's alive."

Brack stood with new motivation. When radio contact had come in, he was told they were *lost*, not alive. He paced around drunkenly. For such a high tech company, they had serious communication problems.

"Why would they take a hostage?" Prossman chimed in.

"We don't even know who *they* are. This whole time we've been focused on the Yotogi... but Kyra," Brack's eyebrows perked up. "Kyra doesn't have any ties to the Yotogi. She's always been a little sympathetic towards them, but she'd never join their cause. That's what's been off about this entire ordeal. We knew there was a leak, but there was never any reason to suspect her."

"They were Russian." Hal was the only one who wasn't drowning in liquid.

"Russian?" Brack looked puzzled.

"Claire spoke to one, briefly, in Russian." Hal responded.

Brack stood in place, no doubt regretting his whiskey that retarded his judgment. "Why the Russians?"

Hal shrugged his shoulders, taking a guess. "Kyra is Russian."

It had never occurred to Brack. Kyra had been with the company for more than a decade, but it wasn't unheard of to plant a spy for years, decades even.

"I don't think the Yotogi are your guys, Brack." Hal was trying to be calm in presenting the idea, but so far they hadn't shown that much hostility.

Brack didn't like the idea, but he couldn't dismiss it either. Now they'd created two enemies, one of which was under their nose the entire time.

"Is there any way we could contact the Yotogi?" Hal approached the topic carefully.

"No. They have never responded to our requests, and they sure as hell won't now." Brack raised his palms to his face, trying to work out the conspiracy in his head.

"What about Michio?" Hal asked.

"Michio? The plant?" Brack knew of their contact that was working both sides of the fence. "How do you know Michio?"

"He was one of Claire's contacts you guys frowned upon so badly." Hal took another sip from his whiskey. He was almost enjoying Brack's struggle.

"But we don't even know if he was at the Mirada," Brack protested.

"He was, but made out safely." Hal knew more about what was going on than he did, but it didn't say much for his knowledge. Brack worked from the secure position behind his monitor and under Troy's thumb.

"We lost communication with Michio a day ago. The Yotogi are fleeing the city. Some have been apprehended, but if Michio is alive, maybe... maybe we have something to bargain with." Brack's eyes lit up at first but sank again when he considered that their actions had only pushed them farther away.

172

"Michio won't talk. He thinks the raid on the hotel was because the Yotogi discovered he's a mole. He won't come forward here because he thinks you'll kill him." Hal was speaking as if he'd had some personal contact with the man.

Brack paused. He was stuck and Hal let him stay there for a moment.

"I know how to reach Michio." Hal still didn't care much for the Yotogi at this point, but if it meant they could have just a glimpse of hope towards recovering Claire and Ortiz, he wanted to be part of it.

"How?" Brack was still clueless.

"I..." Hal paused. He wasn't sure how much information he should give out. Michio was running scared and hadn't regrouped, so the Yotogi were being rightfully paranoid. "Remember Claire's contacts that I met in Miami?"

"Westford. I know the name." Brack was referring to Howard and Ruby.

"He's with them, but, and I don't say this to offend you, but I don't think they'll respond to you." Hal backed up, preparing for Brack to lash back.

"Why?" He acted clueless.

"Well, for one, you hate them, and two you blew up their building then sent marshal law after them." Hal was being somewhat sarcastic, but seriously, Brack had known this.

He held his head down. Brack was not a likable man, and his personal vendetta towards their organization had been blown way out of proportion.

"Let me talk to them," Hal offered.

Brack's face lit up with hope. He knew Hal had no obligation to them, but maybe his tactics needed to change. He was the only one on their side now that still had any leverage.

Hal walked over to the computer console. He'd seen others make video phone calls, but he stood awkwardly at the screen. "Call Westford."

The screen lit up and dialed into Claire's directory of contacts. Several minutes passed before the macho-man himself appeared.

"Claire dear..." Howard paused as he looked at the stranger, obviously not who he expected. "Oh, excuse me. Mr. Brent himself.

What can I do for you?" They'd never met, but there was an informal friendship between the two.

"Is Michio still with you?" Hal asked.

"Yes, but he's... well, he's unavailable at the moment." He looked behind him in the quiet room.

"Listen, Howard, I know we haven't met, but I need to ask a favor from you." Hal sat down, this was going to take some explaining. "Claire has been taken hostage by a group of people. We believe they're Russian, but we don't know. I need to get in touch with the Yotogi. They weren't involved with the ARCA project being stolen, but they were somehow still receiving information on it. I need to get in touch with one of their leaders. If they somehow got their information second hand, I need to know who it was from."

Howard was listening intently without reaction. "Claire is their hostage?"

"Yes. The hijacking of the freighters was by someone else. We don't know who yet, but that's what we're hoping the Yotogi can help us with." Hal was laying it all out on the table, despite any objections Brack may have been considering.

"You don't need Michio for that, and I'm keeping him here for now. The Yotogi are regrouping, but there's opposition. And Brack!" Howard knew he was in the room listening. "You stay out of this."

He looked back at Hal through the camera. "Meet at the Mia Marina docks in two hours. Come alone."

The screen went black and Hal turned towards Brack who stupidly stood there, inebriated.

"Can you get me a boat to the docks?" Hal asked him.

"Yes, but..." He wanted to object somehow. It was in his nature.

"No. No followers this time," Hal insisted.

Brack had been beaten, and he was in no position to weigh in. "Follow me."

They exited to the south on the dock that outlined the front of the complex and approached a large motor boat.

The wind was turbulent and the circumstances of the weather were shitty at best. Of all times to go out to sea, they were forced to attempt this during a hurricane.

"Take these." Brack shouted to Hal as he tossed a set of keys.

He didn't offer any words of advice or thoughts on the situation. Not that he was capable of it in his drunken state but he knew Hal was in control. He'd burned his own bridges, and it was their only avenue.

Hal nodded and fired up the boat as it violently shook on the waves.

The trip from Soldier Key to Miami was a fairly short distance, but difficult to navigate in the weather. The glare of Miami hovered in the fog and stood out as a bright beacon.

He pulled the boat close to the dock and jumped, anchoring the board to the pier. Most of the residents had already transported their boats elsewhere, and Brack's ship bobbed carelessly on the waves, colliding into the docks.

It was awkward, having just been here, chaotically fleeing the scene as the destruction unfolded. The docks were empty and Hal began to travel towards the city, wrapping his arms around his chest, trying not to tip over from the violent winds.

Hal stopped at the edge of the dock just before the city and looked around, but Howard was nowhere to be seen.

Without warning, ten men sprung up around him, guns perched and aimed. The Yotogi meant business this time and they weren't taking any chances. They circled him in a twenty foot radius and shouted orders back and forth to one another in Japanese. He didn't understand, but their body language and tone made it obvious they were in disagreement.

"I'm unarmed!" He wasn't sure if they understood him, but they shifted their focus back. "I'm alone. I don't have a wire."

One of the men pulled his gun to the side and approached him, checking his pockets and behind his coat. He was clear, but the other men didn't lower their aim.

"Where's Howard?" He asked, and they all looked back and forth at each other. They clearly didn't understand what he was asking.

"Howard Westford?" He asked again hoping the name might ring a bell, but they didn't move.

The screech of tires on wet payment rippled through the air and a car sped onto the sidewalk, driving directly towards him. The men dodged out of its way. Shots were fired into the air and Hal ducked to cover his head, but he remained in place as he crouched down.

The car skid to a stop about three feet to his side and the door flung open.

"Get in!" A man yelled from the driver's side.

The Yotogi quickly jumped back to their feet and took aim, firing recklessly as bullets ricocheted off the side. Hal obeyed and lunged into the passenger seat. He didn't know who was driving yet, but there wasn't a choice.

Before the door even shut, the car took off, skidding down the wet docks towards the ocean.

"Wait, wait!" Hal screamed at the stranger as it approached the water.

"Hold on!" The man yelled as Hal gripped the interior, bracing for impact.

He jerked forward, his hands bracing the dashboard, but it didn't slow him enough before his head hit.

The vehicle slowly submerged and the operator pulled a lever to his side and began to accelerate deeper into the water.

Hal began to panic and tried for the door but it was locked. He frantically looked over at the driver who had reached for an interior light switch. It was Howard.

"Good to meet you, lad!" Howard smiled and was entertained by the shock Hal was going through. "Don't worry. This baby was designed for this. Well, not the gun fire, but she's a water cruiser. I don't know if any bullets made it through, but we'll find out soon." He looked over at Hal with a serious face. "Nah, I'm just kidding. It's bullet proof."

Hal shifted and looked behind him to see another passenger in the back seat that he recognized – Akira Eiji.

"Why the hell are your men after me?" Hal directed his question at Akira.

"The last time we encountered you... Well, lets just say there is some disagreement between your employer and my followers." Akira was stern and suspicious of him now.

"They're not my employer," he shouted back. Akira knew this, but with their lack of organization in the current chaos, communication between their group had been scattered.

176

The car fell quiet and Howard switched to a type of sonar panel to navigate under the dark water.

"I'm taking you to a safe house. Many of the Yotogi have regrouped there, but, as you can see, not everyone was in agreement." Howard glanced into the rear view mirror. Not that he could see anything in the pitch black ocean, but he was referring to the men he'd just encountered on the dock.

Hal looked into the back seat at Akira. He'd taken quite the heavy fall when he did a base jump from the eighteenth floor.

"I'll recover," Akira answered, knowing what he was going to ask.

The boat traveled north a few miles under the water, which was calm compared to the surface.

They resurfaced a few minutes later, bouncing off the waves as the tires shifted into driving position and grabbed the sand beneath them.

"Ugh, I hate sand." Howard seemed remarkably calm during all of this and even found it somewhat humorous.

Hal could feel the car lurch forward then stop before going forward again. It was almost like being stuck in snow, but the fight of the ocean waters around them kept pushing them back. A separate engine engaged and they grabbed hold of the land, lunging the car forward onto the beach and then onto the solid ground.

He pulled around onto a driveway that wrapped around a well lit beach house. Hal looked out the windshield and saw the several men looking out the huge bay windows overlooking the ocean.

"Welcome home." Howard looked at Hal before opening the door.

They were now parked in a dark garage, and Hal took a minute for his eyes to adjust before exiting. Howard leaned his seat forward and helped the old man out of the back, gripping his arm around his waist for support and walking him into the building.

Hal followed and relaxed. These were his allies, supposedly. He didn't know why, but so far he had no reasons to question them.

The condo entrance was filled with twenty or so men, all dressed in their black robes, but their faces were revealed. As he walked in, they held their heads down with one hand over their chest.

What the hell? They greeted him as if he were some sort of royalty. He still didn't know why they'd been so fascinated with him

"Come into the den. We have matters to discuss," Howard said as he walked Akira into the room and gently sat him down in a plush recliner chair.

Howard sat across from him in an office chair and made a gesture for Hal to sit next to him. He did, and two men approached the exit before sliding the doors shut.

"Are you wearing a wire?" Akira leaned forward and looked into Hal's eyes.

"No." He lifted his shirt to show his chest and tilted his head to show there was no communication device in his ears.

"Your wrist band." Akira pointed at his arm, which still had the device for his vital signs attached.

He slid it off and handed it to Howard who placed it into a semitransparent bag and sealed it.

"So." Akira reclined again, wincing in pain as his knees unfolded.

Hal looked over to Howard. He wasn't sure who to address about what had happened, but Howard seemed like the natural choice given his connection to Claire.

"Tell us what happened," Howard asked.

Hal took a moment. He didn't know exactly where to start. "The attack on the Mirada was Brack's order. I didn't know that he had planned it. I don't even know the reasons I was sent in to contact you. They believed that your men had hijacked their freighters with certain military equipment on it. Or at least that's what I was told. I was sent to make contact with you, Akira, because they claimed I was the only one you'd give answers to." He paused. That wasn't the reason he volunteered to go, but at the time he didn't have much choice.

"You came to me with other intentions." Akira was calm and soft. He was sympathetic to Hal and he knew the real reasons.

"Your men tried to capture me when I had first arrived at A&H." Hal held his head down in shame, knowing that he blindly turned towards A&H because they appeared to have his best intentions at the time. He made a motion with his hand. "All of this... I'm lost. I don't belong here. I thought your men were trying to kill me. You said something to me when we met at the Mirada. I'm a complicated subject, that I made it back. All I wanted in this was to find my flight team, and you lead me to believe there was a way."

"You did not have a choice, my friend."

Hal could see why Akira was such an influential leader. He spoke very softly and felt the same painful questions that burned in Hal's mind.

There was no point dwelling on the subject now, so Hal continued. "When we arrived at A&H, one of their scientists went AWOL. She stole the remaining ARCA device and fled on a ship heading towards Puerto Rico."

"Kyra." Howard said her name with discontent.

"Yes, Kyra. At the time Brack thought she was working with you to steal the research, but when we approached the vessel, it was their own. It was one of the missing freighters that A&H supposedly lost at sea, but we quickly realized that the occupants weren't who we thought. We were out numbered and out gunned. Claire and I made it to the ARCA, but it had been reprogrammed. She couldn't disable it, so we attempted to take it back." Hal held his head down in his hands and felt his heart sink. "They captured Claire and two other men. The signal went dark and I went back to A&H. I didn't know what else to do."

"You did what you had to. A&H has been blind for years, motivated by their company's welfare. They lash out at anyone who questions their research, and meanwhile, they overlooked their worst enemies within." Akira took a sip of some tea and relaxed.

Howard was starting to grow impatient with the conversation. He had his own concerns with the situation, and even though the Yotogi were his guests, he didn't agree with their priorities.

Hal was still somewhat suspicious of Akira. "You have been receiving information about the ARCA for a while now. I want to know your source."

"You or A&H?" Akira could sense his intentions.

"Me. Whoever those men were, they have the only two people that matter to me. I don't give a shit about the ARCA or A&H's research. Ortiz is the only person I can remember from my past and Claire..." He couldn't put her in the same category, but he needed her back.

Howard spoke up. "We need Claire back." Their relationship was still unknown, but it was the only thing that concerned him, too.

Akira shifted uncomfortably. He didn't want to reveal his connections. Maybe it was out of fear that someone unsavory had provided him with this information, or maybe he was protecting them.

"We acquired our information on project ARCA from a black market source. We never met face to face, but we were able to locate their transmissions to a place in the Gora Kharan mountain range." He paused to sip his tea before continuing. "It was a satellite transmission and yes, the man had a Russian accent. About three weeks ago we had caught wind that this ARCA device was going to be used on the island of Bermuda and we wanted to intercept it. We had no intentions of harming or hijacking anyone's vessel!" Akira was growing somewhat defensive.

"You don't need to prove that to me." His response allowed Akira to compose himself again.

"So how do we find these Russians?" Howard lit a cigarette and leaned back into his chair. "I don't suppose you have them on speed dial?" He phrased the question to Akira.

"Not exactly. We offered money in exchange for their information and we do have a location for the bank and the man who signed for it. Pavel Ockstrov." Akira pulled a folder from behind his chair and handed him a photo of a mean looking grunt. "He's not with the military, but after some research we've seen his name come up several times for weapons purchases on the black market. Mostly small things like assault rifles and grenades – nothing nuclear. We were suspicious about his intentions when we contacted him about the ARCA because it's not a weapon. It's a tool. It was meant to clean up nuclear waste in the lower atmosphere. It's no secret that Russia has its share of waste, and we left our suspicions at that."

"Small things like assault rifles?" Howard asked inquisitively. What the Yotogi considered small was almost laughable.

Akira shrugged it off. He didn't like being questioned and he already felt the guilt of having it slip his attention.

"So how do we find him?" Hal asked.

"We don't." Akira was blunt. "He comes to us."

"We don't have any leverage or anything to bargain with." Hal objected.

"That's not entirely true." Akira held his head down again in shame. "You see, the ARCA is unstable unless it's in its current location, which is why we were so interested in it. This may sound like science fiction to you Mr. Brent, but there is a very unusual phenomenon in this region that we also experience just off the coast of southern Japan. You know it as the Bermuda Triangle. We called it the Devil's Triangle, and before you object, let me explain." Akira put his hands in the air as he and Howard both let out a sigh of disbelief. "You are a product of this phenomenon, and you can't deny it. You can't explain it, and neither can we. The problem lies with the electromagnetic fluctuation you only experience here in this area. The ARCA was built in tune with its frequency and would have worked precisely as designed. If our suspicions are correct, then you're looking at a massive weapon of destruction if it's used in another location such as the Gora Mountain range. What this means is that we have some time. The ARCA will not function unless it is properly calibrated for a given region. The fail-safe will not allow it to function unless it can be reprogrammed by someone that understands the reasons for its functionality." Akira looked back and forth between Howard and Hal.

"That's why they have Claire alive," Hal stated.

"Most likely. Kyra was never the head of the project and she lacks the knowledge to successfully convert it to a new region. Claire will not volunteer this information, I'm sure. It won't be long until they figure this out and will search out other sources who are capable physicists." Hal still wasn't sure where he was going with his statement.

"So what? We use someone as bait and then track them? No one will volunteer for that, and even if they did, Russia is a large land mass. We can't just sneak onto their shores and walk to one of the most desolate mountains. They won't let anyone affiliated with the Yotogi fly in, and as far as my resources stretch, I don't have any pilots," Howard argued.

"Yes you do." Hal perked his head up in response.

Akira acknowledged that he was exactly the candidate they needed. "We can provide the wings. All we need is a volunteer to get in."

Hal shrugged his shoulders. "I have nothing to lose."

Howard struggled with the idea. He didn't know Hal well enough to judge his commitment or character, but he had a persuasive argument. It's not like he had a family or business connections to lose like he did, and he was an experienced pilot that could handle the flight in.

"If this goes, you'll be stuck in one of the most desolate places on earth with no exit. We'll tail your location as closely as possible and try to provide back up, but it may not be available. We don't need to make contact with them. We just need to know where they're located," Akira told Hal, phrasing it more like a question than a statement.

"When do we leave?" He was motivated to jump on a plane here and now. It had been years since he'd been in the air, but flying was a natural bonding with your plane, and Hal would never lose that connection.

"Tomorrow morning I will put out the word that we have an experienced physicist that's looking for another avenue of employment. The specifics aren't important, but when they realize the ARCA doesn't function as they've planned, they will look for available resources under the radar. Hopefully they will seek us out." Akira said, placing his folder back behind his chair.

Howard stood, bored with the whole sci-fi theory. Hal couldn't blame him. Neither of them understood half of what Akira had mentioned, and the whole topic of the Bermuda Triangle brought his credibility down a notch.

"So that will be it then? We'll just put the word out and sit on our hands until they call us. Fantastically productive," Howard sarcastically said as he walked over to the nearby bar stand and poured himself a drink.

Hal leaned in closer to Akira. "When I spoke to you in the Mirada, you mentioned my men that went down with me on my last flight. What connection are you implying about the Bermuda Triangle?"

"Every myth has its truths, my friend. You cannot explain it, but you cannot deny the mystery behind it. This whole matter in front of us now – manipulating matter, moving it into another frequency and essentially out of our dimensions indefinitely. Do you really think it's so impossible?" Akira answered his question with more questions, but his point had been made. There was no reasonable explanation for what he'd come and gone through, but the ARCA was proof it could be done.

Akira sighed. He wanted to offer an explanation to Hal more than anyone, but his theory was just that.

"We must sleep. The calm before the storm is always the worst part." Akira slowly reclined and closed his eyes.

Hal looked at Howard from across the room, still occupied by his television. "Where do I stay?" He asked, interrupting his focus.

"Make yourself at home. There are several bedrooms down the hallway. Take your pick." Howard waved his hands before turning back to the warm glow.

Hal stood and exited the room only to find himself the center of attention in the main living area. Twenty or so Yotogi members all looked at him with intrigued eyes. What was with these guys?

He tried to brush it off and approached the kitchen area. He hadn't realized it until now, but it'd been over a day since his last meal and the emotional drain was taking its toll on his stomach.

The kitchen was stocked. Two refrigerators, two stoves and an indoor grill were stretched along the long counters and island bar table.

He must have looked like an animal shoveling handfuls in his mouth, but he didn't care. He washed it all down with two beers and stumbled over to the hallway, looking for a vacancy.

The Yotogi were lounged about on little mats lining the floors of the large house and left the bedrooms untouched.

Hal took the last door on the left, trying to get away from the crowd as he quietly latched the door. The room was huge and had a small kitchen, private bathroom and an enormous, plush, king sized bed. The tin roof was an added comfort as the rain hammered down on its surface. This was the lifestyle of a king, he thought before collapsing onto the heavy covers and blacking out, fully dressed in his soaked clothing.

Chapter 22: The Beast Consumes

His head ached and he tried to raise his palms to his face but they were restrained by the harness around his chest. He breathed in and could feel the new bruises that pushed into him from the belt.

The hook unlatched as he pressed his thumbs on the release. He fell forward onto the flight controls and the plane tilted forward with his movement. Disoriented, he pressed up, straining the muscles in his chest and arms. The plane was nose down in a tree, surrounded by fog. He could see the ground below him about twenty feet.

"What the?"

Hal looked around at the tree that had wrapped itself around his plane. It was unnatural and its grip twisted around the hull. It didn't just catch him. It clenched him.

The hull began to cry out as the metal came crunching inward. He reached for the belt around his lower waist and released it, allowing gravity to pull him towards the spider cracked windshield. One way or another he needed to get out. He grabbed the ledge and with a few swift kicks the glass pried from its edges and hit the mushy soil beneath him.

He swung his legs out and hovered in the air before releasing his grip and sank into the marsh.

The tree groaned as its branches tightened onto the plane. It was collapsing inwards, strangling the plane and shattering the remaining glass windows as shards rained down.

He tried to pry his feet from the soil and with a few steps he found firmer ground. The plane squealed above him and he watched in terror as the tree came alive and engulfed the mangled metal.

Where the hell was he? He looked around in the dense fog and could see about forty to fifty feet in front of him. It was a marshland, spotted with bare trees and no green vegetation. He shook his head and looked up again at his plane as it slowly quieted its rebellion and fell still. He must have hit his head hard.

"Hello," he yelled in every direction. "Can anyone hear me?"

There was no response as he spun his head around in hopes for an answer.

"I've crash landed and I'm badly injured. Is anyone there?" He yelled again but to no avail.

His chest ached and his arms were sore from the impact. He squinted his eyes to see, hoping for some movement. The fog swirled around him and clung to his skin. It was cold and oily, unlike anything he'd seen or felt before.

He got to his feet and walked forward, peering through the mist to see. There were no landmarks he recognized, no buildings and no living creatures.

He looked behind him, but in the dense fog he couldn't see his plane anymore. The mud quickly erased his path of footsteps as it sank back into place. If he just walked forwards in a straight line he would be able to find his way back, he thought to himself.

He continued about two hundred feet before there was a change in the terrain. The fog was darker and he approached a rock wall that had an opening into a cave. It wasn't exactly shelter, but the fog was thinner and the ground was solid.

He reached for his lighter as he entered and immediately the walls began to shift. Roots dangled in through the sides and began to retract upwards as the light bounced off of them.

He jumped, fearful of the images his imagination was displaying. He closed his eyes and rubbed his head. It didn't feel as if he'd suffered a concussion, but this couldn't be real.

Opening his eyes, he expected the chaos to stop, and he jumped back, started, and shook the flame out. The movement of the roots sloshed through the damp soil as it moved.

He caught his breath and relaxed. "This is a hallucination. I've had a head injury. That can't happen," he told himself as he built up the courage to strike the lighter again.

He moved inward with his lighter in front of him, looking behind at the entrance, which still lit the way. He stopped for a moment and let the lighter die out as his eyes adjusted to the darkness.

The surroundings grew quiet in the darkness and he felt disoriented. How far did this cave go? He continued forward, pressing his hands against the cave wall for direction as the light from the entrance slowly dissipated.

There was a whimper in front of him somewhere and he paused. It was human.

"Hello?" Hal whispered. There was almost zero visibility now, but someone else was definitely here.

Whoever it was sensed his movement and groaned, desperate for help.

"Hello? Are you hurt?"

"Help me." The voice was quiet. "Please."

Hal tiptoed forward, squinting his eyes to see. Reflections of light flickered from the walls and the roots twisted on the sides. He flicked his lighter again and lurched backwards as he saw the man chained to its surface. The roots had grabbed him and were penetrating his body. His legs and arms were wrapped, pinning him to the wall.

Hal quickened to the man's side and reached for the roots on his left arm. He pulled backwards, but its grip was relentless.

"Help me." The man looked down at Hal. His face was immobile and his white glazed eyes focused on him.

"I'm going to get you out. Hang in there." Hal pulled, but the more he tried, the more it fought back.

The man winced in pain. The roots were now active, as if they'd become hostile and were fighting back, sinking into his skin.

"No. No. No. Stop." It was a desperate, hopeless plea, and the roots slowly tightened their grip on the man, strangling him.

There was a snap as a root reached around the man's chest and pulled in, collapsing his rib cage. The air escaped his lungs in a wretched scream.

Shock took over and Hal lurched backward. He didn't know what he was witnessing. He ignited his lighter again and watched, frozen in fear. Small vines trickled down the man's forehead and buried into his skin. His mouth opened but no sound escaped. Black lines writhed under his skin as they moved down his face to his gaping mouth. There was another snap and the man's jaw dislocated and breath escaped with a gurgle. The vines twisted around the remainder of his body and pulled him back. His bones snapped and a warm trail of blood slid down his body.

Hal adjusted his footing and sprinted towards the light at the end of the tunnel, back to the cave entrance.

He slowed, looking to his sides and the roots squirmed in rebellion from the light. Laying on the ground around him were bones, and he looked up to see bodies tangled into the walls.

He lunged towards the entrance and stopped, turning back towards the cave and the fog welcomed his presence as it clung to his body. There was no shelter, inside or out, and death surrounded everything here.

He had to move. He didn't know why or where he was going, but he couldn't stay.

Climbing the rock face adjacent to the cave's opening, he rose above the fog. The top was desolate. The ground beneath him was solid and he sat breathlessly, listening for anything at all. There was absolutely no sound and everything about this place seemed unnatural. No wind, no insects chirping. Everything was eerily still.

"Hello!" He yelled. "Is there anyone out there?"

He leaned back onto a rock and waited, listening to his surroundings. This place doesn't exist. It can't. He took in another deep breath. This is a hallucination. You're hurt. You're delusional. It will pass. Just rest. Just rest, he repeated in his mind.

The light through his eyelids faded to dark and his pulse calmed to a normal level.

"OK, I'm going to open my eyes, and when I do, I'm going to be alright," he chanted out loud, as if it'd somehow make it a reality.

His heart quickened. This couldn't be right. A dark cloud began to roll in from the distance and he looked around at the withering trees. Their branches began to stoop lower and lower. Their roots heaved up from the ground beneath and writhed through the hard, dry soil. He scurried backwards against the rock as they approached.

There was no choice, no time to think. He jumped to his feet and ran forward. Branches lashed out towards him, grabbing his arms and side, whipping his flesh as he darted through.

Looking back, he could see the cloud approaching even more quickly.

It was too close to react as he ran straight into a barrier. The large square-cut rock appeared so quickly out of the mist, he didn't have time to stop. His feet skidded on the ground and he stretched out his arms for impact. His hips made contact with it and the momentum sent him careening over the top. He landed on the sandy soil beneath,

187

which was much different than the previous. This was light sand, almost like a powder, and white in color.

He peeked his head above the barrier. The black cloud had stopped, just hovering in place a hundred feet outwards.

He stared for a minute, anticipating it to charge. This was crazy, but delusional or not, it was happening.

He placed his hand on the rock in front of him and began to stand, pausing as he looked at the stone. This was different. The rock had carvings on it. It was a straight edge and he scratched its surface, breaking small chunks with only his fingertips. Sandstone. What the hell was sandstone doing in a marshland?

Hal turned to look behind him at the very different terrain. The fog was light here, almost absent, and the air all together felt thin. His jaw dropped as he got a closer look at the formations around. These sandstone blocks were everywhere. Some were toppled over onto others, some stacked into larger formations and smaller ones were bricks, creating what looked like small houses. Whatever these stones were, the architecture was definitely man-made.

The sky was dim but he couldn't tell what direction the sunlight was coming from. In fact he couldn't actually pinpoint the location of the sun at all.

He walked inward towards the ruins. They were just that – ruins. Pillars were stacked on the ground, although most had fallen over, but several were still in an upright position. Where on earth was he?

The light yellow sandstone almost glowed. It gave off its own illumination, and as he pressed his palm to it, it actually felt warm. There were etchings on several of the walls, but they were hieroglyphics and he couldn't make anything of it. There was a small passageway through the center of the fallen blocks and he began towards it. The sandy ground was more like a powder, which billowed under his feet as he took each step.

He'd walked about two hundred feet from the main stone before the light began to fade. There was still visibility, but he was reaching the edge of the light area.

He stopped abruptly as his foot slid out from beneath him. He squandered backwards, kicking in reverse, as he looked back into the darkness. A large sink hole extended beyond his vision and there was no way to gauge its distance downward. The round hole extended from his sides at least a mile in each direction before its edges faded out of sight.

Hal slowly crawled to the edge and looked down into the darkness. It withered beneath him, as if sensing his presence, and attempting to swallow him. Roots clung to the walls and slowly crawled upwards, reaching for him. Hal jumped back and retreated, springing to his feet and taking several clumsy steps backward. He dodged towards the light again, running back to the sandstone formations.

He was blinded and shielded his face with his arms. Rays of light streamed through the sandstones, as if a giant spot light were now being shone directly at him, growing in intensity as he ran. He paused, pressing his hands over his eyes, but it refused to fade. He was blind, spinning with his arms outstretched for balance. It was a brief struggle and then there was silence again.

Chapter 23: The Bait

Hal sprung up into a sitting position. His body was drenched in sweat and his heart was racing. His chest ached and he lifted the shirt in the morning light. He stepped into the restroom and gazed into the mirror in disbelief at the new scars and bruises on his chest. They were in the same pattern as his flight harness used to be, but these were fresh. There's no way he could have just acquired these.

His hands were covered with a white powder, leaving a trail on his clothes as he pulled his shirt back down. Powder? His mind froze, recalling his nightmare. The bruises, the powder... How the hell was this possible?

The clock on the wall read 8:43 AM. He'd been out for almost eight hours, but he hadn't left the luxury suite in Howard's home.

He felt this unbearable need to wash the sandy residue off his body and jumped into the shower. The water was cold, but it felt good on the new wounds. Like before, when he was at A&H, he was somehow bringing these dreams with him into reality.

He stepped back out in front of the mirror. His naked body was still much thinner than he remembered himself, although he'd gained several pounds in the last few days. The bruises and marks on his body were a new addition to his side wound from before.

He began to dress as someone knocked on the door.

"Rise and shine, friend." Howard entered the room without warning and Hal walked out to greet him with only his bottom half covered.

"What the hell happened?" Howard approached, gazing down at his torn body.

Hal covered his side with one arm, not necessarily ashamed, but he didn't know how to answer the question. "These are from something else." He said and quickly pulled his damp shirt over his head.

"You're about my size. A little taller, but I'm sure there's something that will fit." Howard was partly trying to change the subject as he walked over to the closet doors, revealing a huge walk in area with a wardrobe most women would be envious of.

Hal walked in and sifted through some of his belongings. His own clothes were damp with sweat and God knew what else. A&H

had only given him one new set of clothes and it was a welcomed change to have so much selection suddenly.

Howard's collection ranged from the super casual boxer-pants and exercise shirts to full formal attire with bow ties. Hal grabbed something in between with a black T-shirt and denim pants, some new socks and, to his thankful surprise, a package of unopened underwear.

Howard still hovered in the doorway looking down at his battle scars.

"You're ripped up pretty bad. Those are claw marks."

Hal tightened his belt and tucked in the shirt before looking at Howard again, who was still somewhat in shock.

"Did they take the bait?" Hal asked, changing the subject. It wasn't that he didn't want to talk about it. It was that he didn't know quite how to explain it.

Howard tilted his head and his mind jumped back into business. "Not yet. We've had some random requests though and Akira is trying to determine if the source is Russian."

"Alright. Well, let's check on his progress." Hal walked passed him towards the doorway. He didn't want to dwell on his haunting nightmare, which, like before, left him catering to his injuries.

"Wait," Howard interrupted.

Hal paused and turned towards him.

"If this pans out..." He paused. "Claire is a good friend of mine. She paid the way for my Ruby to come here and I owe her my life. Akira wants the ARCA destroyed, just as I'm sure A&H probably does at this point. But if they for one second hurt Claire, you kill those men. You have my word that you will have a place here in this family." Howard looked down, ashamed he couldn't be the rescuer. He was a tough man, but he had his weaknesses.

"I want her back too." Hal held his head down, admitting it out loud for the first time, and Howard could appreciate his intentions.

Akira was standing with a cane over two men in front of computer screens who were using a satellite surveillance system to triangulate the transmissions. Several people had requested their help, all from foreign sources. Most were poorly masked and it was easy to eliminate them as suspects.

Ruby stood in the kitchen and approached Hal with a glass of juice. She wasn't dressed in her normal corset and lace and her hair was pinned back. Hal couldn't see her face before when it was covered in make up and hiding behind long bangs. Now, dressed in her pajamas and in the light, he could see why Howard had fallen for her. She was a pretty Japanese girl, only about five feet tall with a soft complexion and gentle eyes.

"Good morning Mr. Brent. Good to see you're well." She handed him the glass and sat on the couch, curling her legs up and wrapping her hands around her knees.

"Any progress?" Hal asked and all three men turned to face him.

"Not yet. We're still trying to pin point some new connections, but they're dynamic and keep changing." Akira was still optimistic, though.

Hal walked over to one of the couches that stretched along the room and winced as he sat down. Like before, his nightmares had left a wound that came through into his reality and Akira noticed as he tried to ignore the new pain.

"Bad dreams?" Akira asked.

He simply nodded and took a sip of his juice.

Akira limped over on his cane and adjusted his legs as he tried to sit next to him. "Let me see." He pointed at his chest and arm.

He lifted his shirt, revealing the fresh bruises of a flight harness.

"It's following you back here." Akira leaned in closer to look at the marks.

Hal didn't want to dwell on the issue. It was traumatizing enough and so far he'd been able to shrug it off as a nightmare, but the eerie feeling kept creeping up on him. The dreams were unlike anything he could fabricate even if he wanted to. They were more like flashbacks, reliving a memory that simply wouldn't disappear. It wasn't something he could escape.

"Your memory is clouded. It's being suppressed. When you let go, your mind and body are free to remember. These dreams of yours, they are a peek into that void." Akira spoke about the visions like he'd had personal experience with them.

"How do you know?" Hal didn't want to think about the actual events in his dreams, but he wanted to know why they kept recurring.

"When we are awake and conscious, our mind can block things out to protect us. When people are subjected to something traumatizing, it's a mechanism that can kick in and help us cope with the reality afterward." Akira paused and repositioned himself to become more comfortable. "Your plane crash and the events that followed are confusing. What you're remembering doesn't make sense, but you freely dwell on it while you're asleep when your brain is allowed to observe. This," he motioned everything around him. "This is what your brain accepts as reality. Your visions are what it remembers. It's like hypnosis. When you accept that these events happened, they will come to you more clearly."

Hal held his head down remembering the man in his dreams. He wasn't exactly a creative person and there was no way his mind could have concocted something so horrific.

"Tell me about the triangle." Hal's curiosity overruled his sense of reality. If there was any truth to it, and if there was any small chance that he'd been a part of it, he was willing to listen.

Akira reclined on the couch, uneasy about the subject he was so intrigued by the previous nights.

"The triangle is an unexplainable phenomenon. You've heard the myths. Ships and planes disappear. People who find themselves stuck in its wake, disoriented for minutes, maybe hours, return home to realize they're days behind. The cause for this disturbance is unknown, but we know it happens. We experience a similar phenomenon in southern Japan, although not as often. No one knows for sure what happens to those who don't return." He looked over at Hal with fascination. This is why they were so interested in him. They thought he was the missing part to a global, mythical puzzle.

Hal held back the urge to laugh. It seemed ridiculous, but he stopped and held his head down. A man disappearing for twenty-six years, then suddenly reappearing without aging a day. That was also ridiculous.

"So what happens if the Russians contact us?" Hal wanted to switch the subject.

"Well, a lot of it depends on whether or not we can trace the exact point of their signal. If we can, we have several planes that might be able to go the distance. If we can't we may have to send you to scout the area and locate their base. For research on the ARCA, they have to have a fairly large area to test it, so it should be visible from the sky." Akira explained.

"We know they were heading to Puerto Rico. Why can't we intercept them there?"

"They've long moved on from the territories. The hurricane has made it almost impossible to travel by sea now. Our best bet is to intercept them on their own soil. The Gora Kharan is a remote, frigid place, far from authorities. We have a much better chance taking them by surprise where they least expect it." Akira began to sit up as one of the men motioned for his attention.

"I think we have something, sir," the man announced. "We have an offer coming from Russia. It's being rerouted through their capital, but we can trace it. It's coming from the Gora Kharan prison."

"Excellent." Akira stood and waddled over to the man, leaning heavily on his cane. "How soon until we can be in the air?"

"In this weather..." The man checked his watch. "About a day, sir."

"The hurricane is passing. Mid afternoon I'd like to head back to our home. Along the way we can plan." Akira looked over to Hal. "We have five pilots still among us that can accompany you. One is a cargo chopper large enough to make the trip back with a large crew, but it's slow. It will be behind by several hours. Use that time wisely, and the exit route will be waiting afterward."

The hours couldn't have passed slower as Hal looked out the windows overlooking the ocean. The weather was calming and debris lined the shore with branches and grass that had been swept out and washed back up. Rain still fell, but the wind had died down and Howard's home was now dismally quiet.

Ruby sat on the couch, constantly checking her watch. Howard was focused on the television, still watching the reports of damage from the storm. There was mention of the attack on the Mirada hotel, which was now being described as a failure with their furnace on the top levels. Seven people had died and twenty were injured. The Yotogi and A&H's names were surprisingly left out of the report, which was no doubt Brack's doing through bribery.

Akira was patient and he sat Indian-style on the sofa with his eyes closed. He'd remained this way for the past two hours and everyone was uncomfortably silent because of it. He was channeling some sort of Chi through meditation, and despite his mild intentions, Howard was annoyed by it. Akira wasn't asleep, but every time someone moved or made a noise his eyes would open and frown in disapproval. The Yotogi had taken over his own home. Albeit they were friendly, they showed great disapproval for his lifestyle and silently protested him.

Hal felt comfortable around Howard and was also annoyed by the overtaking. They were supposed to be resting. Akira may have made himself comfortable, but he was putting everyone else on edge.

A man walked in and bowed his head as everyone turned their attention. "Sir, the jet is ready."

Howard sighed with relief that the men would be leaving. He grabbed a bag from behind the counter and approach Hal. "Here. Just in case."

He followed the men out and ducked his head down, shielding his face from the light rain that was still sprinkling. Several men entered the four luxury cars that were lined up along the circular driveway and Hal accompanied Akira in the limo at the rear of the line.

Akira again assumed his meditation, silently ignoring the passengers. There wasn't much to say anyway, and Hal watched out the tinted windows as they passed through the city he once remembered, quietly observing the differences twenty-six years had made.

The jet was a privately owned, medium-sized plane that seated forty or so and Hal made himself comfortable in solitude as the remaining members boarded. They were all quiet, and the large seats put some distance between them.

It was the first time he'd been in the air since his crash and he was thankful to be alone with his thoughts. He recalled what Akira had said about the Bermuda Triangle and somehow it still bothered him. It was a myth, a legend used to scare and fascinate people. Hal was an exceptional pilot and a part of him refused to believe he would get caught up in it. He wasn't lost. He'd made the route dozens of times and he could have flown it with his eyes closed. Being disoriented over the ocean was something you adapted to. Getting lost was something that an inexperienced or stupid pilot did, and he didn't feel comfortable with Akira questioning his record. It just wasn't the case.

He closed his eyes and thought back to that day. The weather was beautiful and clear. There was little turbulence and the ocean was quiet beneath him. Bimini was a short distance in the air, and you could see the ocean floor in the shallow waters.

They were flying through some low clouds when they were suddenly engulfed in a thick fog. His instruments went off their circuits and there was zero visibility. They weren't losing altitude, but it was disorienting without any visuals. They just needed to fly straight through the pass and they'd be home free.

But it didn't end. The further they went, the thicker the fog became. There were flashes of light and they made spider-crack arks as they touched the glass. His students were starting to feel uneasy as Hal tried to reassure them everything was fine. But it wasn't and he couldn't hide it anymore. They were only a few miles from the shore and at their rate of travel, they would soon be on top of their landing zone.

Hal's eyes sprung open. He didn't want to recall the rest. It was a long time ago, but to him, it seemed like only a few days. He didn't have an answer for what happened and his heart was heavy with guilt as he remembered the young men that were lost under his watch. He'd give anything to go back to that day.

The flight was going to be long and he needed something to occupy his time. Dwelling on the past only lengthened the struggle with patience.

The bag that Howard had provided sat on the adjacent seat and he unzipped it. A small bag containing his arm band was on top and he pulled it out. A&H would still be monitoring him to some degree, and in the Yotogi's presence it wouldn't be welcomed, but he didn't care. As much as he disliked Brack, he still had a right to know. He pulled the sleeve over his left arm and gripped it. It was like secondary skin and felt so natural. The circuits illuminated and gave his location, time, vitals, etc. Amazing.

The nice thing about owning a private jet was the lack of security, which would have flipped backwards as he peered into the bag. A small briefcase sat inside, and contained an assembly of parts that could be pieced together into anything from a sniper rifle to a silenced pistol. Other belongings such as black market grenades and canisters lined the sides. Hal found it somewhat humorous that these were *normal* for Howard's travel attire. Out of everyone he'd dealt with throughout the past few days, Howard was the most prepared. It may have been overkill, but considering everyone else simply equipped him with a stun gun and good intentions, he welcomed overkill.

He zipped the bag and checked his watch, setting the time for 4 AM, which was the estimated time they'd be landing in Japan.

He closed his eyes as the plane elevated above the clouds. Even though the day had been restful, he was still exhausted.

Chapter 24: Home Base

He was startled when his alarm went off, completely unaware of how much time had passed. The windows were dark in the early morning and he gazed around at many of the Yotogi who were still asleep during the flight. Leaning over towards the window he could see open land sprawling below them. He didn't recognize their location, but it was far from any major city. The plane circled around before bouncing on the runway, making a rough landing and startling the passengers. Hal smiled to himself, finding amusement in their inconvenience. Having flown for years, rough landings were his specialty, and these men were clearly distressed by it.

The plane stopped and he gathered his gear before heading towards the stair ramp that led onto an empty landing strip. There were several other planes and two helicopters on the strip, but it was no airport. One building stood out at the edge of the field. It was a traditional Japanese temple, built on the shore overlooking the ocean. It was beautiful. The Yotogi had great taste in architecture and it was secluded on the shore, perched up on the rocky hillside before extending down to the waters below.

The men finished exiting the plane and started towards the complex, stretching and complaining as they walked. Hal couldn't understand their language, but their expressions gave the hint of discomfort. They were tree hugging, meditating, peace lovers, which wasn't a bad thing, but they were easily agitated.

"Hal Brent." Akira's voice stood out among the noise as he called him to the side.

He approached and stood next to the three other men.

"Two of our pilots have declined this mission. We only have two men who will accompany you in. Jomei will stay behind until you've reached the base and will plan for your extraction. Your planes have been equipped with two extra fueling canisters, which will then be used for the trip back." Akira nodded towards Jomei, who acknowledged his role and then handed each a set of keys.

Keys. That was old fashioned, then he looked at the planes they'd be flying. They weren't exactly modern and Hal guessed they may have even existed in his time.

His key chain had an image of a black falcon on it with a Japanese number, which he couldn't read, but he started down the strip and instantly saw where it belonged. It was a small four-man shuttle plane manufactured in 2001-2003, he guessed. At least he'd be familiar with its controls.

The hatch popped open and the metal rack of stairs clanked down. It was missing two of the footholds and he jumped the gap, pulling himself upwards into the plane.

"What a piece of junk," he quietly muttered to himself. He was about to fly to Russia in this thing? A plane is only as good as the pilot, he reminded himself, and continued to pull in his bag of equipment.

He closed the door and looked around as the light bulbs swayed back and forth on a slim rail of wire.

"This gets even better."

There were two large metal barrels in the back that smelled of fuel.

He sat down in the pilot's seat and pulled up his sleeve to access his wrist band. There was a communications icon and he tapped it.

"Call Brack." A small screen came up with Brack's unpleasant face before a message came up stating he was unavailable. He touched the icon for messages and suddenly saw his own face on the screen. This was the current age of video voice mail, he guessed.

"Brack, this is Brent. The Yotogi have taken me to Japan and we're going to attempt flying into a Russian prison in the Gora Kharan mountains. We're going to try to locate the ARCA device there. They believe Claire was taken to modify the device for this area. I don't know half of what Akira's been talking about, but the device doesn't work here, so there's still time to disable it. It's about 4:32 AM here and we're leaving now. I'm not sure if I'm even doing this right, but if you get this message, well, I just thought you should know. I'll bring her back." He hit the send button and a confirmation message came up stating it was in the virtual mailbox somewhere.

He slid his sleeve back down and turned the key. The old girl's engine purred and he closed his eyes, remembering the feel and control at his finger tips.

The readings on his dashboard were in Japanese, but there was no need for labeling.

In front of him were the other pilots and they saluted him as they began to stroll forward down the runway and take off. He followed, last in line.

It felt good to be in the air and he looked below at the beautiful ocean as it rocked beneath him.

It was about two hours of travel before land appeared in the distance and the sun was beginning to rise behind them. They were taking the long route, heading south over the land before proceeding north as to not attract any attention.

The land quickly changed as they headed inward. It was the warmer season now, but the farther north they went the colder it became. Small towns scattered the outskirts of the main cities and they flew to a higher elevation above the clouds.

The navigation on the craft was foreign and he depended more on his wrist gear than the controls. He was following the two other craft in front for the long flight and he tried to make himself comfortable on the old tattered seats.

It felt good to be flying again and even though the Yotogi weren't exactly his friends, he wasn't being held as a hostage or used as some sort of leverage against his enemies. He'd chosen to do this, and they had provided him with all the means to make a clean getaway, yet they trusted him not to.

Akira's words still bothered him. He wasn't a superstitious man and didn't believe in supernatural events like the Bermuda Triangle, but he couldn't deny the feeling that there was some truth to it.

There was no explanation for his disappearance, and he'd asked himself a million times why or what was driving him into doing any of this. It started out as a frantic chase for his life; a fight for survival. Claire had opened up to him from day one, and in a world he no longer belonged in, he didn't owe it to any long lost family members, friends, or even co-workers. But he owed it to her and to his fellow pilots to push onward. There was no benefit in giving up now, however bleak the situation grew.

His wrist beeped and he pulled his sleeve up to see Brack's ugly mug appear in a small window.

"Brent here."

"What's your status?" It was Troy who responded.

He dreaded the sound of his voice. He pitied the man, but he still couldn't help this overwhelming hatred either. "We're about an hour south of Gora mountain. The Yotogi believe that's where the Russians are taking the ARCA."

"You're working with the Yotogi?" Troy's first concern was the Yotogi... of course. "They're trying to steal our research!" His voice was shaking with anger.

"They're not your enemy, Troy. They know more than you think, but they're not the ones you should be focused on right now," he snapped back.

There was a pause of frustration on his end. "Mr. Brent, you have no idea who you're dealing with here. They're terrorists."

"No, they don't like you, but they're not the ones with a weapon of potential mass destruction." Hal was sarcastic in his response. He wasn't exactly friends with the Yotogi, nor did they get along, but they weren't the ones who blew up a building or planned a hijacking.

Brack came onto the line, but he could still hear Troy grumbling with anger in the background.

"Brent, think carefully about what you're attempting. You're invading foreign soil and you have no right to be interfering with our research."

"You want me to turn back?"

"No, but you need to be aware." There was a long pause, presumably due to his lack of planning, again.

"I'm not under any orders, and you said it yourself. I'm a dead man. I have no ties or connections that will implement A&H. The Yotogi are onto something. They know more about the ARCA than you realize. The Russians have been selling it on the black market for who knows how long, but it doesn't work!" Hal shouted back at his wrist, knowing both were listening.

"Why are you doing this?" Brack was mild. He had to have known the ARCA wasn't functional.

Hal tipped his head down. He himself wasn't entirely sure.

"I need to know if there's a connection between the ARCA and my disappearance. Listen, I don't have time to argue with you. Just know I'm not trying to sabotage anything. If the Yotogi have any information about..." Hal paused, feeling the guilt as he said it, "about my men, then I need to know. I owe Claire, too."

"I understand your grief, Brent. I do, but we still don't know what the Yotogi's intentions are. If you're able to pull this plan through, please, just be careful with it. In the wrong hands it could be devastating. You're not under orders, not that they'd matter, but I am still encouraging you to resume where we left off on the freighter if it's possible." Brack was understanding and saw the grand scheme of things more than Troy did. "Keep me informed."

"Can do." Hal hit the end button on his wrist and took a deep breath in relief to be off the communications line with him.

The clouds became thick and snow fell beneath them. The limited sight made it difficult to follow the men in front. The plane shifted side to side in the turbulence, and he again referred to his arm band to read its gauges. They were flying low, but in the dense clouds there was no visual of the ground.

A man yelled over the old style radio, but he couldn't understand.

He pulled up on the controls. The other pilots weren't in sight but his instincts told him they were too low.

He gripped the controls hard. This was bad. They were almost to their destination at the ice shelf and snow stuck to the windshield as the temperature plummeted.

From somewhere behind him he heard a loud explosion. A man came over the radio repeating something frantically, but he was no longer in sight.

"We're too low!" Hal yelled, not knowing if he would hear him. "Up, go up."

The man was still frantically shouting, but there was no response from the other pilot. Shit.

Hal saw it all too late as the tree tops quickly came into view. He pulled on the stick, but the hull squealed as the underside scraped, and the plane quickly jerked to the left as a wing hit a tree side.

Hal's harness tore into his side as the inertia pulled him. He panicked and yanked harder on the stick, but it only flung him farther sideways.

The engine sputtered and gave out, and just as quickly, the plane tossed over onto its side and slammed into several more trees. Hal held his breath. He'd never actually been in a plane crash and with adrenaline surging through his veins he instinctively gripped the steering column, bracing for impact.

The realization of what was happening went by in slow motion. He ducked as the windshield shattered and glass rained inward. The clanking sounds of the fuel canisters behind him hit the ceiling and then the floor as it rolled. He violently flung from side to side, his harness gripping into him with every turn and then a thundering hit.

Hal opened his eyes as the world stood upside down. He was still held in by the pilot's harness. The plane had landed on its roof, and he looked out of the empty frame that no longer contained a windshield. Snow blew in with a gust and stung his face and hands.

The clamp on his belt let loose as he hit the release and he quickly shifted his arms above his head to catch his fall, then curling onto his back. Broken glass shifted beneath him as he wiggled out the front and into the snow.

"This is Brent, can anyone read me?" He spoke to his arm band, but it was silent. "I repeat, this is Hal Brent. Can anyone read me?"

He crawled on his knees and reached into the plane, fumbling around for the radio. "May day, may day, my plane is down. Can anyone read me?"

He looked again to his wrist band, which was now showing that he was about three miles east of the ice shelf where they were supposed to land. If the other pilots had made it, they should be there, but the fuel canisters were far too heavy to haul that distance.

He sighed and looked back at the wrecked plane. The left wing was split in half and the propeller on the front was missing a fin.

The mountainside he'd landed on was covered in snow. He was almost at its peak and the thin trees didn't do much in the way of slowing the heavy winds.

He tightly pulled his jacket and tucked his hands under his arms. West. He had to go west to the ice shelf.

He reached into the wrecked plane and found his bag that Howard had given him before setting out.

It was cold and Hal quickly found himself wondering why the hell he didn't plan for this. Miami was hot when they'd taken off and it had entirely slipped his mind. His feet were numb as he trotted down the mountainside, occasionally checking his wrist band to make sure he was on track.

He was about two miles out when a branch snapped and he spun around. The gusts of wind blew passed his ears, making it difficult to sense direction.

There it was again. He grabbed the .357 from his shoulder harness and spun.

"Who's there?"

The sting was brief and he tried to fight it as he turned to his side, swinging his gun and firing one careless shot. He'd been hit, but he realized it too late as two men shuffled closer in the snow. The tranquilizer's effect was almost instant, completely paralyzing his senses in a matter of seconds.

Chapter 25: A Rude Awakening

The smell of salt stung his nerves and he jerked his head up. A man stood before him with a small packet dangling in front of his nose. He flinched, but his arms were restrained behind him, sitting on a cold metal chair with bare feet on the broken concrete below him.

"Who sent you?"

He was still disoriented and the room spun as he looked from side to side. He wasn't alone.

The man swung his arm, slapping Hal back to his direction. "Who sent you!"

"I'm an escort. I was hired to fly a man here, no questions asked. I don't know what you're talking about." Hal knew they were expecting a physicist.

The man seemed to back off to his surprise. "Where is he?"

Hal shook his head. "I don't know. I crashed. He must have bailed before we hit."

"Tell me, then. Why does an escort carry such weapons?" He dangled the bag of his belongings in front of him. On the table behind him, Hal could see his tranquilizer gun and .357 revolver.

"It was a precaution." He looked up at the man. One eye was swollen and blurred his vision.

"I don't believe you," he said and straightened his jacket before walking out with his bodyguards. "Leave them."

Two men gathered the weapons from the table and piled them into the bag before following and shutting metal gate. He was in some sort of prison with brick walls and small barred windows. The concrete floor crumbled under his feet. The broken window let in a heavy draft and Hal sat tied to the chair with nothing more than a T-shirt and pants. His boots and socks had been taken from him and his feet were pale from the cold's exposure. He wiggled his toes. They weren't frost bitten, yet.

There was a man chained to the wall, his arms behind his back. He squinted to see better and shook his head.

"Ortiz." Hal whispered.

He lifted his head in recognition. "Hal?"

There was almost joy as he responded.

"Are you OK?"

"I took a hit to the leg. Smithers is..." He trailed off, remorsefully. "They got you too?"

"Not exactly. I made it back to A&H." He paused as a guard tapped the bars.

"No talking." His English was bad, but understandable.

Both men acknowledged him and turned away, waiting for him to resume his patrol. He stood for a few seconds, trying to intimidate his prisoners as he tapped a baton against the bars.

Hal looked over at Ortiz who still had his head down. The guard lost interest and started back down the hallway. He could hear other people farther down the hall. Some were crying, others moaning or whispering to one another. Just how many people were being held captive here?

"Is A&H sending reinforcements?" Ortiz perked up again.

Hal shook his head. "No, I don't think so. I came in here with two other pilots, but I don't think they made it. The Yotogi are the ones planning this."

"The Yotogi? Why?" Ortiz had learned that the Yotogi weren't the ones interested in the ARCA, so why pursue it?

"It's a long story. I lost radio contact with them, but we were supposed to mark the territory for them to send back up. I don't know whether or not those plans still stand."

He wiggled his hands behind his back. They were tied loosely to the frame of the chair back and allowed him to move around a little bit, but the rope was tight against his wrists. He moved his arms up and down against the rails, sliding the rope on the edges, but it was too smooth to cut through.

"How long was I out?"

"I don't know. Two, maybe three hours." Ortiz shuffled around, trying to sit Indian style with shackles around his ankles. His feet were bare and cold as he tried to tuck them underneath his legs. "They came in about fifteen minutes ago. You were mumbling, but not making a whole lot of sense. I recognized when you muttered the word ARCA, and it peaked their interest."

"Shit," he whispered under his breath. So much for his cover.

"So..." Ortiz was confused and his hopes were beginning to fade. "How long do you think the Yotogi will take?"

"I don't know. We were supposed to mark the spot a few hours ago. By now they must realize something has gone wrong. If they're still going to attempt making the trip, it should be an hour, maybe two." Hal was shivering uncontrollably. It was below freezing and he had no way to curl up and preserve his body heat. His feet were beginning to go numb and he clenched his fists to try to bring some warm blood down his arms. The breeze coming in through the window was relentless.

"Did you see Claire?" Hal asked.

"No. Why?"

Hal held his head down. It pained him to think about that night as he helplessly watched her fall to her knees inches away from their escape. She fought the tranquilizer, but like so many targets he'd taken down the same way, the effect was too strong and quick.

"The ARCA?" Ortiz continued to ask.

Hal shook his head. "Almost. We were twenty feet from the life raft and they took her. She's alive, I think, unless they changed their minds." He looked over at Ortiz who was confused. "She was stunned. I don't know why they chose to spare her, but the Yotogi believe they needed her all along. She's the only one capable of fixing the ARCA."

Ortiz's eyebrows lifted. It made sense. He didn't know anything about the success or failure of the operation. All he knew was that most of his men retreated, which was the only option, but he and Smithers had fallen too far behind.

"So Claire is here?"

Hal nodded. "I think so."

Ortiz chuckled. "Well, good luck to them."

Hal chuckled too, remembering as she walked down the dock with gear strapped to her back. Her expression burning with vengeance. She was down right scary. She wouldn't volunteer peacefully under any circumstances. Hal almost felt sorry for whoever was around when she woke up.

They both quieted and held their heads down as footsteps trumped closer. Hal lifted his head and met his gaze. He tried to hide his anger, appearing to be a victim; just a pilot escort, dazed and confused. For all the man knew, that's what he was.

The man huffed and smiled with an evil grin as he looked down at him, thumping his baton in one hand.

What a stupid brute, Hal thought to himself and pretended to wince. The man responded with a brief chuckle. Yep, just a stupid, dumb, tall, and intimidating brute. Hal was no man of sizable comparison, but he knew that wasn't what mattered. He'd been in hand to hand combat before and had years of training. Everyone had their weaknesses.

Hal studied the man as he stood. His neck was exposed, he had nothing to guard his head and he envisioned a good swing to the throat. He'd be down on the ground gasping for air before he knew what hit him.

There was a distant thud that shook the ground and the guard spun in its direction before clumsily running down the hall.

Hal looked over at Ortiz who was hopeful. He tried to lean forward and get a glimpse, but the chains held him to the wall.

There was noise everywhere now. People in the nearby cells were shuffling around. Some of them were unchained and looking down the hallway, yelling to one another. Most of them were speaking Russian, but Hal didn't understand the language. Something was happening and Hal sat at full attention listening to the ruckus.

In the distance he heard the distinct pop of gun fire. Another boom sounded from the other end of the hallway. Someone was coming in with force.

There was a scratching sound on the outside wall and Ortiz stood to look out the small window. His chains pulled him down, but he stood tall enough to get a glimpse. Startled, he fell back to the ground as a man's face appeared before them, gripping the barred windows. Hal didn't know him personally, but his attire was all too recognizable. He wore a mask covering the lower portion of his face and his hair was pulled back into a tight ponytail. The Yotogi were making their entrance.

He looked at Hal in recognition and nodded. "Get back."

He disappeared from the window and fastened a small explosive to the brick wall, starting the countdown for ten seconds. He hoisted himself back down the building side as the beep continued in quicker intervals.

The deafening blast blew bricks and debris inwards, creating a two foot hole in the wall. It blew Ortiz's chains out of the cement and he rolled onto his belly as the force blew him over.

Hal's chair tipped to the side and the deafening shock muted his hearing.

With the remaining bricks loosened, the man outside climbed back into position and kicked a larger hole in the wall. He slid in through the gap and pulled a knife from his left boot and began to cut his way through the rope restraining his hands.

Hal quickly loosened his shoulders as it gave and propped up on his side as the man did the same to Hal's ankle restraints.

The frigid wind rushed in through the wide gap. Hal had been released and the man ran to Ortiz's side.

"Push your hands back." He yelled at Ortiz, knowing he also was temporarily deaf from the blast. He obeyed and the man pulled a small blow torch from his backpack.

The metal chains that bound Ortiz were heavy and it took a full minute before the torch burned through one of the latches. With his hands free, he held them out to grab the torch and proceed with his own foot shackles.

The man stood to face Hal and he pulled the large sack off his back. "For you."

He opened the sack as its contents burst out of the zippers. A large, white down coat puffed out and he quickly pulled it tightly around his arms. Hal reached into the bottom of the sack and pulled out a pair of wooly, padded boots.

The metal snapped on Ortiz's last chain and he sprung up, stretching his back and shoulders, leaning on his good leg. He was still badly injured, but not incapable of standing.

"Stand to the back." The man pointed towards the far wall and they obeyed.

He turned his back to them and molded some sort of putty around the door at its weakest point. Attached was a wire that would allow him to detonate. He approached them both and held out his arms to embrace them, pulling them to the ground and covering.

He motioned for everyone to cover their ears as he pushed the trigger switch. It was quiet compared to the first explosion and with a quick pop the putty burst the metal lock into pieces.

Hal stood and parted from the group. The man still sat with Ortiz, looking at his leg and rigorously rubbing his arms and shoulders as he tried to generate some body heat.

Hal stopped in his tracks as the patrol brute intercepted his exit. He was quick on his feet, unlike the brute, and swung his new steel-toed boot directly into the man's groin.

The man heaved and fell to his knees. Hal was swift and kicked the baton from his hand, catching it as it flew from his grip. He swung the club back, extending the weapon, and then lashed it like a golf club. It curved and hit the man's throat dead-center. The force of it collapsed his airway and sent him flying on his back. He gasped for breath and gripped his throat as Hal stood over him. He pulled his arm back and then halted. He had so much rage at that moment building up, but he held back. Killing a man was a hard thing to do, especially with your hands. One good swing to the temple and that would be it, but Hal wasn't like these men. Maybe it was his weakness, but he just couldn't do it.

"I'm going to need your boots and coat," he spoke calmly.

The man didn't understand. Hal reached down and yanked on his collar. "Your boots and your coat."

He was gasping for air and his face burned red as he struggled. Hal pulled harder on the jacket, sitting him in an upright position, but it was no use. He continued to wheeze and shake on the ground.

Hal loosened his grip and let him gently fall to the floor. Ortiz would freeze to death before he could make it to the escape helicopter. He began to tug on the man's collar and pulled the zipper down his chest. Shifting his weight, he pulled the man's shoulders off the concrete floor and wiggled his arms out one by one before continuing to his boots.

The Russian was a good four or five inches taller and significantly heavier than Ortiz, but the size of his clothing meant more protection for him. The man's breathing had become relaxed but he still wheezed as he inhaled. He'd live, but he wouldn't dare attempt the threats he'd made before.

Hal pulled off the last boot and took them to Ortiz. He lifted his foot and gently tried to pull the boot over without moving his wounded leg. Ortiz flinched, but it couldn't be avoided.

The Japanese man still stood beside them and helped pull Ortiz to his feet, swinging his arm around his neck and carrying him towards the exit.

"Take the stairs four flights down. You will come to a passageway that leads into a new building. Claire is being held there. Our men will provide back up, but we are not many. Get what we came for." The Japanese man nodded his head in the direction of the stairwell door about eighty feet down the hallway.

"I'll meet you at the ice shelf." Hal looked in the direction of the doorway before pausing and letting the two continue outward. There was one last thing he needed to do.

As Ortiz and their rescuer hobbled down towards the exit, Hal crouched down beside the Russian man. He was breathing normally now, but the cold air and struggle had left him drained. He lay still, watching intently as Hal began to rummage through his pockets.

"Keys." He wasn't asking for them.

Hal sighed and continued to rummage through his pockets. A leather vest wrapped around his chest to his back. Hal pushed with all his force to move him onto his side, and although he didn't struggle, pushing the massive man's weight was a task in itself.

He smiled as his eyes fell upon something familiar strapped to the backside of the vest; his .357 revolver. It may have only contained a few shots, but if he had to, he would make every one of them count.

The man's belt loop jingled and Hal grabbed what he was searching for. He pulled the loop and with a hard tug it snapped the denim material that bound to his pants.

The key ring contained four large, old keys. They looked like they belonged in the 1800's with a long round shaft and a hook at the end. He hadn't put much thought into it as he gazed around at the long prison corridor, but this place must have been at least two centuries old.

The hallway was filled with noise as the prisoners reached out of their cells and begged for Hal's attention. The language was entirely different, but the question was all the same.

He approached the closest cell just across from his own and began trying each key. The second attempt was successful and the door clanked open to the side. The two men inside were gaunt, cold and malnourished as they hobbled out the exit. They looked to him in gratitude, and also sad bewilderment. Who knew how long they'd been here, and where they'd go now.

Hal approached the next cell and began to unlock the door as he looked inward. An elderly man sat with his back to the wall and his head hung low. Who the hell were these people that the Russians considered criminals? They were all worn, old and useless. Not a single one of them looked like a threat. What the hell types of crime could these men have committed? The thought burned in his mind and a hatred grew for their captors.

He swung the door and left it open before approaching the next. He had to hurry. They were already well aware of a break-in and on guard, but he couldn't just leave.

"I can help." A voice called from behind him and to the right.

Hal turned his attention towards the man and ran towards his cell. "You speak English?"

"Yes. Little." He pointed towards the keys in his hands. "Give to me. I open."

The man behind the bars looked fairly healthy in comparison to the others, and considerably well dressed. He unlatched the door and the man exited.

"My name is Bernard." He extended his hand to shake Hal's. "Thank you, sir. I help."

Hal smiled at the man's eagerness to pay back the favor. He didn't know how to respond to him, or whether or not he'd even understand. He placed the keys in his hand as he shook it, and Bernard vigorously nodded in acknowledgment before waddling over to the nearest cell.

This was good. The situation here was taken care of. It didn't take Hal more than a crash landing to find himself beaten into a prison cell, and most of the men were weathered, old and frail. They were no harm to anyone, and at the very least he'd given them a chance to stretch outside of their chains.

He cautiously opened the door at the end of the room, prepared for someone to greet him at gun point, but it was empty and quiet.

The spiraling staircase extended downward eight levels and the bottom hid in the darkness. There was no electricity here and the only light came from above where a giant hole in the ceiling shined in.

He counted each floor as he descended four stories and leaned his back against the wall just outside the door. A small window was inlaid in the frame, letting light in and he looked down a long modern hallway. The arch of the ceiling was glass, supported by metal beams. This must have been the passageway to the other building. Its architecture was unmistakably different from the building he currently stood in.

He waited a minute, looking through the small window for any movement. In the distance he could hear a few shots of gunfire. The Yotogi were a small group, or at least he thought, but there was commotion not too far away. The guards were distracted from where he stood and their attention was currently on the intruders.

He checked his weapon. The metal was cold on his hands and without gloves in this temperature, it clung painfully to his skin.

The door handle was unlocked as he pulled it inward. A warm gust of air came at him from the heated room as he entered.

Walking down the hallway, he glanced out of the huge arched windows that covered the stretch. It was a beautiful view looking down the mountainside that the buildings were perched on. Directly in front of him was another large complex with a much more modern build. Its frame was built out of concrete, supported by steel beams.

He peeked into the nearby door that led into the complex and saw a large room lined with computer screens and what looked like an older server rack from his time. They definitely weren't as advanced as A&H, but their ability and man power was much more aggressive.

The room was well lit, but vacant from his viewpoint and the door was unlocked. There were no palm or vision scanners to verify a person's identity before entry, and their security was definitely lacking. But then again, the base was far outside of anyone's typical reach and those who dared to even venture into their territory were immediately spotted and apprehended.

Inside the confined walls of the complex the outside gun fire was almost mute. He could hear the hum of fans cooling the computer equipment, but all else remained quiet. The room had three levels, starting at a staircase that led to the above floors. He approached it and ducked below the wall just before the next level.

Peering his head above, he held his breath at the disturbing sight. The bodies of two men floated in large containers of murky fluid. Tubes were inserted in their chest and arms as if dangling from the wires. Their skin was a pale blue, but their bodies every so often twitched, still reacting to some sort of stimulation. What the hell sort of experiments were these people doing here?

Hal was dazed and he slowly approached one of the chambers. He pressed his hand against the glass and squinted closer at the subject. His veins were black from the injections being fed into his body.

His eyes opened and Hal jumped backward, startled, dropping his revolver on the ground with a loud clank. He was alive!

The man twitched and his eyes begged for Hal's help. A mask over his mouth fed him oxygen, but his eyes screamed in terror that couldn't be expressed.

Hal fumbled back. The man in the container twitched uncontrollably. He began grabbing the tubes in his chest and pulling. Panic and pain flashed on his face the more he moved.

"NO!" Hal unconsciously screamed at the man as he watched. He let go of any consideration for being quiet. "Don't move!"

The man continued to struggle, pulling at the tubes in his chest. The look of anguish spread across his face as one detached. Draining from its end came a black fluid that swirled in the container, turning the murky blue fluid into a hazy gray. Hal pressed his palms on the glass and peered inward, but it clouded quickly into a solid, hiding the occupant.

The swirling slowed and the liquid started to congeal as the mixture turned into a thick paste and the man within fell still.

A deep feeling of guilt set in as Hal turned his back from the scene. The Russians were doing much more than experiments with weapons here, and from the looks of it they were dabbling in everything from bio-weaponry to reanimation. He looked at the equipment that surrounded him. None of it was familiar to him and the language on the various consoles was all Russian. There was no way to disable the machines that injected the subjects in the tubes, much less release him from his chamber.

A door opened above him on the next level. Hal sprinted for cover behind a solid metal desk a few feet away, but he was clumsy and his new boots were loud.

The man above him was alerted and yelled in his direction. There were several other men that he could hear responding from various directions. Footsteps approached quickly and Hal could hear them running towards his location. He gripped his revolver firmly and took a deep breath in as he tried to hold back his panic. They were surrounding him.

Hal counted four different voices as they spoke back and forth. He didn't understand what was being said, but they were careless with their approach. Two were grouped together, coming in from his side. Another was still in the distance in front and he could see the fourth approach from his other side.

He knew the .357 would be loud, and it would have to be quick. He propped his arm up on his knee and crouched further under the desk. His aim was sharp and the jerk of the pistol was a bit more than he remembered as the first shot struck the first man to his side. The force of the bullet grabbed the side of his chest and spun him off his feet.

Hal spun on the balls of his feet and changed his target. His aim was quick, almost instinctual, as he squeezed. He braced his wrist with his other hand and he fired, jerking his hand back with a loud bang. The man flung backwards in the air and landed on his back. A third shot released before the man next to him even had a chance to react. He flew back with force as it impacted his chest, pushing him into the table directly behind.

A panicked yell from behind the desk pin pointed the fourth man. Hal was covered by the desk, but the noise throughout the room was enough to alert the whole base.

The man remained on the above level just beyond the desk. Hal estimated he was about forty, maybe fifty feet in front of him, where he remained as he called out in a panic towards his comrades that lay lifeless on the ground.

Hal wasn't about to give him much time to call for back up, and he raised his head just above the desk top, swinging his arms onto its surface and squeezing. It took him less than a second for his vision to set on the man's chest. He breathed in quickly and pulled. The ring of the last shot echoed through his ears as the room suddenly grew quiet.

Hal waited. He crouched below the desk with his head just above the surface and gazed around at the three entrances that led into the room. They remained still and he let out a sigh of relief, but remained behind the safety of his cover.

A minute passed and his heart rate declined. He checked his pistol, which now only had two shots remaining. Cautiously, he approached the man on the left side. He was motionless, but Hal shoved him with his foot just in case. There was no movement, and he knelt down to search for ammunition.

The men were well armed and carried assault rifles. Hal pulled on the strap that held the gun to his chest and rummaged through his pockets. The man also had a concealed pistol under his jacket, along with a long hunting knife. Hal pulled the vest off his chest and equipped it on himself.

He approached the other two men who were close by and pocketed the ammunition clips for their assault rifles. These men were armed to the teeth, but they were still terrible in combat. They didn't so much as fire a single shot. Perhaps being out here in the wilderness and away from threats for such a long period of time had dulled their skills. They were intimidating, but stupid and slow.

The shock of the situation was beginning to wear off, and he remembered the objectives that the Yotogi had given him. He glanced back at the chamber tube where the man still remained in the silent gel.

"I'll make sure these men will never be able do this to anyone else." He knew the man in the chamber couldn't hear him, but having witnessed the inhumane, barbaric treatment, his pursuit for justice was only growing stronger.

Up the stair case Hal nudged the fourth man with his foot. He remained motionless and Hal cautiously tip toed over his body, avoiding the blood that now seeped from underneath.

He holstered his .357 and exchanged it for a .45 he stole off one of the guards. One of the Russian men wore a fur hat, which served as no protection but Hal took it anyway and held his head low. At the very least he wouldn't stand out as an intruder.

The door was open and he peeked around the corners. A long hallway extended to his right with several doorways. The complex was actually built into the mountainside and was much larger than it appeared from the windows. It was a maze and although the doorways had signs above them indicating their purpose, it was all Russian gibberish to him.

Even in the empty hallway he tried to act normal. If anyone looked out, he would appear to be one of them, just pacing through the patrol routes.

Each door had a small window and he gazed through several of them before passing one of interest. It looked like some sort of interrogation room with a long metal table. Several items were spread out, including his belongings. Unlocked, like the rest of the doors, he quietly pushed it open and waited for any sounds.

Shouting came through a hand-held radio that had been left on the coat hanger. Someone angrily screamed orders, fading in and out with static, but no one made any motion to grab it within the room.

He tip toed over to the table and grabbed the sack. Still silent, he swung it over his shoulder and quickly backtracked out the door.

Inside he found what he was looking for. His tranquilizer gun was still loaded, along with his arm band and several other items of destruction. He quickly equipped the band and wrapped the strap around his shoulder.

"Try to remain calm. Do nothing suspicious," he told himself.

His hand firmly clung to his tranquiler pistol. It was just as effective as the other pistols, but much quieter, as he found from previous experience.

Each room he passed appeared to be empty and the noise faded to the south as he proceeded. A set of double doors ended the hallway and he peered through the windows.

His heart sank with relief. Claire stood at the far end of the room, her back turned as she faced a computer console. Two men stood at the corners of each side, both holding their assault rifles firmly against their chests.

Out of all the open doors in the complex, he was frustrated to find this one locked.

"Oh come on," he whispered to himself.

217

He looked around at the rooms and possible entryways. In the room where Claire stood, the second floor appeared to have an overlook with a window peering downward. He couldn't see the doorway leading to it, but looking up, he saw a series of air vents lining the sides. He followed it with his eyes and saw its main line connected with the hallway directly above him.

The door to his side led to a stairwell and noise bellowed in as he opened it. Several footsteps were rushing upwards and faded. He entered, pistol in hand.

The shaft was well lit and extended downward at least eight stories. Above him was the same and he continued upward to the next level.

The room in front of him was small and occupied. Six guards stood in front of an old TV station watching various camera angles.

Hal reached into his bag and grabbed a sleep grenade. He had yet to try one of these and he closed his eyes before pulling the pin. The door squeaked and the guards turned, unsuspectingly watching as a grenade rolled to their feet. Suddenly they panicked, screaming orders to one another, but there was little that could be done. With a slam, Hal held the door handle shut and waited for the quiet huff of gas to release.

After a few seconds of coughing and wheezing, the crowd went silent.

He pulled his coat collar over his face and the door again squeaked open. The blue gas hovered in the air and his eyes began to tear.

He wouldn't be able to hold his breath for long and he quickly scurried over to the floor vents lining the room. They were loosely screwed shut and he pulled at the edges until the thin metal gave. He took in a short breath through his coat and wiggled his way into the shaft.

The vent was wide enough for him and his equipment as he crawled to the junction that divided into three directions. He was now directly over the main room and the gas was slowly wafting through. He quickened his pace to the next opening, trying to out-run it.

About twenty feet ahead of him he could see light coming in through a side vent. The room was empty, and the light came from several computer screens that were still lit. Whoever had left the room

218

did so in a hurry, but a cigarette was still smoldering in an ash tray on the table. He hit the vent with his palms, ignoring the fact that he was creating noise. He had to get out before the gas took over his nervous system and he passed out.

With a final thud, the metal bent and the screws gave on the bottom, pushing the doorway open. He rolled out and onto his back, taking in a deep breath as he lay there.

Looking at the ceiling he spotted a camera. Shit. It was positioned directly at him and he rolled to his side, jumping to his feet and crouching behind a desk. In the chaos he doubted anyone was even watching the damned camera feeds anymore, but its focus made him uneasy.

He reached into the sack, remembering the EMPs that Howard had equipped him with and tossed one in its direction. Archs of electricity lit the room in fantastic blues and greens before the room fell black. The lights and computer equipment flickered as they were suddenly overwhelmed by the power surge.

Someone had become alarmed by the sudden crash of equipment and they rushed in. Hal had the advantage in the dark, and the beam of a flashlight darted back and forth throughout the room.

He shifted and turned to face him, tranquilizer gun aimed at the man's silhouette as he entered.

There was no muzzle flash and no loud bang as he fired. His body slumped to the floor quietly and watched the door behind him slowly swing close.

The flashlight was still on as Hal grabbed it from his hand. He fired another shot to the man's leg to ensure he wouldn't be waking up anytime soon.

The neighboring rooms were dark, which were also affected by the EMP.

Shouts could be heard in all of the neighboring rooms, and he approached the door leading outwards.

He stopped as six men all emptied into the hallway, frantically yelling back and forth at one another. A sudden rush of panic swept over him but they all just looked passed. Under the coat and hat, he looked the same as them.

He backed up slowly, reentering the room he'd just left and knelt behind the wall. Propping his tranquilizer back up, he aimed for the man farthest down the hallway. The men all stopped mid-argument as he collapsed to the ground. Another fell, and remaining four spun in confusion. They were blind in the dark and completely disoriented. Another one down, and the last three raised their weapons, swinging from side to side.

They went quiet, listening for any indication of his direction. They turned, now with their backs towards him and looking forward at the first man who'd fallen. He squeezed, pivoted, and then again two more times.

Not one of them had a chance to even fire a shot in an accurate direction.

Hal checked the cartridges of his pistol and counted eight more rounds. It was an efficient weapon and completely silent, but he was quickly burning through his ammunition.

The first doorway to his left was now empty and open. It was the overlook that gazed down at the lab below and was still partly illuminated on the far side. The guards were distraught and frantically searching the room below. Claire sat in one of the chairs at the far end with her arms crossed. She didn't appear nearly as afraid as the two men surrounding her and waited with an annoyed look on her face.

The two men below were shouting into their radios, but there was no response.

The overlooking room had a side door leading towards the top level of the lab room and he exited into the shadow above. He propped his wrist onto the railing and squeezed. With a jerk, the first man twisted in his direction and lifted his assault rifle but fell to his knees before being able to fire.

"Show yourself!" The second man spun around. He fired a quick burst at the top level, but Hal was nicely concealed and the man missed by several feet.

He didn't leave him a second chance to fire and Hal pulled the trigger again. The man wheezed and gasped as he fell hard onto his knees. It took him three or four seconds before the drug burned through his veins and paralyzed him, collapsing onto his chest.

Claire darted out of her chair and hid behind a desk towards the corner of the room. She was still unaware of the extraction plan and she curled her knees to her chest and covered her head.

Hal waited. He wasn't going to take the chance that someone might still come barging through. The room remained silent and the lights above flickered.

"Claire," he called out quietly.

She lifted her head and squinted as she looked around.

Hal stood and holstered his pistol before walking into the dim light.

He walked down the stairs and she flinched as he approached. Hal looked down at his coat and realized he probably looked the same to her as the monsters who kidnapped her.

He quickly yanked the hat off. "Claire."

"Hal?" Her tone was surprised and shocked. She sprung to her feet and ran over, her arms reaching outward and wrapping around his neck. She lunged at him and her force almost pushed him backward.

He couldn't explain his reaction as he wrapped his arms around her and pulled her against his chest. His body ached in relief knowing that she was alive and in one piece.

She loosened her grip and cupped his face in her hands before pulling him down to meet hers. Her lips were warm as they made contact and he didn't fight the urge to kiss her back. His hands moved up her back, bringing her closer, and there was a burning in his chest like he'd never felt before. He remembered painfully watching her fall on the freighter and the guilt that he'd been carrying since quickly vanished.

It was brief and she backed away, still holding onto him. She ran her hands along the side of his face. "How did you get here? What did they do to you?" She asked, noticing the fresh bruises under his eye and broken lip.

"The Yotogi escorted me here. I'm fine. Are you alright?" She had a dark mark on the side of her neck and a puncture wound just below it.

She placed her hand over the mark and winced. "I think so. They injected me with a sedative to cooperate, but nothing I can't shake off. So they're here for the ARCA?"

"Yes, and you. Kyra has been working with the Russians, but not just on the ARCA. They're doing experiments on humans too. It's some sort of bio-lab. I don't know. We have to get out of here now." Hal looked back at the door he first tried entering through.

He stepped over to one of the guards on the ground. Claire was still wearing the same clothing from the freighter mission, and it wasn't enough for the frozen wasteland just outside.

"Where are we?" She stood over Hal as he began to strip the man of his coat and boots. "I remember being in the Atlantic but the rest is fuzzy. We boarded a plane, but that's all I can remember."

"Russia." He looked back at her as she stared in disbelief. It'd been two days since her kidnapping and she was still in a fuzzy haze, unable to recall much afterward.

"Russia! We're in Russia?"

He nodded. There wasn't much time to dwell on their travels or the events between now and then.

"Where's the ARCA?" He handed her the coat and boots as she confusedly accepted them.

She paused and held one hand to her head. Still suffering from the effects of sedation, she stumbled and tried to recall the last few hours. "Um. I believe it's..." She trailed off, glancing around at her surroundings. She was lost and confused. She'd spent the last day in this laboratory but was still somewhat incoherent. "They had me in a laboratory not far from here." Pointing towards the balcony on the second level, she clumsily waved in its direction. "I think it's that way."

She still held onto the clothing he'd given her, unsure what to do with it. Her nerves were shot and dark circles under her eyes showed her exhaustion. They hadn't abused her like the other prisoners, but whatever they'd been planning for her had taken its toll. She was medicated and off balance.

Hal grabbed the coat from her arms and placed it over her shoulders, helping her slide into it. It was enormous on her small build and the sleeves extended passed her hands by about six inches.

"Come on. We need to get out of here." He placed his hands on her shoulders as she crossed her arms and nodded.

One hand gripped his tranquilizer pistol and he grabbed her wrist gently with the other as the proceeded towards the stairs escalating upward to the higher split level.

The lights were dim from the EMP and several flickered to give a brief glimpse at what was ahead. The top level was small and it looped around the main floor below them. A long glass panel window stretched along the one side and they cautiously approached, hidden in the darkness above. Looking down was another laboratory with several large glass canisters that contained what looked like the ARCA, but were most likely mock prototypes.

Claire looked inward with a dazed expression. "This must be where they're rebuilding it."

"Which one is it?"

"I don't know." She looked around the room, squinting at the various models as she shook her head. Her focus shifted to the overlooking room. It was a surveillance room, and the three glass walls were tilted, looking down at their research subjects below.

Claire slid her hands along the glass lining the room until she reached a door. It squeaked on the hinges as she pushed in.

"Wait," Hal whispered in her direction as she carelessly stepped into the light.

He rushed in behind her, cautiously holding his pistol in front. The room was empty, but he could hear shouts from their sides and gunfire in the distance. Of all the places to be, this room seemed like the main target someone would be patrolling. He counted two cameras positioned in the corners of the room.

"Make it quick, Claire," he continued to whisper, although they were clearly being watched.

She quickened her pace towards one of the chambers and looked it over intensely before dashing over to the next, and then the next.

There were seven chambers all together and Hal examined each as he passed. He'd gotten a fairly good look at the real prototype while they were on board the freighter, but these all looked so similar.

"It's this one!" She yelled as she pressed her hands on the glass of the forth canister.

"How do we get it open?" He ran to her side and looked at the console.

She looked down and tried typing in some commands, but a red warning sign flashed every time she did.

"Shit, I'm locked out." She spun and looked at her surroundings. "There." She turned and pointed towards the overlooking room above. "The main console is there. We can't activate any of the chambers from here."

Hal's eyes circled the room, following the side entrance that led to it. "Stay here."

He walked over to the staircase and approached the entrance. The room was empty and illuminated by the screens surrounding the walls. Each displayed various camera angles of the complex. There was movement on some of the views and he could see the flash of gunshots on several screens. The Yotogi were coming in full force, and they'd forgotten their policy for a nonviolent approach.

The door pushed open easily and he stared at the confusing console controls. None of it was in English and he frantically looked from one piece of equipment to the next for something to stand out.

Claire was growing impatient down below as she shuffled back and forth. A metal chair lay on the ground, tipped on its side and she began dragging it clumsily behind her.

Hal was startled and jumped at the clash of noise from down below. He looked down through the window to see Claire take another swing, throwing the chair's weight at the glass chamber. The back of the chair made contact and the glass spider-cracked with her force.

She swung again, stumbling to the side as she almost lost balance. She screamed and swung again, cracking it further. The anger was bleeding out and the drugs were wearing off. She raged against the glass, breaking the back of the chair from its body as the chamber shattered.

Shards flew in every direction and she lost her footing, falling onto her back.

Hal raced out of the room and down the stairs to her side. A stream of blood slid down her forehead and Hal dusted the glass shards off her body. She had several cuts, none of which were deep.

"I'm OK." She let out a final deep breath and sat up straight.

She stood, shaking the glass from her clothing, and Hal gripped her arm as she balanced herself. The chamber was open and she crawled up on the platform. The release arms were stiff and with a swift stomp downward she dislocated its grip. The ARCA tipped to the side and Hal reached out to catch it. Claire continued to stomp on the remaining arms, and one by one they reluctantly bent away from the frame.

The shoulder harness gripped both sides and pulled heavily on his neck. This time he took the burden of carrying it.

The device vibrated in his arms and the power canisters began to spin. "Claire?"

"It's powering up. It's completed now." She was calm as she looked at him with pride. The thought didn't comfort him much, and he grew more and more suspicious as the cores began to brighten.

The moment of admiration faded as a door smashed open. Hal's hands were occupied and he couldn't grab his weapon.

"Fire!" She yelled and ducked behind the neighboring canister.

The man stood in the doorway and Hal could see several men approaching behind him, weapons raised. Hal looked at Claire frantically as she smiled in anticipation. All this time she'd worked on the ARCA, she'd never seen what it was capable of in a stable unit. She was brimming with excitement.

Hal adjusted his footing and prepared for the kick. The trigger clicked and in the brilliant flash of light he could see and feel the shift in space that was being created. Time slowed and he could hear the low cries of the men as the void approached them, sucking them inward like a vacuum before vanishing. The surrounding equipment screeched across the floor, the glass cracking and falling inward to the ARCA's projection, sucking everything in its path.

He released the trigger and time seemed to snap back, jerking him forward and he adjusted his stance to catch himself.

Claire screamed with excitement. "It works! It fucking works!" She jumped to her feet and stood beside Hal, gazing down at the weapon and then in the position where the men formerly stood. "Can you believe it?"

No wonder the Russians wanted the ARCA so badly. Every country on earth would be waging war over a weapon like this.

The damage it left behind was devastating. The force of its beam pulled matter inward. The glass containers were warped, bending towards its direction.

"Where did they go?" Hal asked. It was as if they vanished into thin air.

"They're here. Just outside of here." She shook her head. "It's hard to explain. Later. We have to go."

"Wait." He couldn't just accept the explanation. How could they be here?

"The ARCA disrupts the electromagnetic field we reside in. It modifies its target and pushes it into another frequency; one we can't exist in. Matter exists on levels way beyond what we can touch. Gases, solids, liquids – all our atoms exist on a frequency that can interact with others in that zone. If we move matter outside of that zone, they seize to affect ours." She still had a smile on her face.

"So they're not dead?" He was puzzled.

"No. They exist here. They can probably see and hear us, but can't affect it." She stumbled around and placed her hands on the glass on a warped chamber.

Hal smiled in relief. It was actually kind of funny, come to think of it. They were still in the room but confined to a new prison of their own, alone, only with themselves now.

"Come on," she yelled and sprinted towards the doorway, her coat loosely flopping behind her.

"Wait! I'll go first." Hal propped the weapon back up. It was heavier than he realized as he tried to catch up.

The exit was loud as the door swung open, leading them into the large atrium. They were on the bottom level looking towards the main entrance. Several Russian soldiers scurried on the two levels above them and Hal shifted his aim in their direction before pulling the trigger. He braced himself, shifting his feet for the shock to come. The flash took the men by surprise and time again folded around the wave that projected from the ARCA. He watched as the burst absorbed them, slowly sucking them into its wake.

He turned, repositioning the beam, and objects from around the room twirled like the suction of a tornado. Railings bent, desks flew, the glass windows shattered and even the concrete walls around them contorted.

He released his finger from the trigger and the thrust left behind lurched him forward. The room immediately fell silent.

Claire looked at him in amazement. She was proud at that moment, although the implications of this hadn't set in.

The patter of a helicopter could be heard in the distance and they raced to the entrance, which was now just a gaping hole in the wall. Cold air rushed in, and Claire gripped her coat tightly around her chest.

The walkway of the building was long, about a hundred and twenty feet and descended several levels as it climbed down the mountainside. Wind whipped past them and snow blazed from every direction in its shift.

The clouds sat lower at the mountain base and he could hear several voices shouting orders back and forth.

The prison was at his left and made an L-shape before attaching to the newer half of the complex. The newer construction extended from its main body and was roughly seven stories higher from where he stood. The rooftops were lined with several satellites and antennas.

Claire bolted down the stairs as gunshots rang through the air, smashing into the concrete around them.

"Snipers on the roofs!" Hal yelled in her direction as she darted for cover behind one of the dividing barriers.

They came from all directions and Hal backed into the building again. Claire was paralyzed, but behind cover. She didn't dare move.

"Catch!" He yelled and grabbed for his .45 in his holster and tossed it in her direction. It landed five feet out of her reach and as she made an attempt to grab it, a bullet rushed passed, smashing into the barrier wall and she retreated back to her position.

The ARCA was heavy, its power cores beaming with light and he propped it up, supporting its weight with his knees before aiming towards the building tops. He was prepared for the shot as its projection rippled through the air, beaming towards the satellites and warping them to its center. The metal bent, screaming in rebellion as it twisted into the vortex.

He released the trigger and pivoted towards the prison's rooftops. The pull of its shot brought down the top two stories. Bricks careened down towards the ground as the ARCA stopped firing. He pulled the trigger again, anticipating the pull, but it sputtered and just jerked slightly.

"It needs to power up!" Claire yelled in his direction as the power cores slowed.

He ducked for cover and waited. How long does this take? He watched as they spun, slowly brightening, but it would take a minute, maybe two, for it to fully recharge.

Several shots were fired outside and he peered around the ledge to see Claire with the .45 firing upwards at the neighboring mountainside. Seven men were now stumbling down the snowbank towards her and she clumsily shot in their direction.

The cores were still dim, but if they had any juice, he had to attempt it now.

He spun around the corner and took aim before releasing a burst at the men. Its effect wasn't as powerful as before and it pulled in, dragging the men towards its center. Their limbs contorted with the pull before the burst cut out again. They dropped to the ground, squirming in agony as the frequency shift only partially took effect.

He had a moment to pause and observe the reaction. Their arms and legs had been morphed, extending and breaking the joints. The bones were elongated and their chests had expanded. They hadn't vanished, but rather were stuck in the pull before the full burst could displace them. It was a grotesque sight as they squirmed, unable to control their broken bodies and blood began to flow over the white snow.

Claire sat in shock, repeatedly pulling the trigger, but the clip had emptied. They were running out of ammunition and the ARCA's recharge time was slow.

He still had the carrying bag strapped to his back with several grenades and eight more revolver rounds.

Placing the ARCA on the ground, he pulled the magnum and reloaded it. Each shot would have to count.

He charged over to Claire's position and handed her the pistol. "Here's six shots and two more." He handed her the remaining two bullets. "We need to make every shot count. Breathe. Steady your aim and don't blink before you squeeze."

She nodded nervously.

"There's an ice shelf at the bottom of the mountain. Our pick up will be there." He pointed in the general direction down the hill to the west.

Several shots were fired down below where the Yotogi were making their approach.

Claire stared at the men that lay fifty feet away from her, still twitching and gurgling from the weak shock of the ARCA. At full charge the weapon worked as it was designed, cleanly moving matter into another space, but it was still a prototype and without full power, the results were unpredictable.

Another shot came from above on the west side rooftop, snapping their attention back to reality as they ducked for cover.

The power cores were still spinning on the ARCA, slowly gaining power. They brightened and Hal flinched as another shot came from above, striking the cement barrier that Claire crouched behind. She screamed, covering her head with her hands and curling her knees up.

Full power or not, he had to fire. He spun around the corner and squeezed the trigger, firing a weak blast towards the top of the building. He missed the shooter by several feet, but the pull of the ARCA's burst was enough to warp the brick structure below him. They were pulled toward the center of the ARCA's stream and gave inward, collapsing the top two stories above and below.

Hal released the trigger, conserving its power and letting gravity continue its destruction.

From Hal's perspective, the time delay was about four seconds before snapping back to normal and the man plummeted eight stories to the ground. The snow muffled his fall, but his body shook as it made contact with the earth again.

Hal waited in his position for the next shot as Claire remained under her shattered barrier. They were sitting ducks now out in the open.

"Move!" Hal yelled and she snapped into action.

Gripping the revolver in one hand and the remaining bullets in the other, she flailed around as she frantically sprinted down the remaining walkway to the open slope downward.

The ARCA was heavy as he tried to hoist the harness more comfortably on his shoulders. Claire raced forward without looking back and he began to follow, but the weight of the weapon made him slow and awkward.

He stepped into the snow and stumbled as a shot fired from behind him. Snow burst into a cloud as he landed on his knees. Two men stood on the roof directly behind him, sniper rifles perched and aimed in his direction.

He spun on his knees in the icy snow and aimed, clumsily pulling the trigger and missing. The ARCA jolted with a weak shot, hitting a support beam and the whole mass shifted. The lower level collapsed and the floors above began to topple to one side.

The building screamed as the steel supports cried out from the weight being unevenly distributed. The concrete exterior cracked and the windows began to shatter throughout the whole complex.

He shifted his aim towards the opposite corner of the complex and fired one last burst.

The concrete pulled outward and the beams gave. As the discharge of the weapon faded, the second and third stories collapsed. The whole building shifted to one side, its interior exposed and crumbling.

A thud from the center gave out, blowing glass from the windows lining it.

The two men on the roof were no longer in sight and Hal didn't wait for them to reposition as he jumped back to his feet and spun towards the downward slope. Claire had vanished, frantically running in the direction of more gun fire.

The power cores slowly resumed their rotation as he slid the ARCA to his side and began to trot downward.

As he descended the fog grew heavy. They were at a high elevation and the clouds that surrounded him were cold. He clenched his fists as the chill bit into the exposed skin.

Snowmobile tracks were etched into the snow of a make-shift road and he followed along side it through the tree line that led the way.

The run was exhausting and he'd made it about a thousand feet before stopping at a cross section where the tracks split into a fork. The trees were thick and it was difficult to see in any one direction for great distance. One set of tracks led to a side road, but it was far too exposed. The other led downward and probably lead to an outpost farther down.

Engines roared in the distance and began to approach as he ducked behind a large pine tree. The Yotogi wouldn't have had such an equipment here, but if he could hijack a snowmobile, he could travel much faster.

He reached into his pack and pulled out the case that Howard had given him. The hand pistol inside could be reassembled using various attachments. Hal had escaped their visual range and they'd be scattered in loose formations as they split up. He wanted to stay as hidden as possible and being in the open with a loud sniper rifle would only give away his position.

The cold bit into his fingers and he scurried to place the silencer onto the 9mm pistol as the sound of engines approached. There were four, maybe five of them on the ground. He listened intently, but not only for their positions. Claire was still out here and with a revolver, one shot would ring like a beacon, calling over the mountainside.

The thought scared him. He'd already lost her once and she was running scared. She knew where the pick up would be, but the sedatives had left her disoriented and confused. There was no com system here and they were both on their own.

The thought was interrupted as movement caught his peripheral vision, scattering the light that flickered through the trees. His coat was white and blended into the snow as he crouched down.

The snowmobile spun around the corner of the road and slowed as the man peered through the trees looking for their lost targets. He zoned in on Hal's position. Shit! The power cores spun wildly on the ARCA, giving off a florescent glow.

He slowly approached, not yet fully alert, and Hal had to take the shot. It was now or nothing.

The silencer shook on the front of the pistol and let out a muffled pop, striking the guards shoulder and flinging him off the seat. The snowmobile slowed before coming to a stop.

Hal lay motionless as the man sat up and reached for a weapon inside his coat. Another muffled shot hummed through the air and struck his other shoulder.

He cried out in pain and Hal struggled to lift himself and the ARCA out of the snow, sprinting towards the idling snowmobile.

He secured the ARCA to the back carrying cage before slinging the pack onto the seat and rummaged through to find several vials of morphine. The man's arms were immobile from both shoulder wounds and Hal waded through the deep snow to his side.

The forest was quiet, or at least in his immediate area and Hal quickly unwrapped the syringe before stabbing it into the guard's leg. His eyes begged for relief and it came as the drugs rushed through his system.

Hal grabbed his legs and exhaustively dragged his limp body off the main road. They'd be patrolling the area soon and he wouldn't leave any tracks to follow.

He propped his body against a tree facing away from the road, kicking snow over the tracks and blood trail.

The snowmobile purred as he pressed the accelerator and shifted into gear. He pulled his hood tight, and at a glance the Russians wouldn't immediately recognize the difference between him and one of their own guards.

The road twisted around the thick trees and he slowed, listening for anything abnormal.

"Claire," he called out, but restrained his volume. On the snowmobile he would be much faster than her on foot.

"Please let her make it," he whispered.

The repetitive thump of helicopter blades echoed. The Yotogi were close now. "Follow the sound, Claire," he thought out loud. "Follow the sound."

He accelerated forward and turned at a bend in the road that led to an open field. It must have extended a mile in each direction and as he looked closer he could see two small hunting lodges and a tree fort lining the sides. He dismounted and pulled out the case, equipping the scope to the small 9mm and gazed through it.

The cabins were dark, but they were no doubt occupied. The tree fort was covered by brush, but the stairs nailed into the tree's side extended upward about fifteen feet.

There was no way around the field as it extended out of view. Anyone progressing downward would have to cross.

He needed some sort of diversion as he sorted through the sack and grabbed two incendiary grenades.

With a quick swing, the small canisters flew eighty feet to his side into the open field. The shock was more than he expected from an incendiary round and it let out a violent thud as it exploded into a ball of fire. The residents in the nearby cabins were immediately alarmed and rushed out in the open, trotting forward cautiously with their assault rifles raised.

Hal gazed through the scope and counted four men accelerating, then to the tree fort. There was movement, but the 9mm was way out of range and would just attract attention, and there were surely men still in the cabins.

The distinct ring of a .357 revolver echoed through the trees and he jumped. Claire.

Damn it! He lunged back over to his snowmobile and reversed onto the trail, glancing at his front as the men now began rushing to her position. He veered off the trail and raced forward, twisting along an unmarked path through the trees.

He reached into the bag behind him, pulling an explosive grenade and tossing it behind as he pulled the pin and released the trigger. It shook the earth and threw shrapnel within a thirty foot radius as he sped forward.

Another shot rang through the air and there was return fire. Come on! He threw another grenade to his side and heard shouting nearby, followed by the thundering explosion as he rushed passed. He needed them to shift their focus.

He rushed the snowmobile into the field as he approached the four men running along side and a sleep grenade tumbled through the snow at their feet. The muffled puff of its release was muted by the engine and he accelerated towards the closest cabin.

Lights flickered as he approached and a man exited, his gun remained at his side as he ran towards him. The coat concealed Hal's face and he took the man by surprise as he accelerated, swinging out his arm and knocking him to the ground.

He spun the snowmobile around the corner of the cabin and raced forward along the edge of the field towards the gunfire.

"Claire!"

The area was clear and he listened intently for more shots.

Covered by the thick trees surrounding him, he dismounted and reloaded his pistol. He grabbed the ARCA and bag but left the vehicle idling. "Claire!"

Shots echoed in the distance to the west. They were only a mile or so from the ice shelf, but the terrain was difficult to navigate and would be slow on foot.

"Claire!"

The silence was painful.

"Hal!" He breathed a huge sigh of relief and rushed towards the voice as she clumsily stumbled through the snow. Tree branches hung low and snagged at her loose coat.

He ran with the heavy cargo on his shoulders as she closed in.

Hal stopped in his tracks as something caught his peripheral vision.

"Get down!" He spun to his right, gun aimed and fired six shots. Bark shattered off the tree as bullets crashed into the fort a hundred feet from him.

The sniper flinched, returning one shot that struck the ground ten feet from Claire and sent her to the ground.

Hal swung the shoulder harness around his chest and propped up the ARCA. The power cores spun rapidly in their casing, now fully charged, and the bright beam sent a powerful burst through the trees. The gravitational pull snapped limbs and branches towards the center. The steps from the fort ladder pried loose and flew into the path before vanishing. Time was slowed and the sniper was swept off his platform, gripping the edge in rebellion, but it was pointless. The tree directly in the ARCA's path uprooted, snapping in several places before disappearing.

Hal released the trigger and he lunged forward as reality snapped back.

The surrounding trees cried out in protest as their trunks morphed into an unstable position.

"Claire!" He swung the ARCA back to his side and rushed over to her.

She laid on her back, her blue eyes were glossy and wide with shock.

"Are you OK?" He brushed his hand on her cheek before patting her chest and limbs. She wasn't hit. "Claire, can you hear me?"

She was breathing rapidly and shaking, but managed to nod her head in acknowledgment.

"Hey. You're OK." He turned her head to look at him and placed a hand on her face, trying to calm her nerves. She'd been running in a straight line, nerves shot and exhausted as she fought the sedatives still surging through her body.

"We need to move. Come on." He tried to be gentle as he tugged on her arms, swinging her to her feet. He'd just set off a wave of motion and they'd surely be heading towards their position now.

She nodded, catching her breath and gripping reality again.

There was shouting from the south where the other cabin was located and Hal gripped the steering bars, checking Claire behind him, and pushed on the accelerator.

He steered clear of the trail, slowing up as he weaved around every tree that cluttered the thick forest. Claire wrapped her arms around his chest and rested on his back.

The forest came to an abrupt halt as Hal quickly hit the brakes several feet from a cliff that extended down to a frozen river. He pulled up his sleeve, further exposing his skin to the bitter cold as he gazed down at the compass on his wrist band. The small overhead display indicated their location and a small dot marking the ice shelf. He gazed up and down the river that winded around the mountain, but it was nowhere in sight and the patter of helicopter blades had now gone mute.

They were slightly off the mark and needed to head south. It was difficult to read distance for such a small landmark, but south was their best bet.

He reversed and rode along the cliff side. He stopped and cut the engine, startling Claire as he stood. It was quiet. Too quiet. The Yotogi had invaded the complex to their east, but now the land was dead. The water below crashed on the rocks and ice chunks formed deadly barriers peaking up above the surface below.

"What's wrong?"

He glanced at his wrist band. They were right on top of the ice shelf, according to the satellite feed.

"The ice shelf should be here." He spun his head around in every direction, but the only thing in view was the forest to their sides and the turbulent river below.

"Let me see." She reached around and grabbed his arms. Her hands were bitter and frozen. "It needs to be calibrated. The EMP burst must have damaged a circuit." She tapped in some commands and the screen flickered out before fading back in again with the same readings.

She looked around, trying to find a landmark, a twist in the river, anything that might indicate where they were on the geographic image. Wind swept passed, sending a gust of snow from the trees above and rained down on them. They were lost and their target was nowhere in sight.

Hal grew nervous sitting idly in one place. They'd taken more than a dozen men out during the escape, but they wouldn't give up. There was no shelter, no radio contact, and nothing for warmth. Starting a fire and setting up some sort of camp was out of the question. They needed extraction and now.

Claire pulled hard on his arm, tugging him down slightly as she peered at his wrist.

"There." She pointed at the map and zoomed in. She shifted her gaze and pointed at a large mass of rocks on the other side of the river bank. "That's this mark here, and see how the river bends?"

He looked closer at what she was zooming in on. There were several forks in the river. Its main mass winded around the base of the mountain, and several streams fed into it.

"If we head south-west a mile, maybe two, we should come to this junction and follow the river south." She looked certain, but a flicker of doubt still showed. "The terrain is open and level. The ice should be solid this time of year. You said the Yotogi are sending a helicopter?"

Hal nodded. This was autumn in Russia and although ice rippled through the waves, it was a moving mass. The shelf would be unstable.

"We have to try." She knew the implications as much as he did, and they'd freeze to death in a day's time, given that the Russians didn't hunt them down first.

Hal sat back down and started the engine. Its gas tank was quickly depleting and they would soon be riding on empty.

Claire wrapped her arms back around his chest and Hal adjusted his coat, unzipping the front and sliding her icy hands in for protection before the snowmobile jolted forward.

The land flattened and opened up as the trees thinned out. It was quiet, but fear lingered in the air. He knew the Russians would be migrating towards the pick up location where the sounds of the helicopter originated.

The engine sputtered and hiccuped before coming to a complete halt. Hal tapped the gas meter as the needle now sat below the red line indicator. They'd made it about two miles farther, passed the fork in the river, but the ice shelf and the Yotogi were still nowhere in sight.

"Can you walk?" He knew she could, but it would be exhausting.

"I think so." She stumbled off the vehicle and stretched her legs that were almost frozen to the uncomfortable seat. "Let's go."

She took lead, her boots sinking into the knee-deep snow and she tucked her hands inside her coat. Hal dismounted the ARCA from the carrying cage and swung it around his shoulder. The bag was lighter, having expelled some of its contents. It was still going to be a long haul, but he didn't dare part with what was left in his arsenal.

Claire sped up as they came to a bend along the river side, and there it was. She laughed and bent over, perching her hands on her knees as she breathed in and laughed with relief.

The craft sat quietly on the surface. Its blades were still and Hal pulled the 9mm to his eye, looking through the scope. A familiar face looked in their direction as he saw Michio sitting in the pilot's seat.

He lowered the scope from his focus. "Claire!" She was charging towards the chopper at full speed. Michio took notice and the blades quickly began to swivel above the craft.

A shot split through the air and struck the ground several feet behind her and without thinking Hal raced forward. They were waiting for them.

Claire spun on the ice as the shot interrupted her movements towards a happy rescue.

Another shot rang through, striking the ground in front of her.

Hal swung the ARCA to his front and aimed. The sniper was hidden, and he guessed at its orientation before pulling the trigger. Snow flew and the ice in front of him began to heave along the radius of the ARCA's burst. It was a careless move and he released the trigger as matter plummeted back towards the earth, creating a wave underneath that rippled through the ice.

Another shot thundered and caught his peripheral vision. His reflex overcame any logic and he swiveled on the ice before firing a short burst from the ARCA. Its pull was quick and snapped against the snow bank two hundred feet away. A gust of snow flew into the air as the small explosion hit its mark.

He lunged forward, steering towards the craft as his feet struggled to balance on the shifting ice.

Claire stood in place a hundred feet from him, eyes glued to the ground beneath her. He charged towards her as the wave beneath rippled through, tearing cracks in its wake. She glanced up in fear as it gave. Her feet slid out from underneath her as it split, dividing the mass.

The helicopter began to rise several feet off the ground and a man, dressed in a black tight coat jumped to the surface. Hal pulled the bag and harness off his chest and with a swift throw, it slid along the ground forty feet towards him.

Hal slid on his belly, reaching towards Claire as she fell into the void of ice and submerged. His hand gripped her wrist, the water dancing in rebellion below them as the suction pulled her down and he slid further on the surface.

"Don't let go!" He yelled.

A man slid up from behind and grabbed Hal's trunk before pulling back and reaching into the water and grabbing her other arm.

"Pull!" His accent was heavy and Hal glanced at him in shock, realizing he was Russian. It didn't matter now.

They heaved and Claire resurfaced, gasping for air that froze in her lungs.

Hal flipped to his side and struggled to get upright as the other man pulled. He gained traction with his boots and heaved backward, pulling her onto the ice. The enemy beside them quickly pulled at his zipper and Hal defensively grabbed Claire, shielding her as he closed his eyes and waited for the gunshot.

Hal winced as the fur hit his face and glanced up in surprise, seeing the man's coat laying on her lap.

"Stop what is happening here. Go!" He shouted at them.

Hal didn't ask questions. He flung Claire's arm around his shoulder and sprinted towards the chopper that hovered several feet above the icy floor.

He lifted Claire and the Asian man reached down to pull her in.

Hal looked back at the man in shock and gratitude. "Why?"

"Because someone has to!" The Russian pulled out a 9mm and held it above his head, firing eight shots towards the sky. He may have been the enemy, but whatever he'd witnessed here had crossed a line. Anyone in the immediate vicinity would have heard his shots and thought he was pursuing them.

Hal gripped the interior railing and saluted the man, who returned the gesture as the chopper began to lift.

Chapter 26: The Detour

The large cargo area of the helicopter was about two hundred square feet and Claire lay on the floor. Her breaths were shallow and her skin was pale. Hypothermia was beginning to take over and Hal fumbled with the wet fur coat as he tried to peal its icy shell from her chest. A cold draft came through holes and gaps in the hull, but the damp was deadly.

She inhaled deeply as the heavy coat lifted from her chest and her fists clenched as the cold air swept in closer to her skin.

Four other Yotogi members sat in the rear of the craft, each attending to someone injured. Ortiz sat uncomfortably on one of the back seats with his knees curled to his chest and his eyes closed.

The man beside them fumbled with Claire's boots, yanking at the frozen material.

The coat pulled loose and her arms were free as she shook uncontrollably.

"We need something dry." Hal indicated towards the man next to him.

He understood and nodded, scurrying towards the back. They came prepared for the cold, but not the wet.

Hal pulled Claire into a sitting position and shook her arms, trying to create circulation. "Stay with me, Claire. Look at me."

Her head tilted forward and met his gaze.

"You're going to be OK. Stay with me," he begged.

The turbulent wind shook the craft, tilting it to the side and everyone struggled to grab something for balance.

Hal shuffled around, stripping Claire of her wet clothing and cradled her in his lap. The Russian had given his coat to them and he wrapped it around her chest. The man from behind knelt down and continued to cover her before pushing them both farther towards the wall.

There was silence in the helicopter and everyone held their somber head down. They'd lost men, friends, maybe even family, on this excursion. Hal looked at the remaining few that were lucky to survive, but they were scared. Their plan had worked, but at great costs, as he counted eight survivors, nine including the pilot. The Yotogi weren't men of great resources, but they were devout in their cause. He'd witnessed the power of the ARCA, and with the wrong intentions it could be mass produced into one of the worst weapons of its time. The results were grotesque. Without full power it wasn't able to fully remove matter from existence; only horribly distort it. The science boggled his mind. It was beautiful, but there were unimaginable consequences. Claire hadn't had time to explain it. She was proud to see it in operation, but he was terrified. At his own hand he had dispelled men into a foreign existence. It was worse than death. Alone in a foreign world, being able to see those in our reality but unable to touch it, as Claire had described. He couldn't shake the feeling that this was horribly wrong. It was too perfect to imagine, really. He was no physicist, but matter can't just move into another existence. It has to go somewhere.

Remembering the shift, the pull and transition of the ARCA had left Hal with an unshakable feeling of déjà vu. It shifted time. He was able to observe a drastic delay that left him stumbling backwards, like he himself was shifting with it before throwing him back to earth.

The hull shook as they hit turbulence, blowing the craft from side to side. Hal tightened his grip on Claire. She was breathing normally now, but her face remained pale. Her eyes were heavy as she glanced around at the other occupants. Ortiz sat on the opposite side, curled under a blanket that engulfed him.

"The ARCA?" she asked, quiet and muffled.

Hal nodded and lifted his eyes to where the weapon laid nearby. Its power cores were bright, swirling beautifully as it sustained full charge. A smile peaked out as she looked upon it. It was a magnificent piece of technology and this was the first testing area where its full power had been unleashed. Hal still didn't feel right, though. He appreciated its power, but something was wrong. They were crossing the lines of nature and existence.

Warmer air began streaming in and most of the occupants had dwindled into a light slumber. Everyone was exhausted and when reality landed, they'd all step off the helicopter in a state of mourning. Hal suspected Brack and Troy would be waiting, still oblivious, but back in control. The ever looming question of his place in the world would be back, but he'd gotten what they came for, and now he at least had something to hold onto.

He began to close his eyes. It would be a long trip before they landed again in Japan and his body ached for rest. Claire quietly shivered, her eyes closed and her wet hair was matted and messy. He gently brushed it to the side, looking at her pale face that was normally tan from the tropical sun. He was amused, thinking back as she walked down the pier with a sniper rifle strapped to her back. She was tough, but as she lay shivering in his lap, he felt himself scared. This wasn't over yet. As long as Kyra was alive, Claire would always be a target. She had invaluable knowledge that the Russians needed, which is why they took her as a hostage, rather than a corpse. Kyra was vicious, but determined. She could hide as long as she wanted in Russia, but sooner or later she'd have to come back, and no doubt with an army behind her.

He blocked the thought for the time being. That was tomorrow's war, and like them, they'd have time to prepare. Right now they needed distance.

His eyes ached as he closed them. It had been at least a day since he met sleep, and the brief hours he had in a tranquilized state left him more weary than rested. A comforting dark settled and he slipped into it.

The helicopter jolted violently and a siren rang. He snapped to attention, as did everyone. Michio yelled at the front of the craft, swearing at the controls that fought against him in his hands.

"Where are we?" Hal looked around frantically. The windows were dark and he peered out to see a long stretch of dark fog engulfing them.

"We are due south, forty miles from the coast." He pulled at the controls, but as he jolted at the stick the craft remained on its course. "I don't understand. We're losing power!"

The red emergency lights flickered on. Everyone stopped as the rushing sound of the blades above them slowly decelerated and panic struck.

Adrenaline rushed through and everyone fell silent, gripping whatever parts of the interior were available, bracing for what was to come.

He winced, gripping Claire in his arms.

Then it stopped.

There was no feeling of vertigo, no drop, and he loosened, looking around as time seemed to pause. The others felt it too and glanced around confused. They were stalled above the ocean, yet they weren't falling on a collision course to the surface.

"What the?" Hal let go of Claire and began to stand, looking out the small window in the door hatch. Then a new sense of fear took over.

A spark. Faint, but it was there. It came again to the side and others rushed over to see.

"It's happening," he muttered to himself, all too familiar with the fear.

A bright light from within the craft began to flicker, brighter and brighter as everyone's attention shifted to the ARCA. Its power cores were spinning more rapidly with every cycle. Growing, it pulsated into a blinding white beam that spun around the room. Everyone stared, dazed by its aura.

"No. No. No. Michio, get us back online!" Hal yelled but his attention was captured by the ARCA.

His stomach turned as he looked out the front windshield. Electrical sparks were drawing closer, streaking across the glass and creating an arch of spider cracks as it made contact. The lights on the controls flickered on and off by the disturbance.

Through the sparks he could see the shadow that lay directly in front of them. Without power, they were moving forward, being pulled into the gaping void.

The shock was brief and he screamed as time slowed. The light of the ARCA was blinding, and everything faded into its brilliance.

Chapter 27: Déjà vu

Cold. Wet. He pulled his arms to brush his face. They were damp and a green haze filled his eyes as he tried to focus on his hands.

Everything was a blur and he rubbed his eyes, but it didn't clear.

"Claire?" He sat up and tried to yell but it was muffled. "Claire?"

There was the sound of water somewhere, but not the ocean. It sounded more like mud, gurgling and splatting. A fog surrounded him and clung to his skin as he tried to stand on shaky legs that sunk into the mud.

He patted his chest, feeling new bruises. This felt familiar, somehow.

"Claire," he yelled, but the only sound returned was the echo on running water.

The marshland extended into the fog that lingered four feet off the ground. The trees hung long, their branches dipping into the soil and were completely bare. It wasn't wet, but the fog was different. It clung to his skin with an oily texture, unlike water. He smudged it with his hand and left a residue of gray slime.

The fog stretched out over the ground in a green haze and even though the trees were scarce, he could only see a hundred feet in any direction, maybe a hundred and twenty.

"Claire! Ortiz! Can anyone hear me?"

He staggered forward, looking around for any parts of the helicopter. Had they bailed mid flight? Where was the craft?

The muck was heavy and with each exhausting step he continued forward to much of the same.

"Can anyone hear me?" He could hear the echo of his voice travel through the forest, but nothing returned. There was absolutely no reaction. No wild life, no sounds of an engine, nothing. The land was completely dead.

He waited for several minutes, calling out in hope, but without any response, it was pointless to stay put. If others were out there, they'd be searching as well, and he continued to move forward.

A blasting echo stung his ears and he covered them, wincing in pain. A horn rang through the woods from every direction.

Wait. He paused. This was familiar.

"Wake up, Hal. You're dreaming. This isn't real," he whispered to himself, recalling the nightmares. He knew this was a fabrication. He closed his eyes and held his hands firmly over his ears, bracing himself for the wake-up shock. He continued to beg himself to wake.

He peeked open his eyes, expecting a different sight, but it lingered. The fog swirled, touching his skin, embracing his heat.

"This can't be. It's not real."

His only instinct was to run. The trees shifted, the mud latched onto his feet, the swirl of the mist honed in on him. He charged forward as the soil tried to drag him down. Each step was exhausting as his feet plunged into soft swamp.

Noise rose up all around him. The forest was awakening and was aware of a new occupant. Branches lurched out for him as he dodged through the trees and found firmer ground. His boots gripped the rock bed and he stumbled as the friction took him by surprise.

Standing on the hard soil, vines scattered over the earth and slithered under his palms. He had to keep moving.

Suddenly everything halted. The air stopped. The trees remained quiet and the dirt below him fell still as the echoing horn dissipated. It wasn't gone, but something was muting it. His ears were overwhelmed and they ached from the sudden silence. It was like being underwater and hearing something wail just above the surface.

He fell to the ground and perched his elbows onto his knees to catch his breath as he rocked back and forth. This was not a dream.

He remained still, listening intently in the muted haze. The dull sound of running water also surrounded him, but there was no consistency to it. No direction.

The smell of this place was unlike anything he could recall. It wasn't mold, or stale water, or dirt in the woods. It smelt like death, but not decay, and something about it was familiar, but he couldn't place it.

A scream in the distance startled him and he jumped to his feet.

"Claire!" He yelled, turning in every direction. "Can anyone hear me?"

245

He fell silent hoping the voice would come again. Something shifted, moving behind him and he spun in its direction. Again, from the side and he moved.

"Is anyone there?" he whispered as a chill ran down his spine. Something about it was wrong. It wasn't human.

Again from behind it came, taunting him. A groan, low and faint.

The sky darkened and the fog fell low to the ground. Some sort of transition was taking place.

He crept forward, his feet steady and quiet. "Is someone there?"

Another groan from behind and he spun to face it. A dark shadow lingered over the land and he squinted to see.

"I can help you. Where are you?" He remained quiet as he spoke. He didn't want to startle his surroundings as he crept towards the sound, but it fled to the other side, now whimpering.

The sky was like a void. There were no clouds, no sun and no moon or stars; just a gray pallet.

He paused as a figure approached, struggling to see as it flowed and morphed forward. It whimpered and he stood in fascination, watching. No light reflected from the small mass as it came closer, hovering over the land, gliding towards him.

It wasn't nothing, but more like a lack of anything. Light gravitated towards its void of existence. It was the reverse of a ghost, slowly creeping across the earth, and he calmly stepped back, avoiding its path and holding his breath as it continued. It whimpered like a child, crying as it aimlessly wandered over the land.

He was frozen and didn't dare move. Was this hell; where lost souls wandered, lost and confused? It didn't behave like a demon, or at least not how he would have imagined one, but something told him it wasn't an innocent either.

The darkness that followed in its wake faded with it.

His chest ached, breathing in as his emotions sank into his gut. He fell to his knees, gripping the dirt below. Some painful sorrow ached and he bit his lip holding the grief back. He couldn't explain the sudden wave of emotion. What the hell was that?

Slowing his breath, he stood and gathered himself. The world seized to move.

Were there others here? Were they witnessing this same chaos? He had to find someone, anyone that would bring back some sanity. What if the void returned? Was it here for him? Could that *thing* have been a someone at one time?

He didn't want to find out as he resumed his weary walk forward, holding his head down and only lifting it to remove obstacles in his path.

The running water was closer now and the surroundings began to change. The soil beneath him was now a dark sand, void of any color. The trees were thinner, but still hung low as the branches sobbed, digging into the earth like roots. Large rocks spiked out of the ground and the fog had completely faded.

A glare caught his eye as he lifted his head to see a polluted beach stretching out along a dark water line.

He began to trot, glaring down at the various metal chips and spikes that punctured the sand, but he didn't recognize anything from the helicopter.

"Claire!" There was no point being quiet. The world was deafeningly silent and his voice echoed over the massive beach that stretched for miles. Water sloshed against the large debris that remained above the ground. It wasn't the ocean and he dipped his hand into the liquid, which left a black oily residue that repelled off his skin.

He exhaled in frustration. He was lost, and from the looks of things, others had at one time been here too, but they were nowhere to be found. It was hopeless and he was exhausted. He plopped down into the sand and lay still. His body ached, his stomach growled in hunger and his eyes burned as he closed them. This was hell. A personal hell that nurtured fears of solitude. This was it and he shut out the world, calming his thoughts as he fell into sleep, welcoming the peace it might bring. Where ever this place was, he was alone in it.

The cold lingered in, sweeping over silently in the nonexistent wind. He shivered and stirred, clinging his arms around his chest and curling into the fetal position. He didn't want to wake, but a crackling thunder made him flinch.

He opened his eyes but his body remained in place, waiting to see if it would come. The sky illuminated with a violent strike of lightning in the distance and rumbled toward him. A drop of water fell on his face and created a dark stream as it slid down his nose. He wouldn't have cared, but it was unusual and struck his attention, wiping it with his hand and sloshing it on his fingertips. It was dark, more like an oil, and its texture wasn't really wet as much as it was slimy.

He sat upright and held out his hands as it fell more steadily. The land grew darker as it showered on the surface, spreading a thin layer of darkness onto everything it touched.

"What the hell?" He glared around as another rumble of thunder crept in from the distance.

He scurried along the ground and scooted under a piece of wreckage from an old craft that had careened into the earth. The hull was old, probably from the 1950's and he glanced around at the markings that were still visible. They were foreign and the rusted metal was heavily degraded. The small parts that remained looked like the front section of a small two-man plane. Its rear had been torn off and the one remaining wing was split into two pieces. Two seats were loosely attached to the floor, which hung sideways as the plane lay on its side. It was barely enough cover to hide under, and water from the lake waded in underneath.

Rain struck the plane's surface like bullets and aside from the occasional rolling thunder, it was actually peaceful.

He reached around his side and felt the holster vest gripping into the back of his shoulders. Most of his weapons were still in the carrying bag that remained on the helicopter floor, but he still had the tranquilizer and twenty rounds in the cartridge that he'd loaded on the flight back. Not that he'd need them, but it was one of the only comforts he still had.

The rain was short and he waited, dozing into a light sleep as he rested his back against the metal frame. It was less than twenty minutes before the rain faded to a heavy mist; the same that it had been before, and the oil that covered the ground sank into the sand, disappearing within minutes of it falling.

He touched his arm band, but the screen remained dark and unresponsive. Damn it.

He pulled himself to his feet, gripping the hull to help his weary legs push upward.

"Can anyone hear me?"

It was a hopeless effort, but why the hell not?

"I'm here!" Hal spun in surprise, glancing to his side at the response. His previous efforts left him feeling helplessly lost, but a sudden rise of hope lifted him. It was Claire.

"Where are you?"

"Here! Where are you?"

"I'm on the shore." He began to trot forward. "Keep talking! Are you hurt?"

"I'm OK. But..." Her voice faded as something overwhelmed her.

She stumbled off the rough rocky surface onto the soft, unstable sand. Hal saw her emerge from the forest and bolted forward, his heart sinking with relief.

She plowed down the bank and gripped him, crying and Hal almost fell to his knees. He backed away and held her face, which was struck with absolute terror. She was in her underwear, having been stripped of her frozen clothing, but aside from a few shallow scratches, she was OK.

She gently backed away, clinging her arms around her chest in embarrassment.

Hal quickly shoved his heavy coat off his shoulders and wrapped it around her. It was still somewhat damp from the rain, but better than nothing.

"Are you OK?"

She nodded, silently looking down and then peering around at their surroundings.

"Where are we?" She held her hand above her eyes as if it'd make a difference in the murky fog.

His eyes followed hers as they glanced down the long stretch of the dismal beach. "I'm not sure. Have you seen the others?"

She covered her face with her hands and began to sob. "Yes."

"Where?" He asked somberly, but she shook her head violently. There was no explanation needed.

"Can you take me back to the helicopter?" He placed a hand on her shoulder.

"No! You don't understand. We can't go back there. Something took them. It... something, I don't know what it was. It was dark. We woke up in a daze and Michio lit a flare. The hull began to crush inwards and this thing, this shadow, it just seeped through the cracks and engulfed them." She began to shake and tears fell down her face. "I ran. I just ran. I couldn't see anything. I just heard the screams as it consumed them. It was... crying." She looked up confused and terrified.

Hal took a step back, remembering the void that passed by him, whimpering.

"What's happening? Why are we here?" She turned away. "What is this place?"

His gut sank. He knew where they were. "It's the ARCA. We're on the other side."

She spun around to face him, almost angry, but the realization quickly hit her. They didn't know where the ARCA displaced matter, just that it wasn't in their reality.

"Claire, was the ARCA in the helicopter when you woke?" He tried to be gentle, knowing that she'd replay the whole event in her head again.

Her eyes darted back and forth trying to recall the surroundings. "No. And neither were you. Or Ortiz. It was just Michio and two others. Where is everyone?"

"I don't know. I woke up about two miles from here. You're the first person I've seen." He paused, questioning whether or not to mention the void that had passed him. Right now it didn't matter. They had to find the others, if they were still here and lost.

"You think the ARCA did this?" She asked, looking back at the path she came from.

"I don't know, but I've been here before." He had this undeniable feeling of déjà vu, and the longer he stayed, the more familiar this place became.

She turned to face him in disbelief. "What?"

"It's confusing. I don't understand it. It's just so familiar." He closed his eyes and pressed his hands to his face. "Those dreams I had. They weren't dreams. They were memories."

"Hal." She walked closer to him in comfort, but didn't know how to respond. It didn't make sense.

He shrugged, trying to erase any feelings. "We need to find the others before..."

She held her head down and bit back more tears.

"Claire. We need to get back to the helicopter. If anyone survived, they'll be looking too." He placed both hands on her shoulders. "It's OK."

She nodded and turned back towards the direction she fled from and wearily walked forward.

She stepped carefully as her bare feet sank into the mud. The terrain had changed from the oily beach sand to a congealed, cold muck, and Hal struggled to pull his clumsy boots out from each step.

The fog thickened as they continued deeper into the dead forest. Hal tried to swing his arms and move it, but the more he struggled, the more it seemed to cling to him.

Claire stopped, looking from right to left for the trail she came down. She sighed with frustration. "We should be there by now. Ortiz! Can anyone hear me!"

Hal ran over to her. "No, don't!"

She turned to face him before the thundering shock made the ground shift under their feet.

"What's happening?" She looked in fear as the wailing horn echoed through the trees.

He grabbed her wrist and ran forward. Her fear was almost paralyzing as Hal dragged her towards a mound of dirt several feet above the mud and pressed his back against a tree.

"Don't move," he whispered.

The sky darkened and the mud below them began to shift as roots and tree limbs lifted above the surface. Hal could see the panic rising in her, breathing heavily as tears slid down her face.

The green haze transitioned to a dark cloud, moving rapidly over the ground, coming towards them.

"Hal?" Her voice was shaking.

"Don't move."

He watched as she struggled to control her fear.

The whimper came, and she exhaled heavy, about to burst. Hal grabbed her arm and swung his hand around her mouth. His grip was tight as she trembled, struggling to disobey her instincts and run. He held her arms down with his other arm, wrapping around her waist.

The remaining light that lingered around them retreated as the void approached, crying and whimpering in sorrow, endlessly searching for life to consume.

Hal was almost calm. His energy was focused on the beast. He knew better than to run. It would only be attracted to the chaos.

"Shh," he whispered and she breathed in deeply through her nose.

The void stopped, shifting in positioned. Dark rings reached out like tentacles, searching the air and ground, crying in a low tone as it moved.

Claire held her breath, her eyes wide, as it hovered closer. Hal remained still. It couldn't see them.

The creature let out a shriek and lashed the earth behind it. Its noise muted out the roaring horn that resounded beyond them. Another tentacle whipped to its side, and another, smashing the base of the dirt mount. It swung again, hitting a tree to their left, cracking like a whip as it plunged into the bark. Something supernatural was happening and the tree responded. Its roots up-heaved and lashed back. Its branches creaked as it reached out toward the beast.

From below, vines slithered out of the soil, wrapping around the base of the void. It let out another shriek as they spiraled up, gripping the tentacles and pulling them down. The mud lurched upward, exposing more roots that grabbed onto the creature. The roots yanked and splattered in the mud as it fought. Branches whipped through the air, slashing the darkness as it fell further and further into the earth. The fog followed as it was pulled down underneath the soil.

The earth was in turmoil as it consumed its prey. It gurgled and spat, swallowing the darkness. The tree calmed, its branches falling back down to the side, and the heaving roots rested as they sank back into place below the surface.

The echoing horn ceased and the haze reoccupied the space below. It grew lighter as the darkness vanished and Hal released his grip from Claire as she began to breath steadily.

She lunged forward, placing her hands on her knees to catch herself. With a few deep breaths, she was able to compose herself and push down the panic. She turned and looked at him, her eyes wide with confusion and still shaken. "How did you know?"

"This place is at war with itself. I've seen the void before, but I can't explain how I remember it." He looked around at the tree that was now stiff and silent.

"What..." She trailed off, gazing at the ground where the beast had been sucked into. "What was that?"

He shrugged, holding his palms upright as a drop of dark rain tapped his skin. "I don't know. I suspect it's the same thing that was attracted to Michio's flare."

She stood in realization and whispered. "It consumes the light."

Hal nodded. The rain was beginning to fall more steadily and he grabbed her hand. She looked up at him, still dazed by what they'd just witnessed.

"Come on." He tugged gently on her arm, but she resisted.

"Wait. You said you've been here before. How? I mean, if you crossed over, then how did you get out?" Her tone had changed from scared to curious.

Hal struggled to remember anything and shook his head. "Right after I awoke in your doctor's laboratory, I remember this place. The horn, the fog, the darkness." He looked around at his surrounding, more familiar than ever. "There are others here. There was a small group. I remember their faces." He closed his eyes as something flashed back. "Four. No wait. There were five of us. We were in a small camp somewhere, but it was different. We were gathered in some sort of man-made cave. The ground was powder, like a golden sand. Not like this."

He crouched down and placed his hand on the cold dirt, struggling to feel the memory as it rushed back to him. "Someone had left the group. They were looking for food, and they ran back to the base, but something followed him. He was panicked, yelling in a foreign language. I couldn't understand him, but the darkness followed. Everyone fled. We didn't plan for anything. We all just darted in different directions. I must have run for miles. Then there were these sparks and an overwhelming brightness. There was something else, though. Something was following me and then..." He trailed off and opened his eyes to meet Claire's looking down at him in sympathy. "Then it just stopped."

She looked at him with a new realization. "Your nightmares? They were here?" She asked somberly and he nodded. "How long was it?"

"I haven't figured that out yet." He looked up at the sky that loomed an ever existing dusk. "There's no cycle here. With no nights, no mornings, it's hard to tell. Months, maybe a year. I only have fragments of my memory, but some of it has come back."

He was somewhat comforted that he could remember, and also terrified to see the images scrolling through his head. He could see their faces. There was a small camp somewhere on the outskirts where four others remained. The soil was different, almost like a powder, and there was a small amount of vegetation that they were able to scavenge food from. He could remember a camp fire that burned and some sort of animal cooked above it. Then there were the violent memories, being stalked out in the open, much like this place now.

It was painful trying to recall the past; a fight with your own mind trying to remember a dream that was quickly fleeting, but bits and pieces floated back to the surface.

Claire stepped over and sat on the ground next to him. She was calm now, but still bewildered.

He looked at her and smiled a little. It was a shitty situation, but at least he wasn't alone in it. The others were here still, somewhere. At least some of them were, and there was reason to hope. She sat quietly beside him waiting for something, anything. Dazed and confused, it all still felt like a bad dream neither could wake up from, and it seemed pointless to try. They were both drained, physically and mentally, and Claire sat, staring off into nowhere curiously but devoid of any energy to move forward.

He closed his eyes, recalling his last memory. It was like a dream, but parts of it were still clear. The sparks, blinding flashes of light, the echo of the horn wailing from no particular direction, they all came back in small increments.

The doctor's voice came through in those last moments as he ran. It was so far and all the scenery looked the same. Then it all just ended. It was a black spot. His dreams had been so vivid and clear now, except for this one and it was the only one that really mattered. If it were his last few moments before breaching back through to reality, he had to know how.

He sighed in frustration. It just wasn't there.

"We should keep going and try to find some shelter." He looked up and squinted as the rain fell more steadily.

She stood, clumsily, and straightened the big jacked over her shoulders tighter. Hal watched sympathetically. It wasn't necessarily cold out, but her bare legs and feet were pale from the previous hours of hypothermia she was still recovering from. The jacket was large, and came down to her knees, covering most of her body and she began to walk forward without direction. They didn't know where they were going, but she led the way.

Hal pulled on his chest harness that felt tight around his ribs as the leather straps strained against new bruises. The rain beat down on his shoulders and he ached for someplace dry with firm ground.

The rain faded to a drizzle after several minutes and the ground below them began to harden as the soil quickly absorbed what life came from it. Branches hung low, dipping into the dirt like roots and anchoring the mass from above and below. They thrived in the rain, despite a lack of sunshine.

A flicker of light caught his attention from the side. Claire still paced forward, unobservant and confused. She was on autopilot, walking around like a zombie with a blank mind. The realization hadn't hit her yet, but this place almost seemed normal to him.

"Wait. Look." He pointed to the side and she lazily peered through the fog in its direction.

Hal didn't wait as he skipped forward, his feet now gripping the hard, rocky ground that proceeded them.

A late 1980's prop plane dug into the dirt. Its nose was buried three feet into the hard surface, but the hull was mostly intact with its tail in the air and one remaining wing extending outward.

He held out his hand, cautiously telling Claire to wait. He was paranoid, but understandably so. The plane was in fairly good condition, or at least as far as shelter was concerned, but who knew what type of creature might have taken up occupancy.

He pulled the tranquilizer pistol from his harness and held it forward before pulling the side door open. It screeched on its hinges before the metal gave and tumbled onto the ground. Startled, he jumped back with his arms at bay.

The interior was dry and two seats that had detached from the floor rails now laid on their sides.

He cautiously peered in farther, letting his eyes adjust to the darkness. The plane was in good shape considering it took quite a beating upon impact, and he could see the interior had remained untouched as he stepped inside.

"Hal?" Claire knelt down as she crept in behind him with her hands over her mouth, staring at the rear end where a passenger still remained. The man hung from a seat harness, the flaps of his jacket hanging to the sides.

He stepped passed her and grabbed a sleeve as bones and dust slid out the opening.

Claire jerked backwards, looking in the opposite direction. The man had been here for quite some time and probably died upon impact.

"I'm sorry to do this." Hal spoke to the man, regretful of what he was about to do. He released the clamp that held him in, and as it let loose, his body collapsed forward. Claire still had her back turned, nauseous by the sight.

Hal pulled the remaining clothing and threw it through the doorway, kicking the debris from the floor out the exit. He felt a sense of guilt as he grabbed the man's boots and shook the remaining fragments out. All the soft tissue had decomposed and dried, leaving a waif of dust and small bones.

He held the boot to his foot, sizing it to his own. It was a size bigger than the ones he currently wore, and he cringed as he exchanged them. At least he had socks.

"There. It's gone, Claire. We should rest here for a while."

She turned to face him as he held out his old boots as an offering.

She smiled and accepted, dropping them onto the ground and sliding her small feet in. They were a few sizes too big and thumped on the ground as her feet loosely flopped around inside.

He pulled one of the seats back onto the rail. It tilted and wobbled on its stand, but stayed upright and he motioned for her to sit. He began to fumble with the other seat, leaning it against the hull for stability. It reclined backward as he let his body fall heavily onto it.

It was almost comfortable on the worn cotton as he leaned back.

Claire lay across from him. Her eyes were closed and she shifted, lifting her knees under the large coat and curling her arms around.

"Your boots are gross, by the way." Her eyes remained shut and Hal couldn't help himself as he let out a hearty laugh. Everything about this place was a nightmare. The trees, the fog, the inhabitants; they were worse than any dream he could have concocted, yet he found himself struck with humor.

"You should see my new ones." He joked back, holding out one leg to display the torn leather, covered in bone powder, and she returned with laughter. "They fit, too."

Her smile remained as she looked back at him. "You know, when we wake up from this..."

"I'm retiring." He filled in the blank before the humor faded.

"Yeah. Me too." She ran her fingers through her matted hair, trying to give it an organized direction as it fell back from her face. Her head tilted back and her eyes shut again.

"Thank you." She was quiet and calm now. "You didn't have to come back." There was a long pause, holding back emotions that were about to surface.

"Claire..." He lifted his head, trying to restrain what he felt. "I couldn't leave you there. "

She bit her lip, failing to hold back the tears.

Hal felt a wave of guilt come over as he sat back again. "I'm sorry. I never meant to disrupt your world...."

"You didn't." She cut him off, but not assertively. "Our world was a wreck already. Without you, we'd still be chasing the Yotogi, Kyra would have the ARCA and I... I wouldn't be anywhere."

His heart sank. He'd felt nothing but guilt since he'd resurfaced and now... now someone needed him. Someone wanted him.

She stared in reassurance. She didn't want him to feel rejected or like a hindrance. Any debt he owed had been paid, but that wasn't it. He was the only person she could trust. There were no career motivations, no intentions to destroy the company, or the world for that matter. He was the only one eager enough to risk an invasion into Russia for her and not just the ARCA.

Hal never had anyone care about him, or at least not outside of his family. He had married his career and love of flying, and this emotion of attachment was new, but comforting.

He smiled and she returned. "Get some sleep."

There was more to share and things she wanted to say, but exhaustion was taking over and she shifted in the chair. Her eyes fell heavy and she relaxed her arms around her knees. Her legs were still bundled in under the large coat and hung off the edges

Hal yawned, watching as she let go and fell unconscious. The weight of the last few days was heavy and he fought to stay awake, but it was an impossible burden as he stared at her, now peaceful and oblivious to the surroundings.

His eyes had adjusted to the lack of light within the plane and for the first time it was welcomed. It was quiet and he let his eyelids fall. His body sank into the cushion and the darkness grew warm as he slipped into it.

Chapter 28: A New World

Hal stretched uncomfortably as the springs under the thin cushion dug into his backside. The air was chilly and fog lingered in the open doorway. The dim daylight never changed except when a void was present, but it was peaceful now. Claire still lay in her chair, curled up and asleep. He checked his watch, but it was pointless as he tapped on the arm band, which remained dark.

His stomach turned and rumbled with hunger. It'd been at least a full day since either had eaten anything and there was little to no vegetation that was edible.

The plane lay partly on its side and was mostly intact. The rear extended another twelve feet or so from where he sat and several containers and luggage had remained in place for at least a few decades.

He stood and walked down the aisle, still paranoid that something might lash out as he held his tranquilizer pistol firmly in one hand.

In the dim light he scoured through the compartments. A first aid kit was still sealed, some spare parachutes, empty water jugs and a few suit cases were scattered on the floor.

He began to rummage through the suitcases for anything that might be useful. Food, water bottles, clothing, even ammunition was a possibility. There were three suitcases in total and one large packing bag. He unzipped the first and rummaged through its belongings. Clothing, sandals, and more empty bottles. The clothing was light. Presumably the travelers were headed to a beach vacation spot before they tumbled out of the sky. The next bag was much of the same, but he was pleasantly surprised at the third as aluminum cans clanked against one another. A small case of cola, beer and canned fruit rattled onto the floor, waking Claire as one rolled towards her feet.

She whipped her head around in shock as she woke, not fully coherent and conscious of the surroundings. Her eyes settled on Hal as he looked back apologetically.

"There are some supplies here that I think we can use," he explained, holding a can of warm beer with one hand.

She looked around and sighed. "How long were we out?"

Hal let his hand fall to his side, still holding the unopened cans. "At least a few hours. I tried the arm band but it's completely dead. Are you hungry?"

She slid her hand under her coat to her stomach and nodded before slumping out of the chair and onto her feet. She wobbled over in her big boots and stretched.

"There's some canned goods and some rations that the previous passengers were carrying. They're expired but still sealed." He held up a few cans of fruit and something that looked like a toaster tart in an aluminum wrapper.

"Beer?"

She chuckled and accepted. "It's hard to believe this place has remained untouched since at least..." She held up the canned fruit and read the expiration date. "1989!"

Hal smiled back. "You know, I actually remember those years." It was an odd concept to think about, given that her reality was in the year 2039.

She popped the can open and smelled its contents before attempting to pull out a slimy peach with her hand. Hal watched, mildly amused, waiting for some sort of shutter or gross expression. The food was at least fifty years old by now.

She closed her eyes and chewed. "It tastes like the can, but not bad," she said and continued. "So. What were the 90's like?"

Hal snapped open an old can of beer, and to his surprise it was still fizzy. "Well, computers were big. Not like what you have now. We had box monitors with transformer tubes and these huge towers that cost thousands, well, probably tens of thousands with your inflation now. Televisions were the same and we picked up reception on rabbit ear antennas."

"Wow. The stone age," she joked, lifting her eyebrows in sarcasm.

"It wasn't so different from your world though. If someone had asked me what 2039 looked like, I would have imagined people on hover crafts and robots taking over." He relaxed against the ship's hull and for those minutes he'd forgotten where or when they both were.

"Oh, they tried," she said sarcastically. "Japan became the world's leader in robotics and Troy has actually been part of their orthotic program to help his mobility. However, as you've seen, he's not the easiest person to work with."

"He rejects everything." He nodded in response.

"Yeah. That's a way to describe it mildly." She trailed off and finished the can of peaches before crawling over to the remaining luggage.

She unzipped the large bag and pulled out several new pieces of clothing. "Pants!" She pulled them out and over her bare legs.

"How extraordinary!" Hal joked, watching her turn around in them and adjusting the waistline. "A bit big."

"Beggars can't be choosers." She was just relieved to have something covering her bottom half and the thick denim was a comforting addition.

She sat down and leaned against him, popping open an old can of cola. Maybe it was the buzz of the old beer or the lack of food that made his head spin, but he was more comfortable now than he had been since he awoke in Prossman's lab. He raised his arm and placed it around her shoulder, pulling her closer. She was warm and content, wrapped in the coat and under his arm. It wasn't the time or place for romance, but he couldn't help himself as he brushed the hair from the side of her face behind her ear. Her blue eyes were lazy and tired and she leaned forward, touching her lips to his. Her palm touched his cheek and pulled him down farther. He closed his eyes and breathed in the moment. She'd kissed him before in Russia during their escape, but he'd shrugged it off, telling himself it was just a reaction in the chaos. She'd been drugged and confused, and in the rush of the moment she was just glad someone had come to take her away. They were both strangers from different worlds, but he no longer wanted to go back to his past.

She cupped his face in her hands and moved closer. His heart began to race as he pulled her in. What he would give to be somewhere else right now.

The horn echoed, shattering the peace and they both backed away, covering their ears as it rang through the forest.

Hal stood and walked towards the door as the light outside began to vanish.

"It's coming back," she whispered in the corner, straightening her coat as she stood.

Hal ran over and dumped the clothes from the carrying bag and threw what supplies they might need into it. The cans clanked around inside, making more noise than he expected and the forest began to come alive.

The hull screeched as something latched on. The remaining light outside began to creep in through the cracks as it caved in under the pressure.

"We need to run this one." Hal gripped her hand and pulled her out the doorway.

He looked to his right as the light began to vanish, but the beast wasn't in range yet. Something had targeted them and it knew where they were now. He began to jog in the opposite direction, gripping the cans in the bag as he tried to silence their movement. He didn't know where he was going other than away, chasing the light. Trees whipped and lashed their branches as they passed. The soil beneath them fought to grip their feet as they briefly touched the surface.

The ground thumped, shaking the trees and earth beneath them. Hal slowed his pace and looked side to side. As they stopped, the trees halted and the branches retreated. Something was coming, and it was big.

Footsteps approached, shaking the earth as it came closer. Claire gripped his arm and darted a glance in every direction.

A wailing shriek came from their left and Hal shifted to move Claire behind him, extending his arm to shield her.

"Go," he whispered and began to step backwards.

She bolted without further directions and he followed behind, casting a quick glance to his back.

Trees cracked and he could hear the footsteps quicken. Flickers of lights began to spark, catching his peripheral vision as he passed them. They were brief and disappeared before he could focus. Whatever beast was following them agitated the world. The trees made way for it and the ground heaved up as it approached. The soil fell still and solid beneath.

Hal reached for the tranquilizer and fired a shot backward. He couldn't see the creature yet, but his weapon still fired true.

The fog thickened, and the trees started to grow thinner. It couldn't hide for long.

Claire stopped abruptly and Hal almost plowed into her. A cliff side was hidden in the fog as it dropped down into a pit of darkness.

Hal spun around, waiting as the shocks of the earth approached, his gun ready. Claire clung to his back, an arm wrapped around his waist.

The steps were slowing as a deep grumble traveled over the settling fog.

A white dome appeared and Hal raised his weapon, focusing on the mass as it slowly stepped into view. His eyes widened in recognition. He remembered this beast.

The warped body calmly took a step. Its frame was carried by three legs, two extending in the front and a smaller in the back. The knee joints protruded from the milky skin. Dark veins pumped a black fluid through the chest up the collar bones and neck. Its eyes darted open and the black glossy domes that sunk under its brow spotted them.

He squeezed several shots, each striking the creature's chest and neck. It shrieked and charged forward. Forty feet away, it began to stumble and Hal pulled two more shots. Its front leg gave and threw the beast's weight forward, tripping on itself and throwing the massive body to the ground.

It rebelled, trying to stand upright, but the more it fought, the heavier it fell each time. He wasn't going to take any chances and he stepped forward before firing a last shot to the temple.

Spasms overcame the creature as it cried and the echoing horn faded, almost instantly sending the world back into its deafening silence.

He stepped closer and looked down at the beast as it fought the last moments of consciousness. The image of this thing was burned into his memory, recalling the chase right before waking up in the lab. It was no dream.

Claire stepped cautiously behind him, gazing down. "What the hell is that thing?"

"She's an abomination," he said, coldly.

"She looks... human." She knelt down and held out her hand, hesitating before she placed it on the dry white skin.

She was right. There were some undeniably human traits. The skull had morphed, creating a dome that extended back. Its brow protruded forward and the sunken eyes had an outlining iris. Her chest was stretched along the ribcage and what looked like breasts hung to the side. It looked like a human skeleton underneath it all, morphed and distorted, but the anatomy was similar.

"I've seen this," Claire whispered.

"You have?"

She let out a sigh, hiding shame. "Yes. Well, not all of it, but while we were conducting tests on aquatic life, we would sometimes capture things that we didn't recognize. We thought they were some sort of mutated sea creatures from the radiation on Bermuda, but this," she pointed to the shoulder and rib cage, "we have a specimen of this in the lab. Several of them, actually."

"I've seen it, too," he said.

She stood, her eyes wandering and hopeful. "They can cross over."

"Did you see the sparks?" He asked, motioning towards the forest they'd exited.

"Yes."

"I remember them. They were one of my last memories here. They attached themselves to the helicopter as we were flying back, when the ARCA overpowered everything."

Her eyes were glowing through the fading tears. "We need to find the ARCA."

Her enthusiasm grew as she looked back and forth trying to recall anything about her surroundings. They had traveled so far in two days. If the ARCA was still at the crash site, they were way off the mark by now.

She grabbed his arm and tapped on his wrist band, hopeful for any signs of life. It flickered, illuminating some of the circuits briefly before shutting off again.

"Hal, look." She looked down at the immediate area around them. The fog clung to his arm as she touched it. The light flickered and the fog again gravitated towards the band. "I think it's disrupting the transmissions."

"We need to find someplace dry." He grabbed her hand and they started to jog.

Retreating in the direction they came was horribly disorienting. Everything looked the same and weaving in and out of the tree brush only redirected them by a few degrees. Nonetheless, they'd gone off course somewhere.

Their footsteps had vanished into the mud but he kept going forward. There had to be something, a landmark, a rock, a hillside, anything dry.

Claire sighed in frustration. "We should have passed it by now."

Exhausted, he leaned against a tree stump and held his head in his hands. There was nothing but marshland as far as they could see.

"We should switch directions." He looked to his right and began to trot forward. If they couldn't find the plane or the helicopter wreckage, maybe they could find something else; someplace new.

Claire hurried up behind him and grabbed the bag from his shoulder. He was exhausted and carrying the heavy load had left him drained.

"I'll take this for a while. You lead." She swung the strap over her shoulder.

They traveled a few hundred feet further and the terrain began to change again. The ground was firmer and lighter, but not like the hard dirt they'd been on before. It was a fine powder that clung to their shoes, like sand, but lighter. Hal was again struck with déjà vu as the fog thinned away. The trees were also different and had dark leaves lining the branches.

"Hal, look." She paused and slowly approached something illuminating a white rock to their side.

It was some sort of quartz crystal, but it gave off its own light from within.

Hal pulled up his sleeve and touched the arm band. It responded to his touch, and as he approached, it grew brighter.

Claire took notice and grabbed his arm. She was smiling as the band returned to function. Tapping in some commands, a topographical map appeared. It didn't give a satellite image, but red markings came up on the screen.

"These are power signatures. If the ARCA is within a two mile radius it should be one of these markers." She looked up at him optimistically.

"There are so many, though." Hal noted, realizing there were a dozen or so dots, each blinking like some sort of ping transmission.

"Yeah," she said, confused. More and more glowing crystals were becoming visible. It was as if they were attracted to the electronics and amplifying a signal.

It was almost pretty as the lights brightened. The purple hue that they gave off reflected on the white rock surfaces as the fog retreated.

Claire stood and gazed around them. Her mouth dropped open as the land became more visible and bright.

She stumbled forward, tripping on the white sandstone blocks that lined a floor. Massive pillars stood ahead of them. Some had toppled over, but the landmarks were definitely man made.

Hal followed. His eyes were no longer glued to his arm band as he walked inward, the light growing and reflecting off clean surfaces.

"What is this? I mean, how could someone build this and not be..." She trailed off in awe of the sight, placing a hand on the stone. "It's warm."

Hal set his hand on the stone and a small growth of crystals sprouted from its surface.

Claire came up and examined what was happening. She looked at him in excited, confused shock.

Hal removed his hand, but the crystals continued to slowly grow. It was as if he were creating the light, the life, that separated this place from the dead swamp.

They continued forward through the entrance and stood in awe as the land opened up. Pillars lay on the ground and stone structures heaved out, partly buried by the white sand that had spent centuries untouched.

"Where are we?" she asked.

"Atlantis?" He sarcastically guessed.

She laughed, but jokes aside, it was as accurate a guess as any.

"What I would do for a camera right now." She stumbled forward, amazed. "Hal, do you realize what we've found? This has got to be the largest undiscovered landmass anyone has ever seen!"

"You mean this thing doesn't come equipped with a camera?" He sarcastically asked, referring to his arm band. "Even in my generation everyone had a camera on their cell phone."

She laughed, looking at the layout of ruined buildings that stretched as far as they could see.

Hal examined the beacons of light that pulsated on the band's display. One stood out among the others, blinking more rapidly.

"Claire, there's a strong reading to our left. It's a big one." He walked towards its direction and she reluctantly left the scenery to follow.

The sand rose above most of the small buildings, engulfing the rooftops of what were presumably houses at one time. Sandstone walls surrounded the area, almost like a barricade protecting a city. Crystals were scattered along the ground, lining walls and growing brighter, almost blindingly so, as he walked passed.

The ground took a dip as it descended downward and Hal paused before cautiously treading down the slope. The soil gave beneath his feet and he stumbled, sliding down the hillside.

Everything around him darkened as he slid and the fog again started to creep in.

Claire stumbled over, still at the top of the ledge. "Are you OK?"

Hal shook the sand off his clothing. "Yeah. Stay there!"

In the blink of an eye, the ground changed. It moved, now aware of his presence.

His arm band flickered and went dark. He had crossed the zone and the land he now stood before slowly crept closer. Before going out, the arm band indicated a power source should have been several feet directly ahead of him.

A grumble came before him and he stood still, panicked and unable to move. Something snarled in the haze and he reached for his tranquilizer, which now only had eight remaining shots. He wasn't ready yet.

"Claire! Can you break a crystal and throw it to me?" He yelled over his shoulder without taking focus off his surroundings.

"What? Why?" she yelled back.

"Just do it!"

She didn't hesitate and grabbed the nearest crystal she could find, yanking at the base, but to no avail. She removed her boot and swung at it several times before it chipped off the surface.

As she approached the edge and began to throw, the sand beneath her gave out and threw her to the ground. Gravity pulled, sending her down the slide of white powder that quickly transitioned to murky mud at the bottom.

She rolled to a stop and froze as two red eyes glowed in the dark.

Hal tiptoed over to her and reached out his hand. She didn't take her focus off the beast as she lifted the crystal to his side.

The light grew as he approached. His arm band illuminated, sending some sort of electrical signal, sparking the crystal's internal light. The mud slithered away, retreating as it uncovered the ground hidden beneath.

The beast snarled and backed away with the darkness. Hal felt a surge of adrenaline and welcomed surprise as it startled the creature, pushing it back with the dead world it resided in.

He touched his hand to a low hanging tree branch and it immediately began to wither. The branches pulled in, some dropping to the ground, and crystals began to sprout from the remaining surface. He went to another tree and another. They grew brighter and brighter with each one.

Claire stood and grabbed his arm. The marker was here, and he stepped forward.

She placed her hands over her mouth, muting a shriek of joy as two power cores began to spin wildly in reaction. It was the ARCA.

Chapter 29: The Doorway Out

Hal perched the ARCA onto his back and painfully climbed the steep hillside. The sand was volatile and he fought for every solid footstep his boots could grab. Claire did the same, grabbing whatever roots and rocks protruded from the surface.

He flopped onto his back as it leveled off, breathing in heavy, and his body covered in sand. Claire reached a hand up for the last step and she tumbled down onto his chest.

Covered in the white powder, he let out a sigh of exhaustion. It wasn't a victory yet, but he laughed in relief as he held her face and stretched upward to kiss her. She leaned forward onto him and returned, pinning him to the ground and he wrapped both arms around to embrace her. Weathered and beaten, a kiss wasn't uncalled for. He slid his hands down her back and she lifted up onto her palms, staring down and laughing at the mess they both were.

"Ugh. Look at us." She laughed, almost hysterically.

She rolled to the side, landing on her back, but Hal wasn't done with the moment. He slid the ARCA's harness over his head and rolled, placing his hand on her face and turning her towards him. Her arm came up over his head, running her fingers through his matted hair and meeting his lips again. His hand slid down her neck and under the heavy coat. Her warm skin was soft under the cloth and he wrapped his arm under her chest, lifting her from the ground and pulling her in.

Her warm skin was soft under the cloth and he wrapped his arm under her chest, lifting her from the ground and pulling her into an intimate embrace. He kissed her neck and she reached around his back, hugging him closer.

She laughed. "We might actually get out of here."

He propped himself upward and looked over at the ARCA. It was beautiful, glowing as the two remaining power cells spun wildly in their cylinder chambers.

"Will it work with only two chambers?" He asked, suddenly doubtful.

"They function in a parallel circuit. It won't be as strong, but it should work." She began to sit up, still blushed and flustered.

Hal remained sitting as she crawled over to the device. The touch panel was cracked, distorting the image, but it was still functional.

"I reprogrammed it in Russia. We were able to realign the frequency for any zone, so it's stable now, but again, we haven't had much time to test it." She stood, hoisting the heavy device onto her knee and aiming it towards one of the white sand walls. The burst was weak as it made contact, crumbling the wall, but there was far less distortion than he remembered.

She let out a frustrated sigh. "What I would do for a simple volt meter right now. The circuit's been damaged. I can see the wiring that's been broken off from the third core, but everything else looks good."

"What about these crystals? They seem to give off their own energy source." He pulled the crystal chunk from his pocket.

She rotated it in her hand. It did seem to radiate some sort of energy field, and his arm band picked it up on radar.

"Worth a shot. There's no telling how much power is being generated. I don't feel any shock with it in my hands, but if it can even put out a few more volts, it'll help." She clumsily placed it in the position of the missing chamber and held it against the bridge wire. Her expression wasn't promising as she looked down at it.

"Why the hell not," she said, then pulled the trigger.

The shock threw her to the ground as it projected forward. Now laying on her back, she released the trigger and slid the ARCA to her side on the ground.

"Bloody hell!" she yelled.

Hal laughed, reaching out his hand to help her sit up. She was only stunned as she wiped more white powder from her chest.

"That's got some kick!" They both laughed at how ridiculously perfect it worked.

"I want to take this home with me."

"Can we reverse the effect to take us back?" He changed his tone to serious.

She let out a huff. "I don't know. If the frequency is set correctly, yes, but we have no way of knowing. We need to test it on something organic. Here, let me see your arm band."

270

Hal slid the device from his arm that had been attached so comfortably. The air tingled on his skin where it had been as he handed it over.

Claire slipped it onto her forearm and touched in some commands. It illuminated, displaying bits of code he couldn't translate.

Her eyes widened at the readings, looking at Hal.

"What is it?"

"We're on Bermuda." She stood, gazing around at the land that should have been demolished. "These are the coordinates of St. George. It can't be."

"Why? Bermuda is nice." He tried asking sarcastically, but something still worried her.

"In your time it was. But now, if we resurface we'll be in the dead zone. Bermuda was wiped out by a nuclear attack in 2027."

"Is there any place habitable?"

She shook her head, clearing her memory. "Yes, the southern tip. But that's miles from here."

Hal sighed. He wasn't looking forward to another long hike through the marshland, but if they were somehow able to breach back through, they'd be dooming themselves to deadly radioactive levels.

"So we walk." He accepted it, swallowing hard and wincing at the idea. "We take some crystals, make contact with the land, bring it back to this." He waved his hand around, pointing to the surrounding white sands.

She looked down and nodded. It was a painful thought, carrying their supply bag and the ARCA, but at least they knew which direction to head in and the arm band was functional as long as it was within the radius of a power source.

Hal stood, holding out his hand to carry the ARCA and Claire grabbed the bag with its remaining supplies.

As they followed their footsteps back Hal kicked loose several more crystals and loaded them into his pockets. Claire did the same and piled them into the bag. Its weight grew heavier and slowed her pace.

They approached the entrance of the city and Hal touched the white stone with a crystal. It immediately sprouted new ones as he passed. The land cleared, pushing the fog and grim muck that covered its surface. If anything, it cleared a pathway they could follow back.

Exhausted, they stopped and sat on the expanding white rocks. It was warm and light, almost as if it were reborn again. The trail behind them glowed and slowly began spreading in width.

A groan came from the brush to their side and the slithering soil backed away. It wasn't a creature like before and Hal felt hope as he walked forward.

A man lay on his back, tangled in the roots that slowly retreated. Roots punctured his chest and legs as they moved out and a stream of warm blood flowed. He gasped and looked up at them.

Hal reached down and pressed his hand to the man's chest. He was one of the Russian guards, and Hal looked down at him in sympathy as he struggled to breathe.

Claire crouched down to his side and spoke something in his language. He reached up, touching her face. "I'm sorry."

His hand slid down, leaving a bloody print on her skin as the life left his eyes. She held her head down and let his hand drop to his side. There was a feeling of guilt now knowing the hell they'd been sending these men to.

"It's not your fault." Hal placed a hand on her shoulder.

"I know. It's just," she trailed off. "We never understood where the ARCA would place matter."

"Claire." He grabbed her shoulder and nudged her to look in his direction. "These men would have done much worse. Kyra is still out there."

She nodded. Had the ARCA gone into full production, there was no telling what they would have used it for. There was no sign of Kyra in Russia, but there was no doubt she'd continue and no one would be there to stop her.

"Let's keep moving." He stood and gripped her hand, pulling her to her feet.

"Wait! We need to test the ARCA on something organic"

Hal looked down at the man regretfully, but nodded. He was no longer part of any world, and would serve as the first test subject back.

He returned several seconds later with the ARCA and Claire moved in behind him.

"This is for a good cause," he assured himself.

Hal remembered the pushing force of the ARCA from before and braced his footing. The crystal substitute was much stronger and he lurched backwards with its force. The beam distorted time and the surroundings slowly pulled into its wake. Claire's hand slowly moved upward, pointing at the lining of the beams arch. It was a transparent gateway, part their world, part the other. They overlapped and a green haze escaped the lining as the man faded into the neighboring existence.

He released and the snap of reality pulled them both forward.

He glanced back at Claire who looked hopeful.

"Is that our world?" he asked.

She nodded, smiling. Optimism was a feeling of relief.

Chapter 30: The Trip Home

They continued to travel south and eventually found themselves on a beach, which was littered with abandoned air crafts and boats, partially buried in the sand. Hal guessed most were from the early 2000's, possibly earlier.

Claire stood in amazement, staring down the stretch. "How did all of these get here?"

Hal just shook his head. Akira's voice resounded in his mind, and he wasn't so reluctant to consider it this time. Planes, ships and persons have been disappearing for decades, even centuries, in the Bermuda Triangle.

For now, the explanation was still complicated, but more believable, and the possibility of returning to his future home was the only thing that mattered.

"Is this a good place?" He gestured towards any of the nearby surroundings.

"As good as any. St. George was one of the only islands of Bermuda that was relatively untouched. Well, parts of it anyway." She began to position the ARCA on the ground, pulling a loose string from her denim pants and rigging up a remote trigger switch.

"We're not taking the ARCA with us?"

"I think it's for the best. Besides, if it gets thrown into the rift with us, who knows where it'll displace matter." She continued to tie strings from bits of her clothing she'd ripped off, wrapping around the trigger and trailing backwards about twenty feet. "It's calibrated. I can't guarantee this won't hurt, or worse, but I can't stay here."

He nodded somewhat reluctantly, but if there was a choice of dying or staying, he'd choose the former.

She gripped her hands around his waist and he wrapped his arms around her back, pulling close.

She clenched her eyes shut, pulling the trigger and braced for the unexpected. The immediate burst stung as they were yanked forward, but it subsided as the confusing disorientation stunned the nerves, throwing them into another existence.

Hal swung his arms out in front of him, blinded by the light. The force was like a swift kick to the gut and he flung backwards, landing on the soft sand. He lay still, rubbing his eyes, and the faint sounds of water slowly faded in. Squinting, the sunlight breached through and he frantically looked back and forth.

"Claire!" His vision was limited as he yelled, hoping for a reply.

She coughed several feet away. "I'm OK. I can't see."

"Give it a minute." He was just relieved to hear her voice as he stumbled to his feet and wobbled in her general direction.

"I got you." He reached down and grabbed her shoulders.

She squinted, desperately searching for some familiarity. "There's sunlight! Ugh, thank God, sunlight! I hear the ocean."

Hal chuckled. He'd never been so grateful for that glowing ball of gas and the salty air that only an ocean could bring.

With fuzzy eyes she pulled up her sleeve and tried to focus on the arm band.

"This is Claire Kass. Can anyone hear me?" There was silence for several seconds before she made another attempt. "I repeat, this is Claire Kass. A&H, can you hear me?"

Noise faded in and out from the unit.

"Claire? We read you. What's your position?" Hal never thought he'd be so happy to hear Brack's voice.

"Um, we're on the southern island of St. George, Bermuda. Requesting evac." She read back to him, still not able to read the exact coordinates.

"Roger. Evac is on the way." There was a long pause before he came back. "Do you have the ARCA?"

She sighed. For crying out loud, they were still only interested in the damned ARCA. "Negative. It's been destroyed."

Hal laid down in the sand, basking in the warmth of the sun. It would be several hours before anyone would arrive for a pick up, and he anticipated the ring of questions they'd no doubt be asking. For now, he enjoyed the quiet reassurance that at least they were going home.

The sky turned a magnificent orange and red as the sun began to set. A faint beep began to drone from the wrist band Claire now wore. It had some sort of homing device.

She stood and walked to the water, flinging her boots off and stepping into the surf. Holding a hand to her eyes, she glanced side to side before flailing her arms in the air. A ship crested over the ocean with a search light rotating over the water. The beep grew louder and its frequency quickened.

"Over here!" She waved frantically.

It honed in on her location. Not so much because of her outburst and yelling as the transmission signal from her arm band.

"Hal! Come on." She waded into the water until she was waist-deep and he sighed as he left the comfort of the cool sand.

The boat approached and a life raft was dropped into the water as three men gathered into it and paddled closer. Claire was impatient and swam the remaining distance towards them. They grabbed her arms, pulling her aboard and then moving closer to him.

The larger boat was a luxury yacht and on board were several faces he'd seen at A&H, mostly as passerby's.

It was growing chilly as the sun set. He was hoisted onto the boat and fell heavily unto one of the cushioned seats next to Claire, wrapping his arms around and pulling her back onto his chest. She leaned back, resting her head on his shoulder and her wet hair matted to his shirt.

"Ortiz?" Hal looked surprised as the man approached with a blanket.

"How did you?" Claire reached out to embrace him. She backed away and looked him up and down. He was walking without a limp now, completely healed from the gunshot wound.

"It's a long story. We'll get to that later." He smiled at her in reassurance. "We missed you."

Claire accepted the blanket. "I thought you were gone."

"We thought you were too." He returned the gesture of friendship, but he was holding something back. "Rest. It'll be about a day before we arrive back at HQ."

She nodded, rolling the blanket over her chest and leaned back against Hal. She reached up her sleeve, pulling the arm band off and slid it back over Hal's. He squeezed his grip, feeling some sort of security just knowing it was there.

The wind raced around them as the boat sped up, rocking with the calming waves. The salty air was something you'd never forget and the moon was now brighter than the falling sun, fading the light as bright dots above began to appear.

Chapter 31: Welcome Home

The docks were different, somehow, as they anchored the yacht to the base. Their clothes had dried, but the mud and sand still clung underneath. Hal gazed at the familiar surroundings, but things had changed. There was something new he couldn't place and it was unsettling.

They were surrounded by private military contractors, as he expected since the Yotogi invasion, but the men around them were walking with caution. Claire was oblivious to them as she excitedly stepped closer, but Hal remained suspicious. He'd never liked A&H, and it definitely wasn't a comfortable home yet, but there was a sense of dread as they approached the main door.

On the second platform of the atrium sat Troy and his henchman Brack. Their faces were drear, as usual, and Claire slowed, feeling the tension that would no doubt ensue for the long questions and interrogation. Nothing had gone as planned, and even with their lead physicist returning to them, they seemed less than joyful for the victory.

The escorts surrounded them as they both approached. Brack walked forward and spoke quietly to one of them. Ortiz now stood in the back, and Hal looked at him curiously, asking with a glance why he'd been demoted.

"Claire. I'm glad to see you're in one piece." Brack was cold and void of any emotion. "I hope you understand, but we have some questions. You and Mr. Brent are to be escorted to the medical bay for evaluation and be allowed to freshen up. We'll see you again in two hours."

She nodded, glancing a look back and forth at the other officers. It wasn't the welcome home greeting she'd hoped for and although Brack wasn't exactly a caring man, she felt hurt by his cold orders.

Six men escorted them to the medical lab and her eyes were wide with anticipation to see Doctor Prossman as she entered. At least someone would be joyful for her return, but that thought quickly turned to disappointed when a new face greeted them.

"Hello Miss Kass. I'm Doctor Duvault. I'd like to take some of your vitals, as well as yours Mr. Brent, then we'll get you more comfortable." He nodded at both of them with a fake smile as he retrieved some equipment.

"Where's Prossman?"

"The doctor has retired. I'm the new physician on base." He smiled again in confidence.

Claire felt the disappointment sink in. She was looking forward to seeing old faces, old friends and colleagues who would welcome her return, but again was left with the feeling of abandonment. Hal didn't have the same connections, or at least not here, but he also felt the detachment.

One of the guards approached with a pile of linens and placed them on the beds as they sat up on the medical tables.

The doctor did a quick evaluation. No broken bones, no heart or lung problems, and no other immediate abnormalities were detected. He took a few vials of blood into another room and they'd wait for further results, but on the surface they were both healthy, if not a little worse for wear on the outside.

Claire took the first shower and came back in her white linen outfit. They looked more like pajamas than any sort of formal dress code, but they were comfortable compared to the soaked and dried, sand infested garments from before.

"Something is off, isn't it?" she whispered over to Hal as the doctor busily scurried around behind them. Hal was equally suspicious and nodded, but wasn't about to share much more with so many people surrounding them.

The door flipped open as Troy's chair bumped into the frame and Brack followed closely behind.

"So tell us what happened." Troy was firm, disgruntled and unpleasant.

"Where do I start?" she rejected. Surely they had some idea of the recent events, but it was a broad question.

"You were taken by the Russians on A&H's freighter. Two days later we receive a transmission from Mr. Brent that he's allied himself with the Yotogi and is invading another country. Where were you at this time?" Troy was frank and to the point.

She looked back in shock at his accusing tone before gathering herself. Her eyes darted back and forth, recalling the events.

"We retrieved the ARCA aboard the ship. Ortiz and his team were retreating, and rightfully so. We had no idea what we were walking into when we boarded. There were at least fifty men on board, all of them heavily armed. I remember hearing over the com system that Ortiz and Smithers were down, but the Shadow was disengaging. Hal and I made it to the top platform when I was struck in the shoulder." She reached back, recalling the dart as it hit her. "I blacked out. It gets fuzzy from there. I remember being carried onto a large plane and waking up in a lab, strapped down to the table. They injected me with something. I don't know what, but Kyra was there. They kept me in some sort of observation room with the ARCA blueprints and a console. It was defective. They couldn't get it to function in that zone and I was supposed to reprogram it. In the back of my mind I kept telling myself to resist, but..." She trailed off, searching her memory for the answer. "I can't remember. It was like they'd programmed me to obey their orders. They brought me to a new area. It was a large laboratory with other failed prototypes. I remember it later, but at that time I didn't know what I was looking at. They've been trying to recreate the ARCA for years, it looks like, but weren't able to calibrate it. We never tested it outside of our desired sites, and it was something I never really thought about until then."

She sighed, looking down as she placed her hands over her face and rubbed her eyes. "Then I remember an explosion that came from the outside. Two men were locked into a different room with me and it just kept coming. I remember hearing them on their radios shouting back and forth about intruders. Then Hal came in." She looked over at him in fuzzy remembrance. "We escaped to the bottom of the Ghora Kharan mountainside with the ARCA. That was the first time I realized where I actually was. Michio, our Yotogi contact, met us there and we boarded a helicopter that was supposed to take us back to their Japanese base, but," her tone faded to guilt as she recalled the next few hours in her memory. "We didn't make it. We crashed somewhere. Michio is gone, along with some of the other escapees. Ortiz was on board, but I didn't see him after the crash. I just assumed..." She looked over at him, grateful that he'd made it, but still confused.

"And what about the last three months?" Troy hadn't seemed interested in the events, yet.

"What?" She asked, puzzled.

"Our last transmission from Mr. Brent was over three months ago. We aided the Japanese in a search and found several of your fellow crewmen on a life raft. You, along with Mr. Brent, obviously weren't among them." His gaze pierced her with accusation.

She sat in confusion, glancing back and forth to Hal. "Three months?"

"I know this is going to sound crazy," Hal interrupted. "Check Claire's bag. We brought back proof, but hear me out before you try to find reason. There are some supernatural crystals in that bag. We gathered them from the crash site where we woke up. When I first arrived here I was haunted by nightmares of being in a different world. Those crystals are from that place."

Brack approached the bag and pulled out one of the glowing cylinder shards that lit up in his hand as he gripped it. He looked back and forth at the two.

"I don't know how or why, but when we were fleeing Russia the ARCA lit up and overpowered the helicopter. It was my nightmare all over again. The light, the loss of control, everything replayed over again. We vanished into a cloud and blacked out. Ortiz will testify to that." Hal spoke defensively as he glanced back at him, nodding in recollection.

"The ARCA became unstable. It went into some sort of self-detonation as we fled and somehow we were sucked into it. You yourselves know better than me what it's capable of. It threw us into another plane of existence. We woke up in a marshland, but not all of us were accounted for. We spent a day, maybe two, in this dimension. I don't know what to call it, but it wasn't here. Others have been there." Hal grew assertive as he spoke. They were interrogating them like suspects, just as they did when he first arrived, but now Claire was his witness.

"If you crashed in the Pacific, how did you resurface on Bermuda?" Brack asked, still accusingly.

Hal fell silent, his mouth open without an answer. "You tell me. You're the experts." He bit his tongue, realizing the backlash was more of an insult than an explanation.

"I'll tell you what we think. Research on the ARCA has been leaked for several years. Ever since it went into production the Yotogi have been clamoring to prevent it reaching the public's hands. Kyra is still missing. When you went out to rescue *our* physicist, you not only left our cause, but you failed to bring back two major objectives. Now, you two resurface on Bermuda with a bag of glass, no ARCA and no Russian spy. You tell me, Mr. Brent, how does that sound?" He referred to Claire sarcastically as *their* physicist.

"Are you accusing me of treason?" Claire's gaze pierced Brack with hurt and glared at one person to the next. Each person avoided her gaze, even Ortiz.

"Are you denying it?" Troy spoke harshly.

"Yes," she cried back at him as tears formed. Even Brack showed doubt as she responded. He knew deep down that she'd never give up her life's work, let alone feed it to a terrorist group who kidnapped and killed her associates. Nonetheless, there was a large time gap that no one could explain except those who had been there, but Troy remained unwarranted in his quest to find blame.

"Where is the ARCA, Claire? You failed us in recovering the freighters and now you have one last chance to redeem yourself. That doesn't make you innocent, but it'll be easier if this goes to trial. Just tell us where the ARCA is!" Troy struggled to maintain his composure as he shifted in his wheelchair.

"We left it in that God forsaken land!" She screamed back, letting the tears spill out in frustration. "It was our only way back. You don't understand. Those carcasses we pulled out of the ocean, the sea life we've seen on our testing trials, they're part of that world. The effect of the ARCA has caused a disturbance, something we couldn't anticipate, and we've been seeing the results for years, turning a blind eye when something was wrong. And you'll continue to ignore it. You may think you have a clue, sitting over the test trials, watching the thief steal your research, *my* research, then accuse me of being a Russian spy. For what? How many have died? How many people suffered for your botched mission in Miami and on our own freighters. You don't want a solution or an explanation. You want someone to take the fall for your failures!"

"That's enough!" Brack walked behind the medical bed and grabbed her arms, wrapping zip ties around her wrists. "We're placing you under surveillance until this is resolved."

Hal jumped off his platform, but two of the PMC's came to his sides and restrained him.

Surprisingly Claire didn't fight as she shook her head in his direction. "They can't arrest me. You can't!" She turned to shout at Troy. "Because everyone will know what you've done. Your bombing in Miami, your test subjects and how you ordered twelve men into a war zone. You won't make this public, and you can only throw the blame so far, you fucking coward!"

She slumped forward and Brack pulled her shoulders back to catch her weight as the tranquilizer took effect.

Hal struggled, lunging forward, but the men grabbed his wrists and used zip ties to anchor him to the metal bars lining the bed.

"You stay out of this Mr. Brent." Troy's wheelchair crept forward.

What Claire had said was the truth. He, nor anyone at A&H could come forward and bring a real threat to her, and there was worry in Troy's expression. He knew it, but he couldn't execute them either. Without the ARCA, he needed her if there were any hope of saving *his* company.

"Ortiz!" Hal yelled as the group turned to leave, including his *friend*.

"Mr. Brent, this will calm you." The doctor approached with an injection gun and he struggled to back away, but it was no use. The projectile struck his chest and he heaved in a few deep breaths of air before the room began to spin.

The tranquilizer wasn't as strong as before, or at least not the same that the Russians had used. His eyelids fluttered, gazing up at the two men who pulled his limp body onto a stretcher.

"What do we do with him?" The man's voice echoed through his ears.

"Dump him. He was lost at sea," the doctor responded, looking down at Hal as his lazy eyes rolled back.

The stretcher wheels hummed as they traveled down the hallway. Hal watched the lights overhead pass by and then the burning light of the sun. One man grabbed his shoulders and another his ankles before hoisting him onto a small boat. The engine roared and the wind rushed passed as he watched the sun and clouds above roll by.

He was conscious, but barely, and his limbs were limp as the men slid his weight over the edge. The water rushed over his body and he was able to take a breath in before letting his heaviness sink downward.

The serene water was peaceful and the ocean was cool. He held his breath and squeezed his fists, beginning with a light clench and flapping his wrists as movement slowly came back. He tried to fight the paralysis and the air in his lungs began to lift his body. Surfacing, he took another breath, but his whole body was weak. It was a struggle in itself to move his hands. Slowly, his shoulders and elbows came back and he paddled, face up, trying to stay afloat. His neck muscles restored and he lay on his back, bobbing up and down with the light waves as he looked around. The boat was now almost out of sight, and there was no land beyond them. They'd traveled miles in what seemed like minutes.

His toes wiggled. He'd lost his shoes in the struggle and he began to paddle his ankles, but they were so weak.

An hour or so passed and he remained on his back, flapping his arms and slowly pushing with his feet. The sun was beginning to set and the sky was a beautiful florescent orange, mingling with the blue and purple hues as the night began to take over. There were no lights on any shores, no landmarks, and the only directional orientation came from the west as the sun fell.

It grew darker and darker, and the dotted sky became disorienting. He didn't know what direction was north, south, east or west, and even if he did, he'd never have the strength to swim back to land.

A light flashed over the waves. He stared in its direction and waited for it to occur again.

"Help." His lungs were restrained as he let out a cry.

The light grew closer, and as it did, he could hear a motor.

He struggled to position his body upright, but the buoyancy of his legs tried to tilt him on his back.

"Help!" It was stronger this time and he stared hopefully at the approaching ship. They were headed straight for him.

"Help," he continued.

It slowed and a spot light shone down on the water's surface, almost as if they knew exactly where to find him.

It slowly pulled up along-side and a rush of joy took over him as a familiar face peeked over the edge.

"Kind of late for a swim, eh lad?" It was Howard, smiling in sarcasm. "A&H should really strip a man of their equipment before dumping the body." He pointed to his wrist, and Hal shifted his head to see the electronic arm band, glowing like a beacon in the dark water.

Ruby was on board and threw a chain ladder down the side before following with an inflatable chest harness.

Howard plunged into the water and grabbed him around the ribs, heaving him onto the floatation device and paddling to the ladder.

Hal fell with a thud onto the floor and his limp arms were weak as he tried to sit upright.

"They have Claire." He managed to mumble out a few weak words.

"Yes, I know. Don't worry about your girl. She's an animal they dare not play too rough with. If A&H knows what's best for them..." he trailed off and hung his head low in gratitude. "You're part of our family, Hal. You're alive, and Claire. That's enough for now."

Howard looked to Ruby who was driving. "Back home. We'll get back to this in the morning."

He reached down to Hal's wrist, ripping off the arm band that saved his life. "They'll be looking for this sooner or later." Then he threw it over the edge into the ocean and smiled. "You're a dead man again."

It was well past midnight by the time they'd reached the shore front of Howard's home. Hal had regained the use of his legs, but they were too weak to walk on his own as Howard swept one arm underneath, shifting his weight onto his side and carried him up the shallow steps.

The back entrance faced the ocean and the familiar surroundings were more comfortable than any home he'd been in since his own. Howard had a fine taste in design. Oriental furnishings and the dim shoji lights were warming as the cool breeze of an air conditioner swept passed.

Howard pulled him into the living room and he sank into the fluffy couch.

Ruby rustled around in the kitchen, trying to occupy herself. She began blending some fruits together into a tropical drink before catering them over to the coffee table.

"I don't suppose you've eaten much." She was much different now than he'd remembered in the cafe. She wore no makeup and her hair had grown out of the red streaks into its natural sleek, black roots.

"There's a med kit in the upstairs bathroom." Howard motioned for her to grab it. "There's some adrenaline. It should bring back some of the kick."

Hal struggled to sit upwards. It wasn't easy to feel sympathy for Troy, but for the last few hours he felt the rage and incompetence that he must have felt all the time; struggling to control a paralyzed body. No matter how much he mentally screamed at his limbs, they just wouldn't obey and it was an exhausting task just to sit up and breath.

Ruby hurried over to them, pulling along a suitcase that looked more like a large traveling bag than a med kit She reached for a needle before drawing out liquid from a glass vial.

"This is going to sting like a bitch," she explained and quickly thrust the needle into his thigh.

And it did sting. It wasn't like anything he'd ever injected before. The liquid burst into his muscle, burning as it spread. It wasn't just the physical pain either. He felt a surge of anger rushing through him, kind of like being punched from the inside as the drugs shocked his body.

He bit his lip, gripping his leg and squeezing. It worked, though, and he stretched his legs, flexing his ankles as he bit down.

"You said Claire was with you. Is she OK?" Ruby asked innocently.

"Yes. We made it back, but they're accusing her of treason. After we escaped Russia, well, it's a long story, but it felt like we were gone for a day, maybe two. We had no idea three months had passed." Hal didn't want to get into the technicalities, just that there was a long period of unaccounted time, and now A&H was pinning her as a scapegoat.

"Akira filled us in. They've gone back into hiding, but some are still here in Miami. Claire's a big girl. She'll handle herself. A&H has no idea what's coming to them, but they can't put her on trial for anything. They're no better than the Russians, holding her as a prisoner until she complies." Howard was actually optimistic about the situation. "She won't."

"So what do we do?" Hal asked.

"Tomorrow night the Yotogi have something special planned." He simply smiled and patted Hal's leg. "The effects from the tranquilizer will subside. For now, get some sleep. A&H has had their tail between their legs for three months. Their investors have pulled out and the company has been run up and down the harsh media. They don't have the slightest idea what they're doing, aside from dodging bad press. On the bright side their focus isn't on the Yotogi right now, which is a good thing."

Howard stood before returning to the kitchen with Ruby and lowering the lights.

"My home is your home. Help yourself to anything you need. There are two bathrooms down the hall and three bedrooms. Tomorrow we'll get you a new set of clothes and gear." He grabbed some items from the counter and left.

Hal remembered Howard's home vaguely, and things had changed little since he last visited. He'd been distracted before and didn't have enough time to appreciate just how cozy it was. The floors were a dark bamboo wood, divided by white tile that lined the enormous kitchen. Shoji lights gave off a warm yellow tint to the surroundings. He gripped the black velvet couch as strength came back to his muscles. The shot of adrenaline had given a little more strength against the paralysis and he struggled to stand.

The kitchen had eight switches and he turned each one, which triggered the garbage dispenser, the ice maker and compactor. After years of living in such a modern house, Howard probably knew each one, but to Hal, it was a confusing and loud trial and error process.

Two fridges were built into the long line of counters and the first was strictly a beverage center. He pulled three beers and quenched his thirst.

The second fridge was larger and overwhelming as he gazed in at the variety. Cold meats, fruits, vegetables and pasta. His body suddenly craved it all, and as Howard had said, his home was Hal's. He was feverishly hungry and didn't realize it until now, devouring handfuls at a time without even shutting the fridge door.

Howard was a man of taste, and he wondered for a moment how he could have acquired so much wealth. Given that he always had a stash of the most destructive hand held weapons he'd ever seen, maybe it wasn't a subject to dwell on too much.

Quenched and stuffed, he wobbled back to the cozy stretch of couches that lined the living room area. They were more comfortable than any bed he'd slept on before and he sank in.

Howard's words echoed in his mind and he couldn't stop thinking about Claire. She was tough and wouldn't volunteer to A&H any information after their accusations. For now she was at least out of danger, and from the sounds of it the Yotogi were already forming a plan to take the company out once and for all. Waiting for it was the hardest part.

Chapter 32: The Last Stand

Noise in the kitchen startled Hal and he sprang upwards. He didn't even realize he'd fallen asleep as light rushed in through his eyelids.

"Sorry to wake you. Howard's gone to gather some things, but he'll be back any minute. How are you feeling?" Ruby stood in the kitchen and fumbled around with a cooking pan.

"How long was I out?" He pressed his hands to his eyes, rubbing them profusely as his body fought off the last effects of the tranquilizers.

"About twelve hours. It's noon now. I made some breakfast."

Hal stood, looking down at the buffet of breakfast food she'd been working on.

"Smells good." He stumbled over to the counter, pulling a few pieces of bacon from a plate.

Ruby shifted uneasily. When he'd spoken to her at the cafe she was much more assertive and confident. Here, now, she felt awkward and helpless. The past three months had been hell for her, and Howard too. They were close, although he didn't know the history behind it. It was awkward, being torn with joy, but only after a long grieving period.

"How do you know Claire?" His curiosity grew, thinking of their unusual connections.

She smiled in recollection. "We grew up together. She lived in Japan when we were little. The country was devastated by a tsunami and her parents came as missionaries to help rebuild one of the nuclear plants." She laughed. "She was rebellious. Her parents kept trying to steer her towards missionary work, but she was drawn to robotics and would always be building something out of scrap components found along the beaches."

Her tone changed, suddenly. "The power plant failed, and well, we both became orphans. Doctor Prossman was her guardian and she was sent back to the US, here. We were sixteen at the time, but I was a Japanese citizen and couldn't come with her. About a year later I met Howard. He was a drug runner, and I fell into a dark place. I was just a kid when I fell in love with him, but when he was extradited back to the US, I had no one. Claire had turned eighteen then, and inherited a large fortune left by her parents. She remembered her sister and came back for me." Tears started to form and she waved her hands, trying to shake the emotions before finishing the story. "She paid for Howard's bail and we married. The rest is history."

Hal hadn't learned much about Claire, or Ruby and Howard, but they had a deep, long life together, tightly knit in the awkward circumstances of life.

"Do you think they'll really put Claire on trial for treason?" Her tone was concerned. Now Claire was the one in need of bailing, and the tables had turned.

Hal shook his head knowing that A&H was full of hot air and accusations more so than an actual threat.

"No. I think Howard is right. If they planned on that, they would have turned her over to police by now. The ARCA is gone, and without it the company will fall. They need her." His body had returned to normal and Hal adjusted the uncomfortable garments that were stiff from dried salt water and sweat.

The door opened to the side and Howard strolled in, casual as could be, with several bags under his arms.

"Good morning! Ah, it's a beautiful day." He placed the bags on the floor and opened the shades to the front windows. The unwelcome light stung his eyes and he winced as it flooded the room.

"I'm guessing you're a size twelve shoe and thirty-four waist." Howard began rummaging through the bags, pulling out three new sets of boots and several items of clothing. For such a tough guy, he sure had a thing about shopping.

Hal approached and looked at some of the tags.

"Take your pick." He walked over to Ruby and planted a kiss on her forehead. Hal understood their relationship now. Ruby was the only real thing in his life he couldn't buy, and he cherished his pint-sized gem more than anything physical in his life. They were an odd couple, but perfectly balanced.

"I'll try these on." Hal grabbed the bags and strolled over to the nearest bathroom.

He showered, washing down the grit and sweat that still clung to his skin. The clothing was standard and comfortable, with a pair of dark camo pants, black t-shirt and undershirt, a shoulder holster for a pistol, and a few new surprise accessories such as a leg and belt band that could each carry several rounds of ammunition and a combat knife. There was no way to ignore that they were gearing up for another fight.

Hal walked out of the bathroom looking like a new man. His hair was combed back and wrapped around his ears. The new clothes were a refreshing change and, more importantly, his body felt new. The aches, pains and fatigue had subsided.

"Who are you?" Howard joked as he walked into the room. "We had a bum on the couch last night. What did you do with him?"

Ruby laughed behind the kitchen counter and nodded her head. "You do good work, babe. I think you resurrected a dead man."

Howard walked up to him and padded his shoulders firmly. "No, still a dead man, or at least that's what we want people to think. Come. I have some things I need to share with you." He moved to the side and proceeded towards the hallway that led to a series of neighboring rooms.

Hal followed him to the end where another part of the house branched out. It was a room he hadn't seen before and was lit up from a series of screens that stretched out over four large desks.

"Have a seat," Howard gestured as he pulled over an office chair.

He pulled out a glass sheet from underneath and the clear surface illuminated to his touch as the two neighboring screens in front of them came up with a display of various camera angles.

"Doctor Prossman and a few of the workers left A&H shortly after the attack. There were budget cuts and what not, and many were let go, but I think they were relieved to be dismissed after the Yotogi demonstrated how hostile they've become. Bean was one of their primary security officers there and after he was given the boot, he leaked the security feeds directly to us. That's how we were able to track you when they dumped you in the ocean. That and your arm band gives an unique transmission that only A&H can track. Or so they thought." He tapped in a few more controls and a new screen came up.

"Claire is here, on the bottom levels. She doesn't know, but A&H implants all their employees with a tracking device before they're employed to higher clearance. You have one too." He held the back of his neck, indicating where the implant would be.

Hal reached for his neck but felt no scar or incision.

"Don't worry, it's inactive. I asked Bean to remotely deactivate it last night." He turned back to his screen and proceeded.

"The bottom levels are accessible from several points. There's the main shaft here, which you went through several times, and three other channels. A mini-sub bridges the four main complexes underwater. The Yotogi are planning on sending a scout down to the second building where there's a diving station. It's basically a hole in the floor that leads into the deep water. They have been doing some aquatic life experiments and this is the main station for it. There's also a fifth entrance, that might be a good extraction, but no one knows much about it. They were in the process of expanding the station farther south and the monorail shaft hasn't been completed. There's limited security at that point, but it's too deep for my ship to travel. The Sealo-Pax sub can, though. Once we get into complex we'll work our way down to level C, the third building here." He pointed on the screen, which displayed four camera angles. One looked like an underwater garage bay and Hal recognized the string of lights that followed over the submarine's railing.

"Claire is on level C?" He asked and Howard nodded.

"The complex is huge, though, much bigger than I ever thought. We have the floor plans, but many of the rooms are void of cameras or surveillance. I suspect they're conducting research they themselves don't want documented. Also, the Yotogi will be up top creating a distraction. They have several EMPs planted already along the main power grid. Once those go off, it's going to be lights out throughout the entire complex. We'll have night vision and an EMP disruptor that can deactivate any generators. The problem with an EMP is that they temporarily take out our communication, but they're resilient. The circuits don't suffer any long term burnout, but the generators probably will." He looked up at Hal, who was silently fascinated.

"Who's we?" Hal asked, curious at how large this assembled team would be.

"Well, there are twenty-one volunteers from the Yotogi. I'm going with you, and we have a friend of yours on the inside, Ortiz."

He smiled, knowing Hal had felt wrongly abandoned. "He's under cover. He couldn't help you when you landed again, but he's on our side."

"Akira?"

Howard shook his head. "The Yotogi are broken. Akira flew back to Japan after the ordeal in Russia. The remaining members here felt abandoned. Their leader left many of them here in Florida to sift through the chaos on their own. They gained public recognition from the Mirada incident and they've started to rebuild their own faction." He motioned with his hands, indicating the house. "*We've* been rebuilding."

Hal smiled. Neither A&H nor the Yotogi had quite fit his liking. A&H was simply a large, power-hungry corporation. The Yotogi, at least formerly, were peace loving free loaders and showed great distaste in almost everything he'd done. He couldn't blame them, at least not all of them. He had expected some backlash from the Mirada after he'd taken down some of their comrades. He didn't directly kill any of their members, but A&H had sent him into the mess and then sabotaged the raid. To some, he might as well have been the killer.

"So when do we leave?" Hal was anxious and optimistic. Howard was a man of planning *and* doing, something everyone else lacked. The Yotogi had good intentions, and this newly formed group felt angered and abandoned. They still agreed with the peaceful ways, but you can't protect the peace without some degree of violence. That's where they differed from the main body.

"In three hours." Howard looked down at his watch. "Din is our lead officer. I'll be with you, but he'll be directing the operation. There should be eight men here within the hour for a briefing and supplies. We'll be going in with silenced weapons, mostly tranquilizers and EMPs. Our intent is not to kill, but to paralyze. A&H has got to be stopped. Most of their employees have bailed out, but in time they will regrow. If we can knock out their resources, the whole company will fall and no one will want to come back."

Ruby's voice came over a speaker phone and Howard turned to pick up the voice chat. "Yes babe?"

"They're here."

293

"Excellent. We'll be right in." Howard tapped the controls on the keyboard and the screens went blank.

The living room was filled with noise as they entered. Seven men and one woman sat in a circle, some perched on the bar stools and others lounging on the couch, engaging in humorous conversation. It was a drastic difference from how he'd seen the group before when Akira was present.

To his surprise, they stood and greeted him humbly. He expected them to still be hostile after the incident at the Mirada and failed escort in Russia, but they smiled and nodded as he entered.

"Alright, in thirty minutes we're going to be boarding the ship that will take us to a docking station where we'll switch over to the Scout, which will take us to Complex B. From there we will enter the aquatic station through the diving shaft and work our way to building C where the ARCA research is being done." Howard moved to a tablet control that displayed the floor plans on level C on the main television.

"There are several routes to level C, one of which is the main shaft, but it'll be guarded by private military. My guess is that they're under orders to kill, so if we can avoid that route, it would be best. We're making an attempt to keep casualties at a minimum, but understand that the guards are heavily armored. The servers are located at the top levels of the complex and we have men already in place to disable their security feeds and power grids there. Once the power is out, we'll switch to our night vision and disable whatever generators they have below. Our main objective is to destroy any plans and backups of the ARCA prototype and extract Claire Kass from the complex." He moved again to display an image of the last level, Complex E, which was still under construction.

"Building E is currently unoccupied. There's a monorail system being built with a Sealo-Pax sub capable of withstanding the ocean depths. We'll need to take these channels here or here to enter the complex and make our escape." He motioned towards two openings that lead to the last entryway.

"We have a contact within A&H that will be overlooking the operation and we know these points will be vacant. There are no cameras or com feeds beyond this point, so it's imperative that you all study the map and know your exit. We have approximately two hours to accomplish this before the power grid is reestablished and reinforcements can be sent in." Howard looked around the room and everyone nodded.

"Good. Let's gear up then."

Hal rummaged through the bags which were literally bursting out the zippers with various tools of destruction, most of which were non-lethal. The tranquilizer guns had an expanded clip that held forty rounds, and a harness bag that strapped around the shoulder to a carrying bag. He clipped on eight EMP grenades and four sleep before the weight of the harness became heavy. A faithful .357 revolver as a backup with six rounds, an arm band that was similar to the one A&H had provided him, and a scroll out tablet that had direct satellite feed for the floor plans that could be updated as they navigated further into the unknown territory.

The Yotogi followed with their setup and stretched their muscles, adjusting to the new weight of the equipment before heading towards the back door.

"Everyone suited up?" Howard asked, gathering everyone into a group.

He walked over to Ruby who stood in the kitchen with a look of concern. She'd lost her Howard once before and was scared now at the thought of losing him again. She gripped his waistline and gave a long kiss as he brushed her hair to the sides in consolation.

"I'll bring him back." Hal spoke in their direction, reassuring her that he'd be back in one, unharmed piece.

She smiled and nodded. "I know you will."

Chapter 33: The Extraction

The ship was tight as the ten members boarded. The yacht was only comfortable with four or five passengers, but they packed in closely as Howard took to the controls and headed south.

The ride was only about twenty minutes before docking to the Mia Marina docks. They unloaded, diving into the water and swimming to a mini-sub that hovered just above the water.

The shaft descended down a three-foot wide ladder into the belly of the beast. It was dark and blue lights lined the interior, leading to the front controls where two men sat. The latch clanked shut and Howard sealed the door before giving a thumbs up to the drivers. He sat next to Hal, quietly reviewing his tablet as new data was fed into the system. The floor plans were incomplete, as the new building was still under construction, but he studied what was known.

To Hal's surprise he noticed Howard's hands shake as he tapped his tablet. He was nervous on the inside, as much as he tried to hide it.

Hal reached over and grabbed his wrist, catching his attention and making eye contact.

"Improvising is our best defense. A&H isn't a military force and they're terrible at planning." Hal smiled remembering their lack of tactics.

"I haven't seen action in decades." He leaned in and whispered, trying not to show any weakness to the group. He'd always been looked upon as the strong leader, but there was fear of the unknown and he'd been living the softer lifestyle. He hadn't seen the internal workings like Hal had, and his string of petty crime was nothing in comparison to what he thought they'd be walking into.

Hal had seen most of the complex underwater and knew the general layout. A&H had never done anything right, and maybe he was too assured that things were the same, but he actually felt no fear. Anxiety, yes, but not fear.

"I promised Ruby you'd be back. I don't intend on disappointing her," he joked.

Howard chuckled. "You've only seen her on good days, but I got your back too. I wouldn't want to upset Claire."

They had a mutual, informal agreement, but there was no need for promises. Howard was trustworthy and he owed a huge debt to both of them. The same respect was returned. Hal owed Howard his life, and Claire's.

Conversation fell silent as the ship's hull creaked under the immense water pressure.

"We should be close." Howard observed the turmoil, knowing that the Scout could only go a certain depth.

"ETA two minutes." The man at the controls yelled back at the passengers and his voice rang through the ear pieces.

The crew sat quietly, gripping the rails above their heads as the small submarine navigated into the tight fitting just below the diving hole. It scratched the hull, bumping into the walls of the small opening and then slowly lifted upwards. Water rushed over the top as it met the air above and Howard unclasp the lock for the doorway hatch.

It hissed and sprung open to the side, letting water drip in from the edges as everyone stood to evacuate.

The room they entered was dark, illuminated to a blue hue as a string of lights just under the water sent rippling reflections throughout. Each man exited and crouched on the nearby ground into a small group. Howard was last, closing the hatch before tapping the sub's hull in dismissal.

Computer equipment hummed from all sides, but the screens were black. Several of the stations blinked as the LED lights flickered, but the only real light source came from the water hole next to them.

Howard scurried over across the floor back to the group.

"OK, we are here." He pointed to the small red indicator lights on his tablet.

He glanced at his watch, counting down the seconds. "Din, do you copy?" He asked into the com system.

"Roger. Power grid out in 5, 4, 3, 2..." There was a sudden tremble before he could finish and the drowning hum of electric slowly lowered, turning off the computer stations that waited in standby.

"Night vision on." He lowered his goggles over his eyes as everyone followed his orders.

The room turned into a stale green haze through the lenses. They were unique and responded to the tablet and arm equipment without the ultra-bright reaction you'd normally see on a screen. Instead, they worked with the goggle's reception of light, and the equipment itself could only be seen with them on.

"Team Two, you go south to level E and clear a path for the extraction. Brent, Chiyo, Emi, and Jiro, we go east to level C." Howard's voice echoed through the com system as he spoke.

"Din here. Distraction in 3, 2, 1." He spoke and everyone held still in anticipation, but there was no movement. "Servers one and two disabled. You have two hours before power is back up, data is being downloaded."

"OK, A&H will be redirecting their focus to restore power to the server rooms above. We should have minimal resistance here." Howard stood and began to tread along the small walkway that bordered the diving hole.

The doorway on the east was locked, which lead to the main hallway they'd travel down and catch a ride to level C.

"Emi, get us through." Howard motioned and shifted to the side.

Emi was the only woman in the group and she pulled a blow torch from the bag strapped to her back. She tilted her goggles, adjusting the lens to a new function, then ignited.

The beam was overwhelmingly bright through the goggles and Hal adjusted them as the torch began to burn through the hinges of the steel door. As each broke off, they clanked to the floor and Emi kicked away the remaining pieces. Howard came to her side and together they lifted the heavy frame to the side, letting a dim red light flicker in from the emergency lights.

"Jiro, Chiyo, go left and disable the server grids below. We'll meet you at the exit in Complex E." Howard glanced back at the two.

Team Two was close behind them, following down the hallway until they came to another locked doorway that Emi quickly began to buzz through.

The inside was dark, and the five men scattered to the left, which branched off and presumably lead to the next two complexes. Howard grabbed Hal's wrist briefly, indicating for him to follow.

Emi lead the way. Her torch was still lit and illuminated the passageway. They passed several quiet doorways until they came to another fork. Noise came from above as footsteps tread overhead. They were muffled through the thick cement floors but they weren't alone.

Howard pulled up his sleeve, his face lit up slightly from the dim reflection on his wrist band which shone into the goggle lenses.

"Left," he whispered.

The green haze of the night vision made the room easy to navigate. They stood at a junction where the building divided, and the open area extended three stories with them sitting in the middle.

Hal slid over to the railing overlooking the basement floor below. A flicker of light darted across the room as two patrol men searched.

Howard and Emi continued straight forward, unaware of the men below. Hal remained in place though, listening intently as the darkness sapped away most of their vision. The night vision made the rooms easy to navigate, but if they were to cross paths with a guard, the beam of a flashlight would be blinding.

He pulled the goggles onto his forehead and let his naked eyes adjust. There was almost no light here, but what little did exist reflected off the concrete and tile surfaces. It took a moment and he focused on the floors above and below. There were four sets of footsteps, possibly five. Two men below were whispering, and two above were quiet. The fifth may have been down the hallway, just above, but he wasn't sure.

Hal gazed around himself, suddenly in a panic. He'd been so focused on his surroundings he hadn't realized Howard and Emi had continued forward beyond his current vision. He dare not speak through the com system with guards so close by.

The arm band was dark and without the goggles, the dim light was impossible to read.

He peered through the darkness, still intently listening to his surroundings and looking for the path Howard would have chosen. There were four exits on this level, each opening up into a separate hallway at the corners.

His hand hovered over the balcony railing as he followed the main line. Vision was poor, and although large objects were easy to avoid, he kept the bar railing within arm's reach to stay on a straight path.

As hard as he strained, his eyes couldn't focus down the long open shaft of the first hallway. He lowered the goggles from his forehead.

Entry to Level 4C a sign read on the side wall.

He looked down the neighboring corner, which had a similar sign for level 3C.

There was no choice but to attempt radio contact. He was lost and level C had several branches.

"Howard, I've separated. Where are you?"

"We're half way to 3C. What happened?"

The footsteps above him were getting close. There wasn't time to explain and he quietly slid his sleeve back down, hiding any indications of light from his equipment.

The steps continued to his back side. Hal turned silently on his heels, following its direction.

He'd gone right past an opening in the hallway as stairs zigzagged, bridging all three levels.

A flashlight darted off the walls and the thump of feet slowly descended.

Hal scurried across the floor, carefully hushing his feet as they landed, and lay his back against the wall. Swinging his head back, the goggles rose to his forehead and he closed his eyes tightly, listening as the man came closer.

The flashlight shone brightly forward as he came to the second floor, stepping forward three feet from Hal.

His hand lay firmly on the tranquilizer as he extended his arm, reaching around to the man's face. His grip was firm and the man was much too slow to react before the needle punched his neck and almost instantly paralyzed him.

Hal reached out and grabbed the man's flashlight, steadying it from flailing around in alarm, and lowered the man to the ground. He held him under the arms, dragging him backwards towards the corner and propping him against the wall.

"Hal?" Howard's voice quietly echoed through the ear piece.

"I'm surrounded. I'm in the opening of level C, but there are four, maybe five guards. Just tell me where to go and I'll meet you there." As quiet as he'd tried, the stir of motion had caught some attention.

He stood in place, waiting for Howard's direction.

"Level 3C, go down the passageway and take a left at the forth doorway. There's a laboratory with a ventilation shaft at the right corner. We're entering it now."

Howard understood his position and inability to communicate, but he knew he'd be right behind him.

Hal knelt down at the balcony corner and reached into his back pocket, pulling a spare tranquilizer cartridge from his bag. The guards below whispered back and forth, both aware someone was amidst.

He tossed the cartridge down the hallway, which spun to a stop forty feet away and clanked against the wall. The ting of noise sent the two men below on high alert. Their feet noisily tread up the stairs beside him and Hal watched from his dark shadow as they carelessly clambered towards the noise.

One man jolted from the pinch and he extended his hands, reaching towards the floor to catch his collapsing body. The second man stared, watching in fear as his comrade silently fainted, and in the confusion he didn't even realize the same came to him.

Hal lowered the tranquilizer gun, watching both men for any further movement, but they remained still.

With the power grid taken down from the upper levels, the normal com system was mute and the guards only had local radio contact. Each man had a short wave radio attached to their belts that occasionally hummed with static or a brief order. Sooner or later, someone would realize this sector had been compromised and those guarding it were no longer responding. Lack of communication was like a bread trail that would eventually lead security to his direction.

There was still one more man up top, but his footsteps were far down the neighboring hallway.

He wasn't about to stay put and wait for the backup to arrive as he sprinted down the circular balcony on the second level to the next branch of level 3C. He counted the doors as he past, recognizing the burn marks Emi had left on the locks. The room was lit by several emergency LED lights streaming up the walls, which were much brighter in comparison to the hallway and he tip toed through the shadows to the open air vent.

The air vent was large, about three feet in diameter, and had several large fans along the lining to circulate the air below. With the power out, the air was still and stagnant.

Hal crawled on his belly about twenty feet before a stream of light came through the corridor directly ahead. He paused. Howard and Emi were now a good five minutes ahead of him and out of range. Whoever was in the room was on patrol and suspicious.

He reached for the tranquilizer on his shoulder strap as quietly as he could, but the noise further alerted the occupant, whose light was now darting back and forth trying to find the source.

The exiting hatch was open and footsteps approached. Feet appeared, wearing military boots that Hal recognized, but they were well shielded and the tranquilizer wouldn't puncture. He waited, watching the man get down on his knees and Hal took the shot, striking the man's thigh. He flinched and yelled, quickly falling to the side, but his cry for help had already been heard as more footsteps began closing in on his location. He was cornered in a tight spot and hurried his pace, not wanting to become a trapped target in the air vent tunnel.

The door swung open as Hal exited the shaft and he fired on reflex, hitting the man who immediately entered. He fell back and tumbled into the man just outside the doorway. Catching his comrade, he was momentary distracted as Hal fired another shot, hitting the wall just beside him. The man retreated, backing against the outside door frame and called reinforcements.

Hal grabbed a sleep grenade from his belt and tossed it in his direction, rolling on the floor and the muted puff expelled the noxious gas. He gagged and coughed, remaining in his location as Hal rushed to the door, slamming it shut to prevent the gas from seeping its way back into the room. The door lock had been seared off from Emi's blowtorch and was no longer lockable. Running to a nearby work station, he slid a heavy desk up against it. Even if reinforcements came with a mask, they'd still have a struggle getting the doorway open in time.

"Howard, I need another exit route. I'm on level 3C, but it's blocked."

Howard's voice came through, interrupted by heavy static and he couldn't hear further directions.

His arm band had been loaded with the floor plans of the level C complex and he pulled them up. There were two remaining air shafts, each leading to adjacent rooms, but they'd quickly be occupied by back up private military. One of the adjacent rooms would lead to the main hallway, which extended to a large open area, but it was directly linked to the holding area they suspected Claire was being held. Howard's route skirted around the sides the long way, which intercepted the power generators on that level. If he reached that area, Hal would already be in position to extract Claire. It's not like he had a choice now and he was going to have to continue off-course.

The air vent hatch was tight and he loosened the screws with his knife before pulling it to the floor. Chaos was beginning to unfold in the hallway and several men gathered just beyond the door. Their voices were muted by gas masks and the desk screeched on the floor as it began to give way.

Hal ducked into another ventilation shaft and tried to reposition the vent hatch door in hopes that it would be immediately overlooked. He crawled forward, casting a glance back as lights began to stream in. They passed, moving towards the obvious breach from the other vent door, but the gas slowly began to creep in.

He hurried his pace and paused at the next opening. It was screwed from the outside and he pressed hard with his palms. The metal gave in at the center before the screws in the drywall let loose and the clanked to the ground.

The noise was enough to alert anyone nearby, but thankfully their attention was currently behind him.

The dark room was open, extending upwards one level where Hal could see a dozen glass chambers containing specimens in a murky blue fluid that illuminated from lights within. He paused and squinted at the subjects, which he immediately recognized. They were the remains of the creatures he'd seen on the other side; the ones Claire had seen washed up during some of their testing excursions.

Tubes fed into their bodies, partly holding them in place as they floated in the liquid. He approached the closest chamber, recognizing the figure that resembled a type of canine, sending a flashback of his dream where he'd encountered something similar before. The protruding spine that extended from a mutated head all the way to the barbed tail. It wasn't the exact same creature, but very close.

He jolted back as the animal flinched in its container. Bubbles from the bottom rose, sending its body to the top as the fluid began to drain. The noise echoed through the room and he spun around to see the other canisters begin to move.

A flicker of red light caught his eye as a wall mounted camera spun on its axis, rotating and locking onto his position. Even with the power grid disabled up top, there were still generators for the levels below, and he wasn't alone. The controls on the chambers had been activated, the tubes slowly releasing from the creatures within and their occupants shuttered with movement as if they were being jump-started to consciousness.

The tube in front of him had completely drained and the creature within it slipped on the wet floor, trying to get its footing. Claire had mentioned that they'd pulled these beasts from the ocean during excursions, but he'd been under the impression that they were dead.

Hal had an awkward feeling of déjà vu again, remembering the man in Russia that struggled inside a stasis tube. Maybe this was Kyra's main project, or part of it.

He snapped back to reality as the beast stumbled, crashing into the glass and breathing in the new air. He watched in a trance, but his curiosity changed to fear when the distinct hiss of the hydraulic pump below sounded and the glass jolted. Mechanical arms came up from the sides of the chamber, latching onto the glass and securing before it began to lower.

He glanced at the camera, which was still glued to his position. Whoever was watching was taking this to a new level. A&H had some dirty secrets under the ocean, and whatever their intentions had been towards researching this beast had now evolved into using them as a backup weapon.

Movement echoed throughout the room as Hal stumbled, sprinting forward toward the stair case. The canisters all began hissing; their occupants now fighting to breathe oxygen outside of their fluid. They were waking.

The walls hummed as the cylindrical locks on the doors rolled and opened. Whoever was planning this was desperate.

"Howard, this is Hal. Arm yourself now! There's something else down here," Hal yelled into the mic. He didn't care who heard him now. A&H was unleashing their experimental *pets* and they no longer cared that their own guards would be in harm's way. He didn't know what these creatures were capable of, but from his visions, he knew they were tougher and more relentless than their men.

Static came through his ear as he heard Howard respond.

"The doors are unlocking. What the hell is happening?"

"A&H has been hiding more than the ARCA down here. They're breeding mutated creatures. I don't know what they are, but use deadly force."

Hal grabbed for his revolver and checked the cylinder. He had the higher ground and grabbed the doorway to the exiting hallway before looking back. Two beasts had fallen off their platform, sliding on the tile floor as they struggled to stand on the slippery surface.

He yanked the door behind him, but it didn't budge. It was locked in the open position and it was a free range now.

One of the beasts saw his struggle and bolted forward, slipping clumsily as it fought for traction.

He fired a shot, striking its shoulder and pushing it back, but it only aggravated the beast. He fired another shot, this time dead center in the forehead and it slid to a stop. Another beast was alerted, but still getting its bearings and Hal wasn't about to wait for the rest to regain control.

He bolted down the empty corridor as he reloaded the two bullets. The cross section quickly opened up to a larger room, surrounded by two adjacent hallways. The generators were on his left, where Howard would be, and Claire was in a holding cell to the right.

"Are you at the power station?"

"Almost. ETA two minutes. What the fuck is happening? Everything's been open and we're exposed!" Howard shouted back.

Hal paused, now staring down the hallway as an abomination gazed back at him. He lowered his hands, no longer focused on his arm band.

"They're unleashing hell," Hal whispered back.

He reached for his tranquilizer and slowly raised his aim. The beast focused on him intently, swaying on its unstable legs as it hovered back and forth.

It let out a deafening bellow that echoed through the hallway and the slipped on the tile as its feet scurried on the hard surface. The abomination had adapted to a marsh-like climate with claws that dug into the soil. Now on the smooth surface it struggled for traction as it lunged towards him.

Hal fired the tranquilizer, focusing on the chest. He'd shot one of these beasts before and it took several doses to subdue. Five shots released, slowing each time and wailing out in frustration, fighting against the drug. A leg slid out from underneath and it crashed into the wall, shattering the concrete barriers. It regained control and Hal fired another desperate shot, hitting the shoulder.

Every second made it weaker and louder in its protest. Half the underwater complex would be alerted and he charged forward.

He was within ten feet of the beast as it fumbled on its side, unable to regain control. Its legs kicked, lashing out as he approached. He jumped, avoiding its whips of protest as he passed. Within a minute the abomination would be subdued, but he couldn't stay as he dashed towards the last door at the end of the hallway.

He slid up against the door frame that led to the open containment room, reloading the six tranquilizer cartridges he'd expelled. He spun around, aiming low and waited for any movement.

There was a loud thud as he turned and held his gun in its direction.

"Hal!" Claire yelled, although quietly muted from the glass restrictions she stood behind.

His heart sank. She stood in a solitary chamber about ten feet wide and he ran over to her, oblivious to anything else in the room.

"Back away." he yelled, reaching for his revolver and firing a shot from the side.

It struck the glass and ricocheted off the wall.

"It's Sealo-Pax, you can't break it!" She stood to the side, although she knew it wouldn't matter.

Hal knew this too, but he also knew its weakness.

The small carry bag strapped to his back contained several electrical units that would radiate a frequency and shatter the glass. He tapped on the controls, activating a three-second timer.

"Stand at the center." He dodged backward, hiding for cover behind a work station desk.

The beep counted down and a familiar sound began to radiate through the air as its pitch increased.

He watched from behind as Claire knelt down in the center of the room, placing her hands over her ears and bracing for the explosion.

The device was ringing in full stride for eight seconds before a spider-crack appeared. It was almost an instant reaction as the glass exploded, raining outward in every direction.

Hal covered his ears and ducked behind at the final moment. It was brief and he peered his head above. Claire remained in position, waiting for the damage. It didn't come, and she jolted her head up, looking at him before checking her extremities. The blast had sent a burst inwards, like an implosion, but it was pushed back as the oxygen pressure inside the chamber outweighed its force.

He lunged over the desk, crashing into her as she stood, gripping his arms around. He backed away and pushed her hair to the sides, holding her face and embracing her with a kiss.

She didn't object and tears slid down her face.

"Generators down! Servers down!" Howard yelled through his ear piece.

The clock was ticking and Hal backed away.

"We need to get to complex E. There's a sub carriage that can take us out of here." He hadn't let go of her, but backed away.

"The ARCA. They have another prototype."

"We'll take care of that later. A&H has unleashed Hell. We need to get out now." He began to let go, pulling her hand as he backed up towards the door, but she resisted.

"No. I mean, I know now. Kyra wasn't just working on the ARCA. She was working to create a gap, to bring those creatures here. Oh God, I'm so ashamed. I should have known!"

"Claire, we can bring this place down later. Right now we have to leave." He pulled harder on her arm, but she continued to protest.

"No. We need to do this now. Complex E *was* the staging area. It's not an exit. It's an opening. We were never going to make it to Bermuda. We were never going to fix global disasters. Not with the ARCA." Guilt overwhelmed her for the research she'd partaken in, and as desperate as Hal was to simply leave alive, she couldn't just yet.

"So how do we destroy this opening?" There was no point arguing with her, and unlike Brack, he couldn't just tranquilize her.

"There are separate generators in Complex E. I can override their controls, disable their cooling systems. It'll be several minutes before they overheat, but once it starts, there's no stopping its reaction. We'll make a run for the sub and get out in time."

Hal huffed in protest and let go of her hand, reaching behind for his .357 and checking the cylinder before handing it to her.

"Those beasts you've been pulling from the ocean are loose. Take this."

She looked at him with wandering eyes. She'd known about them capturing some of the creature, but it was obvious she wasn't aware that they were alive and in containment.

They shifted towards the open doorway cautiously. Hal readied his tranquilizer, firing five shots as two men approached. His aim was tired and careless, missing twice before striking and sending his victims to the ground.

He moved forward, quietly placing each step. The complex was growing even more quiet than before, but he wouldn't let his guard down.

A staircase led to the lowest level with three doorways open. Claire stepped in front, her arms perched up and aiming forward as she entered the doorway to the south.

The hallway was dark and the lights lining the ceiling flickered, momentarily illuminating the long passage. At the end stood two large doors and she entered a code into the security reader. The door hissed as its hydraulic locks let go, opening up a vacant room with construction equipment.

"Howard, we're at the opening for Complex D." Hal spoke into the com system.

Claire spun around in surprise. "Howard's here?"

"Yes. The Yotogi, too."

She smiled at the thought, considering the risk they put themselves in for her, but it quickly vanished in fear for their lives.

"Right behind you," Howard spoke.

Claire ran towards him, throwing her arms out as he caught her. They'd had a long history before, and this was the first time she'd seen him since their conversation over the video chat.

Hal watched from thirty feet as they quietly conversed.

A wailing screech interrupted everyone and the familiar abomination stumbled off the balcony of the large neighboring room.

Howard spun on his heels, whipping an assault rifle around from his chest harness. He fired a long stroke of bullets, striking the creature multiple times. It fought, but the bullets continued to rip into its flesh, bleeding out onto the floor and quickly falling.

Howard's finger remained on the trigger, screaming as the weapon continued to click, exhausted of its ammunition.

"I'm sick and tired of these things!" He yelled, which was almost funny. "Are these Troy's new pets or something?"

Claire stood in shock, recoiling from the frightening creature and also the memory of the last time she'd seen it.

"We need to get out of here!" Hal yelled from the open doorway.

At the end of the passageway lay another two-story atrium with three branches. Claire led the way with Hal, Howard and Emi all following. The area was empty and quiet, and the remaining Yotogi members would be at Complex A now, making their way up as the land forces cleared the way to meet them.

Claire came to a skidding stop, propping the revolver to eye level. Howard raised his assault rifle and immediately lowered it, recognizing Ortiz, but Claire didn't waver.

"You traitor!"

"He's with us," Howard spoke from behind.

"But he let this happen." She lowered her weapon. "You knew the instant we arrived this would happen. Why did you just stand there and abandon us. And Hal?"

"A&H has changed. I was demoted when we were picked up in Japan. We failed, Claire. I had no choice. I didn't want to! I didn't even know you were alive. Being threatened with treason, we were going to be put on trial with a life sentence. We had no choice! Not without you. We're just security detail. If I had known what I know now," Ortiz trailed off. "This is the first time I've had clearance on the lower levels. I've seen what they're breeding, what they're intending. I'm not here to stop you. My men have been evacuated, but A&H has a new army. They won't need us for long."

"I'm sorry." Ortiz approached, placing a hand on her shoulder before walking past. He had nothing more to say or offer and he hung his head in grief as he abandoned them again.

Claire stood with her back turned and held her head low. She couldn't imagine the circumstances he was in then, or now, but the objectives hadn't changed.

Hal watched as Ortiz left. There were unsaid words between the two. He'd been the only one from his past, however vague a connection, but when this was over they might be able to find friendship again. It could wait for now, though.

They were all on edge as they approached the next part of the complex. The room was open and well lit, displaying multiple canisters on their platforms and each was empty. Several computer screens were lit, showing diagrams of the ARCA prototype, but the weapon itself was nowhere to be seen.

"This was where the project must have resumed, but where is it?" Claire darted a glance from side to side.

There was a scratching sound from their side and everyone turned in its direction with weapons ready.

The creature waddled over with tubes still hanging from its chest and shoulder. It spotted them, limping to its side, but showed no hostile interest. It was some sort of morphed canine, and Hal recognized it, but it was much smaller than he remembered. It was an infant.

A wail came from behind and Emi shrieked as the mother beast lunged towards her. Howard fired a burst from his assault rifle, striking the wall behind as it charged. The ringing boom of Claire's revolver hit the creature's shoulder, sending it to its side as it spun off balance. Emi had a second to catch focus again, grabbing her 9mm from her back and firing.

The beast was shaken and shifted its focus as everyone else got their bearings, aimed and fired. Each bullet now struck with accuracy as new holes tore through its flesh. It desperately cried out, fighting for strength that quickly fled, and she slumped onto the ground.

Hal turned before anyone else, shifting to the new threats that were alarmed. Three infant beasts watched in horror as their mother was slain, and now grew aggressive towards the perpetrators.

"There's more!" He yelled as they quieted their fire.

Everyone spun in place, gazing at the small army that was now gathering. Three canine abominations snarled at them.

Hal reached for his tranquilizer, which was the only force he was left with after surrendering his revolver. He grabbed into his pocket and pulled six more magnum shots, slowly extending his hand to Claire to reload.

She was scared and clumsy, taking precious seconds to reload as the creatures prepared to charge. Howard snapped a new magazine in quickly and unleashed a spray of bullets, striking everything in his path. One of the babies was struck, but the two others darted forward.

Hal pivoted, catching one to their side, and Emi aimed for the other.

Claire was slow to reload, dropping several bullets on the floor. Hal's tranquilizer had a delayed effect. It slowed the creature, but it still approached, lunging one last time as she fired two shots to the head.

Each creature now lay in silence; a pool of dark blood trailing out from underneath them. The new silence was anything but comforting. They stood, arms ready, waiting for the next wave.

Howard clicked in another clip, Emi as well, and inspected their surroundings.

Claire's hands trembled. Her revolver was empty, but the shock hadn't faded as she spun around. She pulled the trigger, clicking without delivering, as an abomination stalked passed the neighboring door.

Howard grabbed her arm and lowered it, walking past and approaching the door. Everyone saw the movement, but the creature hadn't pinpointed them yet.

Hal stepped to Claire's side, grabbing her arm and loading her weapon for her. She was still uneasy and clumsy in combat. Even with weapons training, this wasn't what she'd grown used to. Howard obviously had some combat in his previous line of work. Emi too. They were calm and precise, but Claire was nervous on her feet.

Howard tiptoed into the hallway, his gun aimed. He had the advantage and unleashed his wrath, striking the beast in the back without giving it time to face its attacker. His victim remained unseen from their vantage point in the room, but it shrieked out in agony, its voice echoing off the walls as it stumbled on the concrete floors and attempted to change. Howard didn't let up and exhausted his ammo, quickly reloaded and remained ready.

Hal approached the doorway, holding his arms to protect those still inside. The beast quivered on the floor, sliding its legs and arms helplessly on the ground.

"We need to hurry before more of these things find their way here," Howard spoke calmly.

Claire stepped past Hal and continued down the hallway towards the creature. She held the magnum in front, aiming at its head as she passed. Its eyes were open wide, following as she did. It was almost sad. However hostile it had been, it was also a prisoner of A&H and whatever torture they'd inflicted.

The bottom levels of Complex E were a series of hallways, each leading to various research labs that remained dark. The doors were all open and they glanced in, weapons ready in case any occupants still remained.

A set of double doors stood out among the rest, lined with thick steel rims and a hand scanner. Above read a sign *Complex E* and a note stuck to the door *Construction Personnel Only.*

Claire scanned her hand, but to no surprise it blinked red with rejection.

"Allow me." Emi approached, blow torch in hand and began at the center opening near the handles.

The main lock burned red and collapsed, but two remaining locks fed into the doors and she proceeded upward.

A camera pivoted on its axis just behind them and Claire turned to observe. Whoever was still in control of security was watching and she fired an angry shot, shattering its view.

The door locks gave, letting out a hiss of air as Emi kicked the center, swinging in on their hinges.

Claire took lead, jogging forward on the platform that looped around the level below. The complex was surprisingly smaller than the ones before, extending down another hallway that was only about forty feet long. One door remained at the end, opening up to another room with a familiar submarine.

She ran over to the controls just outside the water hole and the hatch hissed open. Howard and Emi quickly stepped inside the submarine and Hal followed.

"Wait. The generators," he yelled, but it was too late.

The door hissed shut and Hal darted a glance back at Claire as she stood at the controls outside.

Tears were streaming down her face as she looked at them. They weren't tears of fear or sadness, but of shame.

"Claire!" Hal yelled, quieted by the glass chamber they stood in. Fear rushed up into his chest, and Howard rushed over to his side in shock.

"Claire, don't do this!" Hal shook his head, his heart sinking. He knew what she was doing.

"No. No. No. Claire! Don't do this."

She walked up to the submarine's door and placed her hand on the glass opposite him.

"I'm sorry. It's the only way," she whispered.

The submarine began to sink into the water and she knelt down, holding her hand to the glass as it submerged.

"Claire!" Hal continued to scream, feeling helpless and hurt.

Howard screamed in rebellion beside him, breathing heavy as they sank into the dark ocean. He was losing her again, too.

The submarine moved forward, propelling them farther as the light from Complex E grew dark in their view. It was on autopilot, its coordinates already set as they helplessly moved onward.

Hal sunk to his knees, gripping his head as his chest overwhelmed him with pain. He breathed in hard, rocking back and forth. She'd mislead them and everyone was so quick to evacuate, he didn't catch it quick enough.

Howard paced the small area and Emi sat on one of the nearby seats, swaying back and forth with her head in her hands.

A boom rocked the small submarine, tilting it to the side slightly. Water rushed from the direction of the complex, but it was a completely black ocean. Only the interior lights within the Sealo-Pax sub lit the immediate surroundings, but the shock wave from behind moved the mass of water in its place.

Hal raised his head and let the emotions out. His heart felt heavy and the void set in. He knew at that moment she was gone and tears built up that couldn't be held back. Howard stood at the rear of the submarine, holding the glass wall for balance as he ached from the loss.

She was lost to them.

Chapter 34: Reality

The submarine bobbled in the water as it came to the surface.

"Controls online." A synthesized voice came through a small speaker. "Destination?"

"Westford." Howard spoke coldly. He didn't know how to operate the vehicle and simply stated his name.

"Westford, Howard. Affirmative." The voice happily chimed back. Claire must have programmed it to lead back to his home.

The light from his beach house lit the way as they closed in. The submarine slid onto the sandy soil, but its egg-shaped frame wasn't designed for ground transport as it rolled on its side about ten degrees.

The door chimed before sliding to the side and Howard ducked out of the tilted vehicle. Emi followed, casting a glance back to Hal who just stared into nowhere.

Ruby stood on the porch and she rushed down the stairs to greet her man. He held his head low and met her gaze. She stopped and threw her hands over her mouth before falling to her knees and letting out a painful sob.

Hal exited and stepped closer toward Ruby, who was now wrapped in Howard's arms. He proceeded past them, walking blankly into Howard's home through the back door. He wasn't conscious of his actions and strode down the hallway to the last door on the left. It was the same bedroom he'd slept in a few nights before, but this time there was no emotion, not even worry or fear. He fell onto the bed and held his hands to his face. He felt empty. Part of his being had been lost.

He closed his eyes, trying to block out the thoughts and emotions racing through his body. The void let the darkness in and he didn't object.

A rattle at the door awoke him and Doctor Prossman let himself in. Hal looked in his direction but made no effort to move.

It was morning now as daylight came through the windows.

The doctor was somber. His eyes were red and irritated, tears still forming but he tried to hold back. He extended his arm, holding out a tablet with an illuminated screen.

"This was for you." He placed it on the bed next to him and bit his lip before quickly exiting.

Hal sat up to examine the gift and his heart ached as he saw Claire's face on the screen in a video clip. He pressed play.

"Hal, I'm sorry. I can't do this anymore. I've been a part of something wicked. We're tearing the world apart, bringing the void here. This whole time, I knew. Somehow I knew, but I kept denying it to myself." She paused on the video to gather herself before continuing. "There is no generator backup in Complex E. The last ARCA prototype is, but it's not calibrated. I can't bare the guilt of creating this and it has to be destroyed. It has to go back to the void, where no one can reach it. It's the only way. I never wanted to hurt you. You were this beautiful mystery that fell among us, and with it, I see the truth of what we were doing. I don't have much time before the ARCA overpowers, but Hal... I'm glad you came." The screen flickered and she remained in view, sitting in a chair as the room grew brighter and brighter behind her. She stared into the camera, now looking directly at him from the video.

The flash was bright and her silhouette remained in view before going completely white.

Hal fought back the urge to cry and instead abandoned all emotion and went numb. There was nothing to be attached to anymore and he just stared at the last frame on the video.

A knock at the door interrupted his lack of thought and he turned to meet Akira's gaze as he stepped in. He wasn't disturbed or in emotional turmoil like those around him and instead smiled.

"Mr. Brent, you saved many lives that you will never know today." He perched his hands on his cane, closing the door and quietly sat on the bed next to him.

"Don't regret, don't feel sorrow. You did what needed to be done, and Claire..." He paused. "She is still with us."

Rage began to burn as his face turned red, and Akira immediately recognized the warning signs. Hal was in no mood for his spiritual bullshit.

He immediately retracted, holding his hands in the air before reaching over and placing a finger on the progress bar for the video timer.

"Wait for it." He motioned, watching Hal's anger and focus change.

At the last second he saw it too and his eyes widened. Claire's silhouette remained as the light around her engulfed the surroundings, but at the very last second, the image was distinct. The darkness no longer surrounded her... because she was no longer there.

Akira met his gaze and a wink of hope sparked.

"She is still out there."

Made in the USA
Charleston, SC
28 March 2014